ASHMOOR CREEK

SUPERIOR LIES

JENNIFER GIFFORD

Detroit

Superior Lies is published by
Ashmoor Creek Press

ISBN-13: 978-0-9985931-1-1
ISBN-10: 0-9985931-1-7

This book is a work of fiction. Names, characters, places, and scenarios are the products of the author's imagination. Any resemblance to actual persons living or dead, places, or events is purely coincidental.

Cover design: A. W. Gifford
Cover Illistration: Greg Chapman

www.ashmoorcreekpress.com

For Adam,

Partner in crime, my ideal reader, springboard of story potentials…thank you for all your encouragement, support, and most importantly, your love.

And for my dad, James Gross, who gave me the gift of storytelling, and the ability to spin a good yarn. Thank you for years of stories and tall tales. I miss you.

Acknowledgments

TO MY FRIENDS at the Collaborative of Independent Artists, your input and ears were and have always been greatly appreciated, especially Tom Sawyer (yes, that's his real name) who never tired of my endless ramblings, and to Carrie Hall for helping out in the 'what if' scenarios between sisters. Regardless of parentage, you're my sister at heart, and best friend for more decades than I care to admit to.

To Ashmoor Creek and her staff for publishing my first novel. Thank you for not chasing a name, but letting your authors chase their dreams.

Greg Chapman, for your stellar artwork that graces my cover. Words cannot do it justice.

James Todd Courtney, for lending your police expertise on procedures, protocol, and criminal justice in my small town. Thank you for all the questions answered, and the proofing you did.

Finally, two special people deserve a bit more than a line or two. To my husband, best friend, my ideal reader, and first editor, Adam. Thank you for the conversations and encouraging me to finish my first novel. Your endless encouragement and help was and always has been a great source of comfort and inspiration. Also, I've learned my lesson about interstates. I love you.

Lastly, to my dad, James, who never lived to see this novel published. I inherited your gift of storytelling, and I only hope, even now, that I do you proud. Rest in peace, dad.

CHAPTER 1

MAUREEN HATED IT. She hated the drive, hated the cabin, and hated her sister for putting her in this situation. For all intents and purposes, she shouldn't even be on the road heading towards Lighthouse Bay. Instead, she should have been on the road starting her vacation, but insistent phone calls from her mother had changed all that.

As she headed north on the highway, Maureen finally allowed herself some time to unleash the anger she'd been harboring toward her mother. She felt a new rush of anger just thinking of her mother's shaky voice. Tense and concerned, so instant that something was wrong with Hannah.

"Mom, I'm sure Hannah is fine. She's always fine," Maureen said.

Hannah always managed to get herself into some sort of trouble. It was her one endearing quality that her mother thought made her colorful. Maureen thought it made her a nuisance.

"You can't be certain of that, sweetie. I'd check on her myself, but with your dad and I here in Flor —"

"Stepdad," Maureen corrected.

"Either way, we're here and you're only a few hours away. Well, we didn't think you'd mind. You don't mind, do you dear? She is your sister."

"Half-sister, and I do mind. Mom, I love you. And I like Frank as well. Nevertheless, I am not Hannah's keeper or guardian. I stopped doing that in college when I realized my help wasn't appreciated. Sooner or later she has to learn to be an adult, and she isn't going to do that with a babysitter around."

"Maureen —".

"You know I have a life of my own, and I can't just drop everything to go trekking off into the northern woods to see what predicament she's managed to get herself into this time."

Maureen was doing her best to keep calm, but the last thing she

1

needed right now was to play hero and fix Hannah's life.

Hell, she thought, *I can't even fix my own.*

"Can't or won't? I don't know why you can't be more concerned when it comes to your sister. You're her big sister, Maureen. I just don't understand why you two aren't closer. "

"Half-sister. And I am concerned. But, I have a full-time job, and it's not making sure she stays out of trouble. Besides, there's a lot of snow up there; it is November, and I've never driven up there in that type of weather."

"Hannah's never in trouble, not really," he mother said. "She just ends up with bad luck, that's all. She's a free spirit, always has been. People just don't understand her ways, that's all. Now your da —," she paused, "Frank and I would appreciate you going up to the cabin and checking on Hannah for us."

"Mom," Maureen sighed, as she always did when they had these conversations that dealt with Hannah. "I would if it was any other weekend. I'm under a deadline as it is, and Steve and I are in the mid-dle of moving. I just can't spare the time right now."

"Maureen, I'm really not asking you to, I'm telling you. And frankly young lady, I'm a little shocked. She's your sister — "

"Half, sister. Mother."

"Aren't you worried about her? I know she would do the same thing for you if the tables were turned. What if something is wrong?"

There it was. That tense pause as both mother and daughter tread to the familiar territory of their twisted version of cat and mouse. Mrs. Prescott supplying the bait — the worry of the youngest daughter, with all the zeal and fervor of a dramatic housewife — and Maureen as the cat, falling for the shakiness in her mother's soft, fragile voice.

"We've tried for several days to reach her, and the phone at the cab-in keeps ringing. We can't even leave a message because her voicemail is full. We tried her cell phone too, and it isn't working."

"They had quite the storm, mom. The lines might be down in that area."

"Maureen, your dad and I are worried. Now, we've wired some money for your sister, in your name, same as before. And of course, a little extra for you for the trouble. Just call us as soon as you know an-ything, okay sweetheart?"

Maureen bit her tongue, resisting the urge to correct her mother that Frank was her stepfather.

In the end, like always, Maureen reluctantly agreed. *The ties that bind are the hardest to break*, she thought.

Superior Lies

That had been over an hour ago, and she still had another two hours to go. Maureen had crossed Mackinac Bridge, getting off interstate seventy-five onto U.S. two, then heading along Lake Superior Scenic Highway.

Driving the winding road along the shore of Lake Superior, Maureen tried not to think of how this was a waste of her time, and that Hannah had probably been her reliable and irresponsible self and forgotten to pay the bill. That or she'd blown through that month's trust fund disbursement.

She felt a dull throbbing at the back of her temples. A migraine. The scratchiness of the radio brought her out of her remote haze, the range of the radio station losing its signal as her old, blue Pontiac Grand Am headed north.

The gray-black of the water looked bone-chilling cold. Snow lay along the shore in billowy piles. Adjusting her defrosters again to accommodate the gusty winds rolling in off the lake, she flipped through the dial, choosing to switch the radio off altogether.

"It's only going to make my headache worse, no thanks to you, Hannah." Inhaling, she still could not believe that she had had to drop everything, in the middle of moving, to bail out her sister. Again.

Maureen hadn't exactly told the truth to her mother. She and Steve were moving that part was true. What she hadn't told her mother was that they'd broken up. The late night calls from her frantic, and usually drunken sister, the last minute cancellations of plans, had finally taken its toll on their relationship.

Not that she blamed him. She blamed herself.

Maureen had never been particularly close to her mother, with all her pearls, polished nails, and bridge games. She was a daddy's girl or had been. Fishing trips, basketball games, that was her idea of fun.

Her father and mother had a May-December romance, with her father being nearly fifteen years her mother's senior. But when her father died, and her mother had quickly remarried to a much younger man, Maureen saw the chance of becoming close to her mother slip away. When Hannah was born two years later, her mother turned into the quintessential suburban housewife.

In public, her mother would always introduce her as, 'my other daughter Maureen.'

Maureen hated being the "other" daughter, almost as much as she grew to hate the picture perfect family her mother struggled to portray. She told herself it was because her mother had remarried so soon after her father's sudden death.

3

Maureen just thought that she wasn't close to her mother, and didn't share in any of the hobbies or interests that she did. But when it came down to the cold hard truth, it was a simple matter of Maureen not fitting in. She was the outcast, and everyone knew it, including her.

Yet here she was, driving once again to the family's cabin on Lake Superior's shore, in the middle of winter, where Hannah had taken up permanent residence nearly two years ago. Dropping out of one college after another, Hannah had decided to live at the cabin full time to explore her artistic abilities.

Maureen still remembered that day, sitting around her mother's kitchen table hearing her younger sister's plan for life.

"None of the great artists had a lot of training, and this way, I can focus all my free time on my art. It'll be perfect, just me in all that solitude, and my potter's wheel."

Her mother had said that while she didn't approve of Hannah dropping out of school, she realized how important this decision was to Hannah, and she would support her daughter.

Maureen saw what Hannah really meant. She was bored at school, all her hippie friends were making pottery and hugging trees, and she was going to do the same. Maureen knew in the coming months Hannah would find an excuse to quit the pottery, and all her parents would have to show for it were a few hand thrown vases that looked like ashtrays.

The loud honking of a horn snapped Maureen out of her haze as her car veered into the next lane.

The drive might have been pleasant if Maureen actually liked her destination and the situation that lay ahead of her. Truth was, she had liked it at one point, until her mother and her decorator got a hold of it. Now, it was just another rich suburbanite retreat. Gone are the oak floors and stone mantel. The rustic furniture, the rich wines, ambers, and golds that had once made the family cabin seem homey and inviting. They were replaced with white wash Cape Cod paneling. White gauze and blue sailor patterns echoed the cabin's new nautical theme. The cabin had lost its quaintness and charm, and it still burned Maureen to be there to this day. The day her mother had redone the cabin, Maureen felt like she was losing her father all over again.

She drove another thirty minutes on the main highway before veering off onto the smaller, main road of town that led her through Lighthouse Bay and to her family's cabin. Concentrating on the road, Maureen jumped when her cell phone rang. She answered it.

"Hello?"

Static.

"Hello? Hello, is anyone there?"

Pushing the off button, she tossed the phone onto the seat. The phone barely hit the passenger side seat when it began to ring again. Grabbing it, she answered again.

"Hello? Hello? You're going to have to speak up. Hello?" Looking at the caller ID before the phone slipped from her fingers.

It was Hannah's cell phone.

She realized her car was about to serve towards the guardrail, and she pulled her Pontiac back into her lane before pulling off onto the shoulder to a complete stop.

Queasiness washed through her. Her skin felt cold, clammy. Her hands were still shaking. She could feel her heart pounding in her chest that it echoed in her ears as she looked out her driver's side window.

She almost went over the side of the Lenawee pass and into the bay. Swallowing hard, she picked up the cell phone from her lap and hit send to dial Hannah's phone.

No signal. Nothing.

The words flashed back at her with an eerie taunting, making her spine tingle. She pressed the talk button, but still nothing. Maureen leaned forward and rested her head on the steering wheel, closing her eyes momentarily.

After a few moments spent composing herself, she checked the mirrors and pulled onto the highway again, and drove is rigid silence. Not even the comforting illumination from the nearly full moon gave Maureen any solace.

Maureen could hear the wet slapping of her tires inching along the narrow winding drive which then opened into a large clearing. The cabin looked as she remembered it from her last trek here. Even the tiny greenhouse was painted the same blue-gray color to match the rest of the cabin.

She pulled her Pontiac in front of the large stoop, and Maureen could see the lamplight pouring through an un-curtained window.

She never understood how Hannah could live out here, in the middle of nowhere, and not have any curtains or blinds. Maureen lived in a seventeenth floor downtown apartment and still closed her blinds at night.

Stepping onto the porch, Maureen saw a few days' worth of newspapers stacked on the front stoop, a sign that Hannah was on another misadventure like the one her mother had predicted. Picking them up, she knocked, then waited. Snow had blown onto the porch and had nearly covered the rubber welcome mat.

"Hannah? Hannah, it's me, Maureen. Hannah?"

Silence.

Knocking harder, she waited again, cautiously scanning the blackened foreground for any sign of movement. Her heart began to race. For a second, Maureen felt like she was being watched.

But it was something more.

Panic that something was wrong?

Refusing to stay outside in the cold, she reached for the doorknob. It was locked.

After fishing the spare key from her purse, she opened the door. She always expected the scent of oleanders to greet her. They'd always been her favorite and it was a scent her father often used in the cabin.

When she was young, her father had once told her that oleanders were the Tibetan death flower. Her father had been a smart man. An engineer by trade, but a book lover to his soul, he read everything, and shared that love with her. Maureen remembered with bittersweet sadness how her mother had donated most of his books to a local library after his death. Though Maureen managing to keep a precious few, it was another divider between them.

Looking around, it both saddened and infuriated her that there was so little of her father or his handiwork, left about the cabin. All that was left was the familiar tick-tock of the grandfather clock.

"Hannah? Hannah, are you here?"

Walking around the small lower level, Maureen noticed no signs of her sister. Upstairs, she checked each of the two bedrooms, then the third, which Hannah converted to her studio. A tarp lay over her potter's wheel, and from what Maureen could deduce, it hadn't been touched in months.

"Being one with your art, huh little sister. Whatever." Looking at the objects on the shelves, Maureen was surprised to see dozens of slightly exotic looking glazed vases and bowls. Impressed, and a little envious that her sister had a real talent, she reached out, tracing her finger along the smooth line of one of the vases.

"Well, maybe these aren't that bad." Picking one up to examine, she started laughing. If her sister was going to pass off someone else's work, she was going to have to remember to remove the price tags from the bottom. Putting the vase back, she stopped as the stairs creaked.

"Hannah?"

Stepping out into the hall, Maureen froze. She noticed the grandfather clock at the end of the hall had stopped.

Heart beating faster, she cautiously stepped towards it, her hand reaching out to push the pendulum into motion, when out of the corner of her eye, Maureen caught movement on the landing below.

"Hannah, knock it off. I don't appreciate your damn antics after the long drive up here," Maureen snapped.

Stomping down the hall, Maureen descended the stairs with determination to nail her sister once again for her childlike behavior. Stepping into the living room, Maureen looked around.

Nothing.

No one was there. She swore she just saw someone's shadow move past. Turning around, her eyes scanned the room's interior once again.

That's when she saw it.

It hadn't been like that before, but then again she'd just glanced around the lower level before heading upstairs. But the backdoor, leading out onto the side porch was open. Its chain was broken; the door had been kicked in. Her heart pulsed with fearful uncertainty.

Something was wrong. Where was Hannah? Who else was in the house with her?

Her breath came in short, uneven gasps. She walked into the kitchen, grabbing a butcher's knife from the butcher's block. Shaky hands pulled open cupboards and closets.

Knowing the first floor was indeed secure, she locked the door, and edged her way upstairs, checking each room, every closet, and under every bed. No sign of anyone, including Hannah. Just the faint scent of faded perfume.

In the master bedroom, Maureen opened the last closet door and nearly dropped the knife. On the inside of the door were scratches.

Deep and splintered.

Uttering a soft gasp, she stepped closer and noticed that each mark was the same length, gouged into the oak paneling of the door. Above the nearly two dozen notches, Maureen's finger traced along a word.

SEEN.

She felt it first. A cold breeze wafted into the master bedroom.

Then she heard it. A creak of the stairs.

Panic swept through her. Her heart thudded with such intensity that she felt it ball up in the back of her throat. Easing her way slowly to the bedroom door, she peered out.

Nothing.

Stepping into the hall, she leaned over the railing and peered once again onto the landing below. The room was empty.

Her breathing was shallow and erratic, her eyes dilated wide with breathless anticipation of something unseen. Edging down the stairs and into the living room, Maureen reached into her pocket for her cell phone. Looking at its face, tears pooled.

No signal. Her panic turned to fear, then fear turned to that tiny innate part of every human's core: survival.

The hairs on the back of her neck stood on end, her ears became keenly attuned to the sounds of the cabin as Maureen's body went into flight or fight mode.

Catching a glimpse of a light out of the corner of her eye, she turned to see a flash of light, like a helicopter's searchlight, linger then vanish. Breaking into a sprint, Maureen headed towards the back door, half expecting Hannah to pull up in her Volvo. But the clearing was empty, save for Maureen's Pontiac.

Looking down, Maureen stopped.

The porch was covered with snow, except in this spot by the back door. Flipping on the porch light, Maureen saw the outline of footprints. Yet the footprints were distorted, elongating into wide tracks as if they, and whomever they belonged to, had been dragged off the porch.

She fought to keep the taste of bile from rising in her throat, scared to follow them, but her mind driving her with a need to know.

Where was Hannah?

Following them off the porch, Maureen walked along the side of the two wide-angle marks. Her breathing stilled for a moment. Maureen felt transcended, like she wasn't actually doing the walking, but she was watching herself, as if in some weird family video.

As she walked, the porch light provided just enough light to see. Six feet from the start of the woods, the deep groves of the tracks ended.

CHAPTER 2

WILLIAM REAGAN DOWNS preferred to be called Bill. He'd been a deputy sheriff for Leewanue County for nearly two years before his boss asked him to work — temporarily of course — over in the next county until they had found a replacement.

As he was told, the former Sheriff had taken sick rather quickly after returning from a camping trip, and his condition was uncertain. With just two dozen men to cover three bay counties, they needed someone to take command until more permanent measures could be made, or until the Sheriff himself regained his health.

That was six months ago. Sheriff McRainey never recovered. He passed away a few weeks after Bill's arrival.

Bill was presented with the job offer of a permanent post in Lighthouse Bay a few days after the funeral. While he'd only been a deputy for three years, he did have eight years military experience that gave him an edge compared to the others in his field. He accepted the job offer the following afternoon.

"Okay, Bill, I'm gone for the night. You need anything before I go?" asked Edith, Shoshanee County Sheriff's Office secretary, and dispatcher. She was also the widow of the late Sheriff. She sounded tired, straightening a stack of papers before shoving them into a manila folder. She peered over the rims of her bifocals, staring back at the sheriff. "I mean it, I don't want to come back on Monday and find the place out of sorts because you don't know your way 'round the office yet."

Bill had been working at this office over six months, but she still treated him like a simpering child when it came to office organization.

He thought he heard a combination of mock challenge and sarcasm in her tone, but let it slide. *She's probably like this with everyone around here*, he thought.

The County covered the areas of New Winston, Marshland, and Lighthouse Bay. The little towns that encompassed the county never saw much in terms of crime, so it was a job that suited Edith well since she spent most days filing her nails between typing reports.

"After all your help this week, I think I can manage for a few days without you. Just promise to come back first thing Monday morning and bring that cute smile with you."

"With a shovel no less, since it looks like I'll be adding manure removal to my job description. That line may work on the local skirts, but I know better." Pushing her chair back, she turned off the small desk light, grabbed her purse and sweater that hung from the back of her chair, before reaching for her wool jacket.

"Just you remember that, young man." But she was smiling when she said it, so Bill knew she found him charming. "Don't forget to save your gas receipts for me so I can keep track in the books. We have to report quarterly to the County Commissioners. We don't get much money to police the county, but we try to get what we can. Now you be careful. Will I be seeing you in church Sunday morning?"

"We'll see, Edith. I don't belong to any doctrine of faith out right. And I don't know if a person needs to go to a building and pray to find God. Besides, Sundays are my only day to sleep in."

"One of these days, God is going to give you a sign that you need to go. Until then, it doesn't hurt me to keep needling you about it," she said.

"Have a good weekend, Edith. I'll see you on Monday."

"Night, Bill. Lock up tight." With that, the widowed wife of the former sheriff left, pulled the glass paned oak door shut behind her, leaving him to silence.

"How one person acquires so much stuff, I'll never know."

He'd lost track of the time after a few hours of sifting through paperwork. Bill managed to clean out the files both on and in the desk, sorting through what was important, and what wasn't. He was slowly starting to put some order into this random chaos of files and stacks of paper. If he learned anything from being in the military, it was efficiency.

He didn't have to look at his watch because his stomach was telling him it was long past dinner. He thought of the Wild Catch Special and Ida's Café down the street, and his stomach rumbled again in agreement. It was almost nine, but with luck, he'd be able to place his order before they closed.

Grabbing his hat, he was nearly to the door when a car, an old blue Pontiac Grand Am screeched to a halt in front of the station. A panic-stricken woman with chestnut brown hair, a red sweater and jeans ran for the door. His nerves went on alert, uncertain of what was going to happen. A gust of wind rushed around him as the door swung open.

"I need help! Please, you have to help me, I think something is wrong with my sister. I can't find her, and the back door was open, and she's nowhere to be found!"

"Ma'am, ma'am, please, calm down. Here, sit down and take a deep breath." Steering her over to one of the wooden benches that lined the front window, he sat her down, sitting beside her.

"Okay, take a deep breath. That's it, inhale, now, slowly exhale. Once more."

She followed his instructions, and after a few moments, she was finally calm enough to speak without her words coming out in laborious fragments.

"You have to help me. My sister. She's missing. She's gone. I came up here to find her, and when I got here she was gone." Her face etched with worry and fear.

He looked at her for a moment, studying her face. Her pupils weren't dilated, but he couldn't be certain she wasn't high on something. Her shoulder length hair was damp, plastered to her face in some spots. Her boots were muddy, and for the first time, he noticed she was shaking. Standing up, he pulled off his Sheriff's jacket and placed it around her shoulders.

"Please." Her voice was shaky.

"What's your name, ma'am?"

"Maureen. Maureen Welsh."

"Okay Mrs. Welsh, —"

"Miss Welsh, but that's not important. I'm trying to tell you my sister is missing! Why aren't you asking me about her?" Anger was seeping through the panic in her voice.

"I can't talk to you when you're upset. I can't help your sister unless you stay calm Miss Welsh. Now, let's start from the beginning. What's your sister's name?"

"Hannah Prescott."

"Where does Hannah live?"

"382 Chestnut Trail. It's the cabin, near the beginning of the woods by...by the state park." Her hands were still shaking as she stuttered her response.

Bill determined she was neither drunk nor drug impaired. Grabbing the radio from the corner of his uniform, he spoke, his tone even and level.

"Attention all units: do I have a car in the vicinity of Chestnut Trail and State Road Two?"

"Geez, all this formality and we get to wear these pretty uniforms, too." A voice, deep and baritone, came back over the speaker, laughing at the official way the Sheriff stated his request.

Most of his junior officers bristled at the rigidity from Bill's military training.

He didn't flinch though the muscle in his jaw tensed with embarrassment. It was the only part of the job that hadn't squared itself away. He had suffered quite a few jabs about his age since he'd assumed his new post. His first day on the job, he found a box of Pampers on his desk with a tin badge, like the ones kids buy at the local Wal-Mart.

He had brushed them off, but they were still an embarrassment to him.

"All units, we have a report of a missing person, last known location in the vicinity of Chestnut Trail and state road two." He paused, letting the seriousness of his request sink into the other deputies. "So if one of you could manage to put down the jelly donut long enough to have a look around, I'm going to finish taking a statement from the reporting party here at the station. Downs out."

He strode over to his desk and grabbed a blank file. Pulling a pen from his shirt pocket, he stood leaning against the desk in front of her.

"I need to ask you a few questions, Miss Welsh. Any information that you tell me can only further help me in locating the whereabouts of your sister. I just need the facts. So try and remember as much as you can, without being overly sentimental."

"That won't be hard," she muttered. From her tone, Bill didn't detect any lost sentiments between the two women.

"I see. And why is that," he noted, and crossing his arms. His earlier assumptions that she wasn't on anything were accurate, but there was no sobriety test for crazy. The crackling of a radio broke the silence.

"Sheriff, this is Deputy Hopson. I'm responding to your call. I'm out here on the property now. The front door was locked, but the rear entry shows signs of a possible break-in."

"That's right! I noticed that too when I went downstairs —" but Maureen was silenced by Sheriff Downs hand coming up and motioning for her to be quiet.

"I also found footprints, some tracks. It looks like something was dragged from the lower level of the cabin into the woods."

He stared at her the entire time that Deputy Hopson was giving his initial findings. He watched her face, her body language for any sign or trace of emotion.

Nothing.

She was staring back at him with the same uncertainty etched into her features that had been there since she stormed into the police station.

"Anything else, Paul?" he asked, addressing the deputy by his first name, hoping to put her at ease to let her guard to slip.

Killers craved attention and notoriety. They wanted someone to hear their side of the story. Sheriff Downs was starting to get a sinking feeling in the pit of his stomach that this one wasn't going to have a happy ending.

"Sheriff, we have traces of blood in the greenhouse, and leading out of the greenhouse into the woods. There's a trail, then it just…stops."

CHAPTER 3

MAUREEN'S EYES GREW wide, her heart palpitated, her breath held on the edge of the deputy's words.

Blood. In the woods.

Her mind raced with awful imagery of her sister, her creamy complexion and long strawberry blonde hair trailing behind her as she ran from the house in a panic. Images of her being dragged off into the northern woods by someone. Her stomach churned. Her throat clenched.

Keeping his eyes on his new suspect, he spoke crisp and clear into his police equipped portable radio, or PREP, holstered to his shoulder.

"Deputy Hopson, go ahead and secure the area. Set up a perimeter, and get a crime scene team out there. Call in the State Police Forensic Teams if needed."

She looked at him anger rising within her from the crass terminology he'd used in reference to her sister. Grabbing a chair, turning it around to straddle it, he rested his arms on the back and looked at her.

"Is there something you want to tell me, ma'am?"

It didn't look good that he was just a few months into his new post with a possible murder to investigate.

So far, the only trouble he had seen was the occasional drag racing through town on a Saturday night, or the average speeder cruising ten miles too fast along rural route forty-seven.

But a murder.

This wasn't going to make him look good by any means, and any doubt that the County Executive might have had about his ability to take command of his new position, and the new budget, would be crystallized.

14

"If there's something you want to tell me, something that might help us locate your sister, you need to tell me. Right now, I'm going to be straight with you, Maureen," he called her by her first name, trying to appeal to the humane part of her. He still couldn't shake the feeling that something was wrong with this woman's sister, but he also got a sense that she did care for her, too.

"You coming here, reporting your sister missing, then my deputy finding blood at the last known whereabouts of her, well, I'll be honest. It doesn't make you look too good."

"What?" she asked. She was numb, her mind reeling from the events of the last twenty minutes. Here she was, trying to get someone to help her find her sister, and she was being accused of her…what?

"Are you suggesting that I had something to do her disappearance? Are you nuts?" Color flared through her cheeks and as she stood up, the jacket slipped from her shoulders.

"Ma'am, you need to calm down. Please. I'm just trying to find out what happened. Just like you, I want to find her."

"Then why, in God's name," her voice rising with a slight shrill to it, "are you here, here," and waved her arms about frantically, "in the one place where I know she isn't going to be? Why aren't you out there looking for her? Looking around the woods, I mean you heard your deputy, there was blood—" But she stopped. The full force of what he was trying to ask her had just sunk in with shocking realization.

"You think… I did something to her, don't you?"

"I didn't say that, Ma'am, but I think you need to remain calm and just have a seat."

"And I think you need to kiss my butt, Opie! Get off your ass and do your job! Or are you just waiting around for the next batch of donuts to be ready?"

"I'm going to ask you one more time, ma'am," he annunciated and stressing every syllable, "to sit down and be quiet. I'm trying to conduct an interview and I can't do that with you being overly hormonal."

Mouth open, she sank back into her chair in retreat, back stiff with rage. Breathing heavily through her nose, lips pursed tight into a thin line, she looked at him.

15

"Good. Now let's try this one more time. Is there anything, any-thing at all that you need to tell me?"

"No, but I want to ask you something," Maureen said.

"Okay."

"Am I being accused of a crime?" she asked as calmly as she could.

"Not at this time, no."

"Am I under arrest for a crime," she questioned, staring pointedly at him.

"Not at this time, no." His monotone, repetitive phrases unnerved her a little. At any moment, she expected him to lunge across the desk and cuff her.

"Then from my understanding, if I'm not being accused of a crime, or being charged with anything, I'm free to go, correct?"

She stood up and crossed her arms in open defiance of his position and authority.

He stood up; his feet shoulder length apart, placing his hands on his hips, clearly unhappy with where this was going.

"Yes, you're free to go."

"Thanks for the runaround, Friday. Now if you'll excuse me, I'm go-ing to go find my sister. Let me know how the donuts come out." He didn't wait for her to get out of the office before grabbing his walkie.

"All units, be on the lookout for a 1999 blue Pontiac grand am with a female driver. Woman has brown hair, six foot, approximately one hundred and fifty pounds. She is a potential suspect in the reported disappearance up on Chestnut Trail. I'll be following her whereabouts as she's leaving base. I want a known location of her whereabouts at all times. Proceed with caution, as the subject is," he paused, "ex-tremely irate."

Without looking back, she casually raised her arm and flipped him the bird, before slamming the door to the office. She marched to her car, climbing in, and slammed the door in agitation.

Chapter 4

BILL SHOOK HIS head in disbelief. Grabbing the manila folder, he headed out of the office to his patrol car. He followed the Pontiac as it wove around the twists and turns that incorporated the little inlet community. Reaching into his shirt pocket, he grabbed the small tape recorder and pressed record.

"Field notes, case number 14421, missing persons of female, named Hannah-" But he stopped his sentence short, staring off into the night sky. Out of trained instinct, he slowed the car down, careful to keep one eye on the road and the other the horizon. He checked his watch, making a note of when the activity started. Off behind the woods that tapered from Huntington State Park, there was a reflection coming in the direction of the hot springs. He blinked a few times; making sure what he was registering was true. To him, it looked like a faint flashlight flickering above the darkened tree line.

Then they disappeared.

"What in the hell was that?" he asked as he swerved the car to the far left to avoid hitting the car that had also been watching the odd phenomenon, and had careened off into the guardrail. There, about five hundred feet back was the dented blue Pontiac belonging to Maureen Welsh.

Picking up his flashlight, he flicked on his blinkers. He approached her car, one hand on the flashlight, the other on his gun.

She was sitting upright in her seat, a small gash from her left temple. She was breathing, and she was twisting her head from side to side slowly, her hand idly rubbing her neck.

He knocked on the window. She tried rolling down the window, and when it wouldn't work, she opened the door and got out, leaning against the car.

"Are you okay, ma'am?" he asked.

"For God's sake, I'm your age, stop calling me ma'am. Every time you do that I expect my mother to appear, and she's the last person I want to see right now."

"Still complaining I see, you're fine." He didn't mean it as a jab. He'd just observed more about her in the last thirty or so minutes than most people might notice about someone in an entire day. His training had taught him that.

"What's that supposed to mean? You know, you're the reason that people think cops are pigs. I was just in an accident, and you insult me. So much for protecting and serving the community. I should a write a story about the waste of county tax dollars going to squander just to pay your salary."

He cracked his neck to the side, something he always did when he got mildly irritated. His sense of responsibility and oath to his job made him stop, but for the first time in service, he was seriously thinking twice about leaving someone stranded behind.

"Yeah, well seeing as I took a pay cut to take this position, I think I can safely say that your words would ultimately fall on deaf ears. Besides, most folks up here have taken a liking to me."

Most people up here have claimed to see Big Foot, so it's not like you're setting the bar that high."

Now he smiled. Had they met in any other circumstance, he could see himself being friends with this woman. Dating her might be a bit of challenge, but he didn't mind a little backbone in a woman. He snorted lightly at that image, and shook his head, wondering why his brain would think such a thing. Probably because I missed dinner, he mused.

"What's so funny?" There was that tone again, that angelic voice laced with a tinge of venom that brought him out of his daze.

"Nothing, I was clearing my throat. What made you crash? Was it a deer? The truckers frequently nail them this time of year. DNR said it's not an overpopulation problem since there aren't that many deer in the woods but something sure lures them to the highway."

"No, it wasn't a deer. I thought I saw," she paused, "something. It was probably headlights of a car that turned up ahead or the stress of today. Or you."

"Me?"

"You heard me, Helen Keller. We aren't exactly on a friendly first name basis." She was still rubbing her neck, though not as often.

"I've called you Maureen already," he stated with deadpan satire.

"See, that. That's what I'm talking about. First, you come off all macho stern, and do what I tell you to drill sergeant, and then you sneak in your tongue in cheek sense of humor. It's like trying to mix

18

oil and water."

"Master Sergeant."

"What?"

"I was a Master Sergeant. Not a drill sergeant."

She rolled her eyes at him, and he heard her curse. She used her sleeve to dab the cut.

"Do you have a problem with the United States military, ma'am," he inquired, putting a heavy emphasis on the 'ma'am' to let her know she was treading into touchy territory.

"No, I don't. They pride themselves on getting people to follow orders. I have, however, expressed several times for you to leave me alone, yet here you are." He could tell she was agitated with him.

"The military teaches discipline, routine, and most of all, integrity. I can't leave you alone because you are now part of an investigation that I am undertaking. An investigation, that I want to point out, that's a direct result of you," he pointed at her, "coming into my office under crazed hysterics, and begging for help. Help you, I have, but you have to take my attitude along with it, I'm afraid."

She inhaled sharply at his words and crossed her arms again. Was she pouting? Was she angry with him? She didn't offer up much in the way of body language, so he wasn't able to defer much from how she was behaving other than by what she was saying.

"Whatever. Look, I think if you push from the front, I can get unhooked from the guard rail and we can both be on our merry little way."

He looked at the car, and back to her. Had this been any other stranded pedestrian, he wouldn't have hesitated. But she was a stranger, who was claiming to have a missing sister.

That may or may not be true. You could also be the next unfortunate soul who finds out what really happened to her sister.

He looked back at her.

"No. I'm going to call for a tow truck. It's too dark out here for one patrol car, and if I get injured getting out the car, or if the car isn't in drivable condition, we've wasted valuable time."

For a moment, he thought she was going to protest, but she didn't. She simply nodded.

"So, where does that leave us?" she finally asked.

He swung his hand towards his patrol car and offered her a half grin.

"Your chariot awaits my lady."

She closed the driver's side door, and went around to the trunk and pulled out a small tote bag. He stiffened, unsure of what she was reaching for in the bag. When she pulled out a pair of brightly knitted gloves, he relaxed. But she had caught his sudden change in demeanor.

"It's not a hatchet or a gun," she stressed, even opening the bag for him to see. "Ooohhh, scary. Deodorant and wait, oh no, my hairbrush."

He cleared his throat, then led the way back to his patrol car. He opened the back door.

"You're joking, right?"

"Afraid not. Policy. I can't allow civilians to ride in front because of the loaded weapon," he pointed to the shotgun. "And you should, in no way, feel that you are being held against your will. I said that back at the station, and I meant it. I've been pretty upfront with you, and I wouldn't lie to you about something like this. I've got rules to follow, Maureen, and I won't break them. Please, get in."

She reluctantly climbed into the back seat and pulled her bag onto her lap. Then she looked up at him. She held it out.

"You can put that in the trunk or in the front if you want. I don't want you crashing because you are checking me out in the rearview mirror every ten seconds wondering if I'm going to pull something sinister out of my bag." She leaned back and fastened herself in.

Grabbing the bag, he walked around to the trunk placing her bag inside before closing her door, and taking his spot behind the wheel.

They drove on in silence for a few moments, before he spoke.

"How long has your sister lived up here?"

"About a year now, I guess. I don't really remember. Just so you know, Hannah and I are not close. In case you wanted to make a note of that."

"Can I ask why?" He briefly looked up at her in the rearview mirror.

"We don't get along much. Well, we don't get along at all. We have nothing in common, except sharing the same mother, though sometimes I wonder if I was adopted."

"I take it you don't get along with your parents either." He was asking questions, but only those to the information she was already giving out. It was amazing how much information you could gather from an individual if you got them talking and just let them ramble on.

"No, I don't really get along with my mother much. I got along great with my dad, but he died when I was a kid. Frank—that's my stepfather—he's all right. He's a good golf partner, and can make a hell of a

Bloody Mary."

"But you don't click with him either, I take it."

"I'm not his child, so there is no point in us sharing the pretense of a happy family. That's what they have Hannah for."

"I never got along with my stepdad much, either. I was a teenager when my mom remarried, and I never knew my real father." *I don't think mom knew him either,* he lamented, pushing back the bittersweet twinge he felt at the loss. "I saw less of them after high school when I joined the Marines, only coming home on leave. Then they got divorced."

"Mom and Frank are in Florida soaking up the UV rays and working on their handicap."

"Handicap?" he asked, stealing another glance at her in the mirror.

"Golf. They say it's great exercise and a fun sport. I say its old people in tacky clothes, walking. It's a perfect game for people who don't have enough mindless activities to do during the week."

He smiled at the remarks; her sarcasm and wit were a refreshing change from Edith's quiet demeanor around the office.

They drove on again for several more moments before he again engaged her into a conversation.

"So what brought you up here to see her, if you don't get along much?" He knew just from the last hour or so, that she was a smart woman. He was going to have to dance his way around to the tougher questions if he wanted her to trust him.

"I was wondering how long it would it take you to asking that. In my line of work, we usually do the same thing. Ask a few fluff questions, and then go straight for the jugular."

"What is your line of work?"

"I'm a freelance writer. Mostly fiction, editorials, news commentaries that sort of thing."

"Are you any good?"

"I don't know, but it pays the bills. But getting back to your question. I came up here because my mother hasn't been able to reach Hannah for several days. The phone isn't working, and neither is her cell, goes right to voicemail. I tried to tell my mom that Hannah had probably forgotten to pay the bills, and blew through her allowance this month.

She insisted, and being the dutiful daughter I am, I relented, but here I am. It's what I usually do. Babysit and clean up messes. I should be great when it comes to having kids someday since I have been taken care of an overgrown infant for the last decade."

He was listening to what she was saying and what she wasn't. Before he could engage her in anything else, he saw the turn and headed to the cabin. A few moments later, they pulled into the clearing where two other patrol cars waited.

All the lights in the house were on, and two uniformed deputies walked around the outside. Yellow tape stretched across the greenhouse door, and as he got out, a middle-aged officer, slightly robust with just a hint of a limp on his right leg, walked over.

"Hey, Bill."

"Hey, Paul. What've you got?" He had left Maureen sitting in the back of the police car for a moment. He needed a chance to talk to his deputy.

"Nothing but the tracks, and a few traces of blood in the greenhouse. We are dusting for prints around the back door, but other than that, we don't know much. Is that the sister," he nodded in the direction of the woman in the backseat of the car.

"Yeah, that's her. Feisty one, too."

"Feisty, eh," the man teased. "I said the same thing about my sweet Lorraine before I married her. I still say it about her, though not within ear shot."

Bill laughed and patted Paul on the arm. Of all the officers in his unit, he liked Paul the best. He liked the man's no muss, no fuss attitude. He could tell that Paul was the kind of person who'd sacrifice himself to save someone else, and that's why Bill had made him Under Sherriff over the others. His easygoing manner made him a valued team player. It was comforting to know that he had an officer like Paul to depend on if needs be. The only flaw that Bill could fault him with was his relentless pushing for Bill to find a girl and get married.

"Well don't go tying tin cans around my patrol car just yet, Pops. She doesn't particularly care for me."

"Well you leaving the poor lady in the back of a police car sure aren't going to improve your standings with her, either," he laughed, clearly enjoying himself at Bill's expense.

The two men walked over to the back of the patrol car, and Sheriff Downs opened the door. Maureen looked at the both of them for a moment, before getting out of the car. She walked to the front of the house, where she had used her key, but the front door was open and she brushed past a burly officer sporting a full salt and pepper beard.

"Excuse me, Ma'am, but you can't be here. We are conducting an official police investigation and there no civilians allowed behind the yellow tape when we are gathering evidence."

Maureen looked at him, her cheeks flushed.

"Why are you searching the one place that everyone in the damned county knows she's not going to be?"

She went over and to the wall phone, picked it up, and sighed.

Dead.

Heading back out to the police car, she met with Sheriff Downs halfway.

"I need to get my bag out of your trunk, please. The phone is still dead, and I need to call my mother and Frank to let them know what's happened. They're already worried; I always call as soon as I get here."

Paul and Bill exchanged professional glances, and Bill nodded. Heading to the back of the cruiser, he grabbed her bag. At that moment, another uniformed officer approached them.

"Is this the suspect in custody?" he asked.

Bill dipped his head to one side. If there was one problem he had to deal with on a regular basis it was Shawn O'Leary. He wasn't the youngest of the deputies though he was in his mid-forties. It was a sore spot with him that he had been passed over for the position that Bill now held.

Since then he never missed a chance to piss in Bill's Cheerios whenever he got the chance. Before he could reply, Maureen spun to face Bill herself.

"You said I wasn't a suspect. You were lying to me. You still think that I had something to do with this, don't you? Answer me," her voice was on a near shrill with pent up frustration and anxiety.

He was going to speak but she spoke before he had the chance.

"That's it. I don't want anyone else snooping around or setting foot into that house until my parents have contacted their attorney. You never received any permission from any family member to go rummaging through our cabin or my sister's personal effects. I want you all gone! Do you hear me? Gone!" She brushed past the click of deputies and into the house, where Bill heard her screaming a new round of demands.

Taking his hat off, running his fingers through his hair, something he often did when he was in a situation with a confrontational woman, and put his hat back on before walking towards the sounds of an irate female.

"I knew I should have been a doctor."

CHAPTER 5

SHE PUSHED HER way into the house, glaring at the police technician dusting for prints around the front door.

"You have to go. Right now. I didn't give you permission to be doing this. No one did. You don't have the right to be here. Look at the mess you're making," she raged at him, her hands shaking frantically and pointing to the black smudges he was brushing on certain places along the doorjamb.

"Please, Ma'am, calm down. You just need to sit and relax and let us do our job. We will—".

"If you were doing your job, you'd be out there, finding what the hell happened to my sister! She's not here. She isn't in the house, if she was, I wouldn't have had to drive to town to bring back Howdy Doody to go looking for her, now would I?"

The man didn't seem that unnerved by Maureen, but he didn't answer her either. She was heading to the kitchen when she heard that nagging voice, so calm and pristine in tone, from the doorway.

"I am not going to have you going off half-cocked at my men. If you keep this up, you will wait outside or in the patrol car until we are done collecting evidence."

"I will do—".

"You'll do whatever I tell you to when it comes to this investigation. We will find out what happened to your sister, Maureen. But we have to collect evidence to find leads. Your sister might be out there, scared, hurt, kidnapped, or any other number of ungodly things that sick and twisted people are capable of. And the longer you delay my men in doing their jobs, the slimmer the chance we have of finding your sister alive." There, he'd spelled it out for her in black and white: shut up and cooperate, or your sister might die.

That that seemed to stick in Maureen's brain. Hannah might not be alive. She might be dead. Dead. A finite term that hung in the air like smoke rings from a cigar.

She swallowed hard, almost as if she were swallowing her pride, and nodded just once, just enough to let Sheriff Downs know she would do as asked.

She went over and took a seat at the kitchen table, where he joined her.

"I know this is hard on you, and it seems like we aren't exercising enough urgency, but this is standard procedure, and we need to gather the facts to get us leads."

This time, when she spoke, her voice was without the shrill urgency from before.

"And to make sure whoever did this pays, right?" It wasn't a question.

Maureen had only been a freelance reporter for a few years, but she had learned early on how the news was made. She remembered her first full day on the job and telling her editor about her story ideas. He had sat back in his old brown leather chair, cigar dangling casually out of one corner of his mouth with this Cheshire cat trademark smirk.

"Forget that crap, kid. You want to get your stuff published and out there, remember one simple rule: If it bleeds, it leads. Got it? Good. Now go out and get me a cover story." Maureen did, though the memory of some her more unpleasant assignments have haunted her in the years that passed.

She noticed Bill looking at her, as he looked over his shoulder.

"Hey Phil, you done in the kitchen?"

"Yeah, we're done in there."

She watched in odd bewilderment as Bill strode over to the kitchen stove, and turning on the tea kettle. He looked in the cupboards until he found a tea bag, and two mugs. He opened the fridge and frowned.

"You won't find much in there; Hannah isn't much of a cook." Peering at the top of the fridge, he grabbed a box of Saltines and when the kettle started to whistle, he poured two cups of tea. Setting one in front of her, she looked at him.

"What's this for?" she asked. Yet she took it, her hands folding around the ceramic mug, drawing comfort from its warmth.

"You need something to calm your nerves, and you probably need something to eat as well. This will do until we wrap up here, and you can make better arrangements. Myself, I have a Wild Catch Special at Ida's waiting for me." He picked up his mug, using both hands.

Almost like a child.

Maureen didn't know why, but his gesture touched her. No one had made her tea before. Or anything before. His cup of cheap tea and crackers seemed more appealing than any five-course meal in any swanky restaurant. She sipped her tea and realized how right he had been. The warm amber liquid washed through her, a growing warmth emanating from her belly. But there was something more.

It's probably delayed shock of the break-up with Steve, she thought.

She looked down at the tea. The tea had been meant as a peace offering. She knew for the sake of her sister, she needed to be more co-operative.

"I'll try and stay out of your way. I don't," she paused, unsure of where she going with this, "let me rephrase that. Whenever something happens in my family, I'm the sensible one. I'm the one who cleans up messes, picks up the pieces. It's hard for me to just, sit there, you know, sit and hope and wait. I know I should let you guys do your jobs, but I can't. I won't be able to rest until I know where she is."

She watched him, his face slightly softening as he drank his tea. She was putting this poor man, this complete stranger, through the ringer, and he was taking it all in stride. He's just doing his job, and you're being a royal bitch to him, Maureen chastised herself. *Maybe mother is right, maybe I don't really care about anything*, she thought. That brought tears to her eyes.

"What's wrong," he looked her, and pulled a napkin from the napkin caddy in the center of the table and handed it to her. One more kind gesture of his would make her go all girly on him.

"I was just thinking that maybe my mother is right, maybe I don't really care about Hannah or anything for that matter," she spoke, before blowing her nose into the napkin.

"Why do you say that? You're here, upset and scared as hell. You went for help, people who don't care about people just turn their backs and walk away," he sipped his tea, his thumbing idly rubbing the top of the handle of the mug.

"You sound like you speak from personal experience, Sheriff."

"In my line of work, I've seen a lot of things to know what the worst face of human nature looks like."

She peered over her mug at him, knowing exactly what he meant. They were in the same business: neither one of them could go to work until something bad happened.

"You aren't a bad person, Maureen. I'm fairly good at reading people, and you aren't as horrible as you make yourself out to be. Your human, that's not a crime."

"You don't understand. I didn't even want to come up here. I don't like this place. I haven't liked this place in a very long time. I had plans, and Hannah ruined them," she sniffled, tears pooling before streaming down her cheeks. "I had a life, friends of my own, a boyfriend, a good job." She paused, not sure if she wanted to continue.

"But?" He encouraged.

"But when you have a sister who is irresponsible, immature, and lazy, who barges into your life whenever hers isn't working, and ruins things, sometimes those things can never be replaced." She blew her nose again, then sipped the last of her tea. Bill, reaching over, pulled the kettle from the trivet, and poured her another cup. This time, he opened the crackers and put a few in front of her.

"People don't like their parties interrupted, or their vacation plans canceled because I have to run to the middle of nowhere when Hannah can't function as an adult."

He just let her talk, intent on listening.

"When my mother called me tonight, I was packing. She thinks Steve and I are moving. I haven't told her that Steve and I broke up."

She closed her eyes, though the tears still pooled. It felt like such a relief to let it all out, to cry and just break down. Yet Maureen felt odd, doing so in front a Bill and all the deputies around. After a few moments, she was composed enough to speak.

"He and I were planning a two-week vacation to the Florida Keys. We were going to go deep-sea fishing, and I was going to teach him to snorkel. But he came home one night and said we needed to talk.

He told me he was tired of our lives being on constant interruption by Hannah. He felt burdened by her, and I knew where he was coming from. He went on vacation, and I moved out. I was there, getting the last of my stuff when my mother called.

I was so angry I lost my temper and told her I had my own life to lead, but well," she shrugged, "it fell on deaf ears. Like always. My mother has always been overly concerned where Hannah is involved. It's probably because she's the baby of the family." Or because your mother simply loves her more, she pointed out to herself. You're an adult, face up to the facts that mother likes her more and get on with your life.

"Maureen, I think all parents are concerned for their kids, but I think it's natural to worry about the youngest kids more. The first born and older kids, they have to grow up fast and think on their feet. They didn't have anyone to follow or mimic, they had to make a way themselves. The youngest ones, they have examples to follow, so they figure they can take their time growing up, if at all."

"Well my mother is always worried about Hannah," she bit into a cracker, then another. "Even growing up, my mother never liked to tell her no or deprive her of anything. I think it's because Hannah nearly died when she was a little girl, and my mother felt guilty for it. Later on, after Hannah was old enough to understand what had happened, I think she used it to bait my mother into getting whatever she wanted."

"What happened, if you don't mind me asking?" He took a small stack of crackers, into several of them at one time.

"She almost drowned. Or did.

"Hannah was about four I think. I was in elementary school at the time, and wasn't home from school yet." She took another cracker.

"Where was, what was his name, Frank?" He poured himself the last of the tea, before taking another handful of crackers for himself.

"Frank traveled a lot. It's what he did. He was a regional distribution administrator for his company. He spent nearly forty weeks of the year on the road."

He nodded at her, pushing a few more crackers in her direction.

"Anyway, I came home from school and noticed the gate to the back yard was open. I walked around, and I saw Hannah," she paused tensely, "face down in the pool. My mother was drunk. Passed out. Hannah had probably been reaching for a toy that had fallen into the pool, and couldn't get out.

I ran to the neighbor's across the street, he was a cop and told him what happened. He ran over and dove into the pool, and did CPR until the paramedics arrived. They were able to revive my sister at the hospital that day." She shuddered, taking in a deep, slow breath.

Those dark memories, those secrets of her mother's imperfection of the picturesque suburban homemaker had been locked away deep inside for the past two decades. She felt her heart ache at the memory.

"But she obviously made it, that's a good thing."

Yeah, she was in a coma for about a week. It scared mother sober for a while. Shortly after that, Frank took a different position, and we moved."

She felt him looking at her. Maureen noticed that one of the deputies who dusting fingerprints around the back door had stopped and listened in on the conversation. When she looked up, he turned his attentions back to fingerprinting.

"Were child services ever called?" Bill asked.

"If they were, nothing happened. My mother had been drunk since my father died. My childhood was colorful. Though to this day, she will never admit to it. She'll say she only drank to be social." She smiled a little. "That's when I usually tell her that it doesn't count as social when you're the only one in the room.

"But it was more than just social drinking. Mother passed out with no lunch money for me. I'd come home to Hannah screaming her head off after sitting in a messy diaper all day. I was the one who potty trained her."

He was staring at her, and it unnerved her.

"I know, I know it makes no sense that if I took care of Hannah all those years, why I find it hard to do so now. I can't tell you why I feel that way either. The easiest way that I can describe it is like a custody battle, with my mother and I sharing joint custody of Hannah's future. I think after a while, my mother realized that Hannah was becoming more like me, and that's what I think finally sobered her up for good." *Though this last stunt of Hannah's might just put her searching for hope at the bottom of a bottle,* Maureen thought with remorse.

"That's an awful lot of baggage to have saddled to a kid. You didn't have any business taking care of Hannah. Hell, you were just a kid yourself," he interjected, not bothering to hide the agitation in his voice.

"Someone had to take care of Hannah, sign the report cards, and remember to get milk. If I waited for mother to crawl out from under her drunken stupor to do her job as a mom, I'd have starved to death, and Hannah still wouldn't be potty trained," she said.

Maureen's brief sprint down memory lane didn't even cover the tip of the iceberg when it came to how bad things were at home.

But that was some place that she never went. Like a darkened alley at night in the bad part of the city, and meant to be avoided.

Bill grabbed her mug, and his, and got up to place the cups into the sink when another officer, one that Maureen hadn't previously spoken to, came over to him midway to the kitchen.

"We've finished dusting the door and that for prints. There are three sets of clear prints, and maybe a partial on a fourth print," the officer stated.

Maureen noticed he had a slight mispronunciation to his S's and P's. It wasn't a lisp, but she couldn't quite put her finger on it.

"Have you run them through AFIS for any possible matches?"

"We are now. We did find an older police report that listed a Jack Porter at this address. There's an outstanding bench warrant for his arrest for a bar brawl that left one victim with about a dozen stitches in the face. He never made his court date. Bench warrant was issued a few months ago. The prints might belong to him, but we won't know until we hear back from AFIS."

Bill looked at Maureen. "Do you know anyone by the name of Jack Porter?" he asked, pulling his little notebook from his pocket and a pen as well.

"I think that was the name of this guy she was seeing. He might be her boyfriend, he might not. Hannah always had a lot of male," she paused, trying to find a tactful way of not describing her sister as a whore, "friends. I think he was the latest."

"What do you know about him, and how long has Hannah known him," he inquired.

She was about the say she probably knew as much about him as Hannah did when she picked him up, but a loud ringing cut her off.

"My cell phone!" She jumped from her chair at the table, the back of it hitting against the white washed paneling. Grabbing her bag from the coffee table, she searched frantically before finding it.

She sighed and flipped it open.

"Mother, I know I usually, call, but—"

"What's the matter with you? Do you have any idea how long your father and I have been sitting here, waiting for you to call and let us know what's going on?"

"Mother, I said that I—"

"I'm so disappointed in you, Maureen! First your feelings towards your sister, now this. You can be so thoughtless sometimes, do you know that? You never think of anyone else but yourself!"

"Mother, shut up! Just shut up! Please, I need you to just be quiet and listen."

"How dare you speak to me like that young lady," her mother screamed in outrage.

"Something's the matter with Hannah." That got her mother's attention, and silence ensued on the other end of the line.

"She wasn't here, and I couldn't find her. The phones are out, and I had to drive to town and get the police and they're here at the cabin, and," she took breath, rambling on without realizing that she had to take control before her mother went into a complete, panicked frenzy. "But Sheriff Downs is looking for her, and while the back door was broken into, they think it might be from someone losing their house key." Her eyes pleaded with Bill's, almost as if telepathically trying to tell him to play along.

"I'm sure she's fine, mother. Remember that time she left and didn't tell anyone and she went to Vegas because she and that ski instructor were destined to be together? He left her standing at the altar, then ran off with that ex-playmate? I'm sure it's something like that, you know Hannah. Free spirit and flying by the seat of her pants." Maureen was trying to steady her voice, not to ramble on to alarm her mother. The last thing she needed right now was her mother and Frank to come up to Michigan and be underfoot. Besides, what help could they possibly be?

Sobbing.

Maureen could hear her mother's sobs crystal clear across the wireless band of her state of the art cell phone. It was deafening.

"Mother, calm down, please. Please, just take a deep breath."

"You…have…to find…your sister," her choked sobs broke through. "You have to find my baby."

"I will mother, I promise. I'll find Hannah. Now please, just try and get some rest. I'm sure it's nothing. She's probably been out with her friends and lost track of time, that's all. You know how popular she is, even since she was little." Maureen tried to bait her mother's concern for her younger sister.

"Yes, yes I'm sure that's it. She probably went on a little vacation at the last minute," her mother interjected.

"Yeah, I'm sure that's it. You know that artists don't follow a schedule, they follow their creative streak," Maureen spoke softly, hoping the softness of her tone would sooth her mother all those long miles away.

"Maybe you're, Maureen. Please, just find out where she is, and take care of her," she pleaded.

It was the pleading that made Maureen wilt inside.

"I will. I'll call you as soon as I find out where she's staying." She didn't say "at", since that might cause her mother to think of her youngest child alone in a ditch, or floating in some lake.

"Okay, Maureen. You're such a good girl. I don't say it as often as I should, but I mean it. Take care of yourself, sweetie." And the phone went dead.

It was all Maureen could do not cry herself. She knew her mother was depending on her. But her harsh words renewed the hatred that smoldered inside her. And just as Maureen was about to unleash that fire, her mother would put out that fire with some tender moment or kind word, and reduce Maureen's flame to a mere spark.

The constant duality of their awkward and strained relationship was taking a toll. It was an emotional roll coaster, and Maureen wanted it to stop long enough for her to get off.

She walked over to Sheriff Downs.

"I'm sorry about that. You know how mothers can be in situations like this, I'm sure."

"How did she take the news," he inquired, that familiar formality creeping back into his tone.

"Total hysterics and mass frenzy. But she'll be fine, I think, once she's had some rest."

"She sounds like she really reamed you good. I'm sorry."

"Why are you sorry, she isn't your mother," she interjected, feeling herself begin to clam up again at the mention of her family. *It's the secrets that keep us together*, she thought ironically.

They heard footsteps on the front porch, and for some reason, Maureen swore it was her sister, in those retro combat boots she always wore.

Her hopes were disappointed when she saw the familiar face of Deputy O'Leary. She felt a nervous jittery feeling in the pit of her stomach. She knew he had something bad to tell her, and knew he was going to enjoy it.

"Sheriff Downs, I need a word with you. It's about the witness here." He was standing, arms folded behind him, in a cavalier stance of authoritative smugness.

"Deputy, what is it?" Bill was clearly not in the mood for his attitude.

"I was just talking to Irene, the head cashier over at Miller's Food Mart says she heard over the police scanner they have in the back office about the investigation we have going on here. She immediately called me when she noticed that there was a mysterious wire transfer from a Holten Industries to a," he paused, barely taking the time to scan his notes before looking straight at Maureen, "a Miss Maureen Welsh. It's for five thousand dollars."

Maureen felt the accusatory stares coming at her and tried not to let her face flush.

"Do you want to tell me what that money is for, ma'am?" asked Deputy O'Leary, who was clearly enjoying her discomfort and embarrassment.

"The money was for taking care of Hannah," Maureen stated.

"That sounds like a confession to me, Sheriff. Maybe we should continue this conversation down at the station, unless you aren't done playing house" he stated, and started stepping towards her, his smile sadistic and vengeful.

"Now wait just a goddamned minute, Shawn. First off, it wasn't a confession. Second of all, Ms. Welsh has been cooperating with the investigation since it started, and three," he stood, hands on his hips, inching towards him, "last I checked, I was in charge of this investigation. I mean, it's why I get to where the pretty metal star after all."

"So let's just take in her and book her," Shawn said.

"Ms. Welsh hasn't been declared a suspect. So far all we have is conjecture. I'm not jumping the gun because you've want every crime wrapped up like an episode of CSI."

Maureen watched the tense exchange between the two in odd fascination. She felt odd, like her honor was being defended by Sheriff Downs, and it moved her a little. She knew she had better contact her mother's attorney before she ended up in jail.

"We may have a case of first-degree murder on our hands, Bill. We have a suspect in our midst, and you want me to—"

Bill interjected.

"I want you to solve the case within the confines of the law. We uphold the law, we defend it, and if needs be, we die by it. But we don't go around it, because then we're no better than the killers and thieves we are trying to apprehend."

Deputy O'Leary's face flushed with anger and was about to say something when Bill stopped him again.

"And Shawn, this had better be the last time I have to tell you to stop stepping on my toes in an investigation. I won't tolerate you, or any-one else, side stepping every move and questioning my authority. You don't like it; you know where you can go."

O'Leary stormed out, the porch door slamming so hard it shook the panes of glass in the wooden frame. No one uttered a word as the patrol car pull out of the drive and disappear.

Bill turned to Maureen, who was on the phone, speaking in hushed tones. She looked at him, all the while listening to Alfred Meyers, her mother's attorney.

"Yes, Maureen, I just heard from your mother. Now be quiet and listen. I know how these backward town cops do business. Do not let them ask you any more questions until I get there. Do not give them any more information than you need to, and for God's sake, do not let them search the house for anything that they might be able to twist and use against you. I'm out on the one fifteen redeye to Detroit Metro, and then I have a connecting flight to Traverse City. I'll be there before dawn. Call my cell if you need anything."

"Thanks, Alfred, I appreciate it."

She turned and looked at Bill.

"Who was that," he inquired, his eyes questioning her obtuse behavior.

"An editor. He wanted to run by some story ideas, but well, you can imagine I'm not in the mood to write anything now," she lied. "He thinks I'm taking a few days off because of Steve and I broke up, and I told him I had to move out. I didn't want to get into a big long saga of explaining the real situation. Sometimes a lie is just easier than the truth."

Her fingers laced around the Saint Christopher charm from her necklace and began to fiddle with it, idly tugging it back and forth.

For the second time that evening, she felt as though she had read his mind.

"I know what you mean, Maureen."

"Sheriff Downs!"

A loud noise crackled over his shoulder radio.

"This is Downs. What have you got Paul?"

More static, but there clearly a voice on the other end of the line.

"We are about a hundred yards west of the greenhouse. We have Magnus out here, trying to pick up a trail. We found more evidence to suspect foul play."

Maureen's heart stopped. The pulsating throb of life slowed to a cease in her veins.

She hadn't been expecting that. She was sure they would find Hannah, who maybe had hurt herself cross-country skiing, or hiking.

Anything but this.

This was no longer a version of Maureen's reality, but some surreal, altered state that she had become a part of, and didn't know how to wake up. One doesn't wake up one morning, to unpacked boxes in a new apartment and then find a loved one missing. Those things didn't happen to people like Maureen and her family. They were different. This wasn't making any sense.

The hair on the back of her neck stood on end. A chill ran up her entire body finally erupting into a nervous flutter in her stomach. She had the strangest sense that she, the house—everything surrounding the cabin—was being watched. It mingled with a sickening fear that Hannah's outcome might depend on Maureen's actions.

She didn't feel safe, even with a swarm of police officers around her. Driven with a new determination to get these men as far away from the cabin as possible. Maureen stood up. Something serious was going on, but she didn't know what.

"Bill, you still there," the voice inquired.

"Yeah, Paul. What else have you got?" The downward spiral of Bill's tone worried Maureen even more.

"We found a bathrobe, a blue silk one, torn in several places. It's pretty bloody, and from the looks of it, fairly recent. We also found a cell phone. It belongs to Hannah Prescott. The line is still open from this end." There isn't much snow out here, since the pines keep the ground pretty covered."

"Call the boys at the lab and get them out there. Set up a new parameter. Do you know the number she was calling?"

"I do. Sending you a text of it now. The parameters are going up now." The static stopped, and the silence now seemed deafening.

Bill dialed, and everyone looked up when Maureen's cell phone started to ring.

Bill looked at Maureen.

"Why don't we take this back to the station where we can talk more."

"Do I need to call my lawyer?"

Bill didn't answer her.

Maureen's head spun. Her heart, which had ceased to beat with the unexpected findings in the woods, now beat reverently until she started to fan herself with her hands to keep from hyperventilating.

CHAPTER 6

THIS WASN'T HAPPENING. She was dreaming she had to be. Any moment, she was going to wake up in her cramped apartment in downtown Chicago. She was sure of it.

"Maureen, please follow me to the patrol car," Bill was looking at her again.

Snapping out of her daze, she looked at him, fierce determination in her eyes.

"I'm not going anywhere."

"Excuse me," he said.

"I said I'm not going anywhere. I didn't kill my sister. I didn't do anything to her," she looked sternly at him. "And furthermore, I didn't give you permission to search the premises, and I wasn't presented with a search warrant. I know my rights, and you're violating them."

"We are operating within the law. I'm going to ask you to leave, so I can secure the scene. I don't want to contaminate any evidence. That gives us permission. We have probable cause, Miss Welsh. We don't work for you, we are working for the victim, for Hannah Prescott."

Bill grabbed his shoulder radio. "Boyd, this is Sheriff Downs. Do me a favor. Wake up judge Traver and get a search warrant."

"You still have to operate within the confines of the constitution, Sheriff Downs. Any evidence that may have been collected here, without the presence of said search warrant, will be inadmissible in court. Now I want you and your men out of this house, and don't come back, unless you have a search warrant."

Her veins were heated with wild anxiety, rushing through her with all the potency of a heroin junkie's wet dream.

"I was just on the phone with my family's attorney. You may have heard of the firm, Bradford and Black. I'm sure you've heard of them," her voice laced with an underlying maliciousness.

His eyes challenged her, and she watched his jaw muscles clench

37

and release several times. His breathing was laborious, controlled. She knew she was treading on thin ice, but something, some gut instinct told her to get them out of the house.

"I've cooperated and I want to find out what's happening with my sister, but I'm not going anywhere. You have no reason to suspect me, except so you can have a quick an easy conclusion. I'm sorry. The answers I want have to stem from the truth. I don't doubt your abilities," she softened her tone, afraid she might have pushed his buttons a little too hard, "but I have my rights, too. Now please, I'd like you to go." And she walked over, holding the front door open.

She watched as he stared at her, then at the floor for a moment.

"I'm not going to ask you again, Miss Welsh. I need you to leave the premises, or I'm going to arrest you."

"For what?"

"Interfering with a police investigation."

"This is family property, and I'm not leaving. I know how you backwoods sheriffs work. Planting evidence and home by dinner."

He reached behind him, grabbed a set of handcuffs, and grabbed her wrist, snapping the cuff home with a deafening click.

"Maureen Welsh, you have the right to remain silent." Bill continued reading her Miranda Rights, and secured her hands behind her back, leading her outside to the police car.

"Miss Welsh, you have been given your Miranda Rights. You're hereby instructed not to leave town."

He looked at his men.

"Search warrant is on its way. Keep the premises secure and keep gathering evidence. I'm going to take Miss Welsh back to the jail to process her."

The uncomfortable next few moments of silence that ensued could be felt by everyone. She was trying not to fidget, or look worried, or too upset, or not upset enough. She felt any hint of her emotions would betray her. She needed to be strong for her sister. Whatever the outcome she knew it would ultimately be her strength that got her through whatever tough mess she was going to end up facing. It always had.

"This is personal, Sheriff Downs, at least with me. It's my sister. Imagine how you would feel." Why should you care if he gets upset with you, she chastised herself. Why do you care what this man thinks?

Once inside the patrol car, Sheriff Downs began the long, silent drive back to the station. It wasn't until they were out on the main road that he finally spoke.

"Remember Maureen, secrets rot away at the truth. But mark my words, sooner or later, the garbage starts to smell."

"Do you know you do that very often," she tilted her head in bemusement.

He took the bait after a few seconds.

"What?"

"Well, it's two things. First, you assume that you have come up with all possible and rational solutions to everything; therefore, you completely ignore the sometimes obvious details that are right under your nose. You completely ignore anyone else's opinions. I hear it's genetic amongst you males. And two, you assume that everyone is lying to you and covering something up."

Maureen paused, unsure if what she thought next she should utter aloud. Finding the nerve, and the need to show him another man would not bully her ever again, she found her voice.

"She must have done a real number on you to make you think like that," she said.

She knew she hit a nerve as soon as she said it, and immediately felt a pang of regret. She hadn't meant to be hurtful to him; she didn't even mean to get into a confrontation with him. It just seemed to happen whenever she was around him for more than a few moments.

"Yeah you women really know how to stick it in and break it off." His words didn't mask the bitter resentment he was projecting towards her at that moment. She could feel his rage emanating towards her as if she were standing in front of a burning building.

"Why do you find ways to rile me," her annoyance very clear in her tone.

"Why do you rise to the occasion," he bit back.

"How about we end this conversation before we say something we might regret," she said.

Her nerves that had been riding an adrenaline rush like a junkie on a binge were waning, and she was growing tired. She could feel her body just giving out as the energy just seemed to seep from her pores.

"Oh, this conversation isn't over, not by a long shot, Miss Welsh. For the record, and as a reminder in case you've already forgotten, don't leave town. I have to warn you that you're now a prime suspect in this case. I'll be posting Deputy Hopkins outside of the cabin, to make sure of that. However you'll have to make other arrangements as the cabin is a crime scene at the moment."

Patience wearing thin, she snapped at him once again.

"I heard it the first time, Colombo. I don't know if you noticed, but I'm fluent in Neanderthal."

She leaned back in the seat, choosing to ride the rest of the way to the station in silence.

Chapter 7

BY THE TIME Maureen got back to the cabin, she'd been booked, finger printed, and processed through the Shoshanee County Police Department. With the money her parents had sent, she had been able to make bail without having to call her parents.

Alfred would arrive tomorrow, and in the meantime, Bill informed her that she could return to the cabin as the forensic techs had finished processing the scene.

It took just a few hours, due in large to the fact that there were no other prisoners in the jail. Another officer had dropped Maureen off at the cabin, and she pulled away the yellow police tape across the front door before entering.

The silence of the cabin rattled Maureen's already frayed nerves. Every creak, every noise, she found herself looking around. The bone-chilling realization hit her that someone had come into this place, this warm safe place, and violated it with their evil deeds and abduction.

She felt robbed, and she knew this is exactly how people felt when their homes were burglarized. Only to Maureen, something much more precious was stolen.

She forced herself to go through the house, checking every window, every door. Unnerved by the lack of curtains, Maureen found push-pins in one of the drawers of the massive roll-top desk, and sheets from the linen closet, and covered the windows. Her mother would have had a fit if she saw Maureen improvising with her six-hundred thread count brushed cotton sheets as window coverings.

The enclosed main floor made her feel a little better, but not by much. She dragged her weary body to the couch, falling onto it. Gathering the pillow to her chest, she buried her face in it, and started to weep. Uncontrollable sobs shook and rattled her plump frame until finally she lifted her head and took deep, gasping breaths. Her lungs ached, and her chest hurt with the heaviness that always accompanied a profound sense of loss or sadness.

Her sobs ebbing, she ran her fingers through her hair.

"Okay Maureen, you're the writer. You report stories, you find the clues. This…is no different."

Maureen's personal pep talk didn't do much in terms of motivation, but it kept her mind off the fact that it was dark and she was alone. While she longed for sleep, her mind wouldn't allow her body to relax in the house where her sister went missing.

Restless, she went upstairs to the master bedroom and changed the sheets, took a shower. The openness of the cabin loomed around her, suffocating her where it should have provided comfort. She knew if she could stay busy until dawn, she would be okay.

It was a nagging feeling. Something in her subconscious kept telling her that if she could hold out 'til morning, she'd be fine.

Her brain began to rattle off a plan of attack. Start on the main floor; check every crevice, every drawer. There had to be something to help her figure out Hannah's daily routine, she reassured herself. People just don't go up and missing in this day in age. There is always a logical explanation for things, even in small towns.

"It's not like this is pioneer country and the settlers are still wondering what's lurking in the woods. This is the twenty-first century for Christ's sake. People don't just up and disappear."

Unless they wanted to.

She shook her head to dispel the dark thought. Now wasn't the time to linger on such things, there was a far greater task at hand.

She started with the couch and cushions, unzipping them, feeling around on the inside, and ended up at the foot of the stairs three hours later, her back aching, but her mind fresh with the challenge that lay ahead. She was dredging up the stairs, her muscles fatigued but her brain willing her on, when she approached the master bedroom.

Hannah loved color, and her master bedroom was a testament to the wild and crazy patterns that seemed to run parallel to her lifestyle. Maureen had to admit that her sister knew style.

The room definitely echoed a Tibetan theme. The wall behind the sleigh bed was a brilliant vibrant red. The pillows and comforter, even the duvet, were shades of red, amber, and gold. Dark wood, from the bed, to the nightstands, dresser, armoire, and hope chest, were a rich mahogany. Maureen started with the obvious spots, and in the nightstand, she found a handful of condoms, a few votive candles, matches, and the TV remote.

"At least you're smart enough to realize our family's genetics shouldn't be breeding."

When the search in the dressers and armoire came up empty-handed, she doubled checked to make sure she hadn't missed anything by pulling out the drawers and looking underneath. She was just about to open the chest, when a noise from outside brought her out of her task-induced daze.

Loud thwacking, like two pieces of wood banging against one another, echoed outside.

Thwack, thwack, thwack. One, two, three.

Then silence. And again. And again. Her breath stopped in chest. Her ears strained to listen above the heavy hammering of her heart, her backbone stiff with fear.

Thwack. Thwack. Thwack.

Then silence. The burning of Maureen's lungs, depleted of oxygen, finally forced her to take a breath. Faced with the uncertainty of what was lingering outside, but the need to find a rational explanation for the noise, she forced her feet to shuffle towards the window.

Her shaky hand wavered, slowly pulling back the curtain. She caught a faint glimpse, like a reflection of something shiny, above the darkened tree line. Her muscles started to relax, her brain seeking a logical depiction of what she had just seen.

"It's probably a helicopter. The Coast Guard, or maybe a military base nearby." Calming herself, Maureen started to laugh.

It's amazing how fast the mind can just whip up something sensational that makes the rest of the body all tense, she mused.

"Now I know where our society gets its barbarianism. Our brains and bodies function with a sadomasochistic nature."

Heading back over to the chest, she searched it. Nothing.

She searched under the bed, and in between the mattresses. Behind paintings, and picture frames. Nothing. She was just about to leave when she stared at the closet. Her pulse tensed. She knew about the scratches on the door. They were still vivid in her mind.

But Maureen needed to check everything. She walked over and opened the door. Grabbing the chain, she turned on the light.

Clothes hung from every available inch. The closet was jammed at the top with shoes and purses. A tie rack — probably her father's at one point — now hung adorned with various belts.

Fifteen minutes later, she found no clues of real value; expect Maureen now had a good idea of where her sister's monthly stipend went. All of the clothes that were crammed into that tiny closet all had designer labels, many of them still having price tags.

She was at a loss. Maureen figured that she would have found something in here. From all the stories she had covered, she felt with unwavering certainty that something would be found in the bedroom. After all, bedrooms were the sanctuary of any house. It was where people went after a bad day to relax, it's where they hid their pornography, their diaries, their secrets. Maureen was certain that she would have found some of Hannah's secrets here, too.

Her hands idly ran along some of the leather belts. Maybe her earlier instincts about Hannah were still true; she was just a selfish materialistic child that needed babysitting. She let go of the belt, and watched as it slipped off the tie hook, taking a few others along with it.

Bending over, she was gathering the handful of belts back up, when she noticed a screwdriver, tucked in the very back of the closet, hidden along the floor.

Putting the belts back up, Maureen kneeled and grabbed the screwdriver. She moved the shoeboxes, surprised at the weight of one of them. Flipping off the top of the box, Maureen found a candle, matches, a flashlight, and a rosary.

The hair on her forearms raised in perfect sync with her brain as she realized she was stumbling onto something, something that might help her find Hannah.

She shook another shoebox, and its lightness immediately prompted her to flip off the top. Pre-wrapped packages of Twinkies, cupcakes, little packages of cheese nips packed the box. A few small bottles of water lay tucked in between the mass of sugar and salted coated snacks. If this had been in anyone else's house, in any other place in time, Maureen would have sworn that she had just found some teenager's secret stash of sweets.

Why would Hannah keep junk food hidden in a shoebox in her closet? *God I hope she's not bulimic. And since when in the world did Hannah, inventor of the original sin, pray the Rosary?*

Maureen was at a loss. Her parents weren't overly religious. They weren't even part of the church of the good times now crowd, as her grandfather put it, referring to those people who only went to church on Christmas and Easter.

Her head tilted to one side, something she usually did when something wasn't making sense to her, Maureen slid down the wall of the closet, and sat cross-legged.

Junk food, water, and a screwdriver, she wondered. Something just wasn't making sense.

She kneeled in the closet, her eyes catching sight of the scratches in the door. Running her finger along one cautiously, the wood of the

44

oak door running under her fingertips. The wood was freshly splintered.

Maureen wasn't sure what made those scratches, but the wood wasn't worn smooth from age and time. Whatever and whoever had made these scratches, had done it fairly recently. Probably within the last couple of weeks or so.

Picking up the screwdriver, Maureen rolled it around in her hand. Looking at the door again and then back to the screwdriver, Maureen was struck with odd, yet exhilarating notion.

Placing the tip of the flathead screwdriver into one of the grooves of wood, Maureen's hand started to tremble with the idea that her hunch was right.

Someone had sat in this closet and carved these notches. She could feel the heat rise to her cheeks with sudden excitement. Her stomach also fluttered, knowing that it was more than likely Hannah herself who had made these scratches.

"Why would you make these scratches, Hannah? It just doesn't make any sense."

Nothing was making sense right now. Looking down at her watch, she noticed it was nearly four in the morning. The tension in her muscles was slowly starting to ebb away as she relaxed on the floor of the closet.

She traced each scratch with her finger, counted them — twenty-three in all. She was unsure of where to look next, yet certain that she was onto something. Hannah didn't like the dark, never had. To sit her closet and do this didn't point at any normal characteristics of her little sister.

Unless she's gotten herself into something much bigger than a bottle this time around, she mused sadly. You know the old saying, 'the apple doesn't fall far from the tree.'

"What a nice legacy you've passed on mother," she muttered.

As her mind wandered, so did her finger. Eventually trailing onto the floor, where she felt a sharp sting across her fingertip.

"Son of a-," but she trailed off. Her finger had run over something sharp. Kneeling at eye level to where her fingers had been, Maureen saw a tiny chip of one of the floorboards slightly chipped away. When Maureen pressed on the board, she thought she could feel it move gently, barely noticeable.

Realizing with an epiphany what the screwdriver was for, she jabbed the blunt end into the floorboard and pressed. Without much resistance, the single wooden floorboard gave way to an open spot in the closet floor.

Grabbing the flashlight, Maureen shined it into the hole, and spotted the shiny brilliant red of a book. Grabbing it, and surprised by its weight, she pulled it free from its hiding place. The book itself was a rich wine red, the cover adorned with sequins. Maureen knew immediately that the journal belonged to Hannah.

Embossed on the front cover, in silver embroidery were her sister's initials.

Jubilation and guilt washed through Maureen with equal saturation. She had found something, a piece of a puzzle that just wasn't making any sense right now. But Maureen felt a horrible guilt knowing she might have to invade her sister's privacy to find any real answers.

She remembered her reaction when her mother, in a drunken state of denial about her daughter being the perfect child, read her diary when she was younger. It was then that Maureen learned how to keep secrets, and most everything else, to herself.

Looking at the scratches again, she already knew her choice.

Dear Diary,   *April 4, 2015*

I know that I moved here to harness my creativity and my inner chi, but sometimes it gets really boring here. I have to drive at least an hour to get to the nearest mall, and even at that it doesn't really count as a shopping center. I think there's a rule that if there is more than one outdoor sporting goods store within a five block radius of one another, it doesn't count as shopping. No one here knows what real shopping is. I told the salesgirl at the super Wal-Mart in Lancaster that I missed Saks, and she asked me, 'sacks of what.' I could have died.

But still, the lack of things to do is more than made up by the nice selection of Park Rangers, State troopers, and the few coastguard guys that hang around. Which reminds me, I spent all last weekend with Gabe, and he hasn't called back yet. Oh well, men should be like Kleenex — soft, strong, and disposable. Or like cars, always a better model to upgrade into.

Well, I'm off to take a nap. I don't know why I'm tired, I just woke up a few hours ago, but I did walk down to the lake to paint.

Superior Lies

The entry was signed with a simple H, and Maureen tried not to laugh. Maureen called these lines Hannah's golden moments. One minute she was hitting the nail on the head, like she did with her sporting goods store observation, and the next minute she was wallowing in the shallow end of the intellectual pool.

Dear Diary,   *April 27, 2015*

I think I'm going to have to call someone, like a critter person or whoever does things with wild animals. Something has been spilling over my garbage cans in the back. There were maggots, it was gross city! I almost gagged. It's times like these that I wish I had a man around, to do little stuff like clean up the icky messes, and do all those chores that I can't do, like fix the loose step on the porch.

I think I'm going to start going for walks in the morning to the lake. I like the adrenaline rush, and the water is gorgeous! So blue and pristine. Which reminds me, mom just sent a gorgeous blue sapphire pendant to me. She got the bowls and vases that I sent her and she couldn't believe how remarkable they are.

I feel sorta bad, taking the necklace when I really didn't make the bowls. I mean, I made bowls, but I didn't know all the work that was involved in getting them all the way done. I mean, I needed a kiln, and then there are these variations of clay and glazes that refer to cones.

I know it has something to do with how fine the clay is, and the glaze, if it's too heavy or light, might not work out right. I didn't know that much work is involved. I don't want to spend all that money and put that much time into something that I might screw up. So I've been buying these bowls at this local potter's place. I send a few to mom at a time, and she thinks I make them. I mean, I could probably make something like that with practice, but well, pottery is losing my interest. There are no famous potters, and only sculptures like Michelangelo ever became famous.

And I have decided that I want my riches and fame while I'm still cute and young enough to enjoy them.

Oh! Speaking of enjoying something, Dwight, this new guy I met at the Pink Elephant Bar, is teaching me to play pool! He says the way I hold my cue I'm a natural for hold-

ing the stick. Being up here sure has helped my creative juices.

Well, I'm off. I have a date tonight with Dwight! Wish me luck!

On and on the diary went. Page after page of useless drivel and run-ons about her love life. In the twenty minutes that Maureen had been reading it, she made it through all the entries for April, May, and part of June, and had counted nearly six guys that Hannah had more than likely been romantic with.

What do you care who she was bringing home?

"Maybe I'm jealous," she uttered aloud. Truth be told, her sex life, either with Steve or anyone else, was pretty much vanilla. That's how she compared it to plain vanilla ice cream. Not great, not bad, just vanilla.

She closed the book for a moment, her heart sinking with despair that her golden opportunity in finding the journal, was quickly tarnishing. She leaned her head back against the wall of the closet, drumming her fingertips on the top of the journal. Residing to give it one more go, she reopened the pages and began reading again.

The same useless ramblings were written on page after page. However, an entry, towards the middle of August, finally caught Maureen's attention.

Dear Diary,   *August 14, 2015*

I feel awful. It seems like I haven't slept in days, though I know I have been catching a few hours here and there. Something strange is going on.

I was in the greenhouse last week, unearthing the bulbs from the oleanders, when I heard this odd sound. It was a loud wind whooshing sort of a thwacking. It seemed to just come out of nowhere, and at first I thought it was a helicopter from one of the local news channels flying overhead. But I went outside, and the noise got louder, and there was nothing in the sky. Nothing. It was near dark, so I thought maybe it was a hot air balloon, since I know that they have them in Traverse City for the Aviation Festival. But I looked, and didn't find anything.

But it's more than that. Every time I set foot into the

woods lately, I get this weird feeling. Like I'm being watched. At first I thought it was Dave — that jerk from the Pink Elephant — who I later found out was married! When I told him to drop dead and lose my number, he was pissed. He threw a beer all over my car and kicked the door before Lenny, the bartender, came out and hustled him off. But it wasn't him.

And lately when I go for walks in the morning, I started noticing something wrong with some of the trees along the path I take. The bark is peeling off, literally peeling off like a banana! It's creepy strange. And when I get to the lake, the geese and swans are rarely there anymore. Do swans go south for the winter? I should look that up somewhere when I go into town.

But it's just odd that's all. And my garage cans are still being molested by whatever is hungry. I'm thinking of putting them in the greenhouse where the raccoons, or badgers, can't get at them.

I'm tired now. I want to sleep. The loud noise woke me up again this morning at three thirty, and I haven't been able to get to sleep since.

Maureen's eyes stared at the page. Was that the same sound she had heard? Maybe Hannah was right, maybe it was a helicopter, only it wasn't from any of the news channels.

"Maybe it's like the Fedduchi's," she said. The Fedduchi's were a wealthy Chicago family that came from old money. The eldest, Joseph, had a known love of aircraft. He collected them and stored them in a private hanger he had on the family estate. His son was also a collector, but he was into illegal artifacts.

Using one of his dad's helicopters, he had lifted a box of stolen Spanish coins and was transporting them to a mutual friend via that helicopter. What he didn't know was that the coins were bait, from a governmental task force that had installed a small GPS tracking system to the inside of one of them. They were waiting when he landed to make the bust. The informant who tipped off the feds had mysteriously disappeared.

Oh God, what if Hannah witnessed something she wasn't meant to.

Things like that could happen. People see things, hear things they aren't supposed to know ever happened to begin with, and the next minute, that person is gone. Or worse.

49

Jennifer Gifford

Maureen flipped through to the next entry, her palms hot, and her blood racing with anxiety.

Dear Diary,　　　　　　　　　　　　　*August 28, 2015*

Something is really wrong here. I went to the lake this morning, and there was all this, well I don't know what it was, but it looked like hospital gauze, strewn all over the beach. I mean, it looked like someone's Halloween prank. It was scary, but a little breathtaking too. There wasn't really a pattern to it, not like you'd think of like with a spider's web, thank God! You know I hate them! But it was sorta pretty. It looked like the remains of wings, or something ethereal like that, all silky and shiny in the new light of the morning. The stuff had an opalescence to it, and it was just such a breathtaking sight. I ran back to the cabin to get my camera and when I came back, it was gone!

I drove into town, taking to one of the DNR people, and some guy named, Shawn (I think) and he said that it wasn't anything I should worry my pretty little head about. He said it's what happens when birds are getting ready to fly south for the winter, that they 'shed their nests'. I told him I had never seen anything like that before, and I've been here almost two years now, but he assured that it does hap-en, and sometimes it's in abundance.

He said Michigan has a lot of birds that migrate here for the summer, then leave. But still. It was just, well, it doesn't mix well, as my sister would say.

He seemed like he knew what I was going to ask before I asked it. And I didn't like the way he was looking at me. Creepy old men gross me out. I felt bad for him. Here he was, in his forties, and still playing the role of park ranger. How sad. Even sadder was that I think he was hitting on me.

But it still doesn't add up. I hear those noises all the time now. Always in the early morning hours. And I have no-ticed that the greenhouse, on the side that faces the lake, had the glass broken. Someone has been fiddling around with my Lilly bulbs. Why would anyone want to steal something that they can get down at Jake's Feed and Greenery?

And another thing. The trees that are peeling are only on the path from the back of my property leading to the lake. I

50

*went back to Mr. DNR guy, Shawn, and he said that it's a
form of Dutch Elm disease. On pine trees? On oak trees?
But he says that's what happens when these environmental
problems occur, they manifest into something else.*

*But I don't know. Dutch oak disease? I called Maureen at
work, but she hasn't called me back yet. I figure she might
know.*

*I'm just really tired. I don't sleep well now a days. I had
new, stronger locks installed. Something in the woods is
giving me the heebie-jeebies.*

Maureen stopped, and looked in the box, searching for and finding a
pen. Flipping to the last page of the diary, she used the blank page to
start making notes from the information Hannah had left in her journal entries. Sitting back and stretching her legs, she leaned her head
back, the words of Hannah's diary blurring before her in her mind.

What is that noise from? There has to be a logical explanation for all
of this. She made a few more notes, jotting down things that she
would need to look into.

First thing in the morning, she would be going to town, and using
whatever library sources the town had to get some answers. She continued to read, her lids growing heavy with fatigue.

Finally, her head tilted to one side, resting against the doorjamb of
the closet door she drifted off to sleep.

Chapter 8

A LOUD, REPETITIVE pounding woke Maureen from her restful slumber. She blinked a few times, unsure of where she was. When the familiar sight of her blue bedroom didn't come into focus, she bolted upright, feeling a sharp pain shoot through her shoulders and neck.

Blinking, she realized she'd fallen asleep in the closet, still clutching Hannah's diary.

She got up, stretched and walked over to the banister. The loud rapping was coming from the front door. She cautiously made her way half way down the stairs, peering at the frosted windowpanes beside the front door, before relaxing.

The figure of a short, stout individual was rapping on her door. Her muscles immediately relaxed as she opened the front door.

"Alfie!" The jubilation in her voice surprised the older gentleman, but he none the less returned her greeting smile.

"My gosh, Maureen, how you've grown. You look more and more like your mother every day," he said as he hugged her. She smiled, despite the sting of his remark.

It hadn't been intentional on his part, but any comparison made about her in reference to her mother always made her feel ill at ease.

"That isn't the first time I've been told that. Please, come in." She held open the door for him and motioned to the couch.

"I'd offer you some coffee, but well, Hannah isn't much of a cook. I just woke up myself."

"I'm sorry to disturb you, but I thought I should head out to the cabin right away. I know how these small town sheriffs' operate. They spend their whole lives throwing drunks out of the local tavern, and when something outside the norm happens, they suddenly see themselves as heroes. The need to break away from the repetitiousness of small time life drives the need above justice, and sometimes innocent people," he paused, looking around, then at Maureen, "sometimes they get blamed for something that they didn't do."

"I've already been given my rights. I was Mirandized last night by Sheriff Downs as I was arrested."

"What were you charged with?"

"Obstructing an investigation."

Alfred opened his briefcase and started taking notes.

"All right, but you should know that if Sheriff Downs or any of his men come back here, you ask for a warrant," he said.

"If they have one do they have to read me my rights again?"

"Miranda rights have nothing to do with anything they find, Maureen. It just deals with your speech representing your rights. But given that you've already been arrested, we should get down to business. Now, tell me everything."

Maureen didn't know where to start, so she started at the beginning. Forty-five minutes and a half a legal pad later, Alfred took off his glasses and rubbed the bridge of his nose.

"Maureen, I'll be honest with you. I don't think you have to worry about the obstruction charges, but I wouldn't put it past them for trying to stick you with it. What concerns me is Hannah's disappearance and you're perceived role."

"Why? I haven't done anything. I didn't even meet them until I went into the Sheriff's office yesterday. Why would they want to pin me with a crime I didn't commit."

"Because crime in a small town consists of two main elements, the guilty, and the hero. Everyone has a part to play, child, and I'm afraid your role has already been chosen for you." His Louisiana drawl still crept into his speech from time to time.

Her frustrated hands flew into the air, a look of exasperation spreading across her milky complexion.

"All I want is my sister found, safe and unharmed. You know this isn't like Hannah. She has never run off without telling us about it. I think it might be this new guy she's seeing. The sheriff seems to think that he might have something to do with what's happened. God, I hope she hasn't saddled herself to another loser."

Alfred was making notes and looked up at her.

"You think its drugs? Be honest with me, Maureen, I can't help you and your family unless I know all the facts. The last thing I need is to have something surprise me in the middle of all of this mess. What do you know about him, this boyfriend? Was it serious?"

"With Hannah? Come on Alfie, you know Hannah. She changes boyfriends faster than she changes the sheets. It's always 'love at first sight' then it runs cold after a few weeks. They're never really serious,

Frank and mother see to that."

"Well, someone has to keep an eye out for her. It's a full-time job, and Lord only knows that you've done it long enough," Alfie said.

Maureen didn't say anything, but she couldn't help but feel a little comfort knowing that someone — even if it wasn't a direct member of her family — saw how hard she worked at making sure Hannah was all right. She found the acceptance in Alfred that she was looking for from her own family.

"Well, I don't know anything about this one. That's not my job. My job is to come bail her out of whatever trouble she's in, pay the bills, clean up the messes, and be on my merry little way until she falls into the next pitfall. Her diary didn't mention him all that much either."

"Do you still have it?"

"Yeah, I," she paused, really what she was about to say was going to sound stupid. "I fell asleep in the closet while reading it."

"Why were you in the closet," he questioned her, his eyes peering over his wireless rimmed glasses at her. For a few brief moments, tension ebbed between them.

"I'm not crazy, and I didn't fall off the wagon like my mother, Al-fie. I don't even drink. So stop worrying. I was searching her room and I found the diary while I was ransacking the closet."

"Where is it?" he asked.

Running a hand through her tousled hair, she sighed.

"Well, I think it's still in the closet upstairs. Let me go grab it," she spoke softly and headed up the stairs. Walking into the master bedroom, she went to the closet and grabbed the journal, heading back downstairs.

It's probably not a good idea to tell Alfie about the scratches just yet, she thought.

Walking back into the living room, she handed Alfie the diary.

"I want it back, Alfie. I think I might be able to figure out where she is from whatever she wrote."

"You're a writer, Maureen, not a detective. Let the police do their job."

"She's not their sister, Alfie. I mean it; I want the diary back as soon as you're done with it."

"Fine, I just want to look it over once first, take some notes." He looked up at her, as her head snapped to the side as she heard a car door slam. Going over to the side window, she peered out.

"Dammit," she cursed.

"What's the matter?" He stood up.

"Nothing, it's one-half of CHiPs, and he looks pissed."

"So I take it that you and this sheriff have already had an altercation," Alfie inquired, doing his lawyerly duties by asking question after question.

"You might say that. You might also say that he's not a bad guy when he isn't out to try and keep the balance between good and evil single-handedly. He's a decent guy, who likes to play things by the book from what I can tell. What can I say, Alfie, the man has convictions. Last time I checked, that wasn't a crime."

Alfred took the journal and put it in his briefcase. Maureen watched and looked at him.

"Alfie, what are you doing? You know Howdy Doody out there might have a warrant."

"I'm counting on it. Your parents pay me to keep their family safe, and that means you out of jail. But unfortunately for the sheriff, that warrant won't cover my personal property, will it. And it's not illegal, it's a gray area."

"It's illegal, and you know it."

She didn't give him a chance to knock, she just opened the door.

"Well good morning, Ponch, where's John?" She hadn't meant to be sarcastic. However, after the last twenty fours, the last thing she wanted to do was to get into an argument this early with Sherriff Downs without any caffeine in her system.

"Cut the crap, Maureen. You know why I'm here." He handed her a thick tri-folded pamphlet and waited. Looking at it, it was a warrant to search the house and property. "That gives me the legal right to search, without permission or interruption. You can read it over if you want, or have a lawyer look it over."

"I think that's a fine idea, Maureen. You don't mind if I look that over," Alfie's voice bellowed from behind her.

She didn't move to allow the Sheriff in just yet, she wanted to savor the moment. She was half hoping he'd get ticked off and leave, but he didn't.

"So, you already got a lawyer. You know that lawyering up makes you look guilty, don't you?"

"And you know that barking orders all the time makes you look like a bully? I'm sure you have donuts in the car, but I have a splitting headache from the lack of caffeine, so you wouldn't happen to have any more coffee in your patrol car, would you?" she asked, crossing her arms.

He brushed past her and looked to the man on the couch. Maureen watched the exchange and knew first thing that Sheriff Downs and Alfred were sizing each other up. Geez, it's like having two alpha male lions in the same cage, she mused.

Sherriff Downs walked over and handed Alfred another piece of paper. Alfred opened it and nodded.

Walking over to Maureen, he pulled out his handcuffs.

"Maureen Welsh, you're under arrest for the kidnapping and disappearance of Hannah Prescott. You have the right to remain silent..." He finished giving her the reading of her rights, before grabbing her hand, and placing the cuff around it. The link closed with a metallic click. Maureen felt a surge of anger, towards her sister, her family, the Sheriff, well within her. She turned around and placed her hands behind her back.

"I was just going to cuff your hands in the front; we are only going to my cruiser, then to town. You aren't a hardened criminal."

He's a class A, certifiable asshole!

"Shove it, Deputy Doolittle. If I'm going to be arrested, you will arrest me, cuffed behind the back and all. My tax dollars are paying for this circus; I may as well get my monies worth."

"Look, Ms. Welsh, you've been given your rights. Whether or not you choose to follow them is entirely up to you. My morning isn't going well as it is, so don't force me to treat you as a hostile suspect."

Laughing, she marched out to the police car, nearly half a yard ahead of him, only to stand near the back door of the cruiser to tap her foot like she'd been waiting all morning for him to get there. Alfred followed her out, shutting the door behind her.

"I'm right behind you Maureen, don't worry. You'll be home before lunch." He climbed into the rented Cadillac.

Maureen turned and saw out the rear window that Alfred was indeed keeping his word. She turned back around. A small measure of calmness drifted through her, but she was still madder than a hornet, and she stared at the back of the head that was the source of that anger.

They drove on in silence, her back rigid in the seat, hands behind her. A small part of her wished she had taken his offer; it would have been more comfortable to have her hands cuffed in front, but her pride often overrode her normal senses. Every time the car lurched from hitting a pothole, she winced as the cuffs pinched her arm.

Guess I am just a masochist at heart, she thought.

"Would you like to listen to the radio, you know, to pass the time?" he asked, taking his eyes off the road briefly to look back at her in the rearview mirror.

The man was unbelievable, she vented silently. She could feel another surge of anger, or maybe it was annoyance, boiling in her veins. Rather than say something she might regret later, she simply bit her tongue and remained quiet.

"I see. Tell me, why is it that all you females sweat the small stuff, then give us poor old men the silent treatment when we are just trying to make the situation better," he shook his head. "No wonder you girls have to have fifty million magazines devoted to your species. It's like giving the rest of the world a manual on how you all operate."

"You're one talk! And how dare you group me into some random pile with the rest of your cast offs from your bedpost! Maybe women like me," she emphasized through gritted teeth, her voice slowly rising in octave, "act like we do because men like you give the rest of the bottom feeders a bad name!"

"Honey, you don't know enough about me to fill a shot glass," he was tapping the steering wheel with his thumb, his annoyance evident to Maureen, even from the backseat. "And you should be so lucky to even be considered to be close to my pile of cast offs."

She kept quiet and stared out the window.

The radio flicked on, and she rode the rest of the way to the station listening to classic rock.

CHAPTER 9

WHEN BILL PARKED his police cruiser in front of the sheriff's station, he immediately knew his day was going to get worse. Parked in the space next him was car number three. Shawn O'Leary. The last thing he needed was Maureen, her lawyer, and Shawn all in the same room.

Getting out of the car, he opened the door for Maureen. He noticed that she paused before getting out.

"I'm not going to assume that you opening the door is any indication or measurement of chivalry," she snapped.

Stepping out, she flipped her chin up at him and marched to the door of the Sherriff's station, where she again turned to him and tapped her foot.

Christ, she can be annoying when she wants to be, he mused to himself.

"Patience is a virtue, Miss Welsh. Has anyone ever told you that?" he asked as he opened the door for her again.

"No, never."

Walking inside, he saw Shawn O'Leary sitting at a desk. Looking up, he nodded, a wicked grin on his face.

"You can sit in here," Bill motioned, escorting her to a seat in a small alcove that was enclosed into a small office. It was bare, save for a table, three chairs, and a picture on the wall of the Old Mission Lighthouse.

The door opened and a stout man walked into the station. Dressed casually in navy trousers, dress shirt, and blazer, he beheld the look of wealth and education.

"We meet again." Reaching into his pocket, he pulled out a card, handing it to Bill. "I'm Alfred Morris, I'm the lawyer for Miss Welsh, so if you will just point me in the right direction of," he paused, looking around the cozy confines of the Sheriff's office, "wherever you have put my client, we can get down to business."

"We put the suspect into the interrogation room where she belongs.

58

And that's where she'll stay until we get a confession, and then she'll be going to jail."

By this time, Shawn had stood, and leaned against his desk, arms crossed.

"Unfortunately, you can only detain my client for a certain period of time. Confession or not, whether my client is guilty or not, is mute. She has the right to a fair trial, and the right to an attorney. You might have heard about that little Supreme Court ruling," the lawyer turned to Shawn, "though I imagine you were around when that was grand-fathered in." Alfred's words had meant to be a direct insult to Shawn's age, and it had worked. Shawn grabbed his files, and walked into an adjacent office, slamming the door.

"Thank you," Bill replied, turning to the man.

"I beg your pardon," said Alfred.

"I have been dying to find a way to get him to shut up since I've met him. I'll have to remember that."

Bill motioned to the door, and the two headed in.

He grabbed a tape recorder from the filing cabinets near the door before heading into the office and closed the door.

"This is the interrogation of Maureen Welsh, arrested on November 14, 2014 on kidnapping and suspicion of murder."

Bill stated the necessary information that was typical protocol for any interrogation, though in truth he'd only had to do this once before since he'd been in Lighthouse Bay. He'd caught two teenagers drag racing, and one had ended up ramming a light post causing serious injury to the driver, and damage to several parked cars nearby.

"When was your last contact with your sister, Hannah Prescott?"

Alfred leaned over and whispered to her, her head nodding slowly as Alfred spoke in hush whispers.

"My client isn't going to answer any questions. We have elected to contact the judge on duty or your magistrate. We are demanding a bond hearing."

Bill was afraid of that. Not that he didn't see this coming. He knew that while Maureen and her automobile were reeking of blue collar, her family's cabin and background reeked of money.

Bill looked at him. "The judge isn't here this weekend. He signed the search and arrest warrant, and headed to Deer Creek Lake for the weekend with his grandson."

Alfred looked squarely back at Bill. "From my understanding, we would be asking in the," he paused, shuffling through some papers, "thirty-second district courthouse. I took the liberty of checking this morning before I arrived. We're scheduled to appear this afternoon before a Judge Hatfield."

"I wasn't given any notification that we were adjourning to a bail hearing," Bill stated trying to mask the irritation in his voice.

"Call the district courthouse. We're scheduled for an early afternoon session," Alfred challenged.

Getting up and walking outside, Bill grabbed the phone. He was on hold when a courier showed up with the paperwork, indeed stating they were scheduled for a bond hearing later that afternoon, and a request for prisoner transport.

Bill swore under his breath not so much, because the old man had been right, but because he was being cavalier about it. Bill didn't mind being bested as long as it was done fair and square.

Walking back into the interrogation room, Bill sat down. Her lawyer was shrewd. He would give him that. "Well, it seems that we have a date later this afternoon. If I would have known that, I would have put on something a little more formal," Bill said, even though he was wearing his police uniform.

"Oh my yes, I can imagine the tongues wagging your fashion faux pas since Lighthouse Bay is such a thriving metropolis and would no doubt be on the cusp of etiquette."

"Well, until the bail hearing, I think we get some things squared away. And just so you know, Maureen," Bill looked at her pointedly. "I'm not looking for a confession. Just answers. Now then, when was the last time you spoke to your sister, either on the phone or in person?"

Maureen looked to Alfred, who in turn nodded his head in agreement. "The last time I spoke on the phone with Hannah, was about a month ago. She called to say she was sending a vase to Steve and me. A new design that she was working on. I told her thanks."

"Did she seem her usual self, or did she seem like there was something wrong, something that might be bothering her?"

"She seemed like Hannah." Just then, Alfred leaned over, whispering to her. She nodded her head, sideways looking at the Sheriff.

"Can you explain your last statement?" Bill asked, writing down notes on a legal pad, even though the tape recorder was recording their entire conversation.

"Well, Hannah was, aloof a lot of the times. She wasn't responsible, with money, her bills, personal life. She sorta flies through life by the seat of her pants. Sometimes she gets into trouble, and then I'm the one who gets to come and smooth things over, fix things, put her back on the right path."

"What exactly does that entail?"

Looking at him, then at Alfred who signaled the question was okay to answer, she went on.

"Well, often it means paying bills that she has forgotten to pay. Electricity and gas are paid directly by my mother and stepfather. Her cell phone, house phone, credit card bills are her responsibility. There isn't a mortgage on the cabin; my mother and father owned it outright. I know there are taxes, but I'm sure that my mother and Frank take care of those."

Bill continued to make notes, and then looked at her.

"So, your sister didn't act any differently than she normally did? Did she mention a falling out with a friend, a fight with a boyfriend?"

"I really don't know much about her friends, save that they like to drink and party, and that they are pretty well off. None of them, as far as I know have jobs. But I never talked to them, and I wouldn't be able to give you any names since they're never around when I come here."

"You can't name any of your sister's friends? What about the boyfriend?"

"Again, I don't know. You'd probably have better luck asking the bartenders at the local bars since that's where she probably met them. She never dates them long. Usually about a few months, then they are upgraded to a new model."

Maureen crossed her legs, placing her hands on the table.

"So you have no idea who she hung out with, who she was dating? You don't know much about your sister, do you, Miss Welsh?"

"I know she's naïve, and deep down, has a good heart. And stop talking about her in the past tense. It's rude. If it were your loved one out there, I think you could understand where I'm coming from."

He felt her eyes, pleading with him, and he hadn't been aware that he had been talking about Hannah in a past tense until Maureen had pointed it out. After years of detective work, the job and conditions harden a person's humanity. Sometimes the small details in a case can mean the world to people.

"I'm sorry; I didn't mean to refer to your sister in any negative aspect." He paused before adding, "These are just standard questions."

Bill had made a few more notes, before looking at Maureen.

"I need to know about her personal life. Remember, I'm not trying to assume anything about your sister or her lifestyle. And I don't want you to think that these questions, depending on what information you give me, will change the outcome of how we solve crimes here. Do you understand?"

She was looking at him and then nodded. "Yeah it means if my sister was a tramp, you're still going to find where she is, and if needs be, whoever did anything to her."

"We aren't a department that lets the bad guy get away just be-cause the victim lives their lives in a different manner than what society deems as normal." Bill was trying to reassure her, smooth things over from their last conversation, attempting to make an effort to get her to relax and trust him.

"It's okay. Thanks."

"Did Hannah have a lot of boyfriends, male friends?"

"I guess so. Most of her friends were male, and I couldn't give you any names to go with them. I couldn't even point them out if I were face to face with them. Most of the time I had the privilege of meeting them, they were either drunk, passed out on the couch, or outside at the fire pit while I dealt with Hannah. There was one girl, though, oh what is her name," Maureen paused, then nodded," Chloe. Chloe Buchannan. I remember her name because her dad owns a Buick deal-ership near Cadillac."

"Can I ask you how you can remember that, but you can't remember the names of the guys your sister was hanging around with," Bill in-quired, his eyebrow rising slightly in interest.

"I could say it was because they were the hottest men I've ever laid eyes on and their names seemed pointless at the time, but it's because Chloe was making fun of the car I drove. People have a tendency, I think anyway, to remember bullies names more so than everyone else. Don't you agree, Sherriff Downs?"

Was she calling me a bully? He thought bitterly. *Who the hell did this broad think she was anyway. Here I am trying to do my damn job in finding her sleazy nutball of a sister, and she's blatantly accusing me, on an interro-gation tape no less, of being a bully! Women.*

"Sometimes people can be cruel like that. I often find that sometimes people who are labeled as bullies are often people who are simply try-ing to deflect emotion away from themselves, out of fear of getting too close, or getting hurt. I'm sure you can attest to that at some point in your life, right." Bill looked at her, he didn't phrase his response in the form of a question.

The two sat in silence for a few minutes before Bill spoke again.

"Okay, being that your sister had a lot of male company was there any one person, male or female that she mentioned? Maybe she was in a fight with someone, had a falling out, or had a disagreement over something?"

"As I've stated, not to my knowledge. I don't know a whole lot about her personal life," Maureen answered.

"Do you know if she had a current boyfriend?"

"She did, but I don't remember his name off hand. She did mention she met him in a bar."

"Do you happen to know which one?"

"It had an animal in the title. I don't drink and I don't know much of what's around here, save for what's on main street."

"I think you mean the Pink Elephant." He wanted to smile, then decided not to.

"Yeah, it might be that. I know that one of Hannah's old boyfriends was a bartender or a bouncer, and another was in the coast guard. She sent me a picture postcard from Mackinac Island last Halloween. But she never stays with any one man for long."

Bill was still taking notes, then spoke as he continued to write. "Based on our conversation from yesterday—"he began but was cut off by Alfred.

"And you know that anything she may or may not have said is inadmissible since its hearsay."

"I know that. I was going to say, we did a background check on whom we think is currently Hannah's boyfriend. Has Hannah ever been involved in any sort of troubled relationships, as far as domestic violence is concerned?"

"Not that I'm aware of. My mother has never said anything like that to me either, and I wish someone would have told me since I'm the one who usually comes up and takes care of everything. My parents live in Florida full time, so it's easier for me to drive here than for them."

Bill made a note of that and continued. "What I was going to say was that we did a background check on the guy we talked about last night. Not a shock he has a record, though nothing hardcore. A few speeding violations, a bounced check charge that was later cleared. We have one DUI, but that was over six years ago. He does have one outstanding warrant for domestic assault, from a charge in Kenosha a few months back."

A knock at the door interrupted him, and looking through the small Plexiglas window, and waved for the okay to enter.

"Hi Paul, what is it?"

"Bill, can I have a word with you?"

Bill nodded, excused himself, and then stepped outside. Paul handed him the fax authorization and read it over.

"So he was never picked up, and the warrant is still outstanding, right?"

"As far as I know, Bill. You know how it is with these types. They beat up their old ladies and ride their bikes into another town, find a new old' lady, and do the same thing all over again."

The phone was ringing in the background. Bill was going say something when Edith spoke up.

"Hey Bill, you have a few messages here regarding your case. Mayor Carlisle has called you twice. I suggest you get on the horn and call him back. He didn't sound too pleased the last time he called for you." *And the hits just keep on coming*, he cursed silently. *I knew this damn thing would snowball sooner or later. Merry freaking Christ-mas in July.*

"Well if the Mayor calls back, tell him I'm in the middle of an investigation and I'll get back to him as soon as I can."

"But he's already left two messages for you. I don't think —"

"I know, Edith but there isn't anything I can do at the moment." Bill ran a hand through his hair. He felt Paul tap his shoulder and sighed.

"Bill, there's something else. We had run a background check on Hannah Prescott as well. She has a standing prescription for Colophon, a pain medication. She gets its filled every month down at Drexel's Pharmacy. The pharmacist there says sometimes she comes in with a tall fellow, dark hair, rides a Harley."

"Well, at least we are getting leads. I bet you good money she got tired of living in the woods in the middle of nowhere and drove off to Vegas or California." Shaking his head, he pulled a small notebook from his shirt pocket and scribbled down a few notes.

"Come on' Bill. You know as well as I do that domestic violence is on the rise. It's contagious it seems. How many times have we broken up fights down at Benny's Pub over someone smacking someone around? It seems the kids are getting younger and younger these days.

Look at that boy in Escanaba, who punched his girlfriend into a coma. They transported him to a maximum-security facility in Jackson after she died. I swear that stuff is getting closer and closer to us."

The phone rang again, and Bill looked over at Edith. "One second Mayor Carlisle, I need to see if he is still interrogating his suspect," she put the phone down. "Bill, your number one fan is holding on line one."

"And I'm still unavailable. Take a message and as soon as I finish sorting out this mess, he will be my first priority."

"All right, Bill." She made a disapproving face then went back to her call. *Sometimes it's like I'm working with my mother,* he sighed. From the corner of his eye, he saw Shawn O'Leary coming out of the file room, heading towards him.

"Excuse me, Paul, I hate to interrupt," he paused.

Like hell you do, Bill thought.

"I was just finishing up the background check for our suspect here, and it's about the wire transfer we found out about last evening. That wasn't the first. She gets them every time she comes here. From a holding company. I contacted the branch that does the wire transfers and it's from her parent's account. That confirmed what she told us last night. But as it turns out, she has a pretty nice nest egg built up over the last seven or so years. Reporters don't make that kind of pay, Bill. I told as much to Mayor Carlisle just this morning when I ran into him at Drexel's Pharmacy. Loretta said she came in last night to pick up a few things and she saw the yellow wire paper when she pulled her wallet out of her bag."

Bill looked at him, shaking his head slightly. "We know the reason why she gets the money."

"See, I thought you were right on that one, Bill. But as it turns out, her bank gets a deposit shortly after she gets the wire."

"Her parents send her a little extra for her troubles. That isn't un-heard of. Again, Shawn, we need to find the facts, not the facts that just back up our suspicions. We could be missing a clue or two if we don't look for everything." *How many times do I have to say it?*

"Well I agree, but the Mayor said he wanted to have a word with you about it, though I'm sure you already knew that." With that, Shawn walked off and headed out back.

"Paul, do me a favor and escort Miss Welsh to the courthouse. I'm going to need to do some digging before that meeting in front of the Judge. You know, sometimes I hate working in a small town."

"Sure thing, Bill. Yeah, I know what you mean. Sometimes living in them isn't all that fun at times, either. Especially when your in-laws live within walking distance of you."

"Betsy giving you a hard time?" Bill asked, referring to Paul's mother in law.

"Isn't she always? She's nice as far as mother-in-laws go, but I told her to stop calling the sheriff's station every time the Wilson's cat traipses through her flower beds. Those aren't emergencies, except to her. But I'll get Miss Welsh down to the district courthouse for you. You gonna be there or should I wait it out?"

"No, I'll be there. I didn't like the idea of arresting her in the first place. Too much circumstantial evidence, but you know politics in a small town. Sometimes they outreach the long arm of the law."

If Paul agreed or disagreed with him, he didn't say anything. It still ticked off Bill at having to get dragged in and forced to play the games that happen in little towns. He'd just about had enough.

The phone rang again, and this time, Bill marched over to Edith's desk and grabbed it before she had the chance to answer it.

"Sherriff's Department, Sheriff Downs speaking." He recognized the voice on the other end of line.

"Well, here I was starting to look for a new full-time Sheriff. I was expecting a call from you earlier, Bill." Mayor Carlisle did indeed sound irritated, which made Bill smile. It was the first time he'd done that all day.

"Well you might have heard I'm in the middle of an investigation. I'm sure someone in the sewing circle has already told you." Bill let the comment linger before adding, "That's probably why you called. You knew I'd stepped out of the interrogation long enough to grab a fax."

"I suggest, Bill, you watch your tongue. I may be a small town Mayor, but I'm the goddamned Mayor none the less." Silence. "Now, what's going on with that girl we've charged? Has she confessed yet?"

"No, we have a hearing this afternoon."

"A bond hearing?"

Something in the tone of the Mayor's voice sounded surprised, but not in a pleasant way.

"Yes, a bond hearing. It's the arraignment. I don't know if the judge will let her post bond or not." Bill had a gut feeling that not only didn't the Mayor know about the bond hearing, he wasn't happy about it either. Tread lightly, he told himself. Something's stinking like yesterday's garbage.

"Well, I'll have to get a hold of Judge Hatfield, and he's fishing isn't he?"

"Yes, with his grandson. We've already put in a call. But it's hard to get a hold of man in the middle of a lake. Let alone, Lake Superior."

"If you hear from him, tell him I need to speak with him before the bond hearing." The Mayor hung up before Bill had a chance to say goodbye.

Going over to his desk, he grabbed the file and started making copies of Maureen's files. Then, he folded his copies and shoved them into his security manifest that all the deputies were required to carry in the patrol cars for paperwork.

"Bill, I know you're in a pinch for time right now, but you need to stop and think about something."

Bill turned to face the voice of his secretary. She walked over, a navy blue sweater draped around her shoulders, her glasses hanging from a pearl chain around her neck.

"Now you know me, Bill, I never try to interfere in anyone's business, least of all police business. I know you've taking a liking to this girl, and she seems sweet enough. But these things happen, they are tragedies, but they happen. Life needs those tragedies to keep the balance of good and bad. Sometimes, no matter how hard we try, we never find the answers we go looking for. Sometimes happiness in life, means knowing when to let things go, and sometimes it's best, well, to just let sleeping dogs lay, you know what I mean?"

"Edith, you know who came up with that phrase, 'let a sleeping dog lie?'" Bill asked, hands on his hips, but a soft smile on his face.

Edith didn't answer, and he didn't wait for a reply.

"A dog."

Chapter 10

HEADING OVER TO the courthouse, Bill made one stop at the Heritage Mutual Bank to do a little business. Stepping inside the branch, his senses were immediately assaulted by the scent of potpourri and musty newspaper. Glancing around the teller counter, he spotted who he was looking for: Gwendolyn McFee, a short, perky brunette with bouncing curls and dimples.

If Shirley Temple had a long lost twin, Gwendolyn might have been her. She had more energy than any woman he'd ever known, and he'd never known her ever to be in a bad mood. She spotted him and waved him over.

"Hiya Bill, still fighting crime or are you off the clock? Don't worry, I have your account pulled up," she spoke, her voice dancing along as her words came out a mile a minute. "What can I do for you to-day?"

Bill smiled at her. "It's not for me, it's for a case. I'd appreciate it if you could help."

She likes you idiot, Bill lamented, so try not to take advantage of her generosity.

"Well you know I'd do my best," she said. Bill thought he could detect a slight blush to her cheeks.

"I am investigating this female who gets wire transfers. I know this is her primary bank, though not this branch. Can you still get access to her account? I'm looking for any suspicious activity."

Gwendolyn looked at him for a moment, then bit her bottom lip. "I really shouldn't be giving out that information to you, Bill. Not without a warrant or something."

Bill had to think fast. "I know, I said the same thing to Shawn at the station. But he wouldn't listen. I told him, 'you don't know Gwenny, she runs things by the book.' I had to defend your honor; you've been too nice to me not to."

God, you're pushing it buddy, he told himself.

"Well Bill, that is the nicest thing anyone has ever said about me,"

She paused, and smiled at him. "What do you need?"

After spending about fifteen minutes, Bill left with definite answers to his nagging questions.

Not only was Maureen Welsh thrifty, she didn't spend a whole lot either. Cautious with her money and her life, he mused. What was she so afraid of? There was nothing unusual about her spending habits either. All the money wired this time, was deposited into a savings account. Maureen had never made a withdrawal from that account, which he also found odd.

Looking at his watch, he knew he had just enough time to swing by the Mayor's office before haul ass in order to make it to the court-house. He wasn't looking forward to the bond hearing, but it was a necessary.

Bill's gut instinct said that his suspect would be let go on her own recognizance, and he would be back at square one. Climbing into his cruiser, he veered onto county road fifty-three and headed towards the Mayor's office. While in the bank, his walkie went off three times, and his pager as well.

Whatever was the matter could wait. The short drive to the Mayor's office only succeeded in allowing Bill to brew longer over his sullen situation. He didn't like being told how to run an investiga-tion. He didn't like being told how to handle a job he'd been doing longer than the Mayor had been in office, and though he didn't want to admit it, he didn't like the idea that Maureen Welsh thought he was an asshole. She was obviously an educated woman; surely she would have seen the situation from his point of view. *And why do you care if she does hate you*, Bill wondered silently. *Why are you wasting your time on someone who would rather spit in your face than say hello?*

But Bill had to admit that her stubbornness and tongue in cheek sense of humor made him smile, and he didn't mind holding a con-versation with her when she wasn't reaming him for something. He didn't even mind the nicknames she called him either, at least not most of the time. Stepping inside the Mayor's office, Bill recognized the secretary from Ida's Café, but couldn't recall her name. He'd seen her there a few times with a small boy, though Bill noticed she wasn't wearing a wedding ring.

"Hello Sherriff Downs, I'll let the Mayor know you're here." She picked up the phone and spoke quietly. After a few moments, she put the phone down. "He's just finishing up an important call, if you'll have a seat; he'll be right with you."

She gestured towards the two large brown leather over chairs. Taking a seat, he casually glanced at his watch.

So, we're going to play this game, he mused. Bill had a sneaking suspicion that the Mayor was going to make him wait it out in the lobby of his office, since Bill had made him wait on the other end of the line in his office.

The pettiness of small towns reminds me of high school, he thought. Then again, he really didn't fit in there either.

After about ten minutes of sitting perfectly still and quiet, he saw the secretary's eyes dart to her computer screen, then look over at him. She quickly typed something, and then went back to her stack of files she was going through.

Oh how cute, they are both playing this game. After waiting another ten minutes, Bill stood up and walked over to the desk. "Please give the Mayor my," he paused, wanting her to know the little waiting game they were playing wasn't going to sit well with him, "sincerest apologies. But I have a hearing I have to be at, so if he needs me, he knows where he can find me." The surprised look on the young woman's face lifted Bill's spirits as he headed back to his cruiser.

He didn't even have his seat belt buckled when he heard a tap at the window. Mayor Carlisle himself was rapping at his passenger side window. Unlocking the door for him, he climbed in.

"You know Bill, I realize we don't see eye to eye, but it wouldn't have hurt you to wait for me."

"I did wait for you, Mayor. For twenty minutes. I have a bond hearing."

Which is why you kept me waiting, he thought.

"Well, now I can see how that's more important than me doing the town's business, Bill. Hell, you should be Mayor for thinking so smart," the older gentlemen growled.

Bill didn't much like Mayor Carlisle, and he sure as hell didn't like the man insulting him in his cruiser. But rather than answer the urge to punch the man in the face, Bill took a calming breath.

"I meant we are both pressed for time doing our jobs, Dwight. What did you want to talk about?"

Carlisle's face seemed to soften a bit. He looked around, almost as if out of caution, then finally spoke. "Look, it's a terrible thing what happened to that girl in the Bay. But this is a small town, Bill. A small town that makes it's living off tourists. Are you following me, here?"

It wasn't a question.

"We need them in the spring when the fishing season opens up; we need them in the summer when the beaches open. We need them in the fall for the wine tasting tours, and we need any help we can get to make it through the winter months. If a scandal got out, that we have a murderer in our quaint little town, this could hurt us. I mean financially, Bill. In the pocket."

Bill said nothing, but a small part of him had to agree. Everyone — from the Mayor, the local restaurants, the hotels — feel the pinch. Even him. What town needs a Sherriff if they have no one in the town left to watch?

"I know you think I'm a real son-of-a-bitch. You're probably right. But my first concern is making sure this town stays afloat. Now I'm not asking you to convict her off the bat, we have a court of law for that. I'm just asking you not broadcast that we've had a murder. We don't know all the facts; what if this girl turns out to be a roaming serial killer?"

"First off, Dwight, we don't even know if a murder took place. We don't know that any foul play has taken place. It's unlikely since most serial killers usually have a fixed idea of their victims, method of killing, and often disposal."

The look on the Mayor's face was worth ten cases of beer to Bill.

"I was in the military. I have a degree in criminal psychology, remember. We have to study that sort of thing in order to prevent it. Besides, Miss Welsh doesn't have any of the signs of being a closet sociopath."

"Still, I want you to keep this sort of thing hush-hush. At least for now. We don't need any negative publicity about this, you hear me? We need to keep it quiet. The only thing I want to see on the news about this town is the upcoming Christmastide Celebration.

I think this could be the year that Lighthouse Bay finally starts to find her place on the map. I just want you to know how important it is to understand that whatever little tourism we get, we need to keep."

Bill sat as patiently as he could, though he felt like he was being talked down to by his father for doing nothing wrong. He was quickly losing patience with being told several different ways to do the same thing.

"I understand your concern, and respect your need to want to keep this private. But I won't be pressured into keeping an investigation quiet, not if it will help me solve the case, especially if other people might be harmed. The most important thing is finding what happened, and if something did happen, whoever did it to prevent it from happening again. I know we live in a tourist town, and they are the ones that keep us going.

I'm not going to push through this investigation and risk screwing something up. If I do that, not only will justice be denied, but it might let a criminal go free."

He paused briefly.

"Besides, the evidence just isn't there that I can see. I don't think she did it. From what I have been able to gather, it sounds like her sister may have run off with the latest loser she was dating."

The Mayor didn't say anything, continuing to look straight ahead for a few moments. He then reached for the door handle, before saying, "Someone has to pay for this crime. Someone needs to be punished. We need answers, and we needed them yesterday."

Getting out, he slammed the door before Bill had had a chance to retort. This is turning to be one hell of a week. Can't wait to see what the weekend might turn up. Wildfires in the state park, maybe aliens will land on Griffin's Warf and decide to open a canoe and livery to help out the dying industry of this poor town, of which I can go there to find my new job.

Yanking the gearshift into drive, Sheriff Downs headed down the county road to the interstate, his previously sullen mood now worse. Driving along the interstate, Bill took turns turning on and off the radio, before he decided to pull off to grab a quick snack. Pulling into the quick mart, he grabbed a coffee and a bag of pretzels, then headed out again.

Arriving at the district courthouse, he checked in his gun, hiking the four flights of stairs to the courtroom rather than the elevator.

Opening the courtroom door, he spotted Maureen sitting quietly behind the defendant's desk. Bill nodded to Paul, who was standing close by. Bill also saw Thomas Deveroux, the prosecuting attorney. It was his fault that Bill was here. An overzealous attorney from a small town, who returned to that small town because he found work-ing in the bigger cities actually meant work, Thomas was quick to sign arrest warrants, only to suffer the embarrassment of having his cases plead to lesser charges.

Those that didn't plead out, were often dismissed due to lack of evidence. However, Bill didn't pay him too much attention. He was watching Maureen's attorney who had a stack of papers piled in front of him. Something in his gut told him that his bad day was just about to get worse. When the chamber door opened, Bill stood, out of habit, as judge Hatfield took the bench.

"All rise," bellowed the short and stocky bailiff.

"Be seated. Go ahead Josey," he nodded to woman sitting at his right.

"Case number 120828, State of Michigan verses Maureen Welsh for obstruction of justice in serving a search warrant."

"Is the prosecution present?"

"Yes, your honor. Thomas Deveroux, head prosecuting attorney for the Bay area."

The beginning formalities came and went. Then Alfred stood.

"Your honor, at this time I would like to move to dismiss these charges, as well as institute a restraining order against the sheriff's department of Lighthouse Bay."

"Present your evidence."

Judge Hatfield didn't appear too amused or even happy to be here, Bill noticed. He swiveled in his chair back and forth, like an annoyed bystander watching two children fight over the last piece of cake.

Alfred was smooth. His tone was understated, yet firm. Bill admired the man, even if he was becoming a bit of a thorn in his side.

"Your Honor, deputies from the Lighthouse Bay police department were responding to an inquiry by my client in regards to her missing sister. They searched the grounds and house, without a warrant, and questioned my client, without being given her Miranda rights so as you well know, but for reasons I have to state here today, any evidence, whether or incriminating or not, is inadmissible."

"Mr. Deveroux, did your men have a search warrant?"

"Not at the time, Your Honor. They were responding to a call and felt it—" but the judge cut him short.

"Necessary to operate outside the law? Let me ask you this then, when the officers came to search the home, was," he had to look at this paperwork to remember Maureen's name, "Miss Welsh given her Miranda rights."

"No, Your Honor. She wasn't a suspect at the time."

"While you were searching for evidence at the place of residence where the defendant was, was she was being questioned without knowledge of her rights?"

The pause was brief, but his silence said volumes.

"Yes, Your Honor. We have reasonable suspicion that someone inside might be injured."

Bill could almost smell the stench of Thomas's case going bad. It was all going to snowball from here. Bill had been in court enough to know when a judge gets irritated that his time was wasted for lack of procedure.

"The defense may proceed."

Alfred went on to explain that all the evidence they found was circumstantial at best.

Then he went on to explain that Hannah Prescott, while a sweet girl, was extremely naive and lacked judgment when it came to relationships. Alfred pointed out that it was a pattern with Hannah to be irresponsible. He also pointed out that it wasn't a crime for an adult to disappear, and that Maureen was only trying to get some answers to appease her family.

In addition, since the current boyfriend was also missing, and Hannah lived off a trust fund, frequently taking short trips throughout the year; it was more than likely Hannah was on a mini vacation and hadn't felt the need to tell anyone.

Bill listened as Alfred presented his evidence, including past account statements showing her trips, various letters to her mother about several men she had dated. When Alfred said that, Bill noticed that Maureen blushed. Was she embarrassed by her sister, or for her family? He couldn't tell. Bill thought the information that finally clinched it was that Maureen would make these trips, a few hundred miles one-way several times a year or more, and there was no motivation for harming her sister.

Alfred also pointed that there was no evidence of foul play, no hard evidence that a murder had taken place, and importantly, no body. When the defense rested, the judge sat quietly for a few mo-ments. Maureen's back was stiff, and she turned her head slightly towards Bill's direction.

Quit staring at her you moron, he scolded himself.

"Approach the bench." Alfred and Thomas stood at the judge's bench for fifteen minutes before returning to their seats.

"It is the judgment of this court that due to lack of evidence, improper protocol on behalf of the Lighthouse Bay Police Department, a violation of Miss Welsh's civil rights has taken place, and a gross misconduct of charges by the prosecutor's office, that the charges against Maureen Patricia Welsh be dropped. The defendant is free to go."

The smack of the gavel confirmed Bill's gut instinct. He watched as Maureen stood up, and patiently, yet proudly, offered her hands to Paul to be unshackled from the handcuffs. Turning to hug Alfred, Maureen started walking out of the courtroom when she passed him. He was half expecting her to stop and spit in his face, or maybe slap him.

Lord knows I deserve it. Instead, she walked right past him, like he wasn't there. So what if she didn't say anything to you, he sulked.

Why should it bother you?

He didn't have time to think about it because Alfred was standing in front of him.

"This is for you and your men, Sheriff. It's an order of protection against my client. I will not have her harassed." Bill glanced at the personal protection order and nodded.

"But it will still allow me to question Miss Welsh on official business related to the open investigation of her sister."

"You assumed correctly. Now if you'll excuse me, I'm taking my client to lunch."

Bill just stared at Paul, who shrugged his shoulders. He knew he was back at the drawing board. He looked at his watch. One thirty. Hell, all this chaos and it's not even dinnertime. Walking over to Paul, he tucked the personal protection order, into his pocket. Paul had a huge grin on his face, and Bill hadn't the faintest idea why.

"Why the hell are you looking like you just won the lottery," he barked. His patience and manners had left the building along with his suspect.

"Well, I was just thinking, if she had stopped and the two of you had had a chance to speak, her lawyer and I could have taken you down to the second floor and made it official," Paul smiled, and continued to laugh.

"Funny. Keep that sense of humor when it comes time for me to do your yearly review, then see who's laughing," The two headed out of court and back to Lighthouse Bay.

CHAPTER 11

THE RENTED CADILLAC pulled into the parking lot of a small diner off Main Street. Maureen knew the place well; Ida's Café was one of two restaurants that the town had to offer during its winter season and was a part of Lighthouse Bay for as long as Maureen could remember.

It was an old-fashioned, clapboard building with a wooden railed fence and a wraparound veranda that allowed customers access to wrought iron tables and chairs on the porch if they desired.

"This isn't such a bad little town, Alfie," Maureen commented, noticing the frown as he pulled in. "Granted, you won't find a La Petite Françoise but it's still nice."

They got out and walked up the bricked path, surrounded by the brick flowerbeds. Old-fashioned brass lanterns, with small votive candles in burgundy, silver, and gold hung centered from the under hang of the porch roof. A scrollwork screen door, faded with chipped blue paint revealed the main seating area. Hardwood floors, worn with time, spanned the entire building. Oak tables and chairs were scattered across the dining room. The long oak bar had soft brown leather stools and brass accents.

Muted earth tones, the rich browns of the leather furniture, and rustic feel from the natural wood made it just worth seeing for the presence alone. From experience, Maureen knew the food was equally layered in taste. Taking a seat at the table, a waitress came over and handed them two small menus.

"Hi I'm Abby; I'll be your waitress. Our special's today are the acorn squash salad, perch filet with lemon butter and garlic toast, or Ida's famous one pot supper stews."

"What is a 'one pot supper stew'?" Alfred inquired.

Maureen tried not to laugh at the look of obvious social discomfort on his face.

"It's Ida's famous one pot supper stew. You have your choice of chicken or lamb. Both come with a ton of seasonal vegetables and spices, in addition to fresh herbs from Ida's garden."

Maureen perked up, "I think I'll have one of those. The lamb please," she stated before the waitress could ask.

"And for you sir?" the waitress asked. She waited patiently, pen poised at the ready. Shaking his head, he looked up finally but with hesitation. "I think I'll have the perch. How is it prepared?"

Without missing a beat, the perky blonde replied, "It's cooked."

Maureen waited until after the waitress took their drink order, before laughing in spite of the events of the day. It seemed odd to look at her watch and see it's only after two thirty. It felt like it was the end of the day. All she wanted to do was go back to the cabin, crawl onto the couch, and sleep. She had three more days, and then she'd have to call work and use some more of her personal and sick time.

It's a good thing I never get ill, Maureen lamented. *Then in addition to being Hannah's keeper, I'd be unemployed as well. Hell, I'd just live there, full time and we could both mooch off the trust funds.*

Disdain and pity washed through her as Maureen tried to push past the guilt she felt over feeling that way about her sister.

"Maureen, did you hear anything I said," Alfred interrupted.

Shaking her head out of the fog, she smiled faintly. "No, I'm sorry I didn't. I was just thinking of Hannah. Do you really believe those things you said in court today, Alfie? That she just ran off."

Alfred looked at her, the way a parent looks at a child about when delivering bad news.

"Maureen, I've known your family for nearly as long as you've been alive. I've come to care a lot about you girls. Now, I love Hannah as if she were my own child. However, it's time to face facts, Maureen. She's irresponsible. She's bad with money, bad with relationships, and too naive for her own good. You don't know this, but Frank and your mom went through a little financial trouble there. Hannah's monthly allowance," he paused, stressing the term in a childlike manner, "had been cut in half. So maybe she got tired of having to cut her spending in half and took off with a man who'd keep her in the manner to which she is accustomed. It wouldn't be the first time something like this has happened. "

"No, I didn't know that. It's just after the way my mom and step-dad are always apart and fighting when they aren't, I just assumed she didn't want to get married."

Then again, how much do I really know about my sister? She thought. As if on cue, Alfred echoed her thoughts.

"How well do you really know your sister, Maureen? You can list her faults without any problems, we all can, but other than that, what do we know about her? She lived like a recluse up there in that cabin. It made your mother half-crazy at times, going for weeks on end, with sporadic phone calls and an occasional email."

This wasn't news to Maureen. She knew that her sister's haphazard methods of communication all too well herself.

"I know, Alfie, it's just—" she paused, as Abby brought their food.

"Will there be anything else today, folks?"

"No, I think we're good for now, thanks." Maureen grabbed her spoon and dipped into the rich smelling broth, bringing up a spoonful. "I know Alfie, it's just not like her typical behavior is all. What if this is the case of the boy who cried wolf?" she asked tasting the stew. She missed the authenticity of home cooked meals. Any chance she could get, she would take homemade mom and pop diner food over something from a sack.

"And I'm saying that sooner or later, that wolf is going to get antsy and want to roam. She's a grown woman, Maureen. Maybe she finally found a man and wants to settle down for a while. You know what that is like."

Not anymore, she thought bitterly. But the truth of it came down to she was fine with the breakup. It hurt at first, sure. Yet after crying for a bit, she realized that she and Steve weren't that compatible after all. There was no point dwelling on it, because what's done is done, and the past can't be changed. Besides, a real man would have taken your dedication to helping out your sister as a sign of faithfulness and being family oriented, not a sign of selfishness. She was stabbing at her stew with a spoon when Alfred interrupted her.

"Something the matter, Maureen? If there is, you'd better tell me. There's no since taking it out on a bowl of stew."

Looking up, she smiled softly.

"Steve and I broke up. I've already moved out, and I was stopping by to get the last of my things when I got the call from mother."

"Oh, I'm sorry Maureen. You two seemed like you were going to make a go of it for the long run. Guess some things are never certain."

He bit into his perch, and she noticed he seemed pleasantly surprised.

"Well, it's for the best. And there is no sense in me staying upset over it since that won't solve anything," She said faintly, picking up another bite of her stew. The hearty herbs and savory richness of the stew wasn't much help in lifting her sullen spirits.

"I'm sorry Maureen, I wouldn't have said anything at all, but I just wanted to point out to you how you and Hannah are different. If she had half your brains, you wouldn't be in the middle of this mess, and she'd be better off, too." he continued to eat his perch in silence.

Maureen stabbed at her stew but didn't take a bite.

"Enough, Maureen. Quit that brooding, it's not going to do anyone any good. If by the rare chance that that boyfriend of hers did do something, Sheriff Downs will catch him. He may seem like a bit of a prick at times, but deep down I think, he's a good cop."

Maureen, completely taken aback, just looked at him, spoon in mid bite.

"You're sticking up for him now? Whatever special sauce they put on that fish, can you share it," she smirked, taking a huge bite of her stew.

"I did my homework. He did two tours with the Marines. He's decorated; he passed his exams in the top five percentile. His work towards his degree is also impressive; he had a double major, you know."

"No, I didn't, and thanks to you talking about him incessantly, that's now three and a half minutes of my life I'll never get back."

Alfred eyed her but said nothing.

"What were his majors, anal retentiveness, and chauvinism?"

"So, you're picking on him already. Must mean he's gotten under your skin a little, which means you've taking a little bit of a liking to him."

"Have not," she replied before she realized how ridiculous she sounded. Why not just stomp your foot like a three-year-old, too. That'll show him.

Alfred grinned and finished the last of his perch. Looking to Maureen, he handed her a wrapped present from out of his briefcase.

She played along, but she knew it was the diary. She knew he had to disguise it, and in front of anyone here who saw, it would look like a gift. Shrewd, Alfie. Very Shrewd.

Taking it, she smiled.

"Thanks. We should probably get going. I'm sure you have a lot of work to do and I have a lot of reading to catch up on." She hugged the present to her and waited at the counter while Alfred paid the bill.

The ride back to the cabin was mundane with the occasional idle chitchat that permeated the silence. Dull comments about the weather, how pretty it was up here, clear air and the like helped pass the time.

When they pulled into the driveway, Maureen half expected to find police cruisers there, with officer O' Reilly twirling a freshly made noose like a cowboy spins a lasso, but she didn't.

The yard was empty. No police cruisers, no yellow tape marking off the doorways as there had been last night. The house looked strangely quiet and peaceful.

Putting the car into park, Alfred reached into the breast pocket of his jacket and handed her two small silver keys.

"I had the liberty of having the doors fixed and the locks replaced. It was no easy task, finding a locksmith up here. Once I did, he didn't have a problem coming out for a little something extra," Alfred said.

Her fingers curled around the warm pieces of steel. She hated to admit it, but she felt safer knowing that Alfred was helping. Or maybe she felt safer because a man was helping period. As much as that chaffed against the rebellious, self-sufficient streak she prided herself on, she knew as soon as she thought of it that that's what it was. It has to be genetic, she scoured. The drive to be that rescued Scarlet O'Hara had to be a defect in the female genetic code.

"Thanks, Alfie I appreciate that." She was reaching for the door handle when he grabbed her arm.

"Keep your cell phone on you, and call the police if there's trouble. If Hannah ran off, odds are they might be back. If she didn't, whoever dragged her off might come back as well. I want you to promise me if you see any signs of trouble, anything at all, you'll call the police."

"I promise, Alfie." His precautions hadn't so much unnerved as they should have. Truth was, she had already been thinking about alternate possibilities of Hannah and her hippie boyfriend coming home to ransack the house for drug money.

Getting out, she shut the door when Alfred rolled down the passenger side window. "If you need anything, call me. I'm staying at the Serendipity Motel. Room 4B."

She wanted to tell him that she'd be fine, but she wasn't so sure. She also wanted to tell him about the scratches on the door in the master bedroom, but decided against it. Besides, that information wouldn't do anyone any good. The only person who knew the real significance of the marks wasn't around to share it.

"Thanks, Alfie, but I think I can manage. Remember, I live in the big bad city."

"I want to do one more thing. Let's go inside; check the rooms, the closet. Anywhere where someone might be hiding. I want you to lock the doors and windows behind you. When it's all clear, flick the porch light on."

Maureen thanked him and went into the cabin. She went upstairs, going from room to room. Checking under beds and closets in broad daylight would have probably seemed strange, if not funny to someone else under normal circumstances. But after the last few days, nothing would ever surprise Maureen again.

Finally making her way downstairs, she flicked on the porch light and watched at Alfred's rented Cadillac drove off. Leaning against the wall, she looked around. Everything was as it had been this morning. Heading into the kitchen, the wrapped present that was disguised as the diary still under her arm. Grabbing the teakettle and turning it on, Maureen leaned against the kitchen counter and opened it.

Inside the brightly foiled wrapped box was Hannah's diary.

In addition, there was a small book, Famous Quotes from Famous Folks inside as well. The book wasn't a hardcover, but a glossy soft cover, double the thickness of a magazine. Inside was a gift receipt from the Barnes and Noble in Whiting, in addition to a small hand-written note by Alfred, scribbled on a tiny piece of legal paper no doubt tore from one of the corners. On it, Maureen found another set of instructions.

Ripping the note to shreds, she set the two books onto the counter and went into the small half bath from around the kitchen. Flushing the pieces, she watched the yellow bites of paper swirl and waited for the tank to refill before she felt safe enough to go back to her books.

She walked in the kitchen. As she waited for the kettle to boil, she reached for a cup above the microwave. It was then she felt an odd sensation of being watched. Turning around, she didn't find anything. Looking out the window, her spine chilled, though she saw nothing. Pulling the gauzy white curtains shut, Maureen waited.

She was going to need all the fortitude she could find to get through the rest of Hannah's diary knowing full well it might be the last thing that Hannah ever wrote.

Leaning against the counter, she rubbed the bridge of her nose. This hadn't been how she had envisioned this visit. She could feel her body start to sag, a few tears pooling in her eyes before the whistle of the kettle snapped her out of her sorrow-laden daze.

Pouring a hot cup of tea, she settled onto the couch. Maureen flipped through the diary until she found the place where she had left off. She started reading, but her mind kept wandering off track, thinking about Alfred's comments. Maureen knew Hannah could be off the wall and flaky, but to just up and leave?

Deep down, Maureen knew she was a little envious of Hannah's carefree nature and spirit. Then her mind kept wandering back to Sheriff Downs face when she walked past him in the courthouse. He looked like she had just kicked his dog, but in retrospect, what did he expect? He accused her of kidnapping her own sister, implying that she had done worse, and then arrested her. She put the book down and grabbed the cup of hot tea.

After taking a few sips, she ran her fingers along the gilded edges of the pages. *What would it be like if I didn't have a sister anymore?* she wondered, then shook her head to rid herself of the negative thought. *Don't be stupid, Maureen. Hannah is fine. She's probably taken up a new hobby that you just don't know about, and more than likely won't approve. I Just hope she doesn't come home all tattooed at pierced.*

Picking up the journal again, she started reading. A few pages in, she had the oddest sensation that someone was watching her. Looking around, she didn't see anything. She reached for her mug of tea and took another few sips. She had never been much of a tea drinker, but this blend was nice.

Getting up to get the remaining tea out of the kettle, she sat back down, looking over the notes she had made in the back of the journal. Picking her place where she left off, she started reading again. The journal entries, which had basically started out as fluff about her love life, what she did with her friends that day, what she wore to the bar, had changed.

Like an onion, the entries were layered; little was mentioned about Hannah's life, except the occasional mention of the lack of sleep, her bad dreams, and the strange things she started to notice about the landscape and lake.

Maureen felt an odd sensation when reading over the entries. It left her with a mixed feeling of guilt, anger, and curiosity. The old adage that, 'things like this could never happen to me' didn't have a better poster child than Maureen at this moment.

Running her hand through her tousled hair, she picked up the journal and began reading the entry for August 17th.

Dear Diary,   *August 17th, 2015*

> *Sleep has eluded me. The loud thwacking kept me up again. I spent all night sitting in the closet, debating on whether or not to hide with the flashlight on or off. I don't*

know why, but I can relax a little in the closet.

I stopped going for walks altogether. Even in the middle of the day, even with the sun beating down, as soon as I step foot into that forest, I feel an instant chill. It's always dark in there, even on the outskirts. The last time I went walking, I heard a noise similar to the loud thwacking that I hear at night and ran as fast as I could to get out of there. I nearly fell into a ravine.

It was so gross.

I stopped before I nearly toppled over the ledge, and I saw the picked apart carcass of what I think was either a small dog or a possum or something. I nearly threw up.

My lungs hurt by the time that I made it back to the cabin, but I made it. That was yesterday, and I've been in this closet ever since.

I found a pocket watch, sticking out of the ground a little bit near the ravine. I managed to clean it up, but it looks old. It might be older than what I think, but it doesn't look recent, you know? On the back, there are some initials that were put on it. It was probably a gift that some tourist lost. I hate losing stuff.

I'm still trying to figure out whatever it was that was chasing me. An animal? But it sounded high up, a hawk maybe? Shawn, from the DNR, has been a little nicer to me, answering my questions about the wild animals and game around here. He thinks it's a hawk. They have expansive wing spans, from what he says. He told me to plant a few oleanders because they don't like the sweet smell of them.

I mentioned that the garbage cans were still knocked over, and the lid on the one was dented. He said that the lake levels were down this year, from lack of rain. The perch haven't breed as much, which means no food supply for the hawks, so they go looking where they can find it. I guess that that makes sense, but I just didn't think that a bird could be that aggressive. I just didn't have all these problems last year. And I've asked at the hardware store in town, but they just tell me to call the DNR. So I'm back to the drawing board with Shawn again.

But I did what he suggested, and bought a box of oleander bulbs, and cleaned up the greenhouse and started planting them. Hopefully, that will do the trick.

But the watch. There are three letters on the back; I'm as-

suming they are initials. The last one is too tarnished that I can't see what it is. I took a picture of it with my camera phone and showed the local jeweler in town, but he said he doesn't sell pocket watches.

He said they, 'just aren't practical for working folks and farmers.' He made me feel so stupid for asking. He acted like he didn't even want me in his store in the first place.

I get that a lot of that from some of the townspeople. Like I'm a burden to them. Makes me wonder if they are members of my family that I just don't know about. Except for Mrs. Potter. She runs this cute little bakery type coffee shop in town. She is always happy to see me, and she even gave me some of her famous homemade chocolate chip walnut cookie crunch bars for free. It's nice to know not everyone in the town is mean. I bought a cute tea set from her since it went with the kitchen, and well, I feel bad she is so old and still has to work. Guess she didn't marry very well, did she? She was really generous and gave me all these tea samples she makes. Everything is organic, so at least I won't get chubby like my sister.

Maureen put the book and cursed. "You bitch." Then she felt immediately guilty. *It's a normal reaction,* she chided herself. *You've always been sensitive about your weight, and probably always will be. You would call her that to her face if she were here, too.* But her soothing in-ner voice did little as she languished over the guilt of hating someone close to her who might have met fate in a gruesome way.

Maureen picked up the journal again, wanting to finish the last part of the entry.

"*But Maureen can't help how she is any more than I can. At least my parents don't buy her off with money. They actually talk to her, not at her.*

I called my mom two days ago to tell her that I think something is wrong around the property, but she didn't want to listen. She just said she loved my bowls I sent. I bought those bowls.

My parents seem interested, proud almost, of Maureen. My parents show their love for me with a check and a pat on the head. They should have just had Maureen and bought a dog. Maureen seems to be the only one who cares by coming

84

up when things get jumbled for me, but lately, it seems like even she can't stand me.

I hid the watch in the closet, in a shoebox from Macy's. It's in the shoe itself, pushed down by the toe. I don't know why I'm writing this. To be used as a reminder of where I hid it. I don't know. My memory has been so foggy lately. And my fingers and toes have been extremely cold a lot. I hope I'm not getting sick.

At times, I'm starting to feel like I'm just making this all up in my head. But a part of me still feels it's important. I plan on writing Maureen to let her know and see what she thinks. My sister the reporter, she's good at figuring out stuff like this. But I'm tired, and I think it's nearly morning. I'm going to go try and get some rest.

Maureen put her marker in the journal and tapped her fingers on the cover. She opened it to the back and started taking notes. She wanted to see the pocket watch for itself. Getting up, putting her tea-cup in the sink, she headed upstairs to the master bedroom.

Opening the closet door, she got an idea. Closing it, she sat down and got the flashlight, turning it on. She reached up and felt for the knob, and found the little latch there. The door locked from the inside.

Maureen's heart skipped and her pulse started to quicken. Hannah switched the doorknob around so it locked from the inside. What was she so scared of? Maureen's jaw tensed slightly, the adrenaline rushed through her veins. Imagine the panic that Hannah must have felt to barricade herself in this tiny closet for hours on end, a voice whispered to her. You can almost smell the fear.

Maureen had enough and tried to open the knob. Flicking the latch to unlock she tried the knob. It wouldn't budge. Maureen didn't like tight places. Why had she closed that door? In her hurry to get the door unstuck, she dropped the flashlight.

Panicked, she turned the knob, then started shaking it until finally she heard the pin click and the door open. She all but spilled onto the area rug in front of the bed, but she was glad she was out. Leaning back against the bed, she rested her arms on her knees and took several deep, calming breaths.

Maureen crawled the few feet to the closet, grabbed the flashlight turning it off.

Remembering the journal entry, she grabbed the Macy's shoebox and pulled out a pair of gold sequined heels, and reached in to pull out a nylon ball. The watch was inside. Pulling the pocket watch from the stocking, Maureen looked it over. It was old; Hannah had been right about that. The watch was heavy, and Maureen suspected it was real.

Opening it, the glass of the watch face was cloudy and cracked. The time was three eighteen.

The scene on the front cover was a mountain landscape. One or two small pine trees were in the foreground. Closing the cover, she flipped the watch over. There were initials on the back of the watch. First a "W", then an "X". Her brain rattled out an answer that she didn't have a question for. William. William Xavier. William Xavier Welsh. The weight of the watch felt like a ton of bricks in her hand at that moment. Her father, William Xavier Welsh, died in a car accident when Maureen was little.

This had to be a strange coincidence. Making her way back to the liv-ing room, Maureen flopped onto the couch.

Should she tell Alfred of the watch? The scratches? Her mind raced with horrible what if scenarios, crazy notions, and random bits of information that she had learned over the last few days. Something wasn't making any sense.

There was a puzzle piece missing, and the rest of the information didn't fit without it. Rubbing her eyes, she leaned back on the couch, her eyes slowly starting to close. It had been a long morning.

She'd take a nap and then head into town to try to find the questions to the answers she already had. She thought for a moment and tried to remember if her father ever having a pocket watch. She'd have to call her mother, but there had to be a logical explanation for this.

Maureen was beginning to think that nothing made sense in Light-house Bay.

CHAPTER 12

BILL WANTED TO avoid the station, so he swung past the Burger King, grabbed a burger, and ate in his patrol car while figuring out his next move.

Mayor Carlisle was certainly anxious to jump down his throat about making an arrest that would stick, but damned if Bill could figure out why. No one liked having crime in their town, but for him to think that Lighthouse Bay was exempt was not only cavalier, it was foolish. No town was safe from crime, no matter how small the town.

Bill tried to assume that the mayor's sense of urgency in wanting things kept quiet and wrapped up was to make sure that the town's reputation survived, but Bill had a sneaking suspicion that there was something else behind his motivation. He also didn't like the fact that Shawn O'Leary seemed to be aware of information regarding the case before he did.

Shawn was too cocky about what he knew, and how he knew it. He didn't know much about Shawn, but Bill suspected he should find out.

Finishing his burger, Bill's thoughts drew back to Maureen. He wanted to apologize for arresting her, but she didn't know the little eccentricities of this small town. An incompetent prosecuting attorney, who only got the job because he was dating the Mayor's niece, was another dysfunction of Lighthouse Bay. The town's foundation was based on the motto, 'you scratch my back and I'll scratch yours.' Bill had seen it firsthand.

He drove outside of town to the county records building. He wanted to do a little homework, without making it obvious at the station.

For some reason he just couldn't bring himself to trust Shawn. The man did everything he could to undermine Bill's authority. At worst, he was manipulative, at his best; he was shady about the business that went on when he was on the clock.

Heading into the records building, Bill was glad that no one was at the front desk. Odds are, no one was going to stop him coming out of the building, being in Sheriff's uniform.

He took the stairs rather than the elevator. He didn't like the cramped, closed in feeling of elevators. In the military, he learned not to be shut into close quarters, and an elevator did just that. But Bill's latest nutritional intake consisted of diners and fast food. Fitting in a little exercise couldn't hurt.

He wasn't sure where he was headed, or what he was looking for, but he knew if there was information here about Maureen's family and the cabin, he'd find it. Heading into the real estate archives, he asked the woman at the desk for all deeds related to the Welsh property. It took her a few minutes, but she was able to locate them.

"Can I get some copies made of those?" he asked her.

"Sure, but it'll cost you," she remarked, a smile on her face. Bill could see she had a huge overbite.

"That's five cents a copy. And we can't do front and back on the copier up here."

"Fine." Bill was just glad she hurried off; he wasn't in the mood for idle chit-chat. She came back a few minutes later, a small stack of papers in her hand.

"That'll be a dollar ten." She waited for payment. Bill suspected her chubby little hand would have stayed closed around those papers until he paid. Fishing in his pocket, he brought out exact change.

"I don't need a receipt thanks."

He turned and headed out into hallway before looking at the papers. Glancing over them, Bill didn't notice that anything wrong. It looked like the standard sale of property to Maureen's parents forty years ago. They bought it from the McMahon's, a local family. Bill stopped, searching in his pocket for a pen. He had an idea.

Going back the way he came, he headed up another flight of stairs to the historical archives and again, made the same request for information on the property. The clerk—a woman in her late sixties, Bill guessed—wore silver framed glasses that hung from a matching chain around her neck, came back, carrying a small manila folder.

"That will be six fifty." He dug the cash from his pocket, and thanked her.

Stepping into the hallway, he was able to compare census records to deeds, to historical information in regards to the property. Looking around for some place to sit, he saw a bench over in a quiet corner by the stairs when his cell phone went off. *Sometimes it just doesn't pay to get up in the morning*, he thought.

"Sheriff Downs." The voice on the other end of the line registered in his brain, and immediately he could feel the heat rise in his cheeks.

"Hello Mayor, did I forget something at your office this morning?" he asked.

"Don't be cute with me, Bill. I just found out she had a bail hearing, not with Ben Traver, but with a Distract judge! What kind of investigation are you running, anyway?" The anger in his voice seemed to drip into the phone as it took on a low rumbling quality. An honest one, he wanted to retort, but didn't. This man didn't sign his paychecks, yet Bill was going to have to be nice and play diplomat for a bit.

"It was a bond hearing, she has a legal right to one. I don't have any control over who goes where for what. The prosecution failed to gather enough evidence to legally hold the suspect; the case was thrown out of court. It was a laughing stock. I'm sorry, Mayor, I know he's dating Colleen, but he didn't do his job. I arrested her for obstruction, but that didn't take. But arresting her only made the department look like we jumped the gun. And we did."

"Now you wait a damned minute. I don't like what you're implying," but Bill cut him off.

"No, you wait. Every time I turn around your prosecutor is screwing up cases that are open and closed. I'm tired of your little patsy Shawn mucking around in my investigations. If he has so much damned free time that he feels the need to watch my back, maybe I should make an appearance at the next budget meeting and suggest that since we don't have near enough police work to do, we might be able to save the town some of its hard-earned money and downsize. I wonder what that would do for a re-election campaign."

He left the threat hang in the air just long enough for it sink into Mayor Carlisle of how serious he really was.

"This investigation has too many hands in the fire, and frankly, I'm tired of it. I was hired do a job, and I can't do that job with you second-guessing the way I run things. Now, I'm doing the investigation my way. End of discussion."

He slammed his phone shut, then turned it on vibrate. He was starting to feel a headache fast approaching and it was nowhere near quitting time. Heading back downstairs, he went past the reception area without an eyebrow lifted in his direction.

Once in his patrol car, he headed back to the Bay. Twenty minutes later, on the edge of town, he pulled in the Clark station for gas. Reaching for the company expense card from his wallet, he started filling his tank up when he noticed a vagrant sitting down on the side of the station.

Growing up, his mother had often told him his dad was a bum. His real father split just before Bill entered kindergarten. He wondered, as he usually did in these moments between mundane tasks, whatever became of him.

Years ago, he thought about looking up his father, seeing where he was, who he was. His absence left a large gap in his childhood, and Bill wanted answers to close that chapter of his life.

But after a while the desire to find his biological father faded, along with the need to find out what happened. A man just doesn't go out for a pack of cigarettes and keep walking.

Bill looked back to the man, who was just sitting there, starring off into space.

He knew that most of the homeless, whether in Michigan or in other parts of the states, were not really homeless; they were in need of hospitalization. Most of the vagrants he'd had the pleasure of running into were about five beers short of a six-pack, but they didn't choose to be that way.

They simply had no family, friends or support system on which to rely. As much as Bill hated to admit it, he often saw such people as the ones society threw away. *Shadows on the outskirts of our reality.* He went inside and grabbed a root beer, then thought a moment.

Grabbing a bag of chips, a wrapped sandwich, and a bottle of water, he went outside and knelt next to the homeless man.

"Hey, I bought these for my lunch, and I just got a call," he lied. "I was wondering if you wanted them. It's not a handout, I just can't eat on a call, and I know they won't return them. I'd rather see someone eat them than just throw them away."

Bill hoped the man would believe him, rather than see his gesture for pity. Sometimes people looked at a hand up as a handout. The old man thought about it for a moment.

"You sure you were just gonna throw it out?"

"Yeah, it's a shame, too. I've been craving a chicken salad sandwich all day, and then I get a call. It's just my luck."

"Well, if you're sure." Feeble hands, shaking and wrinkled with age, reached out and took the items.

"Thanks, mister, I sure do appreciate this," he said to Bill. He tore open the bag of chips and ate a handful before washing it down with the water.

Bill looked at him, and felt that tug of empathy again. *This man isn't your father, Bill,* he chided himself. Deep down he knew it, but at the same time, he knew that this man — gratefully accepting what little Bill had offered like it was the King's coffer — might be someone's father, or son.

When everything was said and done, Bill just couldn't in good conscience turn the other cheek and walk away.

"Well, take it easy out here, try and stay warm. The old mission shelter always has room," Bill said before turning to leave.

"You do the same Mister, especially since it's the end of breeding season." The man bit into his sandwich, chewing slowly as if savoring every bite. The old man's words got Bill's attention, and he turned.

"What do you mean, 'breeding season?' "

"Ah you know, with those big bug-like creatures. They always breed in the fall storing up for winter. They're late this year, probably since we had such a hot summer. I don't think they like the heat much."

He assumed the man crazy, and wondered now if leaving him here was in the interest of public safety. Bill, for all his good intentions, had forgotten that this vagrant might actually be dangerous. He walked over to him, resting his hand on the hip where he kept his revolver, ready to use it if need be.

"Have you seen these things? What do they look like?" Bill didn't know what to make of the man's rambling.

"They stay 'round the lake. Near Gull's Fall, and Gull Rock. That's why they moved the lighthouse near Gull's Peak, and made it bigger. It used to be on the island out there, but they had to move it. Couldn't keep no one in their long enough to staff the lighthouse 'cause of those things. I remember helping take out the lens and boating 'em back to the new lighthouse.

"All those steps. One man fell and broke both his legs that day. But it's nothing compared to those things when they were hungry. We had us a ten-man crew to clean out the lighthouse on Gull Rock, and we were on the last day. I think they woke up, or sensed we weren't a threat to them. We had to fight to get off that island. But," his voice got very low, "we only came back with seven. They said it was the storm, but I was there, I know."

"I'm sorry about your friends," Bill remarked, hoping the man wasn't about to get belligerent. "They sounded like hardworking men."

"They were. We were a gruff lot, but those who love the water, never stray far from it. A sailor's dream is to die by the sea. That's what I'm having done when my time comes. You mark my words."

Bill's sympathy for the man immediately turned to pity as the only

91

thing that seemed to make him happy, the only thing he had to look forward to, was his inevitable death.

"So these things, they live in the water then?" Bill asked trying to stick to the subject.

"No, they came from up above, like they were hovering above us, just waiting for us." The old man bit into his sandwich again.

"You know, I never heard a sound as scary as the sound those things make when they're flying. It's a loud, deep thwacking. Like someone is beating wet wood with a towel. It's creepy strange. Made all of us nervous."

So far, his story was interesting at best. Bill didn't have any reason to doubt what the man said because to him, what he was saying was real. However, Bill didn't have any reason to trust him, either.

"I can imagine things can get pretty hectic out there in the open waters."

"The water we could have handled, no one," he paused, fiddling with the top of his water bottle. "No one knew what was out there. None of us did. If I could do one day differently, that'd be the day, mister. When you watch another man die, well, it leaves a mark on you."

He grew quiet, picking at his chips. Bill knew exactly what the man had been talking about. Bill, though a decorated veteran, had seen his share of battle and the sudden loss of human life was something he never got over. The old man broke him out of his reverie.

"That's why they moved the lighthouse, you know. Those waters weren't safe." Bill was about to ask him some more questions, when his walkie went off.

"Sheriff Downs, over." The voice on the other end was Edith, who informed him that if he didn't get back with the Mayor, she would take all the phones in the station off the hook. The people of Lighthouse Bay and the surrounding counties could sue Bill for negligence, because she wasn't taking one more message from that tyrant. Bill assumed she was referring to Mayor Carlisle.

"Will do, Edith. Now calm down. I'm calling right now." He held out his hand to the old man, who took it and shook it in return. Though he was old, he still offered up a firm handshake.

Bill admired that. A firm handshake was symbolic of integrity and honesty.

"Well, duty calls." He left the old man to finish his lunch, and as Bill cruised along the highway back into town, Bill wondered about the old man' story, Maureen, and what really happened to Hannah Prescott.

CHAPTER 13

THE SNOW COVERED brush crunched under Maureen's shoes as she set out down the small path behind the cabin. After reading Hannah's diary, Maureen finally had clues. She had a good idea of what to research, but she felt if she was going to find out where Hannah was she was going to have to walk a mile in her shoes.

Making her way through the slightly overgrown brush, Maureen fished her digital camera out of her pocket. She had a small spiral bound notebook she'd bought in town, along with some basic supplies.

Hannah's cupboards were bare, just like her fridge. While Maureen didn't mind cereal, it was apparent that that was all her sister ate most of the time. Basic staples like dish soap, paper towel, and toilet paper were also apparently not high on Hannah's grocery list.

The bare cupboards made Maureen wonder exactly how long Hannah had actually been missing. What if she did run off and just never told anyone? Certainly, anyone could look at the contents of her kitchen to know either she wasn't much of a shopper, or she didn't spend much time at home.

That also made Maureen wonder with whom she had been spending time. She knew her sister well enough to know that Hannah wasn't always the most honest, or most faithful of individuals.

Maureen had only been on the path for about fifteen minutes when she noticed the underbrush wasn't overgrown. According to Hannah's diary—and assuming it was true— Hannah hadn't been on her morning walks in nearly two months. The underbrush should have been overgrown by now. The path was too well worn in most spots.

She kneeled down using the zoom lens to take several pictures with the camera. As a reporter, she knew that it sometimes paid to look at things from different angles.

Continuing on the path, she noticed that it did get darker in the woods, despite the bright sun of midafternoon.

Nearly halfway down the steep slope that a ravine ran off to the right. *This must be the ravine that Hannah mentioned in her journal,* Maureen thought. Getting near the edge, she peered over. Tangled weeds, bushes, and overgrown vegetation peeked through the patches of snow-covered ground. She wanted to find a way down there, just to look around. But she'd forgotten to bring along her cell phone, and no one would know where to look for her if she got into trouble.

Going against her gut instinct to search the ravine, Maureen kept walking. About an eighth of a mile later, she came to a fork in the path. *Now what?* She thought. *Nothing in Hannah's journal mentioned this.*

She decided to keep heading straight, and in another half a mile, the path started to open up, the darkness clearing from the edge of the woods. Stepping out from the path, Maureen saw nothing but open, icy water. She had a beautiful view of the rocky cliffs of Lake Superior's shoreline. Even in winter, it was breathtaking.

The sand was wet, and the chill immediately began to seep through Maureen's jacket. *I forgot how cold it gets up here.* She wasn't sure what she was looking for, and where to begin was another question that stumbled into her mind. She pushed her hands into her pocket, surveying the long beach, the tree line, and just decided to head north to see what she could find.

It wasn't too long before she started to notice fine white string dangling here and there on the trees near the far end of the lake, where it neared the rocky slope that led to the cliffs near the dunes. At first, she thought it was part of the snow covering.

Getting closer to it, she pulled out her camera and started to take pictures of it. It looked like quilt batting, fallen and listless, over a few of the tree branches. She wanted to reach out to touch it, see what it was, but hesitated. Was it poisonous?

"God I wish I had something to handle this with," she uttered aloud.

"You rang."

She jumped at the voice, spinning around to stare into the face of Sheriff Downs.

"You know there is a restraining order from you coming near me unless it's on official police business. Or is restraining order too complicated a term for you to understand?"

She crossed her arms, irritated at the sudden interruption to her solace. She was also concerned. Not thinking to have brought her cell phone, she decided, she could be in a real pickle if the Sheriff started harassing her.

She quickly scanned past him, to see how far the path was from where she was. *I could sprint it if I had to,* she thought. She may not exercise on a regular basis, but she walked everywhere in Chicago, and that had to account for something.

"Relax; I'm not here to harass you. I'm here looking for clues, which is probably what you are doing. Secondly, this beach, like all the beaches in Michigan, are public property. The restraining order only covers your personal property and dwelling. It doesn't cover public beaches."

He grinned. Maureen stood glaring at him for a moment. Her body, running on a mind of its own, immediately folded her arms across her chest, back stiff in agitation. Her editor, Jeff, had repeatedly called it the 'mommy dearest stance' on more than one occasion.

"Look, I'm not sure what you have against me. I came to you for help, and so far the only things you've done is look for Hannah where we all know she isn't, then blame me for it. You just accuse and assume," she challenged, the pent up frustration and anger towards had boiled over, and her ranting at him was the direct result of a fuse that had been lit.

"Worse, you're supposed to uphold the law and be all honorable, but when it comes down to it, you're just a bully. How do you sleep at night?"

"I guess I just dream about you and I forget everything else." He smiled, his words dripping with icy sarcasm.

"And here I was hoping to be Mrs. S.O.B. Unfortunately, I have work to do. You know, a job. It's kind of like what you do when you collect your paycheck, only on my part, there is actually work involved." She turned, walking off and continued to take pictures of the web like material. She was kneeling, looking around in the brush in hopes to find whatever it was that made the mess like material.

"What are you looking for?" he asked.

"I'm not sure." She almost slipped and said she was looking for whatever made the webbing that Hannah had mentioned in her journal, but she didn't think it safe to mention that.

"I saw this, and thought it might be something. It's probably nothing, though." She kneeled, and then looked over her shoulder at him. "Do you know what this is," she held up some of the stringy mesh material with a stick. He kneeled next to her, looking at the thin material repeatedly.

"Well, I know what it isn't. This isn't from any arachnid that I'm familiar with, either in Michigan or elsewhere. Spider web material

96

usually has a shine to it, almost opalescent, and it's very fine. This stuff is too thick, if that makes sense."

She was listening to him, wondering whether or not he was telling her the truth.

"You're certain of that?" she asked.

It was more of a challenge in her voice than an actual question. She was naturally skeptical of everyone, and Sheriff Downs was no exception to that rule.

"Yeah, I'm certain. Michigan has only one venomous spider, the Black Widow, though, in all my years here, I have never seen one. Sure we get reports of a spider bite and someone gets rushed to the county hospital, but they have always been harmless. The Wolf spider is native to Michigan, and it bites, but it's not deadly. And this stuff," he held his fingers up before wiping the residue off onto his pants, "isn't from a spider. Unless we have some new breed I'm not aware of. Besides, spiders don't generally make their webs this close to the ground and this close to the water. They're usually higher up, to catch mosquitoes, flies, that sort of thing. Any animals that wander this close to the ground are going to break free of the web and take off, so it defeats the purpose."

He looked up to find Maureen staring at him again. "What?" he asked.

"How do you know all this? They never went this in depth in any of the public schools I ever went to."

She took a few more photos of the webbing.

"I was in the military. I watch a lot of the discovery channel, things like that. And there are these things called books, with words inside, and sometimes pretty little pictures."

"Why do you always try and irritate me?" she asked.

"Why do you always find a way to comply?"

She had to admit, that in any other set of circumstances, her and Sherriff Downs might have actually been friends.

"You're doing that thing again, are you sure you're okay?"

It was his turn to stare at her.

"I mean, you don't need any medication or anything for something like a seizure or something?" He asked, looking at her.

"No, I'm not currently on medication, though being drugged and oblivious to the world does sound nice right now. Why do you ask, or is that one of your standard pickup lines?"

She started to walk, looking in the same direction that she had been before. Looking for something but uncertain of what exactly you were looking for, turned out to be a more difficult exercise than she first anticipated.

She started scrutinizing everything, from fallen leaves to the way a branch was laying. Then realized it was probably a hopeless cause. Turning, she started to head back towards the cabin when something in the tree line caught her attention. Sherriff Downs must have noticed it too, because he turned as well, and followed her gaze.

"Did you see that?" she asked him.

"I saw black movement at the top of the trees. But it's nothing," he said.

"Are you sure? Those trees moved a lot, and there isn't much wind out here." Maureen was chilled to the bone. The cold dampness had seeped through her jacket and the appeal of the warm cabin pushed her forward.

"No there isn't much wind here, but remember, we are technically below the cliff line, so it might be an Alberta Clipper rolling in from the bay. It does get windy more along the lakeshores than inland, Maureen."

"I know it gets windy, but I thought, no I saw," she stressed, "something in the tree line. It was bigger than a bird, and dark."

She pointed towards the tree line, below it, the path that led back to the cabin laid beneath it.

"It's probably a hawk of some sort, or maybe a crow. They get pretty big up here, feeding off the dead fish and all," he concluded.

"Don't do that," Maureen snapped.

She shook her head, marching towards the path, with him in tail.

"Do what? Answer your questions, be civil to you." His voice held the same level of irritation that it usually did when he got into an argument with her.

"Dismiss me because you think I'm some kind of overactive female, who imagines things, who freaks out at every little noise. I am not," she stopped in mid stride long enough to emphasize her point, "some simpering female who needs to be rescued."

"For once we both agree, Sugar. You are definitely not some simpering female; you are nowhere close to even being in the same ballpark."

Why do men do that? she wondered. *Why do men, when referencing a woman in an argument or debate, refer to us as food or bring in a sports analogy? Because they are all Neanderthals*, she answered herself.

She turned to him, ready to tell him what he could do with his 'sugar' and 'ballpark', but just shook her head and kept walking.

He was following her, but he stopped when she stopped short of where the path began.

"What is it?" he asked.

"It's more of that webbing stuff. And it looks fresh." She pointed to the spot where the brush opened to the well-worn path. Sherriff Downs walked around and in front of her, kneeling down towards the underbrush. It was too heavy to be snow. This appeared glossy, almost with snot like consistency that clung to the branches.

"I don't know what it could be," Sherriff Downs said.

"Well, I'm certainly not going back up that path. You're a cop and a marine, how do we get off the beach back up to the mainland," she looked at him earnestly.

"We aren't going anywhere. I am going back up the beach and find a path somewhere up there. You, "he paused, "are free to do whatever you want."

"You're seriously not going to help me get off this beach," she crossed her arms, her voice rising in pitch slightly.

"I thought you were the non-rescuing type that didn't need help." He was grinning at her. A broad, laid back Cheshire cat grin that sometimes made Maureen's stomach flip, and at other times like now, made her want to slap him.

"Yes," he said. "I would Maureen, but knowing my luck, as soon as I escorted you safely back to the cabin, your hotshot lawyer would be there ready to turn me in for violating that restraining order. I have enough people trying to take a bite out of my hide; I don't need to extend any new invitations," Bill said.

"Believe me, your hide is the last thing on my mind. But isn't it your civil duty to help me?" Maureen asked, arms still crossed. She knew she had him cornered now.

"First off, it's civic duty. And actually, no I'm not obligated to do so. You are in no danger, and there is no threat of violence. In fact, if one would look at this situation carefully, one might say that you might be purposefully playing the damsel in distress to trap me into breaking that restraining order that you slapped against me. You know the one I got for doing my job?"

It didn't take an interpreter to notice the sarcasm in his words. Damn, she wanted to slap that smug smile off his face. The nerve of that jerk to think that she was plotting. Plotting to trap him! Into what? A hot date?

"Hello, Earth to Maureen." She blinked and looked at him.

"I'm sorry, I was just trying to imagine what my life would be like without you in it to always nag me, and I guess I got lost in the fantasy."

"Funny. Wasn't it five minutes ago you were asking me to escort you outta these scary woods. You know for someone who supposedly hates me, you sure do an awful lot of referencing to not fantasizing about me."

Sherriff Downs turned, heading towards the break in the rocks near the beach. Maureen stood there for a few moments, wondering what she should do. As much as her pride refused her feet to follow him, a small inner voice warned her it was better to be safe than sorry.

Undecided, she went against gut instinct and started back the way she came, up the path and back towards the cabin. She was nearly fifteen minutes into the wooded inlet when she started to notice a slight movement out of her eye. Keep walking, act like you don't notice anything, she reasoned, trying to calm herself. Another few minutes and she'd be in the clearing by the cabin.

She kept her eyes moving, looking around in her peripheral line of vision. Whoever or whatever was in the woods, Maureen didn't want it or them to know she knew she wasn't alone.

Sometimes the element of surprise works wonder, she thought. Her old copy editor had told her that. It saved her ass from being fired several times when Maureen had managed to find a breaking story. She only hoped now it would work to save her ass in a different manner.

She felt her fingertips throb with the icy ache of the cold that seeped into her jacket.

Shadows crept along the dimly lit path to the cabin, and for the first time since Maureen had arrived, she felt how remote this area was. Even the birds seemed to have quieted to a hushed whisper.

Above her, in a graceful motion unlike the usual pop up villain in some third-rate horror movie, a dark shadowy figure flew past her line of vision.

Maureen stopped.

Everything stopped.

The noises and sounds sporadic for a Michigan forest in winter, stopped.

So did her heart.

Off in the distance, Maureen's ears picked up the same thwacking she had heard that first night at the cabin.

Her heart drummed in her chest like an allegro vignette. When the burning in her lungs brought her out of the shocked awe that had temporarily paralyzed her, Maureen's ears picked up the loud thwacking, and knew that whatever was making that noise was getting closer. Rationalization left her reality, and Maureen did what anyone in an uncertain situation would do: she ran.

She didn't consider herself out of shape, but she wasn't the athletic type either. The fifteen minutes of walking she had to go until she reached the clearing near the cabin bolted by her as her body leaped into an uphill sprint.

The muscles in her legs ached, her lungs felt on fire as every chilly breath ignited a new burning sting that seemed to spread throughout her body. Her temples pounded as she heard the loud thwacking first grow near, then stop.

She stopped too, her throat dry and burning, her chest pounding with the rapid succession of her pulse. Bent over, she felt her stomach flip-flop, churning with the acidic desire to rid itself of its breakfast.

It's quiet. Too quiet.

Taking in deep gulps of air, she looked around, behind her, and focused on the area surrounding the trail.

Nothing. Not a bird or human in sight.

She closed her eyes for a moment wishing her stupid pride, something she had apparently inherited from her father as her mother was always quick to point out, hadn't gotten the best of her. Otherwise, she'd be walking alongside someone with a gun.

As much as the feminist in her hated the idea, the thought of being with a man in the face of danger gave Maureen a little comfort. She'd be safer. She'd be with Bill.

Snorting at her clichéd romance book reaction to her current situation, she stood upright, stretching her sore limbs. She was just getting ready to laugh at herself for running off like some lunatic in an eighties horror film when she saw it.

It was the only way her brain could register what she'd seen. The figure that Maureen knew she had seen earlier wasn't just some hallucination. There was no mistaking that someone was watching her. Some shadowy figure stood behind a bramble of bushes, its head and shoulders barely visible in the limited light.

She backed up, and before her brain could register what was happening, she was running. Her mind was racing with a hundred worse case scenarios of various monsters amalgamated into some hideous being. That monstrous subconscious creature was coming for her, and someone, someone was screaming.

Is that me? She wondered briefly before spotting the edge of the clearing. Her body was tense from a rush for which that any addict

101

would have gladly sold their soul. She saw the cabin, and looked over her shoulder only briefly, her veins pulsing, before she looked forward and ran clear into Bill.

Hormones, adrenaline, and fear were more than Maureen's body could handle. At once, tears started to flow, though Maureen wasn't actually crying. Somewhere in the distance, she heard inaudible sobs, and realized with a shock, that they were coming from her. Embarrassed, she pressed her face closer to him, desperately trying to hide her tears.

She also realized that he had a protective arm around her, his body angled in a way that whatever might be chasing after her, would have to get through him first. His other hand held the sleek black metal of a Glock nine millimeter.

CHAPTER 14

THE SHERIFF'S OFFICE was relatively quiet in the middle of the day, and Shawn waited for Bill's perky secretary to go to lunch. The staff's skeleton crew could only be in a few places: not on duty yet, out patrolling, or at the courthouse in the next county assisting on a case.

With the office all to himself, he was able to nose around more freely. He started with a search of Bill's desk. There was nothing, but he knew that already. Bill was a thorough leader and never left anything of importance out where it might be misplaced.

The military training in him had not only made him an organized boss, but he instilled that same routine into everyone at the office whether they liked it or not. He was orderly and meticulous when it came to paperwork, office rules, and cases, which irritated Shawn's extremely laidback manor.

Shawn tried the desk drawers.

All locked.

He was constantly checking the window to see if any returning men were heading back to the station house. He tried the filing cabinets behind Bill's desk. They too were locked.

He needed to find out exactly what Bill knew, but it wasn't proving that easy. He never left anything out in the open where prying eyes might see it, and he never discussed a case unless he needed help with it. Assistance was one thing, Bill always said, and gossiping about a case was another.

Shawn hated Bill, and Bill knew it. What goaded him most was that the rest of the team in the office had taken a liking to Bill almost immediately, almost as fast as the rest of the town. Shawn had been the local 'it boy' until Bill had rolled into town. Bill just didn't step on Shawn's toes he jumped on them.

Finding everything locked, Shawn looked out the window once more and started to riffle the pockets on one of Bill's jackets hanging on the back of his chair. A pocket full of loose change in the zippered inside pocket, a few loose dollar bills in the left side pocket, and a phone number from some girl named Carly. The number was local.

Shawn felt the heat flood his face as his blood pressure slowly started to rise.

The bastard even gets the locals girls as well.

Uttering another soft curse, he reached in and looked at the change, taking two-quarters and pocketing them before zipping the pocket and replacing the jacket as he'd found it.

Heading over to another officer's desk, he picked up the extension and dialed. After a few rings, a voice at the other end picked up.

"Hey, it's Shawn. So far I haven't found anything."

"We have a deadline. The last thing we need is the bigger papers or the bigger stations picking up this damned story. If people start investigating, we are in a sinkhole full of shit, O'Leary," the voice on the other end of the line barked.

"Tell me something I don't know. You think I don't know what would happen if word got out? Christ sakes, we'd have Katie-fucking-Couric camped out on our damned doorstep just to get a freaking interview."

"Bet your ass we would. You're forgetting there are too many people who have too much at stake to see that happen. Our livelihoods are on the line while you're out there picking your ass or whatever else itches."

"Wait just a goddamned minute. If you had gotten that little problem taken care of, I wouldn't be here cleaning up your damned mess!"

"We have a deadline, O'Leary."

"I know, I know, before the Yuletide Festival. Finding out what he knows isn't going' to be easy, but I'll see what I can do."

"Do it, and do it fast. We need this thing fixed and forgotten like yesterday's news. And don't go getting any ideas about our agreement, O'Leary. Remember if I go down, I'm taking people with me."

Shawn didn't have time to reply before the line went dead.

Slamming the receiver back down himself, he grabbed the half-empty packet of Pal Mal's from his shirt pocket and lit one, before his radio went off. A call about some teens speeding through downtown on the sidewalk on a snowmobile had to be taken care of before he headed over to Bill's place to look around.

Hoping to deal with the snowmobile incident and make it to Bill's place before he got back, Shawn headed out of the station without leaving a note for Edith on where he was going, or when he'd be back.

Shawn pulled his police cruiser down the dirt trail that led to Bill's rustic two-bedroom loft cabin. The cabin had belonged to Edith's cousin and had been in the family since God was a boy. Bill made an offer to take care of the place when Edith's cousin had passed away, and a few months later, Bill bought the place from her family at their generous asking price.

Double-checking his mirrors, he got out and walked towards the front door. The detached one car garage was in back, so he didn't know if anyone was home. If by the random chance that Bill had been home, Shawn had a file in his hand for Bill to sign off on for the tickets he'd issued for the incident with the snowmobile earlier that day.

He knocked and waited. Nothing. Leaning casually to the left, he peered in the window, only to meet drawn curtains.

He had no visibility into Bill's place. A new rush of angry frustration washed over him and pooled in his belly. He would have sworn that Bill did this on purpose, like he knew that Shawn was coming. Bill operated on angles as the criminals did, only from the other side.

Looking around once again, he tried the doorknob. It was locked.

Taking a closer look at the windows, he realized that they'd been replaced not too long ago, and were far sturdier than he'd hoped for. Walking around the back, Shawn was met with the same thick curtains that obscured his view into the cabin. Swearing, he reached the back porch and tried the back door.

Locked.

If Bill had anything relating to the case in his cabin, Shawn was going to have to break in and risk getting caught to snoop around. That was banking on that there was something to actually be found.

He paced back and forth slowly, pulling a cigarette out of his pocket and lighting it.

Shawn got a certain satisfaction from smoking on Bill's back porch; He didn't understand why Bill hated smoking so much. It was always what you expected it to be; right there when you wanted it, it was the perfect escape.

He took another long drag from the unfiltered butt and stared at the windows more closely. They were all locked, and after further inspection, he noticed fine black knot at the top of the windowpane.

Alarms.

Was Bill hiding something? Why would the local Sherriff of a small town in northern Michigan need security? Shawn went around to the side of the cabin, stubbing the butt of his cigarette out in the porch railing before checking the last of the windows.

Every window had the same small black box in the top left corner. Shawn looked for a company logo, but there wasn't any. Either Bill had hired a private company to do the job, or Bill had done it himself. Maybe something related to Bill's military background.

Taking off his hat, he ran his fingers through his hair, contemplating what to do next.

Hayes would be on him for not getting any information. He'd been told on numerous occasions that he had messed this whole thing up, but Shawn refused to share the blame alone.

Hearing the radio crackle from his patrol car, Shawn picked up his shoulder mic and answered Edith's perky voice.

"This is Shawn, over."

"Hey Shawn, those kids on the snowmobile are back again. Cornelia Davis just called from the Sweet Spot, and said they were racing up and down Magnolia and knocked her sign over again."

Shawn reached for the pack of his Pal Mal's and noticed he had two smokes left.

"I'm on my way, Edith."

Shawn climbed back into the cruiser, backing down the dirt trail eliminating any possible tracks from him turning the cruiser around.

Heading west towards town, making a stop at the mart for more nicotine reinforcements before dealing with those snobby tourists.

CHAPTER 15

BILL COULD FEEL her body shake against his, and he tightened his arm around her. She was sobbing softly against his shoulder, and a small part of him wanted to lift her face and brush her tears away with his fingers. Yet the trained soldier in him was able to acknowledge those base feelings, and he knew that he had to secure the area and protect Maureen from whoever, or whatever was after her. In one fluid moment of grace and training, he shielded her body with his.

"Maureen." He nudged his shoulder, trying to get her to look up at him. "Maureen. I need you to be quiet, Maureen. I can't hear when you're sobbing."

She lifted her chin, and his eyes caught hers for a just a moment. They locked onto her icy blue pupils, pooled with fresh tears that threatened to spill at any moment.

"Okay, Maureen. Quiet, for just a moment."

She nodded.

He looked around, careful of keeping his body in front of hers, blocking anyone on the path from reaching her.

Off in the distance, behind the tree line where the path crept into the darkened forest around the lake, a loud screeching rose above the trees. Startled birds spanned their wings and flew, fleeing from the area where Maureen and had been only moments before.

He closed his eyes momentarily, allowing the temporary blindness to aid his other four senses. His ears pricked, concentrating on the sounds around him. Maureen's breathing. The rush of the leaves in the trees. His own heartbeat.

Still, when he opened his eyes a moment later, the clearing near Maureen's cabin was as it was before. His patrol car and her beat up old Pontiac.

Glancing down at Maureen, then back over his shoulder, he loosened his grip, which caused her to look up at him.

She said nothing.

107

Neither did he.

He pulled her towards the back door of the cabin but stopped her before she entered.

"I need to look around. To make sure that there isn't anyone inside. Stay here."

"Like hell I am," her voice quaked, attempting to gain entrance past him.

"I said you will stay here."

"Not with that thing out there, I most certainly will not. You must have taken one too many grenades to the head to think that I would for one second—"

He cut her off. "Why do you never resist the chance to find a way to irritate me?"

"Why do you always rise to the occasion?" She looked at him, wiping her tear-streaked face with her fingertips. Her pale skin glowed in the afternoon sun, and he turned his head a moment to shake his mind of the base reaction to touch her.

"Maureen," he turned to look at her once more, "whoever attempted to scare us on the beach might have had help. Someone might be lurking inside, and I sure as hell am not going to allow you inside without a look around."

"Fine, but I will be right behind you."

He opened his mouth to protest, but she countered with a plea that rendered him speechless.

"Please," she paused, her voice softer than before, "please don't leave me out here alone."

Resolving that she wouldn't budge, he grabbed her by the wrist and motioned for her to stay behind him.

He turned the knob, slowly pushing the door open. He fanned his gun left to right, sweeping the room before walking to check closet doors on the main level.

The small bathroom on the main floor, two closets, and laundry room were all clear.

He checked the front door: locked. Making his way upstairs, he swept his gun across the landing, moving from room to room, closet to closet, securing the premise before he headed back downstairs.

Closing, and locking the back door, he shouldered his weapon and looked at Maureen.

"Okay, Maureen. What happened?"

"I. . . I don't know. One minute I was pissed at you, walking back towards the trail to get back here, and the next thing I knew I heard noises."

"What kind of noises?" he asked, helping himself to a cup of coffee, and pouring one for her as well.

"I don't know. Just, noises. It sounded like that hissing screeching we heard earlier. Only more close up," she swallowed. "I felt watched."

Bill had the same feeling while on the beach, but he chalked it up to the heat of the argument.

"What else? Think Maureen, I need to know every detail that you can remember."

Reaching to accept the cup of coffee he offered her, she sipped it, cradling the warmth of the cup in her hands almost as if the heat of the mug would chase away the cold shivers pricking her skin.

"There isn't much to tell. One minute I was walking along, the next I got this hinky feeling, and I was running for my life."

"Hinky? I haven't heard that term in a while."

She looked at him.

"I'm a reporter, and I've interviewed my share of cops to pick up on your private lingo."

He smiled at her observation. "So something felt hinky. Then what? Did you see anybody? Hear anyone?"

"No and no. I keep telling you this isn't a person or a group of people. It's something else. I don't know how to put it into words, but I knew I was being watched. My human instincts kicked in, and somewhere in my brain, that primitive notion of flight or fight sounded off. But I just didn't feel watched, Bill. I felt hunted."

"We may be looking at a rabid bear or cougar. There are reports of the occasional wolverine spotted up near Isle Royale."

Sipping her coffee, she shook her head.

"This wasn't an animal, in the familiar sense." She opened her mouth to say something, then looked at him. "Why? Do you think it is a person doing this?"

"I've been in this business long enough to recognize some signs that don't get chalked up to animal behavior."

"So you think that someone is behind what happened out there, maybe to cover up something else that you aren't supposed to know about?"

He looked at her, and whether she knew it or not, the reporter in her reacted just as quickly as the soldier in him.

"Is that on, or off the record?" he asked before sipping his coffee.

Her head snapped at him. "How dare you!" Clearly agitated by something he'd said, and got to her feet and marched over to him. "How dare you accuse me of scooping out a story when that, that thing was after me! Is after me! How dare you when you know that that thing probably killed my sister!"

He looked at her squarely, pushing aside his male feelings and intuition, sticking to the case at hand.

"That's the first time you've mentioned your sister in the past tense. It's the first time you've mentioned that she was dead." He didn't finish the rest of his sentence, he didn't ask 'how do you know she is dead', but the silence that hung in the air was apparent to Maureen as well.

"She's been missing for nearly two weeks. Never in all of Hannah's irresponsible and selfish day trips to other cities or her flirtations with stupidity did she ever stay away this long and not call, not reach out to somebody. Besides, I don't think that my sister's capable of living two weeks on her own without the financial assistance of my mom and Frank."

"Why don't you call Frank your dad?" he asked over the rim of his coffee mug.

"Because he isn't my father. He's nice enough, friendly I suppose, but he never bothered to take me as his own, give me his last name. He always introduced me as his stepdaughter."

Bill studied her, thinking that he might have seen a brief hint of longing or regret cross her face. It didn't take a psychic to know that she had a serious independent chip upon her shoulder, and it wasn't placed there overnight. It had taken years to chip away her self-confidence in herself, and the immediate effect had been that arm's length barrier that Maureen seemed to keep up around herself.

She looked up, watching him watch her.

"Look, I didn't create the distance between us; he'd been introducing me as his stepdaughter long before I was old enough to figure out that it wasn't necessarily out of love. All I did was keep up my end of things and introduce him as Frank. There just didn't seem to be much point in pretending we were anything else but what we were."

A part of him wanted to tell her that he knew how she felt, as he had been there once or twice before himself. But he kept to his original train of thought. He had to know if Maureen did indeed know anything about her sister's disappearance.

110

Bill had been in law enforcement for long enough to know that people, who knew anything about a crime, would eventually slip up and acknowledge it. His perception of the human race was that if people knew about a secret, it was only a matter of time before they ended up divulging it to someone.

"You still didn't answer my question, Maureen. How do you know that Hannah is dead?"

Fresh tears started to well in her eyes and she looked at him.

"I don't really. Because she isn't here, is she? Every day a person is missing, the odds of them being found safe and sound, decreases, doesn't it? She was immature and irresponsible, Sherriff. There is a reason that her inheritance had to be doled out in bi-weekly or monthly disbursements. She would blow throw it if allowed. She had no concept of financial responsibility because my mom and Frank spoiled her rotten." She sniffed, reaching for a Kleenex on the coffee table.

"She was a fraud. She lied to my parents about what she was doing here. Do you know that? She was unstable. She was on antidepressants and anti-anxiety pills. I think that Hannah is dead because she has had so many brushes with danger and death in the past it didn't take me long to figure out that it wasn't 'if Hannah died,' it was simply a matter of 'when'."

Bill took in the information, studying Maureen's face for signs of dishonesty. She had maintained eye contact with him the whole time she had been telling him about Hannah. She had divulged things about Hannah that he'd suspected but hadn't been able to confirm. He would have to tread lightly if he was going to coax any more information out of her.

"What do you mean that she was a fraud? A liar?"

Maureen stood up and motioned for him to follow her upstairs. He did so wordlessly and entered the spare room that he had searched a few times before, first for clues and more recently for intruders.

A multitude of clay pottery pots gleamed in the early afternoon sun. Lined neatly on rustic looking wood shelves, he watched Maureen reach for a large red and black bowl.

"My sister fancied herself an artist. But she wasn't. Look," she commanded as she handed him the bowl.

"Flip it over. It has a price tag on it. They all do. I bet that she went to some local craft show, bought a lot of them, and sent one or two to my mother stating that she was busy at work in her pottery studio."

Bill looked at the vase, and he did indeed notice the handwritten price tag on the bottom.

"How do you know it's from a craft show? Can you be certain that this isn't her handwriting," he inquired, putting the bowl down back in its place on the shelf before picking up a matching pitcher and turning it over to examine it.

"Jesus, and you are supposed to be finding my sister. It isn't Hannah's handwriting because I did what any crackpot newbie would have done with a mail-order detective kit and compared the handwriting to that in her diary. It isn't a clear match.

Second, your crafters are a zealous lot and treat their finished products like works of art. They aren't going to put some generic grocery store price tag on things. They are going to make every effort to create that handmade effect right down to the price tag.

And lastly, Sherlock, these price tags are written on nontransferable mini sticky notes. This way they leave behind no residue to ruin the piece itself."

Bill watched with her a mixture of amazement and humor. She had gone back to calling him Sherlock and wondered if she used nicknames as a term of endearment.

"Touché," was all he could muster. He put the pitcher back on the shelf and looked around again. Indeed, nearly every piece of pottery that he picked up had a price tag on them.

"Okay, so let's say that I buy this theory that Hannah didn't make these. What possible motive would she have for sending your parents this junk and passing it off as hers?"

"Because my mom and Frank," she corrected him, "like to keep tabs on Hannah, especially since she flunked out of school. So they make inquiries as to what Hannah is doing, she sends this cheap knock off pottery, and both parties can be ignorant until something happens."

"Then you get called to come and see what the problem is, fix it, and wait until the next problem happens, is that it?" Bill crossed his arms.

"Do you have siblings?"

"No, it was just my mom and me."

"Was?"

"She passed away three years from breast cancer. I don't remember much about my father."

"Did he pass away too?" she asked, pushing a loose strange of auburn hair behind her ear.

"No, he went out one day and never came back. He smoked, he had big feet, and if memory serves he liked Mexican food."

"That's all you remember," Maureen spoke softly.

"I never had any brothers or sisters because my mom and I had enough to deal with after he left without adding another man and more kids to the situation."

"Do you have cousins or aunts and uncles," she inquired, her voice laced with something that Bill could almost believe was concern.

"Why do you want to know?" he asked. He turned and headed back down the stairs, looking around the living room and its contents. No pictures, no knickknacks. Clean lines and endless open spaces, both on the walls and on the surfaces of the furniture as well. For the first time, Bill noticed that the house lacked personality. It lacked life.

Maureen followed him, making her way back to her usual spot on the couch.

"Because it's sad to think that you have no ties to anyone."

"Careful, Miss Welsh. That almost sounds like concern."

"Your family tree and biological roots are of no concern to me, but I write about this stuff all the time. How do you know where you are going, when you don't know where you have been?"

"Save it for Hallmark. I know where I'm going. I made a good life for myself, and I am not missing anything. But just so you can get your beauty sleep at night, I have several cousins and aunts and uncles that take pity on poor ol' Bill and invite him to the family reunions and holiday suppers. I'm touched by your concern, Maureen."

An awkward pause hung between them.

"So your sister isn't entirely honest with your mom and Frank. She's an adult. What she's doing doesn't necessarily make her a liar. She's a grown woman who doesn't want to divulge every detail about her personal life with her parents."

Shaking her head at Bill's comment, Maureen sighed.

"What?" he asked.

"You approve of her doing that? Unbelievable, no matter how hard I try and help her, to get her help, the people who are always supposed to help her always end up feeling sorry for her."

"You sound jealous, Maureen. Jealousy can be a motive you know." As soon as he said it, he instantly regretted it. The friendly banter that he had established was immediately replaced by the cool façade of her ice queen exterior.

"You know it's been a trying day. I think I'm going to take a long hot bath and make a few phone calls." She got up walking over towards the door, unlocking it and opening it for him in a gesture to leave.

Bill grabbed his hat and nodded to her, heading towards the door.

"I just meant that it sounds like you were jealous of the attention that she got."

"Yeah, maybe so. One gets tired of being the dependable wallflower, only thought about when it's time to clean up a mess."

She closed the door in his face.

"Be sure to lock it behind me."

Without hesitation she did.

Out on the porch, Bill looked back at the door and pulled out a small notebook out of his pocket, scribbling down some notes on it before heading back to his patrol car.

"Believe me, Maureen, only a fool would think you were a wallflower," he commented to no one in particular.

Pulling out of the driveway and heading back towards the station, Bill realized he had his work cut out for him with this case. He had the pieces to the puzzle, but they were fitting too easily for his liking. He had a person to find, a mayor's motive and angle to figure out, and worst of all, he had to find a way to preserve whatever existed between him and Maureen long enough for him to ask her out on a date.

Chapter 16

MAUREEN LEANED AGAINST the door, trying to ignore the desperate hunger that gnawed at her empty stomach. *I guess being in near life and death situations makes a person appreciate the simpler things in life like drowning your sorrows in a large bowl of Captain Crunch.*

Heading into the kitchen, Maureen looked around the cupboards and refrigerator, but nothing wetted her appetite.

She wasn't sure what she was in the mood for, but she knew she wanted something else other than dry cereal or bologna sandwiches, which appeared to be staples in Hannah's life.

Reaching for a can of soup, she dumped the contents into a bowl and popped it into the microwave. Leaning against the kitchen counter, she stared out the side window towards the wooded path to the forest and the beach beyond. The sane, single woman in her told her she was lucky to have gotten out of that situation without getting hurt and she should have been more careful before going out alone.

Just because you aren't in the city doesn't mean that crime doesn't take a vacation.

Sitting at the kitchen table, she ate her soup, feeling the warm broth of the vegetable medley seep into her body.

She also started making notes in her notebook. Some things had question marks next to them, possible theories about what happened to Hannah, people to contact and a list of those she had already burdened with the pitiful inquiry of, 'have you heard or seen my sister,'.

Maureen also had a list of possible subjects and places to check out in town. Whatever happened to Hannah, Maureen couldn't shake the feeling that it hasn't happened to someone else.

She would check tourist information, and then the town hall for records to the property her family owned. Maureen made a mental note to contact the town's surveying office to see where her family's property ended. Maureen hadn't spent a great deal of time here in the last decade, just breezing in and out of town depending on Hannah's troubles.

Her last stop would be the library. There had to be a collection of old newspaper articles buried somewhere in some ancient circulation desk.

People just don't go missing in today's day and age, Maureen kept reminding herself. It's the twenty-first century. Modern technology and the industrial age have nearly made it impossible to get lost in any sort of wilderness and truth be told, there wasn't that much wild undiscovered country left available.

Putting her empty bowl into the sink, Maureen realized that maybe Hannah hadn't actually vanished because of some mysterious circumstances, but maybe she vanished willingly.

The thought never occurred to her before, because her sister's codependent relationship with the rest of her family was too strong to enable the emotionally crippled woman to stand on her for any length of time.

Hannah had to be around people. She was never out of a relationship; she was simply in a waiting period until she reeled in the next man. Constantly surrounded by friends, by men, and a circle of social acquaintances, Maureen thought long and hard about the last time that Hannah had actually been on her own.

With a sad realization, she remembered it was probably in childhood when both Maureen and Hannah received a crash course in self-preservation. Maureen had learned that the only person she could depend on was herself while Hannah had searched in vain for the one person to give her what Maureen now knew she had lost and never felt: security.

If Hannah actually had vanished, then Maureen was going to have to find her, and fast. She had close to a month saved up in vacation and personal time, but she really didn't want to use all of it looking for her sister. It would put Maureen in a terrible bind should she get sick during the remainder of the year.

She wasn't financially worried that she would have to worry about her bills. Her father's social security and death benefits were in a trust for Maureen when she turned twenty-one, and most was still there. She lived a life of pursuit, her dreams and goals came before snagging the latest designer outfit or decorating with the latest trends.

Her oddly non-materialistic habits were often a topic of discourse for her mother, who believed that weekly trips to Neiman Marcus were a part of the recommended daily allowance for good health and nutrition.

She thought about the reasons why Hannah would want to leave but came to a dead end. There seemed to be no logical reason why Hannah would want to just up and leave. Not to mention that Hannah had left behind many of her precious possessions including her hoard of designer clothes and accessories that were essential to her daily survival.

Maureen had to remind herself that her sister probably had wandered off to think, yet her purse had been at the cabin. While she might have had some cash on her, without her credit cards, checkbook, or passport, Hannah wouldn't get far.

Grabbing her blue knit angora sweater, Maureen grabbed her bag and decided to head out towards town in search of some answers.

Locking the door behind her, Maureen made her way to her old Pontiac and looked in the backseat before getting in.

The drive into town was always beautiful no matter what time of year it was. In the spring, thick lush blankets of green, ivory, and pink lined the rolling hills and beaches.

In the summer, hues of vibrant blues etched the scenery into shards of silvery glass that reflected the sun's brilliance in all its wondrous facets.

Maureen preferred the looming hills and winding roads of Michigan's Upper Peninsula in the fall. Autumn had always been her favorite time of year, and it sparked a creative streak in Maureen that required no effort on her part. There was something about the rich and bold colors-fuchsia, amber, gold, and burnt oranges that both appealed to Maureen's creative nature, but also seemed to sooth her as well.

Winter in Michigan was equally beautiful, though slightly more dangerous. Thick blankets of ice and snow froze the life underneath it and created a translucent world of sharply distorted images. But the weather and storms often trapped people in their small hamlets and towns, and during those long winter months, many in Michigan's Upper Peninsula felt cut off from the rest of the world.

Maureen was still in awe as she drove, taking in the blanketed scenery. There was snow on the ground, not enough to cover all of the fall foliage beneath, but enough to give it a light dusting.

She found the local surveyors office, but an illness in the office had them closed. Resolving to check in again in the next day or so, she moved on towards city hall.

Most towns held county records, but Maureen knew from experience that depending on the tenacity, organization, and the size of the town, those records could tell a town's history, or barely give enough to sketch together a paragraph.

City hall was a two-story structure of faded red brick that housed the county's records had a front facade that boasted two large white cylindrical columns and a flight of concrete steps. In the front, there was a large circular garden area, scattered with a few wooden and wrought iron benches.

Lining either side of the small manicured gardens, was a row of burning bushes, the bright fiery red botanicals that bloomed with rich bold colors.

In the center of the garden, a single concrete circular platform that upheld a single flagpole boasting the state flag under a larger United States flag.

The main level housed the licensing division and traffic court offices, the magistrate, the notary, as well as the county seat.

Heading up to the second level, she waited in line until it was her turn at the counter. A large, gray-hair woman in her late fifties, with an oval face and pinched pug nose, turned around to stare at Maureen.

"Can I help you, miss?" The woman, Maureen could tell, had probably been born and raised in this part of Michigan all her life if her northern accent rang true.

"Yes ma'am, you can. My family has property here in Lighthouse Bay, and I wanted to get any information on it that I could."

"Have you just returned to the Bay area, miss?" the woman asked, grabbing a few forms and a pencil.

"Well, I haven't been here for long periods of time, but I have been thinking about coming back here. It's such a friendly and quiet town."

"Well, friendly enough and it could stand to be a little more quiet if you ask me. Too many of those teenagers cruising up and down Main and Little, revving their engines and causing trouble. Kids today have no respect if you ask me."

"Yes ma'am, I couldn't agree more. Makes me wish for the good ol' days."

"Oh honey, you aren't that old. I'm the one who should be longing for the good ol' days." She handed Maureen the papers.

"You need to fill these out, and then I can process the information you need."

"How long will it take, do you know?" Maureen asked, filling out the forms with the pencil.

"Well, it takes as long as it takes me to find the file and the size of the file. Some files are more easily located and are smaller than others. But it usually takes at the very least, about fifteen minutes, and at the most, a few days."

Maureen finished filling out the paperwork and handed the papers back to the woman.

"Well Miss," she paused briefly, "Welsh, you are in luck. It just so happens that I know the precise location of your file, so it will take me all of about five minutes or so to make you your copies."

"I can't look at the originals?"

"No, I'm afraid not. Government rules. The Freedom of Information Act allows you to obtain a copy of public and semi-public documents, but the originals must be kept within the confines of the government building in which they are housed."

"Ah, I see. I was just wondering. Copies work." Maureen was fishing her wallet out of her bag and counting her money after looking at the list of copying fees posted on their information board. The woman had disappeared, and just as Maureen had made the exact change, put away her wallet, and reread over her notes, she reappeared.

"One more thing if you don't mind, ma'am. How exactly did you know where to find this file?" Maureen asked, folding the papers and stuffing them into her large leather shoulder bag.

"Oh, well that's easy. Sherriff Downs was here earlier and asked to have copies made as well."

Maureen nodded curtly to the woman, took her copies and stormed out of the courthouse.

He had lied to her. She was still a suspect, and worse, he was looking into her family's personal information. If he had known something that would certainly explain why he had shown up at the beach. He wanted to confront her.

If he'd found something that he didn't understand, he also might be trying to coax Maureen into revealing some more information that may or may not ending up being used against her.

One thing was for certain, Maureen was going to be very careful about how she went about investigating things in this town. And she was going to smack Sherriff Downs the next time she saw him.

❦

It turned out that Maureen's chance to make good on her personal to-do list of smacking around Sherriff Downs presented itself earlier than she had expected.

After about twenty minutes of getting lost and finding her route again, Maureen finally managed to remember the location of the Lighthouse Bay Public Library. There weren't many cars there, and when she didn't see Sheriff Down's police cruiser and felt a little more relaxed about going inside.

The old man at the front desk was more than helpful in pointing the way to the basement where all of the county's old periodicals were stored.

Maureen noted the man's hands shook slightly even at the simplest tasks, and wondered briefly if the man had Parkinson's. Her grandfather had had the terrible nerve disease, and it wasn't a fun ride watching him slowly wither into a former shadow of himself.

She had only been thirteen or fourteen at the time, but it was the single most defining moment of her life. Researching her grandfather's disease is what inspired her to become a journalist.

The basement of the brick story building smelled. Not just musty, although there was that all too familiar scent of closed in boxed up history. But it there was, a secondary scent, an odd mixture of old wood, lemon, mingled with a fragrance of some retail chain room freshener. All in all, it was a little bit overpowering as well as a little bit nauseating, but after a few moments, Maureen didn't seem to notice.

The floor was paneled in wooden sheaths that probably dated back from the early nineteen seventies, which is when the library was built according to the stone marker on the side of the building.

Floor to ceiling wooden shelves lined the two long walls that were parallel to the entry of the room, making the small space seem larger than what is actually was. Several rows of smaller wooden shelves ran perpendicular to the larger shelves and were broken up intermediately by small square wooden tables with four wooden chairs. Each table boasted a studious looking desk lamp, its shade not in the traditional hunter green but in a softer shade of mauve.

It's definitely a woman's touch, though Maureen as she inspected the rest of the area. Little feminine touches were placed here and there throughout the area to try and breathe life into an otherwise seldom used room.

Superior Lies

A painting, obviously a reproduction, of the ill-fated liner Edmund Fitzgerald hung in the small space above the doorway. The Gordon Lightfoot tune started to play itself inside her brain, and she uttered a soft curse. Songs played on repeat in her brain for days on end, coming and then replaced by another tune regardless if Maureen was singing it or heard it. It was like some random puppeteer had an eclectic selection of music ranging from Bach to Dolly Parton and he just picked a song at random and hit the repeat button for days while he contemplated the next acoustic mind assault.

She put her bag on the nearest empty table and turned on the light. It flickered a moment before coming on completely. Once Maureen was assured that the small halogen bulb was on, she rummaged through her bag. Pulling out a small book size notebook and pen, she flipped through pages of notes, to-do lists, until she found a blank page.

Going over to the large apothecary-like wooden dresser, Maureen started to think about what years to start looking up the periodicals. She tapped her pen for a moment and started writing down a few dates. Her parent's graduation years, the year they married, her birth year, the year of her father's death.

She wasn't exactly sure what it was she was looking for, but like any good reporter worth their weight in ink, she would know it when she saw it.

Some people called it writer's intuition—like a cop—only she was tracking down the information many times before it happened.

Maureen chose to think of herself, not as a sleuth, or a detective, or even a reporter. Maureen fancied herself a thinker. She put together puzzles and figured out riddles to unveil to others what would have otherwise stayed hidden away from the eyes of the public.

She started looking under the years her parents graduated, and found two large tomes of newspapers. The large leather bindings tied together in three separate spaces with heavy string. The newspaper clippings were faded and yellowed, but still readable. Whoever was in charge took care of them.

After two hours, Maureen search for the years nineteen sixty-three through sixty-five turned up nothing. No mention of her parents, the property, or anything else weird in relation to town happenings.

Next on her list was the year her parents got married.

Putting back the leather tombs and exchanging them for three more, Maureen found a break halfway through the first book.

There, in the community section of the paper, she found a wedding announcement for her parents' nuptials that were to be the preceding weekend. She stared at the picture of her parents, not realizing how young they looked.

Her parents looked so carefree, the whole world ahead of them. Funny, it had been so long since she saw a picture of her dad that she had trouble remembering exactly what he looked like until then. Her mother looked so fresh and vibrant, not like the over-tanned, wrinkled drunken socialite that she was now.

Getting up, she went over to the ancient copier and pressed copy. Nothing.

Looking on the side, she noticed a change slot: TWENTY-FIVE CENTS.

"What a rip-off," Maureen muttered.

Fishing out her change purse, she made a copy and went back to the table.

She finished the other part of the tome, then the other two volumes that were on the table before standing and stretching. Her backside ached, and for a brief moment, she remembered what it was like back in catholic school.

Her desk had had hard, wooden chairs that forced people to sit completely rigid and upright, which made every nerve in the lower lumbar area, from hips to shoulders, ache.

It took nearly three months for the permanent ache to go away, only to get a week or two of reprieve before school started up again after Christmas break.

Crossing another year off her list, she went in search of more volumes of periodicals to find something that might help find her sister.

Maureen had spent so much time thinking about Hannah, that it had almost become a subconscious act on her part. Like brushing her teeth or flushing the toilet, it had become such an automated response that Maureen hadn't really sat down to think about her sister.

The weather outside was cold, and the snow flurries were starting to stick.

How is Hannah going to survive out there by herself? She shuddered. *Hannah had no real survival skills save for finding an ATM.*

Guilt washed over Maureen. Speaking about her sister with such disdain when she might be injured or dead. Lost. Kidnapped.

Her cell phone rang and Maureen sighed. She knew the voice on the other end of the line was probably her mother.

To pick it up or let it go to voicemail.

Maureen hated cell phones. She only had one because with all the traveling she did for her stories, it was easier to pick up a cell phone than find a phone she could use. Not to mention that in many cases where Maureen had to go digging for the truth, it wasn't always in the best part of town.

After the fourth ring, Maureen picked it up, not wanting to disturb anyone else that might also be down in the periodical section of the basement.

"Hello." Her voice spiraled downward, unable to hide the underlying resignation in her voice.

"Maureen, oh thank heavens it's you."

"Who else would it be, mom? How are you?"

"I am. . . I guess I'm okay. I mean, I have my moments." There was a long pause, and Maureen knew from the shakiness in her mother's voice that she was on the verge of tears.

"The police are doing all that they can. They have several leads, and as much as he has been a pain in my ass, Sherriff Downs is good at his job, mom. If anyone can figure out this whole mess, it's him." She hated herself for being his personal cheering section, but even as she said it, she knew that it was true.

"Maureen, why are you not out there helping them? I hope you aren't just sitting around, snooping through your sister's things and waiting for her to come home." The heightened shrill in her voice angered Maureen, but she didn't bait her mother this time. She had been through enough.

"No mom, I'm doing all that I can to find her. I'm not just sitting around on my ass waiting for her to stumble through the door. I'm doing my own little investigation, and who knows, in the meantime it's possible that Hannah will wander back home. She's done this before."

"Maureen! How can you still bring that up at a time like this?" Her mother's voice cracked, and she could hear the soft gentle sobbing on the other end.

Great Maureen, why not just find a lame dog to kick while you are at it.

"All I meant was that Hannah," she paused, groping for words, "has to follow her spirit. You know the artist type, they get lost in their work and don't even realize anything that is going on in the outside world. Didn't you tell me that Picasso would lock himself in his studio for weeks on end just prepping before he painted?"

"You think that Hannah is off on some kind of artist retreat or something," her mother's voice sounded hopeful.

"Probably. I mean, people just aren't born knowing how to use clay; she had to learn from someone somewhere. Maybe her mentor. You know artists; they don't worry about calendars, appointments, or clocks."

"Maybe that's it. I bet she is off somewhere, learning some new technique and focusing so much on her work that she hasn't had the sense to call." Her mother's sobs had ebbed as quickly as they had come, and Maureen felt momentarily relieved. She didn't want anything bad to have happened to her sister, but she also knew that there was a possibility that something bad did happen, and she didn't want to be the one to plant that seed in her mother's head.

"That's why I'm at the library checking into these things. I need addresses and contact people, so what better place to find information."

"I hope you aren't angling this whole event into a story to help yourself, Maureen. She's your sister."

There it was. Maureen was wondering when the proverbial slap across the face was going to happen. It always happened. It's why Maureen believed that she and her mother's relationship worked best via email and voice mail. They could keep things short and to the point with just enough contact to acknowledge that they were related, but without a lot of small talk that might launch them into a psychotic meltdown or feud.

"No, mother, I would not stoop that low to use a personal tragedy to get a story or paycheck for myself."

"You have in the past. Telling poor Steve that I liked to drink."

"No mother, what I told Steve is that you were an alcoholic. He figured out the fact that you liked to drink on his own experiencing it first hand at our happy family get togethers."

And we are off.

Maureen gnashed her teeth in disdain. She could feel the underlying anger start to bubble to the surface.

"How dare you! I will have you know young lady I don't appreciate your tone, especially at a time like this!"

"That's the problem, mother, it's always a bad time for you, isn't that why you drink in the first place? Because there is always something going on, some minor catastrophe that requires the medical aid of a martini?" The phone line went dead, and Maureen realized that her mother had hung up.

Slapping her phone shut, Maureen threw it in her bag with more force than necessary.

She ran a hand through her tangled mass of auburn curls.

She hadn't meant to bait her mother, but sometimes her mother just pushed all the right buttons that made Maureen snap.

They mixed like oil and water and always had. They both knew it too, so pretending otherwise just seemed like an exercise in futility.

Her stomach growled, but she had a lot more work to do. Reaching for her bag again, she rummaged around until she found a granola bar and looked around.

No signs that say I can't eat.

She started eating it, woofing down the granola bar in two large bites.

"You know it's against the rules to be eating in the library," a soft voice drawled.

Maureen knew that voice all too well and turned around to see Sherriff Downs.

"Are you going to arrest me Deputy Dan, or is this a social call," Maureen kept her voice cool. She was extremely irritated with him, and then realized with a shock that he had probably been down here the whole time she had been on the phone with her mother.

"As always, it's a pleasure, Miss Welsh." He overemphasized her title more than necessary, which grated her as well.

It must be dump on Maureen day, she cursed.

"So, were you listening in on my entire conversation with my mother, or just the good parts?"

"If you wanted to be a member of my fan club, darlin', all you had to do was ask." He smirked at her, knowing full well that she wasn't going to leave his comment alone.

"You are such a jerk, do you know that?" She shoved the wrapper into her pocket and the rest of her things into her bag. Her research was going to have to wait until she cooled down, got away from Sherriff Downs, and had some lunch.

"Sticks and stones, babe."

"Don't call me babe. Or darling, or any other equally nauseating pet name that your Neanderthal mentality has decided is cute. It's demeaning, offensive, and shows your lack of breeding."

He crossed his arms, the muscle in his jaw tensing slightly in the softly laminated light of the basement.

Had she struck a nerve?

"You are one to talk about breeding after the way you just spoke to your mother."

"How I speak to anyone is none of your concern," she retorted sharply, pushing the huge volumes of newspapers back on the shelves.

"A little light reading?" He inquired.

"If you're looking for the picture stories, they're in the toddler section under young adult, Captain."

"You are some piece of work, has anyone ever told you that before?" His eyes narrowed towards her, sizing her temperament.

"No gee, I have never been told that before. Thank you, oh mighty macho male for pointing out the weaknesses in my character. I appreciate that so much, especially in lieu of what is going on."

"What are you talking about?" he asked.

"Oh, I'm sorry, am I speaking in too many syllables for you to comprehend. Hannah gone. Hannah missing. You big chief, you go find her." Maureen made a little gesture with her fingers in a scissors walking motion.

"We're doing everything we can, and we are exploring every lead as you just stated to your mother a few moments ago. And I really have to thank you for the vote of confidence as well. I didn't know you were such a fan."

Maureen was lost for words. She didn't want to get into a confrontation with her mother, and she sure as hell didn't want to get into one with the Sherriff. So Maureen did the only thing that she could do at that moment. She started to cry.

CHAPTER 17

SHE WAS EMBARRASSED to let Bill see her crying.

"Why are you crying?" he asked.

"Gee, a fight with the mega beast, then this with you. Hannah, Steve, my job. I can't imagine why I would feel the need to start crying."

Though the tears welled in her eyes, she had managed to get them under control.

"Mega beast," Bill inquired softly.

"It's the nickname that I give my mother whenever we are fighting." Even as she said it, she knew she sounded childish and stupid.

"Clever. Does she know you call her that?"

"I never really gave it much thought. It's just how..." she paused then shook her head.

"Just how what?" he asked, unfolding his arms and putting his hands in his pocket.

"Nothing. It isn't important."

"It might be. The more that I know about Hannah's life, the more likely we are to find her."

"Then you should be looking through the contents the cabin. Read her diary. Talk to her friends. Search the places that she frequented."

"We are, Maureen." He almost sounded offended.

"Me telling you about my personal relationships with my family shouldn't matter. How I get along with my mother isn't going to help you find Hannah."

"It might, you know. The smallest piece of information, no matter how insignificant, might help us fish out a new lead. Another clue."

"So your only motive is to help find Hannah, huh? You wouldn't be trying to fish out some new information to frame me again for her disappearance or anything? I mean, after all, you were already snooping around the county records office."

"First of all, I wasn't snooping. I was looking at information in regards to the property your family owns. It's a matter of public record, and I'm in the middle of an investigation, which means I have every right to look at those records. Why are you so bent out of shape about it? Do you have something to hide," he leaned back against a bookshelf, a small smile on his face.

"You want to know something, Maureen. You are some piece of work. You bounce back and forth between caring sister and wild hellcat. You lure people in who show you the least bit of concern, then keep them at an arm's length until you feel like letting them past that holier than though guard you keep up around you. You lure people in, and then cut them loose when they don't do exactly what you want them to do. Only animals play with their prey."

He walked past her.

"You're one to talk, Sherriff Sherlock. It takes that kind of cool aloofness to recognize it in someone else. And so as long as we are casting aspersions on our personal characters, why don't we look at the real reason you are here. I guess your momma didn't raise you better."

She flung her bag over her shoulder, preparing to rush past him after she finished her rant.

"You're here because you couldn't hack it in the military, taking orders from someone else, because you are the type of guy that al-ways has to be right. It's your way or the highway, isn't it? You do whatever you want to, whenever you want to, because hell, you're never wrong. So when it comes down to it, you couldn't hack it in the service, so you came here to be a two-bit cop in a one horse town be-cause it suits you being the big fish in a small pond."

She was almost past him when he grabbed her by the arm. For a brief moment, she worried he was going to hit her.

Instead, he grabbed her face in between both his hands and kissed her.

The kiss was anything but gentle. It was hot, demanding, and un-yielding. It pulsed through her, spreading sensuous warmth that curled into a tight ball in her stomach. Maureen felt like she was a piece of territory he had just claimed.

"You are damned right about me doing whatever I want." He smirked, then brushed a thumb across her bottom lip, swollen from his passionate assault, before taking the stairs two at a time as he left.

Outside, Bill had no idea why he did what he did. It was unethical, completely unprofessional, and out of character for him. He never had to push his way onto a woman, not when he had half the woman in town, single or not, offering him their company. He wasn't hard for attention either.

So why had he kissed her?

Christ, Andy was right. I do like her.

He got into his car and hit the steering wheel twice.

Now, what in the hell am I going to do?

However, she didn't try and push him away either, and she certainly seemed to enjoy the kiss, the way her body leaned into his.

He liked her fire, her tenacity, and her passion for her family. She was a scrapper, as his grandfather would say. And a scrapper was always made sure your days were never boring, and your nights were never cold.

Bill frowned, tapping his thumbs against the steering wheel.

He shoved the key into the ignition, turning it on.

Then he shut it off.

He had absolutely no idea what he was doing, with the case or with Maureen. Why had he come to the library to begin with?

Because you knew the reporter in her would more than likely bring her here, he chastised himself.

Before Bill could decide on what to do, he noticed that Maureen exited the doors of the library, and headed towards town. She had bipassed the beat up Pontiac, and Bill had to smile while looking at the car in full broad daylight.

It wasn't new, but it was well cared for. It showed some wear, some minor dents barely noticeable, but they gave the car character. It spoke about reliability, comfort, and trust.

The car fit Maureen to a tee.

He watched her walk towards Drexell's Pharmacy and go inside. Instantly, the man part of his brain switched gears into cop mode, and once again, the wheels began to spin.

What was she doing in there?

He had been looking into the periodicals himself, only he had been looking at articles relating to the story that the old man had told him back at the gas station.

He had come expecting to find nothing, but he left with a dozen articles and a completely new set of questions that somehow fit into the mystery of Hannah's disappearance.

Deciding to follow her, he got out of his patrol car and locked it, taking the copies of the news articles with him, folding them and putting them into the breast pocket of his jacket.

Whatever Maureen was up to, Bill wanted a closer look. While the charges against her had been dropped, she hadn't been cleared of all accountability in the missing person case. Whether or not she was involved, Bill was determined to find out one way or the other.

Locking his car, Bill failed to notice the dark haired man sitting in the Plymouth Valiant parked across the street, peering at him through a set of high-tech military binoculars.

Any information that Maureen might have been able to discover about Hannah's prescriptions turned out to be useless. Any information was confidential to the patient, which is what Maureen had expected. Truthfully, however, she had hoped that being a small town pharmacy, they might be more willing to bend the rules or let something slip in conversation. Small towns were notorious and predictable when it came to gossip.

Since she was unable to turn up anything, Maureen decided to take care of a few things off of her to-do list and stock up on toiletries.

While her sister had a designer taste, she had no clue how to stock a house with basic household items needed for daily survival.

Maureen picked up a tube of toothpaste, a toothbrush, a package of toilet paper, paper towel, Windex, shampoo, conditioner, and lotion.

She wasn't paying attention to anything but seeking out the items on her list and didn't realize that Bill was watching her until she heard the pharmacist shout out.

"Heya Bill, how's it going today?"

Maureen looked up then around, and noticed that he was in fact in the store, behind her, and watching her. She inhaled sharply, her lips pursed in clear agitation.

"I'm great, Harry. How's Nora?" Bill asked casually, letting his fingers wander over a shelf of various kinds of shaving cream.

"Oh, you know Nora, baking and sewing and whatnot. She is frantic crazy come this late in the year, trying to get the last of her handicrafts done for Christmas, and the last of her canning done."

"Well, you tell her I want to buy another half dozen jars of her lingonberry preserves off of her when she has them done. I can't make it through winter without my usual staple."

Maureen almost snorted at Bill's overly charismatic attempt to hide his snooping, and worse, people bought it.

"Oh, I'll tell her, all right. You know she keeps her best stock in reserve just for you. Well, you and the Reverend Masey that is."

"Well, now I feel privileged being in the same category as a man of God for Nora's preserves."

The old man laughed, then picked up the phone.

"You of all people should know that stalking is illegal in all fifty states," Maureen said, hand on her hip, basket draped across the forearm of the other.

He turned toward her. "I'm not stalking you. This is a public building, and you aren't the only one who needs," he looked in her basket, using his finger to tip it slightly, "toothpaste and toilet paper."

She shook her head in exasperation and marched past him to grab a can of woman's shaving lotion.

"Why do you always have to find a way to irritate me, Sherriff? Shouldn't you be off somewhere making love to a box of donuts?" She smiled, walking past him into the next aisle.

On one side, Maureen saw rows and rows of tabloid papers and magazines, and on the other, she saw her Mecca. Candy. Bins of rewrapped sugary libations, long bars of decadent chocolate, and small wrapped pies of deep fried goodness.

Her mouth started to water just staring at the brightly colored packages just waiting to make their way into her basket.

"Don't tell me you have a sweet tooth," Bill said, watching her seduce the bins of candy.

"Whatever I have is of no concern of yours. Lots of people like candy, Sherriff. It isn't a crime you know. Perhaps that's why you're so bitter about life, you have a lack of sugar. And hair," she quipped.

Bill automatically put his hand to close-cropped hair.

"I don't have a lack of hair, I happen to keep it cut short because it's more professional looking and easier to maintain. Wavy hair is hard to control, you of all people should know that." he reached out to gently tug a loose tangle of a curl that had managed to escape from her knotted bun at the back of her neck.

131

"You have wavy hair?" Maureen asked, scooping up a bag of miniature Snicker bars, and a bag of Milk Duds.

"Yeah, from my mother's side of the family. She was Irish, and though I didn't get her pretty red hair, I did get the curls."

"I can't picture you with wavy hair," she said, reaching past him for a bag of peanut butter M&M's.

"Please tell me you have company coming and you just want to be hospitable," he nodded towards her candy.

"No, this is mine, actually. I like candy, okay? I'm not one of these twiggy stick figure kind of girls that pretend to eat but in reality is on some stupid diet. I don't like diets, in case you are wondering, because they have the word 'die' in them, which is exactly what you feel like you're doing when you are on them."

It was his turn to smile, and going with the conversation, he picked up a bag of plain sugar-free orange slices.

"What are you Amish or something?" she asked, grabbing the bag from him and putting it back. "You want real gummy goodness, you go for the best," and she grabbed a bag of tropical fruit flavored gummy bears.

"But the orange slices are healthier, and they have less sugar," Bill said, pointing to the little red heart on the packaging.

"So does tree bark, but I'm not going to eat that either."

"So, you have a candy fetish, is that it?" He smiled.

"No, I like all foods, especially comfort foods. Those are the best because they are the worst for you."

"Comfort foods, like soup and stuff?" Bill asked, picking up a bag of suckers to offer Maureen, only to have her shake her head no.

"Um, soup isn't exactly my idea of comfort food, but I guess it can provide comfort on cold winter days."

"What exactly qualifies a food to be a comfort anyway?" he asked, picking up another bag, this time, Fig Newtons and nodding his head and pointing to the heart-healthy label.

Maureen looked at him, then at the Fig Newtons, then at him again, and shook her head.

"You are absolutely clueless and gross, I hate Fig Newtons."

"Let me guess, you prefer Oreos."

"No, I prefer Keebler fudge stripped cookies, which it appears, they are out of," Maureen commented, her voice actually showing the emotional letdown of not being able to have her favorite cookies.

"So, those are a comfort food?" Bill asked, hoping to keep her engaged in the conversation.

She sighed. "Comfort foods are those foods that are totally taboo, that are made primarily of bad things like potatoes, sugar, red meat, and in general make you feel like you need to confess in church that you were a gluttonous pig. Those are comfort foods."

"So it's only good if it can induce a heart attack then," he nodded, smiling.

"Exactly." She smiled and moved further down the aisle to grab two bags of kettle-cooked potato chips.

"What is the difference between kettle cooked and regularly cooked potato chips?" he asked.

"Come on, don't play dumb."

"I'm not playing dumb. I never eat the stuff. Actually, come to think of it, I have never eaten that kind of stuff."

"You aren't serious," she said, shaking her head in obvious disbelief.

"Yes, I am. My mother was a nurse, so we ate healthy nutritional meals. Lots of stemmed veggies and rice, lean pieces of fish and lots of nuts and whole grains."

"So you're saying you have never, ever had anything like this before, ever? I don't believe you."

"I swear on my mother's life. I ate healthy until I joined the navy, and in the navy, well, they watch what you eat for you. When I got out, it never really occurred to me to change what I consumed."

"That has to be the saddest story ever. So, you have never had deep fried potato chips, or ate cookie dough right out of the bowl," she lamented.

"I don't eat cookies, Maureen. They make you," but he stopped.

"What fat?" She smiled. "I admit I am no skinny Minnie, but I am hardly fat. Besides, why should I change what I eat for a man," she retorted, putting back the bag of Doritos she had picked up.

"So," he said, following her to the counter, "what's your favorite comfort food?" he asked, hoping to smooth over his last comment.

"Well, it's all in moderation, you know. It isn't like I eat like that this every day. It's okay to try something new and indulge once in a while," she said and handed her money to the cashier, who was smiling at the exchange between the two.

"Maureen," he said, grabbing her bags for her, "I didn't mean that you were fat. Any man in his right mind can see you're only fat in all the right places," he said, before heading outside.

Maureen didn't know if she had been just been insulted or flattered, but it was too tempting an offer not to bite, besides, he had her bags.

CHAPTER 18

"WHERE ARE YOU going with my bags?" she asked, coming after him.

"I am being a nice gentleman and helping out a lady," he said, heading towards her car across the street in the library parking lot.

He made it across the street and to her car, forcing her to keep up with his long determined strides.

Unlocking the door to her Pontiac, she motioned for him to put the bags in the bag seat.

"So, now where to?" he asked, smiling as she shut the car door.

"Why, is this your personal way of keeping tabs on me again, snooping around waiting until I slip up and say something that you can take as an admission of guilt," she crossed her arms, staring at him.

He looked at her, hands in the pockets of his jacket.

"I was looking for information. It probably never occurred to the reporter in you to actually share information so we might help your sister, did it?"

He had her there. She was so busy hating him for making her feel out of control that she didn't even bother to consider that the two should team up.

"Why, what do you know?" she asked.

"You show me yours and I will show you mine," he grinned and then nodded in the direction of a small café. "Come on, let's go get some lunch and we can discuss things."

"That dinky place doesn't look very appetizing. I prefer more home cooked meals and what not. I'm really not into dive food," she said politely.

"That dive," he replied emphasizing his choice of words, "happens to make the best homemade macaroni and cheese in town, or so I hear from Edith at the station house. I figure your expertise as a culinary

134

guru you would be able to tell me whether or not if that qualified as comfort food."

Her stomach growled, and she shrugged with resignation.

"Fine. But I am not, repeat not, going to eat anything green, healthy, or tofuey, understand?"

"Fine, and then we can discuss what each of us knows, for the sake of your sister."

She nodded, following along, waiting for the blinking light at the corner to change before they could cross.

"Have you had any word from her?" he asked, waiting for the light.

"No, nothing. Nothing on my cell phone, or the home phone."

"Do you think she would call if she could?" he asked, motioning for them to cross.

"She might, she might not. Hannah is flaky I keep telling you that. She might call, or she might be so absorbed in something that feels good and just not care about calling. She's selfish, Bill. I just don't know any other way to say it."

The outside of the dive café had seen better years. The awning on the outside was a faded black, with bold freestyle letter boasting the establishment's name, Out of the Box Café.

The name struck Maureen as a little unusual, but she was too intrigued by the wild and crazy artwork in the windows to suggest another place.

Tinted windows with clichéd art nouveau prints lined the windows, and something savory wafted through the air assaulting her senses and making her stomach growl in agitation.

Bill opened the door, and the inside was just as wild and printed as the outside. Black painted tables and chairs lined the length of the wall near the doorway. Each of the chairs at the table was covered in wildly bright prints of red, yellow, olive green, and electric blue.

The tables had old world French prints of different café scenes and bistro eateries on them.

The sign said to seat themselves, so Bill steered them towards a booth.

"We can have a little more privacy in a booth, and it's away from the door where it's warmer."

"That sounds fine."

The booths were just as warm and friendly, stained a deep rich brown hue while the cushions were upholstered in a lush burgundy and olive green.

Each of the booths held a small metal bucket that housed the ketchup, mustard, steak sauce, and Tabasco sauces. In front of it, salt and pepper shakers in the figures of Eifel Towers were tucked in front of a role of a paper towel on a wildly painted wooden paper towel rack.

Bill saw Maureen looking at the surroundings and smiled.

"Granted their methods of presentation can be a little unconventional, but it works with the feel of the place."

"Actually, you're right. Everything is wild and cozy, and it's a soothing mixture somehow. I like restaurants that have a life of their own."

"I know what you mean. I cried when they tore down the old A&W drive-thru to put in an Applebee's."

"Is that the one on the Livingston Court?" asked Maureen, picking up a menu and glancing over it.

"Yeah, how do you know about it?" asked Bill, not bothering with a menu.

"My dad and I used to go there when I was little when my mom went into town to get her hair done."

"Was this before Hannah came along?" he asked.

"Yeah, she didn't come along until another three years later."

"I am sorry about his passing," Bill sais.

"Thanks, but you didn't kill him."

"Oh, I was under the impression that he died naturally," he said, looking up to see the waitress coming over to them.

"Hey, Bill, nice to see you again." The portly woman smiled at him.

Maureen noticed that she was about fifty pounds overweight, her straight mousy brown pulled back into a tight, high ponytail that framed her simple features. She noticed a wedding ring was the only piece of jewelry that she wore.

"Hey Fran, how are you, how's Ollie?"

"Oh I'm good, and you know Ollie, off hunting again." She offered a smile to Maureen.

"I'm Fran, I run this little dive."

"Oh, I love the décor, it's so inviting. You would never guess that from the outside." Maureen smiled.

"I know. I just wish I could get more people to come inside to see for themselves."

"Can I make a suggestion?" Maureen said.

"Sure."

"Take down the awning. It's old and it hides the details of the windows. Put in two small bistro style French benches, wooden ones not the unflattering stone ones and take down some of the window dé-cor and put up some rich curtains. Maybe some velvet or Chanel inspired knockoffs."

Fran had her head cocked, staring at the window as Maureen had been speaking.

"You know, you might be onto something," she said, returning her attention back to them, "What can I get you?"

"Aren't you going to look at a menu?" asked Maureen.

"Oh, Bill doesn't need one. He eats in here three to four times a week. He wouldn't have to if he had a sweetheart who would cook for him." She smiled, winking at Bill.

"Most of my sweethearts turn sour Fran," he confused.

"Isn't that a shame," she grinned at Maureen, who felt an intense urge to crawl under the booth's table.

"It is. Gee, everything sounds so good, but I think that I will have the homestyle meatloaf, loaded mashed potatoes, and the macaroni and cheese."

"Anything to drink?" she asked, writing it down.

"Oh yes, can I have a cup of coffee, with a little cream please?" Maureen said, putting the menu back where she found it.

"Is the Thursday night special still available?" asked Bill.

"Yes, we have plenty of fish and chips left if that's what you mean. Ollie caught some fresh trout just this morning. You still prefer the sweet potatoes over the French fries?"

"Have I ever ordered it any other way?" He grinned.

"Still want the house salad as well?" asked Fran.

"Absolutely, but hold back on the green olives if you don't mind, I'm not a huge fan."

"Anything you want, Bill."

Fran went off and brought back two cups of coffee.

"Your food will be right up," she grinned.

After Fran left, Maureen smiled.

"Do you only drink coffee?" she asked, stirring the cream into hers.

"Pretty much. I drink tea in the afternoon, and other than my glass of orange juice at breakfast, I usually just stick to water."

"How very Jack LaLane of you," she teased.

"Hey, is that that old guy who juiced everything including his shoes." Bill smiled over the rim of his coffee cup.

"Absolutely."

This time, it was Bill's turn to shake his head.

"So, why were you snooping around the records office looking at my family's property?"

"I was checking to see who owned the property now, when it was bought, and who the previous owners were," Bill commented. "I was also looking to see if there was anything special about the land it."

"What do you mean special about the land?"

"About three years ago, a land developer came up here from the Lower Peninsula, buying some land up near Killikirk. He planned on turning it into a luxury ski resort and golf course. The only problem was, once demolition started getting under way, he found out it was a site that possessed Native American burial artifacts and graves. Under federal law, any site that has the potential to be a burial site must be logged into the tribal bureaus as well as to the guys in D.C."

"I still don't get it; you think my family's property is the site of Native American ruins?"

"No, but I didn't at the time. I wanted to check that out. See, this developer was the son of a man who purchased a lot of land up here in the late fifties early sixties. As it turns out, the father knew about the land, having grown up in this area. But he had planned to cultivate the land anyway, federal law be damned.

A representative from the tribal council, someone from the Cherokee nations, went missing. Turns out the son arranged for her to go missing, so I wanted to make sure that if indeed your property was part of the old parcels sold, that somehow your family wasn't mixed up in it, and that Hannah wasn't caught in the middle."

"Did they ever find the woman?" asked Maureen as Fran came back carrying four small plates of food.

"Not in time," Bill commented before Fran interjected.

"Now this macaroni and cheese is fresh from the oven, so be careful because the bowl is hot, okay," she said.

Maureen's mouth watered looking at all the delicious food, and she didn't wait for Bill to start eating.

She dug into the steaming bowl, blowing on it momentarily before taking a huge bite and closing her eyes. Sharp and pungent flavors of cheddar and Munster cheese mingled with the fresh richness of cream.

"So? What did I tell you?" Bill took a bit of his fish.

"This is sinful. It's probably loaded with butter, cream, and so much cheese that any cardiologist would have to slap my hand for even thinking of finishing it all," she said, taking another wicked bite.

"But you are going to finish it."

"What a stupid question, Captain Obvious," she said between mouthfuls. "Of course I'm going to finish it. I might even scrape the bowl."

They ate in silence for a few moments before Bill looked at her.

"Do you remember that noise that we heard in the clearing?" he asked.

"How could I forget," she added, cutting a bite from her meatloaf.

"I started thinking about it as I drove back to the station because it wasn't a sound that I've heard around here before."

Maureen noticed that he had dropped his voice an entire octave, so he was barely speaking above a whisper.

"What is it," she prodded, smearing a generous proportion of her potatoes into her meatloaf before taking a bite.

"At first I thought it might have been chopper feedback, but I did some checking with an old military buddy of mine, and there are no bases, known or classified in the area.

The nearest airport is over an hour away."

"Which means that we can't chalk that up to a routine fly-by."

"Exactly."

"So there's no military base nearby, what about a private chopper company?"

Bill, putting down his fork after finishing off his second piece of fish, shook his head.

"No, because any one with a private means of air transportation still has to have a call sign to patch into the nearest airport or airbus station. The nearest substation is almost a half an hour away. And I asked around, no one's heard any sort of airplane noises."

"Maybe it wasn't an airplane," Maureen said

"Please don't go all X-files on me."

"Why does it have to be a helicopter, why can't it be something else? Like an animal or a person's invention?"

"Are you serious? What paper did you say you worked for, the National Enquirer?"

Rolling her eyes at him, she finished off her meatloaf before answering.

"No, but I mean that you are pigeonholing yourself into one specific explanation. That isn't good. You need to keep an open mind so you don't miss sight of something that may be right in front of your face. Just because it's ludicrous doesn't mean that it isn't possible."

He thought for a moment, picking at his salad before taking a bite.

"Suppose what you say is true, I don't know of any animal that large that might make that kind of noise," Bill said.

"What about the condor?"

"In Michigan, no way. They're native to California. They need the more temperate weather for survival." He shook his head.

"What if it was some sort of new species or mutated breed? I mean, look at dinosaurs to birds. They mutated, evolved. Many species do over the millennia. It's a basic part of nature, you either evolve to work with what is happening in the environment, or you become a fossil."

"Doubtful, though your part about adapting is true, but the problem with that theory is that it's too broad a theory to test."

"Are you saying you believe in evolution?"

"No," said Bill. "I believe that God came and created the Earth and the life on it. Then He let it go and evolve for a while, but he didn't like what came out. Therefore, He wiped it out, at least the majority of it. Then He came in and created other new life and let it go until man evolved out of one of his creations."

"That's a pretty unscientific and farfetched notion," she replied over the rim of her coffee cup.

"It's a religious theory with a scientific background, because it answers the whole divine intervention versus evolution argument, and it's the one that I can live with," he said.

They picked at their meals in silence for a few moments.

"So back to these possible animal mutations, why would they be chasing after you, it doesn't make any sense. You don't live on the property," he looked at her.

"No, but I'm female. What's the most primal urge an animal can have?"

"To mate?"

"That may be true for the male of the species, but for the female it's the urge to protect her offspring."

CHAPTER 19

OUTSIDE, THE SUN began to set, and a chilly wind blew in from the northeast. Maureen pulled her jacket closer around her and threw the scarf over her neck. Michigan nights were always chilly, no matter the month.

"Did you make that?" Bill asked, zipping up his own jacket.

"Yeah. How did you know?" she asked.

"I see things like this all the time around the office. Edith makes them for everybody she knows."

"Did you know that the military used to teach its soldiers how to knit," she said.

"I know what you're searching for, and no, I don't knit to relax or to balance my chi," Bill grinned.

She smiled and started walking towards the parking lot of the library. Maureen was trying to think of a way to say thank you for a nice dinner and conversation but had a hard time thinking of an appropriate way.

It isn't like it's a real date, she had to remind herself.

Thankfully, she didn't have to because Bill's cell phone rang.

Maybe this way you can leave with a dignified exit instead of drooling all over the person who a few days ago, arrested you.

Bill had his back to her. When he finished the conversation, she was unlocking the door to her Pontiac, readying herself to leave.

"I have a question, Maureen."

Instantly, she got a sinking feeling in the pit of her stomach, like he was about to surprise her with bad news or decide to arrest her again.

"What?" she asked after a moment.

"A colleague of mine who works at the maritime museum has some information for me about local legends. It turns out the beach-front that your property and several others are on, was once part of an ancient fault line that ran the length of the Porcupine Mountains."

"The Porcupine Mountains?"

141

"The Porcupine Mountains run the length of Kewanee peninsula. It's the pre-glaciations before the last ice age, Maureen."

"A mountain range in Michigan, who would have imagined," she tilted her head.

"Well, it isn't the Alps or the Rockies, but they still have enough elevation that would qualify them as mountainous."

"Okay, so this colleague of yours, what does he have to show us? Aerial maps or something,"

"She. Victoria. No, not aerial maps, but she did want to show me some samples and a fossil that might be something. Or it might be nothing."

He stopped for a moment, and Maureen knew that he was letting her process what he hadn't said.

"What do you want with me?" she asked.

"I was wondering if you wanted to come with me, to see what she had to say."

"Sure, I mean, two heads are better than one I guess," Maureen said.

"We can take my car," he said and closed her car door for her.

She hesitated.

"I mean my off-duty car, Maureen." He could see the tension release from her stiffened posture a little.

"All right."

On the way to the Maritime Museum, Bill left the radio playing and didn't say much until Maureen finally decided to break the silence.

"I bet the sports utility vehicle gets its use up here in the winter time," she commented absently.

"It does come in handy at times," Bill commented. "The roads get really icy, especially in January and February. We also tend to get a lot more snow than the lower Penn, so yeah, I can say that my SUV gets its value."

"We get snow and ice in Chicago, but not nearly as much as you get up here. What I hate the most is the nasty wind we have. It's like you can't get warm, I mean even in the summer. Since I have been in Chicago, I don't think I have truly had a moment where I haven't been chilly at some point."

"Where did you live before that?" Bill asked.

"Lots of places. When my mother remarried Frank, we moved from the Upper Peninsula to the suburbs of Detroit, closer to Frank's job."

"I'm surprised your mom and Frank didn't want to sell the place up here."

"Legally, he couldn't. The property belongs to my mother, Hannah, and me."

Bill looked at her out of the corner of his eye, and she shook her head.

"We'll get the property after my mother passes away, not before. It's all legal, you can ask Alfie for a copy of my parents will if you want."

"Good to know, but I won't."

"Right. In any case, Frank liked coming up in the summers and stuff, used it as a hunting lodge with his buddies. It was really rustic and gorgeous on the inside before my mother redecorated. It was all natural wood, stained; it was just beautiful. However, she repainted everything in a nautical theme, like old-fashioned Cape Cod style. I didn't go up to the cabin much after that."

"That had to be hard," he said, "seeing a place that you loved completely redone."

"It did at first. But I made such a fit that my mother finally relented and put my father's stuff into storage, and when I moved out of the house at eighteen, I took it all with me. I think it pissed her off a little that I cared more about my dead father's possessions than I did about going shopping for new ones with her." She smiled faintly.

"It has to be hard, losing a parent."

"It was. Still is in many ways, you know. Holidays, birthdays, milestones."

"Yeah, I know what you mean," Bill said.

Maureen had momentarily forgotten that he had suffered a loss in a sense, abandoned by a father that he'd never known.

"So, these places that you lived, where were they?" he asked more out of curiosity than for the case's sake.

"I moved to Bowling Green, Kentucky, where I went to college. I lived there for a few years after college, getting my feet wet and all. But I had had my fill of covering Four-H fairs, county jubilee's and taking pictures of harvest festivals. I mean, when you've seen one Miss Butternut Queen, you've seen them all."

"Miss what?" he asked laughing.

"Miss Butternut Queen. She rules over the fall vegetable harvest jubilee in Beacon Ridge. It was just a way for small town girls to get their fifteen minutes of fame."

"Ah, you sound jealous," he teased.

"Oh, yes. I so wanted to stand up on a stage, covered in bales of hay, wear a crown made out of cornhusks and carrying a bejeweled cornucopia. Yes, jealousy is a staggering understatement," she said.

"But you born in a small town as well, certainly you would have to be able to relate to them at little bit," Bill suggested.

"I was. But I was one of those girls who couldn't wait to get out of that small town and into the big city. I wanted to taste life and blend in with the rest of the world. I got tired of being 'Poor Maureen', because my mother was a drunk."

"I thought you said she got help?" Bill asked softly.

"Yes, once a year she goes on a retreat in some desert canyon ranch to commune with nature and swears she will try and do better. She still socially drinks, always has. If it gets too bad, Frank will threaten to cancel her credit cards and that's when she packs her bags for the retreat. It's a game they have been playing for years."

"I'm sorry to hear that," he said.

"Why, you didn't have anything to do with the equation. They are who they are, and I can't change them. But I don't have to let their lives influence mine." She stopped for a moment, then changed the subject. "What about you? Your mom never wanted to remarry or anything?"

"No, she worked two jobs most of my life. At least until I got into high school and was able to go to work myself. She wanted to make sure that I had the money to go off to college, but I had already planned on going into the military since I was a kid. My grandfather had been in the Marines and it just seemed natural."

"Well at least you had a male role model around, your grandfather that is."

"It still doesn't replace having a real father around," Bill said, turning left down a small two-lane road that had the bay on Maureen's side of the car.

"No, I know that it doesn't. I essentially had two parents there, and just because they were there, doesn't mean that it was a good thing. I would have probably been better off with an aunt or grandparents. Socially, my mother would not have the scandal, though I think it might have been easier on her and Frank's marriage."

"You mean because he would have had only one person to look after instead of three?" he asked.

"Well, two. I learned from a very early age to be self-sufficient. Most of the time I was in my room doing homework or reading. I made sure the dishes were done, dinner was made, and after my chores were done, my time was mine. Frank and mom never really cared if I went to sleepovers with my friends like Hannah, or if I had any hobbies. I think they were just grateful that I didn't cause them any worry or trouble like Hannah did because then it would have given them con-firmation."

"Confirmation of what?" he asked, pulling into a small parking lot and putting the car in park.

"That she was just a bad mother. If both her kids turned out bad, she would have had no one to blame but herself. But because I turned out to be okay, it isn't her fault or the fault of her drinking. She can still pretend to be a good mother."

Chapter 20

THE GREATER LENAWEE Maritime Museum was a small stone building that had once been the water treatment facility in the area back in the turn of the last century. The simple single paned windows lined the entire top of the long twelve-foot walls, which flooded the room with ample natural light.

There were several long freestanding ornately carved oak cases with glass tops, housing the various museums artifacts. Salvaged pieces from several shipwrecks were on display, with small printed scripted cards giving off information about the artifact itself.

The polished wooden floors gleamed in the late afternoon sun, and Maureen noticed that everything was perfectly maintained.

Near the door was a thick leather bound registry that offered a mailing list for patrons and visitors atop a small rounded Edwardian oak table. A clear glass vase, with an etched nautical pattern of seashells and rope lazily strewn about the base, boasted a small display of poinsettias, their brilliant red petals outstretched in the setting sun.

On the wall by the door, there were holders for pamphlets and brochures that boasted Michigan's nature wonderland and all the activities to do in the wondrous undiscovered Upper Peninsula.

She and Bill were standing around looking at faded black and white photos of sailing ships, cargo ships, and a commemorative photo of the Soo Locks.

"Bill you old dog, are you ignoring me," a voice came from behind them. Both Maureen and Bill turned around to see a tall, lanky redhead smiling at them.

Damn, Maureen thought. You can bet she doesn't go home and make love to a bag of Oreos. For a brief moment, Maureen felt the all too familiar pangs of jealousy.

Oh please, she scolded herself, *she probably lives on kelp and tofu and nuts and berries like the rest of the squirrels in the woods.*

Maureen smiled a little deeper and had to stifle a laugh.

146

"Believe me, Victoria, no man could ever or would ever ignore you." Bill smiled and gave her a hug.

At that moment, Maureen had to turn and pretend to examine some salvaged artifact and pretend to find it extremely interesting to avoid from rolling her eyes into her head by Bill's overly flirtatious comment.

Why not just go get a room for Christ's sake, it's not like I'm in the room or anything.

There again was that little pang of jealousy and for a small moment, Maureen thought about faking a phone call to get Bill to leave.

But she inhaled gently, clearing her mind of her childish thoughts and focused on the recovered handheld compass that was placed in the glass display case.

"Who's your friend, Bill?" Victoria asked, walking over to extend her hand to Maureen. The scent of her perfume reached her before Victoria did.

Maureen straightened up, and smiled politely again, extending her hand.

"I'm Maureen. Nice little place you have here," she said and looked around in a vain attempt to look interested in the images and facts on display.

"Why thank you. It isn't much, but it's my life's work."

"You must put in a lot of hours keeping this place up, doing research and all," Maureen commented.

Shut up Maureen, she chided herself. *Why not just come out and ask if she's married.*

"Well honestly, yes it does. Keeps me away from home a lot, but I don't mind, and neither does Carlos. He knows I can get home when I can. Marine anthropology is a new and exciting field, so I have to put in the hours if I want to make it to the top."

"Well, it's nice you have a supporting man who isn't afraid of letting you balance work and home. You're lucky," she grinned, feeling a little relieved that Victoria was married.

She started to laugh and patted Bill on the arm.

"Oh Bill, she's darling. That just made my long day better."

Maureen had no idea what Victoria was talking about, but she had a feeling that she had just said something extremely embarrassing and she bit her lip, to prevent any more of her foot from slipping into her mouth.

"Carlos is my cat. A longhaired male Persian. He's named after the best Latin guitar player ever."

When Maureen didn't say anything, she cocked her head a little. "Carlos Santana."

"Oh yes," Maureen blushed. "I've heard of him. I interviewed him actually when he did the guitar work for Matchbox twenty."

"Bullshit. You interviewed the Carlos Santana," Victoria crossed her arms.

Sometimes being a reporter does have its advantages, Maureen thought, straightening herself a little more upright feeling the confidence lift her spirits.

"I'm a reporter, a freelance journalist actually. The paper I worked for had an entertainment reporter, but his wife went into labor at the last minute and I was lucky enough to cover the story. It turned out to be a great story because I wasn't a huge fan of his; I was able to actually ask him questions from a non-fan perspective."

"Wow, how about that. I guess that theory of yours is true, Bill. Everyone in the world is really just six people away from everyone else on the planet," she said and held up her hand signaling she would be back in one moment.

Bill was smiling at Maureen, and she looked at him.

"What?" she asked a little too sharply.

"You. Her. Two alpha females in a cage. Relax; Victoria and I are good friends."

"That's great. I'm happy that someone on the planet thinks you are worth spending time with." She smiled, then turned to look at the rest of the photographs on the wall.

"Hey, did you know that there used to be a small lighthouse station on the lake, down near where the beach is," Maureen said.

He walked over, standing next to her and reading the caption below the photograph.

"It doesn't even look like the same place," Bill said. "Is that the island that's in the middle of the lake? The one with all the trees on it."

"Stony Beach."

Maureen jumped at the unexpected voice. Victoria stood behind them. In her hand, she held a black folder with the maritime museums' logo in the center of it.

"The locals call it that because the boats have to go into a no wake zone and lift up their motors or they will get damaged. I can't tell you how many times the Coast Guard and shore patrol has gotten calls because some drunken tourist has busted their motor on the rocky bottom."

She handed Bill the folder. "I took the liberty of printing these up for you I hope you don't mind. I know how you always like to have a copy of things."

Bill opened the folder and looked inside.

Maureen didn't say anything, but she was dying to ask what the information was. While Maureen was great at keeping secrets, she had never been able to resist trying to find them out. An ex-boyfriend had told her that that had been the downfall of their relationship; while Maureen had chucked it up the redheaded flight attendant he was sleeping with behind her back.

"So Victoria, what was the news you wanted to tell me about?" Bill finally asked.

"Well, after your phone call, I started thinking about all the questions that you were asking me about. I compiled a list of animals that have predatory stomping grounds around Lighthouse Bay and the surrounding areas. They range from black squirrels to the moose, and even to two reported cases of an actual wolverine spotting."

"Wolverines, in this day and age? Come on Victoria, what are you trying to do, sell me a piece of the Mackinac Bridge as well," Bill retorted.

"They have confirmed reports of eyewitness sightings, as well as two pelts that are clearly gulo-gulo."

"What?" Bill grinned.

"Gulo-gulo. That's the Latin term for wolverine. As in the landing dwelling mustelidae, or weasel family. The Latin tern gulo comes from the Latin base word for glutton. The pelts have been dated. It was determined they were removed from within the last two to three years. Granted, dissecting tanner's oils and lye can't be dated to an exact day, but researchers like myself can get it to within a week or so."

"Tanner's oils and lye?" Bill asked.

"The pelts have to be boiled to remove any flesh and fat. After that they are washed in a lye mixture to remove any infectious dis-eases or ticks that might be burrowed in the fur of the pelt."

"Well, I think I will skip dinner." Maureen smiled faintly.

"The oils that the tanner's use to dye the hide vary from tanner to tanner. A lot of them like to personalize their work by mixing their own signature oils, so it would be very difficult to determine what is in the oils without serious forensics testing on it."

"Okay, animals aside, what else?" Bill asked.

"The webbing that you asked about it probably due to a large nest, some sort of waterfowl. It's usually caused by the mother foaming up a combination of stomach mucus, acid, and water to create the webbing. They use it at first right when their eggs hatch. It helps protect from enemies from getting into the nest, and is usually strong enough to prevent and fledgling young from falling out of the nest as well."

"So the webbing is from a waterfowl then," Bill paused. "Do you know if it's native to Michigan, or if the animals migrated south from Canada?"

"I can't tell you anything because I don't have much to go on. I have no egg remains, no nests to pick through, and no animal car-cass either."

Bill looked at Maureen who smiled faintly, then looked out the window.

Maureen had tried not to get her hopes up, but she'd been continually praying about this being the one thing that opened up a new avenue in the search for her sister.

Maureen was opening her mouth to say something when his radio chimed in.

"Bill?" The scratchy voice over the radio came in.

"This is Bill, over," he said, speaking into the walkie attached to the shirt collar of his jacket. Even out of uniform, he was still on the job.

There was just something about him that demanded respect and screamed leadership.

Maureen knew that Bill could still carry that air about him in a bathrobe and slippers, and the thought made her smile a little.

"Bill, someone from CommSpec called the office because they couldn't reach you at home or on your mobile. They need to get a hold of you right away. An alarm was tripped at your place."

Bill's eyes looked up and held Maureen's gaze for a moment, and she tried to figure out what it was that he wanted from her.

"I see. I'll get a hold of them as soon as possible, thanks, Edith."

"Shawn is out patrolling for the Welsh girl because he believes that she's somehow involved," crackled Edith's voice over the walk-ie talk-ie.

"Why does Shawn think that?" Bill asked, watching as Maureen's face went sullen, her posture slouching slightly before putting brushing a loose strand of hair behind her ear.

"He thinks it's payback for you arresting her. I have the number for you if you have a pen handy," she said.

"No thanks Edith, I have it stored in the memory of my phone. I think my battery is weak which is why I'm not getting the call. I'll take care of it, Edith. Thanks again."

Bill clicked off the walkie-talkie and looked at Maureen, then to Victoria.

"Thanks again Vic, you've really been a big help," he walked over and hugged her once more.

"Sorry to hear about your place being broken into, Bill. I hope it turns out to be nothing." She smiled faintly.

"I'm sure it is. I was playing around with the thermostat earlier, replacing it with a digital one from the old dial ones that many of the homes have, and I probably tripped the sensor myself. I feel a little stupid really," Bill grinned.

"Well, I won't let anyone know that you aren't a picture of perfect mechanical maleness," she said and extended a hand to Maureen. "It was nice meeting you."

Bill chimed in. "I just call her my ball and chain," Bill took Maureen by the arm. "I hate to cut this short but we should get back and check on the cabin, sweetheart."

Maureen nodded and smiled to Victoria. "Nice to have met you." before Bill ushered her out the door.

Once inside his car, Maureen was about to say something when Bill pulled her close into a hug that any person would mistake as a gesture of romantic comfort. Before Maureen could react and pull away, Bill whispered in her ear, "Play along; I'll explain later."

So Maureen did what she thought any girl would do in a situation like this: she buried her face in his neck and returned the embrace.

After a few moments, Bill started the car and headed back towards the Bay, while Maureen shifted in her seat, wondering about Hannah.

CHAPTER 21

SHAWN WASN'T VERY ambitious. Lighthouse Bay was a small town, and it didn't require a lot of work to keep it running. Most of the time, the town ran itself and Shawn busied his day with new training and citing the occasional tourist for speeding. It was a cake job with an easy workload.

Shawn did just enough work to not get fired, which he attributed to Bill's presence in the office. When he'd pointed this out when he had his annual review, they had the gall to suggest that he should take a note from Bill's playbook, and learn to follow his sterling example.

To suggest becoming a better employee he should spend more time with the man that ousted him out of a position that should have been rightfully his, was insulting and demeaning.

Shawn hired some petty teenage punks to break into Bill's cabin. To make it look like a random burglary. He told them to break whatever they wanted because he didn't give a damn about Bill's property. They were to leave no traces that might link back to them or him.

Lastly, he'd told them to wait until the specific time he'd given them to leave himself an alibi.

There was no way Bill could point the finger at Shawn since Shawn had been in plain view at the station, bringing back his lunch to eat while getting a 'mound of paperwork done.'

Edith saw him, and since he brought in two burgers from Moon Dog's—the local burger joint with an alien theme—Edith had hassled him as usual about his unhealthy eating habits. She'd said he was going to have to run five miles to even make a dent in the calories that those burgers were going to pack on, but he didn't care. His alibi was airtight.

So when the alarm company called trying to reach Bill, and Edith took the call, Shawn was busy wiping the ketchup off his shirt and setting his alibi in stone.

Shawn still felt a little nervous about staging the break-in. Bill wasn't your average townie. He was intelligent, trained, and Shawn didn't know enough about his past or background to allow the cavalier attitude to think that he'd wrapped this thing up nice and neat.

Everything about this whole thing made Shawn nervous, and he kept having second thoughts about his involvement.

In for a penny, in for a pound. Shawn had seen too much, knew too much, and was too heavily indebted to the mayor, to think about backing out now.

Shawn had to play it carefully. The mayor was accustomed to the power and fame, and he had planned on stretching his long arm of the law to the state's capital.

The mayor was going to establish some criminal activity, then vehemently clean up the town, sealing his bid for office.

Sometimes Shawn had to wonder which body — politics or crime — first influenced the other.

However, Shawn was deeply in debt to the loan sharks, the mayor's own personal businessmen, and he was going to wipe the debt off, free and clear and all Shawn had to do was help.

Yet he'd been helping for over a year; establishing petty crimes and some small criminal trouble here and there. Little thefts and break-ins started happening a few weeks after the new prison legislation took place. But his debt still wasn't repaid.

The mayor had been a strong outspoken supporter of new prison legislation that would force minimum-security level prisoners who were being shuffled to Michigan's Upper Peninsula to do charitable community work. Normally prisoners were used to re-timber forests, clean up road debris, or help repair or paint public buildings.

However, Mayor Carlisle decided that the towns these prisons were housed in were not getting enough back for taking the risk of harboring these serious lawless offenders. Every prisoner had a running tab, some sort of financial restitution owed to the state once re-leased.

The problem was that many of the hardened criminals that were bused in from the lower regions of Michigan ended up being repeat offenders, with ninety percent of them becoming lifers in jail. With no chance at getting out of prison, the tab they owed the state went up, but the chance at them repaying it went down.

The mayor wanted a portion of the monies allotted to the care of the prisoners to go to the towns in which they housed, but he'd been met with considerable opposition from some of the state's legislature.

Frankly, it had been a thorn in the side of many of the small towns for a number of years. The trolls—as people of the Upper Peninsula often called residents of Michigan's Lower Peninsula because they lived under the Mackinac Bridge—shipped off their socially troubled to the northern wilderness, dumping them on the doorstep of small towns everywhere.

The mayor's protests, along with a few others, went unheard and the state governor had put into law his own personal prison legislation that gave first and second-time offenders' early parole into a program that linked them to job retraining and adult education.

While many in the state thought the idea was a decent one to help reestablish criminal offenders back into society, many had thought that there were just some people who were going to be criminals no matter how much intervention was provided.

Shawn had to agree.

Repeat offenders were always going to be repeat offenders, and there was no reason why convicted murderers, sex offenders, or rapists should have the opportunity to be back in public preying on society.

So, when the call came in, Shawn did the honorable and noble thing and told Edith he thought it was Maureen Welsh getting payback for Bill arresting her, and was going to go out looking for her. He asked Edith, more to cover his tracks and reaffirm his alibi, to have one of the other deputies go over to Bill's place and take a look around and wait there until Bill got back.

So here he was, sitting in his cruiser on a small turn off on route five, pretending to be actively searching for Maureen.

He'd cruised around the property where she was staying and noticed her car was gone. He drove into town, and started in the small square and worked outwards, until he had found her car on the third lap.

She was at the library, and Shawn didn't bother to go in and spy on her. He had enough of books in school. Maureen was the bookworm type. Sweaters and zippered hoodies over corduroy or jeans, always carrying that oversized leather shoulder bag she all but screamed nerd.

The only thing she was missing was the ugly glasses and overbite.

"She isn't all that bad though", Shawn said aloud. Not like the women he dated, but she was doable in his book.

She wasn't at all like the waitresses he dated, with the overly blonde hair and too heavy lined eyes. He liked his girls a little on the trashy side, not the clean cut lip-gloss turtleneck versions like Maureen Welsh.

He checked the clock on the car radio. He would wait another fifteen minutes and swing back through town, then back to the station house. Shawn didn't actually have to find her, or even worry about question her for that matter, he just had to appear to be looking.

He had no legal cause to question her and wasn't going to if he did find her. He wanted it to appear like he was doing his job. Shawn was being extremely careful to make sure he was acting just like normal, and he tried to make sure that he did nothing out of the ordinary that might trigger suspicion.

Still, it was making him a bit paranoid. He was constantly wondering if he was acting like he normally would, or if he was overacting in an attempt to act normal. It was a time-wasting exercise in futility and it was starting to wear on Shawn.

He grabbed a cigarette out of his pack and lit it, planning to finish it off before heading back to town.

For someone like Shawn, whose life was planned out by someone else, there was no need to rush; he had all day.

Bill drove Maureen back to town in silence. While Bill had promised to clue Maureen in on what was going on, he didn't want to fill her in on anything until he had concrete proof.

That was three days ago. He hadn't run into her in town, bumped into her having lunch, and as far as he could tell, she hadn't left the confines of the cabin.

When Bill returned to town, she climbed out of his Expedition wordlessly and walked to her car without so much as looking back at him.

She simply got into her car and drove off.

It shouldn't have bothered Bill to be so coldly dismissed, but something about the way the whole situation happened was still nagging at him.

He was restless and moody. He even went to Out of the Box Café in hopes of running into her, but nothing. Fran was quick to point out that she hadn't been in since the two of them had had lunch a few days prior.

So here he was, sitting at his desk and pushing through the pile of paperwork that his sullen mood had allowed to accumulate on his desk.

After he dropped of Maureen in the parking lot, he went back to his cabin and noticed that Josh Haskelll, one of the deputies in training was at his place.

"Sergeant O'Leary said I should come and check it out, secure the premises and make sure it was safe until your return." The kid was nervous as a long tail cat in a room full of rocking chairs, but he was new and learning. Green was a vast understatement but he was eager and he liked to help any way he could.

"Thanks, Haskelll. I appreciate it. You've done a really good job, why don't you head back to the station and get to work on the report."

"Yes, Sir. Right away," he said. Bill thought for a moment that the kid might actually salute him.

The kids face lit up when he found out that Bill had been in the military. He'd seen Bill as an endless fountain of information. Bill didn't mind so much at first, in fact, he kind of felt like the kid's big brother. After a while, though, his questions did start to bother him, but Bill didn't say anything because he knew the kid was just curious.

So, Bill indulged him whenever he could, answering his questions and trying to steer the kid in the right direction.

When Haskelll came and told him he'd been thinking about joining the military, Bill had been proud. Then the boy's mother came into the office and explained that being a widow, Josh had responsibilities at home to his mother and two younger sisters. She needed his help, both financially and emotionally. Bill sympathized with her situation.

Bill reinforced the kid's confidence, teaching him the ropes while he went to the local community college and earned a degree in criminology.

It wasn't that hard. He looked up to Bill so much, Bill had to just merely suggest something as simple as where to go to lunch, and Josh was all over it.

It would take several years to polish him into a self-sufficient and confident officer, but Bill had to admit that he liked the kid.

So, he got easy assignments, recovering a stolen bike, issuing citations, and as he completed each new case, he started to relay more on his budding intuition and less and less on Bill's reassurance of his line of thinking.

Recently, he'd handled a case in its entirety, and Bill knew that it was only a matter of time before he was going to be able to step up Josh's responsibilities.

Yet, it always seemed that once he had one problem solved, another took its place.

"You know, I've seen that look before, and I'm certain Bill that you have the bug," Edith remarked, pulling open the top drawer of large, red metal filing cabinet.

"What bug?" he asked, a little too grouchy for his own liking.

"The love bug," she said. She started filing trying to hide her smile.

"Well Edith, that would be a problem considering that the only girl I have seen a lot of lately is Fran over at Out of the Box Café, and I think her husband might have an issue with that," he retorted, hoping she would take the subtle hint and drop their topic of conversation.

Edith didn't have to bother to look around to know that the office was empty except for the two of them.

"You know very well who I'm talking about," she said, closing the filing cabinet.

"That lunatic who can't find her sister? Like I don't have enough troubles of my own than to add a crazy woman to the mix," he shook his head, finally managing to finish the single page he'd been working on for the last two hours. A task that would normally have taken him about twenty minutes.

"Well you know what Andy says about dating a woman who is a little on the feisty side," she said, taking another stack of papers and putting them in the box marked 'in' on his desk. "He says it keeps you young and warm at night," she winked at him.

"Edith, I'm not going to discuss the ways in which I can keep warm at night, at least not with you. As for keeping me young, I think he has young and exhausted confused. She's the last person I'd ever consider," he paused trying to figure out the right phrase, before rewording his train of thought. "I prefer my woman a little more on the shy side thank you."

"Sure you do, and I prefer my coffee decaffeinated and my chocolate low fat."

Bill knew that there was no point in arguing with Edith once she got her mind stuck on a subject. She'd nag on the idea until a person relented or agreed with her.

Running a hand over his head, he looked at the stack of papers in his 'in' box and his mood turned even more sullen. He had work to do, and he wasn't able to get it done.

Admit you care what Maureen thinks about what happened the other day, he pushed himself.

"Bill, I know this isn't any of my business."

"You're right, Edith. My personal life is none of your business," he said.

"Yeah, well I'm butting my nose in any way. Ever since your day off you've been moody as all get-out. You aren't getting your work done, you aren't joking around with the rest of the deputies, and this morning you snapped at Josh. So, a little word of free advice: whatever is the matter, you need to go fix it because it isn't going to fix itself."

She crossed her arms, staring at him and Bill felt like he used to when his own mother scolded him. "You're clearly not yourself, so I think you need to go home and have a nice stiff drink, a hot meal, and think about changing your attitude come morning."

Bill looked at her in disbelief.

"Are you ordering me to leave?" Bill asked, still a little dazed.

"No, I'm politely but firmly sending you home. It's for your own good," she stated, her voice sweet and full of concern as she packed up a stack of papers and shoved them into Bill's small leather satchel, closing the flap securely.

"You'll see that, but you just don't know it yet," she smacked his shoulder lightly before turning off his desk light. "Just think of it like you're grounded." She paused momentarily brandishing a wide toothed grin. "Now, go to your room."

CHAPTER 22

HE STARTED DRIVING towards his place, but passed the small paved turn-off and continued on country road twenty-nine.

Whatever was happening, he didn't like it. He was always in check with his emotions and didn't like unnecessary distractions, whatever and whoever they might be.

When he pulled off on the dirt road that led to Maureen's cabin, he still wasn't certain that he was doing the right thing. Yet, it had been nagging him for the last three days of how he had left things and Maureen deserved an explanation.

He had stopped off at the café and gotten three orders of macaroni and cheese, as well two double bacon cheeseburgers figuring he could use the comfort food as leverage and a peace offering.

Fran had smiled, not bothering to ask any questions in regards to such a large order. After Bill had slipped her the fifty dollar bill and told her to keep the change, she told him she had slipped in two pieces of her triple chocolate mousse cake in case he had a need for something sweet.

What is it about married people trying to make everyone else follow suit.

When he pulled into the driveway, Bill felt a little better having the chocolate loaded decadence as reinforcements.

He took his satchel and the bag of carry out with him, and made it as far as the steps to the porch before he heard Maureen.

She was sitting there on the porch swing, a knitted throw of deep green draped across her legs. Her hair was completely down, framing her face in soft curls. The sun was still out, but it was the coppery orange color that it only gets in the late fall before the weather starts to turn colder.

Her pale features looked tan in the light, and she had her knees pulled up tight under her chin. She was staring off over the treetops towards the water, and Bill felt guilty for a moment for staring at her.

When he walked towards her, he could see that she had been crying. On the small wicker table in front of her was a single navy blue pillar candle, and a cordless phone.

"Maureen," he called.

"Today is the third," her voice quaked.

He didn't know what she meant, so he put the bag and satchel on the table and sat down not too far from her.

"Yeah, it is," he agreed.

"Today is the third," she said again. "Today's the third, and it's Hannah's birthday."

Her words hung in the air like a thick, heavy fog. Bill hadn't a clue as to what to say to a person whose sister was missing, and was still missing when her birthday rolled around.

"I'm sorry, Maureen."

She blinked, the tears still pooled in her eyes.

"I know. Everyone is sorry. Everyone is so sorry that she's missing. But is still doesn't change the fact that she's missing nonetheless."

Her words stung with the truth, but he knew what she meant. He'd seen the look in countless people's faces before, and though bound by the same circumstances, the pain was uniquely individual.

"But we don't know the circumstances involved in her disappearance. This is the twentieth century, Maureen. It's very difficult for people to go missing nowadays without a lead. We'll find her."

Bill tried to get her to look at him, but she wouldn't budge. He leaned back and looked around, then out at the lake.

In the dimming light of the setting sun, Lake Superior's water looked like a sheet of black silk.

Its icy cold waters would be freezing at this late in the year.

"What happens if you don't find any clues? After a while, the case becomes cold, right?" She asked, this time looking at him.

"Some leads can grow cold," he said before she threw the blanket off her and stood up, walking towards the rail.

"Don't give me that some leads bullshit! I'm a reporter remember? Don't you think I know what happens when a case doesn't produce enough leads in the first couple of weeks? The case grows cold, and you shove the information and a photo into a manila folder where it sits in a filing cabinet until that detective's retirement."

Bill couldn't say anything. He'd known a few officers like that who just sat on a case and passed it along to someone else when a promotion came their way.

"Maureen, we have leads. We have clues, and we'll find her. One way or the other. But don't insult me by saying that I'm going to pass the buck on your sister's case. I think I deserve more than that."

She looked up at him and sniffled once, wiping at tears that defied her guarded persona.

His gut wrenched hearing her sniffle, and he'd instantly regretted being so hard on her.

"You have to stop crying because I don't know how to deal with a girl when she starts crying," Bill confessed and immediately felt stupid for saying it.

She cocked her head, looking at him with an odd mixture of sadness and humor.

God, she looks pretty even when she cries. Where the hell did that come from, he wondered and reached for the bag.

"I brought dinner."

"I'm not hungry, but thanks," she said softly, pulling the long sleeves of her sweater down around her hands.

"That's a damned shame," he sighed. "I guess I'm just going to have to eat all that hot and gooey macaroni and cheese. Those bacon cheeseburgers are practically sinful. Someone once told me it was comfort food, but I don't know too much about that. Did you know Fran, at Out of the Box Café, always puts double bacon on anything I order? She did mention something about triple chocolate mousse cake. Oh, but that's right, you aren't hungry. Guess I'll just have to throw the extra out."

She eyed him, then the bag, then back at him.

"It's a sin to let comfort food go to waste. I think it's even in the bible." She smiled faintly.

"Well, I don't want to have a pretty girl's sins on my conscience. The only thing I don't have is an ice cold beer," he apologized.

"Will Killian's be okay?" she asked, picking up the blanket and the phone before blowing out the candle.

Bill nodded and followed her in the house.

She pulled two plates out of the cupboard, grabbing silverware from the drawer and sitting on the couch, passing Bill who'd sat down at the kitchen table.

"Bill, I know you're new to the rules of gluttonous eating, but what are you doing?" she asked, setting up the plates and silverware on the square mission style coffee table with the faded and chipped white paint.

"It's called dinner, Maureen. You eat it. You eat it at the table. Then when dinner is done, you wait several hours and do it all over again. Only that's called breakfast. Can you say breakfast?" he teased.

"Bill, Bill, Bill. Comfort food isn't eaten at the kitchen table all proper like with elbows off the table. It's eaten on the couch, in a big comfy chair, or in some cases bed. And you don't eat it politely with knife and fork. You must lick your fingers during the meal, and it's followed by intense feelings of guilt and an immediate promise to start an exercise program as soon as you can move," she patted the couch.

"We could spill something," he interjected.

"Throw order out the window Howdy Doody and live a little."

Bill shrugged, and sat on the couch. Maureen put one burger on his plate, then the other on hers, dividing up the macaroni and cheese, giving herself an extra helping of the cheesy noodles.

"I noticed when I got here, you were crying. I hope I'm not intruding on you tonight."

"No, I was just upset because my mother left me a message on the answering machine while I was in the shower."

"Oh. It wasn't good I take it."

She reached over and picked up the phone, hitting a few buttons before the answering machine came on.

"You have one new message." A crackle and a slight pause before the ragged voice of a woman spoke.

"Oh, Maureen," she sobs, "Today is your sister's birthday. Her birthday," she spoke more vehemently, "and my baby is gone. My baby isn't safe," her mother starts to sob heavier. "Hannah isn't safe, she's gone, gone forever. No one is safe, and it's all my fault. I loved the life your dad and I had, and I loved your dad, too. I know you don't think so, but I did. And it's my fault," she starts to sob again, taking huge breaths between every few words, "it's my fault, that it's, over. I...I am the one who... who made the choice. You don't know, don't know how hard it was," she wheezed, inhaling through her intense emotional heaving, "how hard...You have to make choices, Maureen. Sacrifices, and, I...when it came time to make mine, I had to choose...and God help me I am paying for it now." Then the message stopped.

Bill looked at Maureen, who was staring at her plate, meticulously stabbing the macaroni onto her fork, taking purposely measured spoonfuls.

"I'm sorry," he said quietly, wishing she hadn't played the message for him. But he was curious about the messages content.

"It's okay. It isn't the first time," she paused, "I've dealt with this my whole life you know. I keep telling my mom that she'll turn up, and I believe that. Now I'm starting to wonder if she'll ever be found, or found alive. I mean, I've never sat down and thought about what my life, my parent's lives, are going to be like if she's never found," she spoke, her voice shaking, as she stabbed mouthful after mouthful of food into her mouth.

"Hey there," Bill looked at her with concern, "slow down."

"I'm an emotional eater. I just thank the Lord that I don't weigh more than I do now, otherwise I would end up like my cousin Anna."

"What's wrong with your cousin Anna?"

"She is also an emotional eater, only she doesn't have my metabolism and weighs in at about three hundred and fifty pounds."

"Sometimes people don't know they're emotional eaters. Sometimes they just do it without even realizing it until it's too late and they have woofed down that cheeseburger."

"Yes, but Anna lives alone. She is nearly forty, never dated, and has a house full of birds."

Bill knew that she was painting the picture of a lonely woman who had nothing but pets because animals loved unconditionally.

"I don't see that happening to you, Maureen. And even if it did, if a man objects to weight on a woman, he isn't worth dating." Bill took a huge bite of his cheeseburger, and savored the rich smokiness of the ground chuck.

"Have you ever dated a large woman?" she asked, finishing the last of her cheeseburger.

"I've dated women of all shapes and sizes. Physical features don't bother me. I have one pet peeve when it comes to women: their characters. I find that a lot of women are vindictive, petty, manipulative liars."

She arched a brow at him, before he added, "present company excluded."

"Oh, well, in that case, I won't kick your butt out and take your piece of cake," she said.

"It's okay, I don't really care for sweets," Bill said, eating the last of his cheeseburger, licking his two fingers before rubbing them on a napkin.

"Shut up," she looked at him, opening the box and staring at the large piece of chocolate cake.

"Seriously? You don't like sweets? What are you, allergic or something?" She asked, wiping her fork off before loading a large bit of cake onto it.

"Yeah, I'm serious. When I was little, I choked on a piece of fudge. I was at a babysitter's house, and she had this plate of fudge on the table. She watched several kids, and well, we just kind of helped ourselves to it. I guess I tried to swallow too much at one time, or that I didn't chew it enough. But there I was, turning blue and about ready to pass out when the babysitter rushed into the room and whacked me on the back."

"Oh my gosh, what'd your mom say when she found out?" Maureen asked, unable to resist the chocolaty temptation. She hefted the triple chocolate mousse cake into her mouth, and savored the rich fullness.

"She never found out because I never told her. I knew if I did, she would find another sitter, and I liked going there because all my friends were there. But after that, I never really got into sweets much. I guess nearly choking on a piece of fudge makes one a little gun shy of doing it again."

"That's tragic. I mean, do you know how many simply scrumptious desserts and delectable goodies that you're missing out on? I feel bad for you," she grinned, taking another bite of the cake.

"Well don't feel too bad. I've seen Fran make one of those cakes from scratch, and you might end up regretting come morning if it makes you sick to your stomach," he looked at her, but picked up his piece.

"I thought you said you didn't like sweets?" she asked.

"I said I don't much care for them, but I like something sweet every now and again." He smiled at her, not realizing the double meaning of his statement until it was too late.

"Oh man, is that the cheesiest pick-up line I've ever heard of or what?" Maureen laughed as she took another bite of cake.

"No, that wasn't. I know some of them. Like, 'you smell like Fritos that's why I am giving you this hungry stare', or 'my love for you is like diarrhea, I just can't keep it in'," he laughed.

"That is absolutely disgusting and deplorable," she laughed back. "Where on God's green earth did you pick up those lines, and please tell me you've never used them on a woman."

"I got them from Weird Al, and no I haven't. I don't have a lot of experience with women, but I do know enough to know that they don't like being compared to a bodily function," he said.

164

"Well your friend Al sounds like a chauvinistic pig," Maureen commented.

"He isn't my friend. He's a musician. Weird Al? You've had to have heard of him. Those are lines from a song of his. I just can't remember the name at the moment."

"Oh, yes, I've heard of him. His videos are hilarious. My dad was a huge fan of his," she said softly, brushing the hair back behind her ear.

He noticed it was something she did out of nervous habit, and he wondered what the situation at hand made her nervous.

"Yeah, I like his stuff as well. It helps me relax after a long stressful day."

"Did you notice that a lot of his songs either talk about things on the television or food? I think we're kindred spirits of a sort, only he writes about food, and I worship it."

They both sat in silence for a few moments, before the phone rang again.

Maureen reached over and looked at the caller I.D.

"My mother," she said softly. The mood in the room instantly changed.

"Just let the machine get it, I think you have enough on your plate without taking another phone call from her," he said, reaching over to take the phone out of her hand.

"No, if I don't, she'll continue to call and hassle me. I want to be able to get some sleep tonight without worrying that my mother has drunk herself into a stupor," she sighed, pressing talk on the phone. "Hello. Hi, mom."

She looked up and smiled faintly at Bill before standing, her back stiff as she slowly paced the living room floor.

"I know, Mom, the police are doing everything they can. No, she hasn't called. No, Mom, I haven't been able to find Hannah, and she hasn't come back. I'm sure she will. No, no Mom, I don't think you and Frank need to be here. Mom, mom, listen to me," Maureen begged.

She sighed again, tears forming in her eyes.

"Mom, Hannah is going to live her life however she wants. She always has. I think we need to seriously think about the fact that she might have grown up and decided to go off on her own. I love her too, Mom, but we have to start—" Maureen was obviously cut off.

She wiped at the tears and swallowed. "Mom, I am. I am checking for leads. I went to the bank and got her bank statements with Alfie's help, and I am—" Maureen was cut off again.

"Mother, how much have you had tonight? Did you finish the whole bottle? Is Frank there? I think you should put Frank on the phone, Mother," Maureen's voice changed, going from concerned daughter to stern warden.

Bill stared down at his plate of food and poked his macaroni and cheese with his fork trying not to listen to the conversation at hand.

"Hello, Frank. No, I said when I learned something, I'd let you know. I know she's your daughter Frank, and I know you and mom are worried, but they are—" Maureen stopped, and stared blankly.

"No, I know what you meant by it but that isn't the way it sounds, and it sure as hell isn't the way I take it. I'm glad that you and mom think that I can manage to take care of myself no matter the situation, however I think it's highly inappropriate to say that you wish Hannah and I could switch places right now. I know that isn't what you meant. I know you're just upset, but that doesn't give you the right to lash out at me. No, you're wrong. I'm a damned good sister, and warden. Look," she paused, running a hand through her hair, "go and sober up mother. It sounds like she's been hitting the bottle pretty hard. I'll call when I hear something or learn something new."

Bill got up, taking his plate and empty beer bottle to the sink.

"Remember who owns this property, Frank," she warned before hanging up.

Maureen let out a scream as she threw her phone in the overstuffed chair. "The nerve of that man!" She let out another scream and marched into the kitchen.

As she entered the kitchen, Bill turned away from the sink, raised an eyebrow, but remained silent. Then, she started opening and shutting the kitchen cupboards.

"What are you doing?"

"Looking for the place my sister hides her booze," she said, slamming the last of the large cupboards before coming up empty handed and cursing. Opening the small door to the pantry, Maureen continued her search, rummaging behind cereal boxes and packages of instant macaroni and cheese.

"You don't need liquor, Maureen," he said. He wiped his hands on the dishtowel, walking over to lean on the end of the counter.

Maureen peered over her shoulder to cut an icy stare at him, before slamming the door to the pantry. "You're right." She closed the distance between them, grabbing him by his shirt collar and pulling his head down until her lips met his. Her arms circled him, pulling him close.

She kissed him, fierce and full of passion, causing him to stagger backward until his grip tightened and he was holding her with the same strength that used to cling to him. Everything in her body told her she needed this.

Her hands ran up his back as her mind raced to forget everything about the last few days. Hannah. Frank. Her ex. She willed herself to push all that negativity aside, wanting to get lost in the emotional release that sex would bring.

Maureen didn't want to think, she only wanted to feel. She wanted to know what Bill's skin felt like against hers, so she yanked hard at the ends of his shirt. He was strong, warm, and with him, she felt a sense of safety and ease that had long since eluded her. She felt Bill's mouth slide along her neck, nipping at her ear before trailing slowly back up to her lips.

She pressed against him, her breasts tight against his chest as he scooped her up and pinned her back against the wall. Bill broke the kiss, looking at her.

"Maureen, this…"

"Is exactly what I want. And you want it too." She stopped to catch her breath before looking at him. Her long hair tussled and spilling everywhere. "You do want me, don't you," she asked, her voice sounding smaller than she'd meant. For the briefest of moments, she worried that he would gently place her back on her feet, pat her on the head and leave.

But he didn't.

Instead, he held her against the wall, staring at her while his hands cupped her face, pulling her to him. She kissed him again, felt him slide his hands down her legs slowly, sensually, until they rested on her buttocks, pulling her to him. Maureen didn't need Bill to tell her he wanted her, she could feel it. She moaned, felt him bury his lips against her neck as his hands slide under her long brown suede skirt, hiking it up past her thighs.

A moan escaped her lips, her head tilted back as her hands searched for the zipper on his pants. Then she felt Bill's mouth on her mouth, his body leaning into her, grinding his erection against her. He shifted his movements before breaking the kiss.

"Maureen, look at me."

She obeyed, looking at him with the same intensity that she had when she first kissed him.

"Please, Bill. I...need you." She nearly choked on the words, ashamed at the awkward and wanton way she was pleading with him. Yet neither could deny the physical attraction for one another.

She let her hands pull off his shirt, watching as her hands roamed over his muscled chest, her fingertips slowly caressing his skin. Leaning forward, she kissed his neck, heard him groan when her hand reached into his pants and encircled the length of him. When her lips nipped his ear at the same time her thumb caressed him, he moaned her name.

Maureen felt him move, then realized he'd pulled a condom from his wallet. Licking her lips, she reached for it, looking at him.

"Let me," she sighed. "Please."

His hands remained steady on her thighs, while her hands slide beneath them, sliding his jeans off his hips. She caressed the length of him for a few moments before she unfolded the condom onto his hard length. He inhaled sharply, then kissed her.

It was a gentle, almost chaste kiss before he leaned back and tugged her sweater off over her head. He pushed her back against the wall, wrapping her legs around his waist as he buried himself inside of her in one, deep fluid movement.

She was hot and slick and tight. Her arms encircled him, crying out as he thrust into her over and over, sinking deeper into her and drawing out new moans of pleasure from her. He watched her, loving the way her lips parted when he sank into her.

"Bill," she gasped, making his name sound like it had more syllables that it did. "Please, don't..." Her words were cut off as she felt his hands grip her buttocks tight and pull him to her at the same time he drove himself home.

She gripped him with her thighs, pushing against him, arching her back to meet his thrusts until he felt her legs begin to tremble.

"Christ you feel good, Maureen," he gasped, unable to slow his pace and unwillingly to let go. He leaned forwarded when she arched her back, sucking one nipple through the sheer fabric of her bra and felt her tighten around him.

Maureen whimpered, gasping with pleasure as she exploded around him, bucking against him in sweet rapture. It was enough to draw him over the edge as well, leaning into her to kiss her deeply before trailing the kiss to her neck, holding her tight. His hand came up to brush a stray tendril of hair from her face, his thumb caressing her bottom lip tenderly.

She looked at him, those eyes only moments before that challenged him with fierce passion and tenacity, had softened, and in that moment, Maureen knew she was in trouble. She liked him. A lot. He was peeling away her layers, discovering her vulnerabilities, cracking the tough exterior she'd worked a lifetime to build.

"You and Frank, are you two okay?" he asked, sliding on his pants.

"Frank is Frank. He didn't mean that I should be the one who is out there God knows where with God knows whom, he just meant that if it were me, I would be better able to handle the situation because I'm more practical and resourceful than Hannah."

Bill grabbed two beers from the fridge and followed her to the couch, watching her just slump onto the big soft cushions. He handed her one of the beers and then took a seat at the other end of the couch.

"Did he threaten you?" he asked cautiously. "I only ask because if he is, it might help find your sister."

"Frank didn't threaten me, he just threatened to throw me off the property if I don't stop sitting on my ass and find his daughter. He loves Hannah, but Hannah," she sighed, running a hand to her face to push the hair behind her ear, "Hannah is a hard person to love. But she's also a hard person not to love."

Bill sipped his beer and nodded.

"Did you at least like dinner?" Bill asked, smiling sympathetically at her.

"It was sweet of you to bring it, especially since I'm probably the most annoying female you know." She paused. "I did like dinner, but my favorite part was dessert." She smiled in return then sipped her beer.

He felt his face redden. "No, the most annoying woman I know Edith at the station. She means well, but she can nag a person so bad it would make them want to saw off their ears to just not to have to listen. I mean, if nagging was an Olympic sport, she would be a gold medalist twice over."

"You know I was thinking of something today. I want to rent a metal detector or buy one at the hardware store."

Bill raised an eyebrow looking at Maureen's odd comment.

"I mean, I know that Hannah was here at the cabin when she called my parents the week before she disappeared. Her mail was picked up at the post office. She also had a post office box for her business address as well, and that was picked up two days before my mother last tried to get a hold of her."

"I see. Did the post office give you any information other than when it was last picked up?" Bill asked, curious as to what she might have been able to find out.

"Alfie found out that Hannah came in once every two weeks to ship out a few packages and check her mail. She had a lot of things delivered to that box. Mostly brown wrapper packages, probably lingerie or the like. I found a whole drawer of black lace," Maureen paused. "Teddies, slips, thigh highs. Apparently, she preferred black. So we know that she was sleeping with someone."

"How do you base that just by black lingerie?" Bill asked a little surprised.

"A woman doesn't wear black lingerie with the intent of no one seeing it."

Bill had no trouble picturing Hannah wearing the black, racy lingerie. Yet, when he thought of Maureen, he knew that Maureen wouldn't be caught dead in something so risqué or trashy. No, Maureen would be all silk and white lace.

"I see. Unfortunately, we don't have any evidence to support your Victoria's Secret theory, and ordering kinky lingerie isn't exactly a crime."

"She didn't order it, Bill. The packages were sent to her, but nothing on any of her credit card statements matched the order amounts. Someone was buying them for her," Maureen spoke softly.

"When did you plan on sharing that little bit of information with the police? In case you haven't realized, we are trying to conduct a missing persons investigation. Dammit, I won't have you and your lawyer conducting a separate investigation behind my back that might hinder mine."

"Hey," she stood up, hands on her hips. "I just found out about that this evening. Your office has access to the same information that I do. Alfie brought by her credit card statements and I spent all afternoon going through them. He had to head back to Chicago for business but dropped them off before he left. That's one of the reasons that I was so depressed. Hannah might be mixed up with some sort of sex maniac and we don't even know his name. I might have to tell my mother that her daughter is a," Maureen paused. "She isn't a whore or a tramp,

170

but Hannah needs to feel secure, and Frank worked a lot and I think that she might be," she paused again, swallowing the bitter realization of her sister's flawed character, "looking for the absent father figure she never had."

Bill smacked his lips together, hands on his hips, and looked out the window. He watched the last of the afternoon's watercolors sink behind a row of trees. His mood solemn.

"She'd make an easy mark. She's naïve, willing, and already has money," he said.

"Yep. All that's missing is a movie of the week about her and you have the perfect Danielle Steel novel."

"Maureen, I'm sorry, I don't mean to yell at you, but anything that you find out, no matter how small, how trivial, or —" he looked at her full on, his eyes locking with hers, "how embarrassing it is, I need to know about it. Okay?" he asked.

Maureen got up and folded the blanket that she had had on the porch, draping it over the back of the couch.

"That's why I want to get the metal detector. My sister mentioned in her journals that she had found a pocket watch out on the beach. What if she had found something valuable and was able to find out who it belonged to, only that person didn't want to be contacted, or didn't want anyone to know what Hannah had found —" but Bill held up his to silence her theories.

"I doubt it's that. First off, things are lost all the time on the beach, and not in three years have we handled a case of lost property of any kind being reported. Tourists know the risks taking their precious items on vacation, and most of the locals don't own anything that is extremely valuable and if they did, they have the smarts to not wear it out on Lake Superior."

Even as he spoke, he could see the hope drain from her face.

"Secondly, how would Hannah know where to look or who to contact? Even something with initials would be hard to track down. We took several sets of fingerprints from this house and her car. We ran them through Codas and AFIS and nothing came up save for one hit, and the guy has an alibi."

"Right, because criminals are so known for their honesty and integrity," she retorted, straightening up the coffee table of its dinner wrappers and take out boxes.

"Maureen, he was in Shoshanee County Jail in detox the whole weekend. He had smoked everything but his shoes and he was pulled over on a routine traffic stop when the cop who did the P.O. noticed he was under the influence. He's back in lockup Maureen, waiting processing to go back into the general prison population at a facility in the Lower Peninsula. He's a parole violator, and he didn't have anything to do with your sister."

Maureen inhaled sharply, so sure that her instincts and ideas were going to pan out a lead.

"Well, I don't care, I'm still going to get a metal detector and comb the beach. I'm going to comb the trails and every square inch of the property as well. I have to do something, I can't just sit here and pretend that sooner or later she's going to come home safe and sound because we both know that it isn't leaning in that direction," she spoke, her voice laced with sadness.

Bill looked around the cabin and nodded.

"Fine, we will do this together. I'm going to have the police station take care of it, because if we do find anything, I want to make sure it's part of the official investigation," he looked at her hoping to earn her cooperation and trust.

"Fine. When will you do it? Tomorrow?"

"I'll put a call into a team that the police department uses on occasion for traffic accidents that result in fatalities. I can't guarantee that it will be tomorrow, but Hal and I are good friends, so he might put a rush on it, depending on his case load."

"Good. Now, there's something else I want to show you," she spoke, walking towards the stairs, standing on the base of the bottom step.

Bill watched in odd curiosity because he was certain that she was heading upstairs. For a moment, he was unsure why, but the base Neanderthal in him told 'who cares' and to shut up and follow the nice girl.

"What do you have to show me, Maureen?" he asked, taking a few steps toward her.

"It's upstairs. In the bedroom."

CHAPTER 23

UPSTAIRS MAUREEN WAITED on the landing. Bill took it a step at a time and followed Maureen into the master bedroom.

Bill wasn't sure what to expect, but he was curious.

Remember what happened to the cat, he warned himself.

Maureen opened up the door to the closet and looked at Bill. "I was in here, looking for clues. When I searched the shoes boxes, I found one that was a little odd. Well two actually."

"Did you find something you think might be stolen?" he asked, arms crossed across his chest.

"No, nothing like that. But I did find something unusual. I was searching through all of the shoeboxes — I was expecting to find a bottle of booze or drugs — when I came across one that was heavier than the rest. I opened the box," she said as she reached for it, "and found a flashlight, candles, matches, and a rosary."

"Okay," Bill said, not really following Maureen's line of thinking.

"My point is that I found them stuffed in a shoe box at the back of the closet. Like some kind of secret or something that shouldn't be talked about."

"Maureen, I hate to sound like a broken record and play devil's advocate, but everyone I know keeps things in their closet, often in shoe boxes. I keep gun cleaning stuff in one, and some of my mother's personal effects in another. We're a culture based on some form of hoarding; we're gatherers. It's in our nature."

"That isn't what I mean. A rosary is something personal, Bill. It's usually kept close, in a woman's purse, or in a jewelry box, a nightstand table. It's used over countless hours through hundreds of worries and prayers. It isn't something to be shoved at the back of the closet like some nudie magazine."

Bill slowly nodded, beginning to follow her line of thought.

173

"Some rosaries are really expensive and ornate, costing anywhere from a few dollars to a few hundred dollars. They're even passed along from generation to generation like a bible, or a family heirloom."

Bill walked over and looked at it.

"Go get me a sandwich bag and a pencil, Maureen."

She handed the box to Bill and came back with the items he requested.

He carefully slipped the pencil under a loop of the string of beads of the Rosary and slowly let it drop into the Zip-lock bag, sealing it shut.

"Were you the only person to see this, I mean other than your sister?" he asked.

"Yes, I haven't shown it to anyone but you. Why? What are you thinking?" she asked, unable to hide the hopeful excitement in her voice.

"I want to have this fingerprinted first. Then I want to look into seeing about who possibly made this." Bill eyed the clothes in the closet, looking at the price tags on a few of the items. "And if your sister spent as much on clothes as she did on this rosary, we might have a fresh lead."

"What do you mean, you think you can trace this?" she asked.

"We might be able to. I can't be making any promises, though. What else did you want to show me?" he asked gently.

Maureen turned, pulling out a sleek black shoebox with a white slash design through it. Taking off the lid, she showed Bill Hannah's supply of junk food.

"Did your sister have an eating disorder, Maureen? Why would she hide junk food in the closet when she was the only one living here?" he asked, pushing past her to look at the rest of the closet.

There were no signs of male clothing in the closet, no trace of anyone else's belongings there save for Hannah's.

"I think she got scared of whoever was out there, and she locked herself in the closet. I mean, it locks from the inside; why would a closet lock from the inside?" she asked, desperation in her voice.

"Sometimes the doors were taken from other rooms in these older homes. Most closet doors pull out, and this one swings in. Maureen," he took her by the shoulders, forcing her to look at him, "You need to not jump to conclusions on this, okay? I know you're desperate to find your sister, but you have to stop setting yourself up for these situations. Not every turn is going to lead us to her. I don't want you to give up hope, but just be careful." He smiled softly, and then kissed her forehead.

He took her hand, and wordlessly led her downstairs, and went to get his coat.

"You're leaving?" she asked, her voice was not being able to hide the disappointment she felt.

"I thought you've had a long day and would want to be alone," he said, still holding his coat.

"I think I would really rather have some company tonight, but I don't want to keep you," she shrugged.

"I was hoping you would say that. I didn't feel like going home right now, and I thought we could talk some more about Hannah."

"It'd be nice to talk to someone."

So, they sat on the couch, Bill getting up to make a pot of tea for the two of them while Maureen talked about her childhood and the number of stupid things that her sister had done over the years.

She went on about her hopes of going to college and being free of the role of being her sister's warden, but she wasn't. It had gotten much worse because the type of trouble that Hannah was able to get into was a lot more dangerous because she had more access to drugs and alcohol.

Bill listened, making a mental note of several facts about Hannah's character that he was going to check on as well as a few things he hadn't noticed about Maureen herself.

She was fiercely loyal, a quality he admired. She was passionate about the things she cared about, another trait that he wouldn't hold against her. She put the needs of those around her before her own, and it was a trait that reminded him of his mother.

Bill listened and asked a few questions now again before he finally looked at Maureen.

"What are you hoping to find with the metal detector," he said sipping his tea.

"Hannah wore a lot of jewelry. I mean a lot. I always made fun of her, calling it ghetto gold. Sometimes she looked like one of those dancers in the music videos. But her stuff was real. I thought if she dropped any on the beach, we might find it."

Bill narrowed his eyes at her and she put her head down.

"Okay. I know a cop from Chicago who once told me about a case in Florida he worked on as a rookie. He had used a metal detector to help locate the remains of a body that had been put in a wood chipper and spread into a swamp. He said it was a long shot, but he thought if he could find a tooth with enough filling left in it, he could prove the victim was there, and he could seal his case," Maureen said.

"Did it work?" Bill asked, amazed by her candidness in what other people in this situation might have viewed as a disgusting subject.

"Yeah, it took three days but eventually he combed over every inch of that swamp front, and found two teeth belonging to his victim."

"So you're hoping to find Hannah's teeth on the beach," he looked at her.

"No, but stop looking at me like that. I didn't kill my sister and I'm getting really tired of having to keep saying it to you. But I'm open to anything." She sounded tired.

"I didn't look at you funny, Maureen," he stated.

"Yes, you did. You looked at me as if I was confessing to something, and I wasn't. I just don't get you. One minute you think that I could be capable of killing someone, and the next moment you're kissing me. Has anyone ever told you that you run hot and cold like a woman? I mean, a lot like a woman."

"No, I've never been told that before," trying to hide his amusement over her comment.

The truth was Bill liked her. He liked her more than he would ever admit to himself, much less to her. He was having a hard time keeping his emotions in check while working on the case. He needed to find Hannah, and soon, for both their sakes.

"Well, you do," she said, finishing the last of her tea.

Bill nodded towards her empty cup. "You're out of tea by the way."

"I'll have to pick more up tomorrow when I go into town. Hannah got it at some shop off of Main and Liberty, so I thought I'd go back in there, buy some tea, ask a few questions."

"Do you think you're going to just be able to walk in there and get answers to your questions as easy as that?" he asked.

"I may not know a lot, but I have a way with people. They open up to me, that's what makes me a great reporter."

Bill had to admit it was true. Her demeanor just naturally seemed to put people at ease. The few people in town that he'd introduced her to had taken a shine to her immediately.

"Well, I also think that what you report on also helps out in that matter. Would it be all right if I were to read Hannah's diary?" he finally asked, tired of beating around the bush.

She was quiet for a moment, biting the corner of her bottom lip.

"I think it'd be okay because of the circumstances. But I don't want it leaving the house. Knowing my luck, I'd let you take it back to the station to read, and Hannah would come home, and that would be the one thing she would notice was missing. Then I'd never hear the end of it."

"Well, I could read it here, but what'll you do?" he asked.

"Watch television. I'm too worn out to think anymore. I'm going to make some hot chocolate, and you can get to reading. It isn't that long anyway, and most of the crap in there is superficial and useless."

"Nothing is ever useless in an investigation, Maureen."

"Her monthly cycles and how much it costs to do her nails aren't really relevant to a case," she said, peering at him before getting up to turn on the teakettle.

Bill didn't say anything and was having second thoughts about finding anything useful in the diary. But still, it was a piece of information that he hadn't been able to look at before then, and if it had any sort of clues as to Hannah's whereabouts might be of use.

Maureen made two steaming mugs of hot chocolate, then grabbed the remote as she flipped on the television.

"This isn't going to bother you is it?" she asked, seeing that he had already submerged himself with reading.

"Not at all," he spoke vaguely, turning the pages methodically after reading them.

Towards the end of the diary, Bill ran across one passage that seemed to stick out from the rest of the paranoia about the noises, the house, and the creatures in the woods as Hannah had referred to them. It turns out that Hannah, desperate to find some peace and quiet, went to town to Saint Matthews to consult a priest, who told her to pray the rosary. Hannah mentioned that she went into Hough-ton to the mall, and found a gorgeous rosary from F.C. Fields and Company.

Bill read over the last journal entry and found that it stuck out as odd from the rest of the diary.

Dear Diary,

Maybe I'm just being the drama queen that Maureen is always accusing me of. Maybe I'm not unlucky, just that I subconsciously get myself into these situations because it's a way for me to get attention. Maybe I really am a screw-up. I never take responsibility. Why should I? Everyone else does it for me. I make a few mistakes in my life, and I'm branded as incompetent. Like they have never screwed up in their lives. Remember my childhood? What a circus that was!

I made a few mistakes, fall for a few lines and suddenly I'm forced to holds hands all my life like some incompetent needing to be helped across the street. I am not a child!

One thing's for certain. I'm not living my life, I'm just along for the ride.

Bill looked up and saw Maureen sleeping on the couch, remote in hand. Even in her sleep, she looked unsettled, unable to leave behind the earthly troubles that shadowed her.

He reached up and pulled the blanket from the back of the couch, draping it across her. He tucked the journal under the blanket and reached for his coat.

Going towards the front door, he slowly opened it, then locked it behind him, pulling it gently closed and trying the knob to be sure of its security before heading to his car.

With the rosary tagged in the plastic bag, and his thoughts racing from reading Hannah's journal, he knew that sleep wasn't going to come to him tonight as easy as it did for Maureen.

CHAPTER 24

MAUREEN WOKE UP the next morning with a stiff kink in her neck.

Covered with the large knitted throw from the back of the couch, she was content in the knowledge that Bill hadn't only tucked her in, but left Hannah's diary in her midst as well.

That display of trust meant a lot to Maureen, and she was sure that her first impressions about Bill being a hardnosed chauvinistic pig were off center.

Just admit it that you're hot for him.

She showered and dressed, trying in vain to tame the wild mane of curls that seemed to go in every direction but where she wanted them. Grabbing her Japanese hairpins, she bundled the majority of her curls into a bun before jabbing the mass of hair with the two sticks.

"At least it's out of my face," she told herself in the mirror.

Her editor had once asked her why she simply just didn't cut her hair shorter, and it was days like this that Maureen wondered why she didn't do just that.

"Because long curly hair is sexy, even if most days I look like Medusa," she sighed, still fidgeting with her hair when she heard the phone ring.

Stepping out of the master bathroom into the bedroom, she grabbed the cordless phone from its cradle.

"Hello."

"Maureen," her mother spoke, her voice scratchy and raw.

"Hi, mother. I was just on my way out the door to check on some things."

"So there's news?" her mother asked hopefully, pleading with her daughter for something to hang her hopes on.

"Actually, Sheriff Downs dropped by last night to look over some of Hannah's papers," she lied, not having the heart to tell her mother that she let some complete stranger look through her daughter's personal

179

effects. "He's going to get some metal detection devices and comb the beach. They're going to look for clues, and go from there."

"What do they hope to find on the beach, Maureen?" her mother scolded skeptically, "I mean, it's a beach for Christ's sake. How will they know if whatever they find belongs to Hannah?"

"Because DNA and fingerprints can be traced. They have her DNA from hairs they pulled from her hairbrush, and they lifted some fingerprints of hers from a glass that was in her bathroom," choosing not to tell her mother that the actual print came from Hannah's prescription bottle of anti-depressants.

"I guess modern technology is on our side on this one," she resounded.

"Sherriff Downs is also going to Houghton to a shop there where Hannah had made a purchase, to see if and when she made the purchase."

"Maybe you were right, Maureen. I think your sister has gone on some therapeutic shopping spree and just lost all sense of decency about keeping her family informed."

"You're probably right, mom. I mean, remember that fantastic silk outfit she got you in the British Isles a few years ago."

"Oh, that's right, I nearly forgot all about that."

Maureen hadn't forgotten about that. Maureen had been on spring break in the mountains of North Carolina with Kurt, her boyfriend at the time. A frantic call from her drunken sister from a British police station had cost Maureen nearly $1000 in airfare and her relationship with Kurt.

There it is Maureen, she told herself. *Hear how happier she sounds, end the call here.*

"Mom, I hate to make this short, but I have an appointment to talk to a lady who owns a shop here in town. Hannah, it seems, went there often. I don't want to be late."

"Oh. Oh, that's good news Maureen. Of course, of course. I just wanted to call and say how sorry I was about last night. I sent something for you that should be arriving soon."

"That was really sweet of you, Mom. I'll call you when I hear something, okay," she said and hurried their goodbyes before hanging up.

"With all the help I have lent Hannah over the years, it might be the one thing that gets me out of going to hell for constantly lying to my mother," she uttered aloud, going downstairs and grabbing her bag before leaving.

Superior Lies

The Tea Caddy was in a little Victorian storefront on Liberty off the corner of Main Street in the historic downtown area. The soft pinks and greens screamed an ultra-feminine flare to the place, and Maureen frowned with disappointment to see them packing up the pristine white wicker tables and chairs from the large front porch area.

To the left of the store was a small garden trellis that led to a small stone walkway towards four small metal white chairs and a tiny metal table. A tiny sign in neat script writing read, 'Reserved', and Maureen imaged that it was only for well-paying customers.

Inside the shop area, rugs in rich burgundies lay strewn about with just enough flare to allow the rich honey oak of the hardwoods to come through. Oak furniture, with linens billowing out of the top drawers, was scattered throughout the tiny shop to create cozy alcoves to displays the shops teas and other goods.

Anything for a tea aficionado or novice could be found from basic teakettles to the more ornately decorated porcelain brewing pots. Maureen saw the same basic curvy kettle that Hannah had and knew that her sister had indeed been in the shop.

"Hello there, feel free to smell the teas and browse around. If you have any questions, please let me know."

"Thank you," Maureen said, continuing to look around, noting several hard to pronounce teas and thinking to herself that she thought that tea was either Lipton or Tetley depending on what side of the Mason-Dixon line you were on.

"Choosing a tea is like choosing a wine isn't it," Maureen commented, hoping to engage the woman in conversation.

"It sure is. Teas should be chosen according to the situation and personal tastes of those partaking. Some people prefer black teas, others prefer green teas. Did you have a particular blend in mind?"

"Well, yes actually. I was visiting my sister and she just raves about this place, and I'm afraid I've drunk all of hers," Maureen pulled the empty metal tin from her bag, "Charm...raj Ni —," she started to mangle the words.

"Ah, yes. Charmraj Nilgiri FOP. A lovely tea from a lovely region in southern India. The tea is rolled between metal plates. Some of the tea remains a large size while others are get crushed and broken. The FOP I carry is all the higher quality, larger leaf."

"Wow, I didn't know that there was so much involved in making teas. I'm new at this. Before I went to our family cabin for a visit, I thought the only difference between teas was the brand."

The woman—elderly, in her late sixties or early seventies—smiled at her. Her snow-gray hair pulled neatly into a tight bun at the back of her neck. A soft lavender sweater did little to hide the extra bulge of her large frame, but her face was round and cheerful, reminding Maureen of an old school nurse in some Norman Rockwell painting.

"Well, learning about teas takes time. It's a shame you didn't visit earlier in the year, you could have attended one of our famous Sunday teas. We host little parties here on the third Sunday of every month from April through September in the garden outside."

"How lovely. That's a shame I missed it. You've probably seen my sister then; she loves those sorts of things," Maureen said, dropping her line before picking up a teacup and matching saucer. "I love this print, so Victorian and vintage."

"Isn't it, though? Pink and purple are my favorite colors, and they are so feminine," the lady said.

"I know what you mean." Maureen picked up another teacup and saucer, pretending to try to choose between the two. "I wish I knew which one looked more like my sister's so I can pick up a set that was similar to hers. I want to take it back with me to Virginia Beach when I leave."

"Oh, well, who's your sister and maybe I might remember which pattern I sold her," the old lady took the bait, eagerly waiting to ring up the large sale.

"Hannah Prescott."

Maureen watched the woman's face register her sister's name, and for a brief moment, Maureen saw the flicker of familiarity in her eyes before the woman spoke.

"Oh, I'm sorry dear, that name's not ringing a bell at the moment. Then again when you get to be my age, you start forgetting more than what you originally remembered," she said.

"Yes, my mother tells me the same thing," Maureen said and picked up the teacup and saucer. "I think I will take this one. It looks almost like hers I think."

"Why don't you call your sister and ask what the design says on the bottom, that way we can be sure. See," she pointed out to the bot-tom of the cup and the label read, 'rose garden' on the bottom."

"I'd like to, but she's busy with the baby. Newborn and all and I would hate to call her for something so trivial and wake up her or the baby." Maureen smiled sympathetically.

The look on the woman's face was exactly the look that Maureen had been hoping for. Maureen had a gut feeling that the woman knew Hannah, and she wanted to hammer home the importance of Hannah's life by bringing up the mention of a newborn. It was a chance that Maureen had taken, and luckily, for her, it had paid off.

"Yes, newborns can be a handful but also a blessing," she said and then turned her attention to the two other women who had walked into the shop. "Would you excuse me a moment?"

Maureen nodded and continued to look around. She noticed the tin that the teas were in were empty, and saw the large glass canisters behind the counter, behind the old fashioned cash register and old fashioned telephone that was mounted on the wall.

"Miss," the voice of the elderly woman interrupted Maureen's snooping. "Would like me to refill that for you," she nodded to the canister that Maureen was still holding.

"Yes, that would be nice, thank you." Maureen watched her take the tin behind the counter and open a large glass container, pulling out a silver scoop and filling it to the top with dark little bits of black dried tea leaves.

Maureen casually looked around. Everything was reasonably priced and there were a few women coming into the shop, but she wondered if the tea trade was that profitable.

Going up to the counter, Maureen paid and took her small bag containing the saucer and teacup, and the tin of tea.

She looked across the street and noticed Bill's Expedition was at the Sherriff's station, and wondered whether or not to head over there.

You could thank him for tucking you in last night.

She went to the corner and pressed the walk button, watching, as it flashed orange don't cross signs at her.

She didn't see the person behind her. She didn't see the hand that reached out from behind her and pushed her into the head of oncoming traffic.

Maureen screamed, panic rippling through her as she flailed her arms around in front of her shortly before trying to brace herself.

She saw the grill of the dodge pickup coming towards her and she screamed, unable to control her fall.

Her hands scraped the pavement, pain like liquid fire burned her palms and arms, and a sharp crack preceded the ache that started to throb incessantly in her shoulder.

Wheels screeched around her. People shouted. Somewhere the distinct sounds of metal crunching metal echoed around her.

Maureen's head spun and wave after wave of rolling nausea washed through her before everything went black.

Bill hadn't seen Maureen come out of the Tea Caddy, nor had he seen her at the street corner.

He was deep in the midst of paperwork when he heard the screams and the crash of the vehicle.

Springing up and out of his chair, Bill was out the door before Edith could pick up the phone to dial the fire department.

Bill's chest clenched when he saw Maureen, her eyes closed, lying limp, sprawled across the concrete.

He looked around, making a mental image of the people around her in the crowd, the vehicles, and the faces. This was a crime scene, and he knew some of his evidence was probably walking away.

"Move back people, give her some room," Bill ordered.

The paramedics and fire rescue arrived, then a tow truck and a patrol car.

Sid Walker ambled out of the police cruiser, large robust frame nearly oozing out of his uniform. He walked over as brisk a man his weight and size could, and looked at Bill.

"What happened?" he asked, pulling out his pocket notebook.

"From what I gathered, she fell into the street into oncoming traffic. That truck," he nodded in the direction of the dodge with the newly dented hood and driver's side damage, "swerved to miss hitting her and hit the light pole."

"All right, I'll go see what I can see," he slurred, wandering off to talk to the driver of the pickup truck and a few witnesses.

Paramedics scrambled out of the ambulance with a long wooden board.

Bill recognized the faces of the two-woman team from the ambulance, but couldn't remember their names.

They knelt down, checking her vitals and blood pleasure.

"B.P. is good but heart rate is rapid. Breathing is shallow," the blond paramedic announced. She took out a pocket flashlight out of her chest pocket, opening one of Maureen's eyes at a time, checking for pupil dilation.

"Pupils are normal. Eye movement stable," she announced before looking directly at Maureen.

"Can you hear me, sweetie? I need you to open your eyes."

"Maureen. Her name's Maureen," Bill told her.

"Maureen." The paramedic touched the hollow part of her shoulder and chest and shook her gently, receiving an agonized groan in response.

Maureen screamed, her face twisting in pain.

"I think we have a possible dislocation." The paramedic looked up at Bill, then back to Maureen. "Maureen, we're going to take to Lenawee General. You have some minor scrapes that might need suturing, a fractured wrist and a possible dislocated shoulder. Are you allergic to any medications?" she asked while the second paramedic returned with a gurney.

"No, not that I know of." She winced, closing her eyes.

"On three," the blond paramedic said.

They lifted Maureen onto the gurney and wheeled her to the ambulance, closing its doors and taking off.

Bill stood up, Fran stood next to him.

"Hey, Bill," she said, her voice soft.

"Hey, Fran, I can't talk right now. I have to go and see what happened here."

"I saw, Bill."

He looked at her.

"Okay, what happened?" he asked, taking out his notebook.

"She was pushed."

His eyes looked at her, then to those around them. He grabbed her arm, pulling her out of earshot of the rest of the crowd.

"Why do you say she was pushed?" he asked, lowering his voice.

"I was on the other side of Liberty and I was going to wave to her when I saw her, and give her one of these," Fran pulled a red colored flyer from a manila folder. "I had these made up yesterday at Greg's Print 'N' Press. I took her idea about remodeling and we were planning a grand re-opening to celebrate. That's when I saw him."

"Saw who?" he asked.

"There was a man, or at least I think it was a man. Black hooded sweatshirt and blue jeans. He cut across Main Street against the light, jogging like they were in a hurry or something, and his path was clear. But he swerved right as he started to pass Maureen and pushed her. Gave her an elbow to the back."

"You sure about this," Bill looked at her sternly.

"I am. I remember thinking when he was crossing the street that it was a good thing that it wasn't so crowded out here otherwise someone might end up getting hurt. But I saw him. He was a good three feet from her and he swerved to hit her. He came up behind her, put his elbow and the length of his hand across her back and pushed."

He inhaled sharply, rubbing the back of his neck.

"Bill, I'm sorry, she'll be okay. She got lucky."

"Yeah, she got lucky. It still doesn't change the fact that someone possibly pushed her. The last thing I need is for people in town to start going off and doing their own version of vigilante justice be-cause of something her missing sister might have done. You can't give me a better description than that?"

"No, sorry. I did think it was strange he only had a hoodie on in weather like this. You think that's it, that someone is doing the 'eye for an eye' bit?" Fran asked nervously, staring past him at the crime scene.

"We'll see. Thanks, Fran, I appreciate it." Bill looked over to Sid and motioned him over. "Now I need you to tell what you just told me to Sid, and give an official statement."

"Sure, anything you want, Bill." Fran nodded to Sid, who was probably the café's best customer testing the bounds of the all you can eat weekend buffet breakfast that Fran held every Saturday.

"Sid, Fran needs to give an official statement. Do me a favor, as soon as you have everything, make a copy and put one on my desk. I'm going over to check on our victim at the hospital."

Bill walked back towards the station-house, and as he approached he realized that in his rush to find out what had happened, he had left his files unsupervised.

Once inside the station house, he looked at Edith, taking a mental note that the only other patrolman in the station house was Paul Fiedler, a fifteen-year veteran. While he trusted Paul and liked his character, things were beginning to feel, as Maureen said, hinky.

"Hey, Edith. I'm going over to the hospital and check on the victim of that accident," he said, locking up his files and taking the rest of his paperwork and shoving it into his leather satchel.

"I'll hold down the fort," she said, for once not giving him any grief.

"Thank you. If you need me, you know how to find me. Do me another favor, call in Shawn and put out an APB on a male, late twenties, early thirties wearing a black hoodie and jeans."

"Okay, but what's he wanted for?" she asked, scribbling away on a legal pad.

"He's wanted for questioning in regards to the accident that occurred this morning. We have eye witness reports that Miss Welsh might have been pushed into traffic, so we need to cover our bases before we rule it as an accident."

"You think it was deliberate?" Edith asked, but not sounding too surprised. She had lived in this town all her life, and knew to what lengths small towns went to hide their secrets.

"We won't know until we get all the facts on this case. I had Sid take all the statements and gather the intel. He's going to make a copy and leave it on my desk. Do me a favor and make sure you keep that file."

Edith knew what he meant. She didn't trust Shawn O'Leary more than the rest of them did.

"I will. Besides, today is Shawn's day off. Instead of rousing him in here, I'll just call Andy. He always likes to come in and hassle me anyway. Edna is probably ready for him to leave her in peace and quiet at home. She never was keen on him going into a partial retirement."

Bill nodded, grabbing his coat and keys before heading off.

CHAPTER 25

MAUREEN HADN'T SPENT that long in the triage area of the emergency room before a nurse came in and started poking and prodding.

"Just a little stick and it will be over before you know it," she said before jabbing the needle into her arm to draw blood.

Maureen hated needles, but she couldn't turn away, too fascinated by watching the thin hollow tubes fill with red blood—her blood, into the little vials with the multi-colored lids.

"Why are the lids different colors when they all have my name and are probably going to the same place?" Maureen asked. The journalist in her unable to ignore the obvious curiousness set before her.

"You know, I really don't know the answer to that. I think it has something to do with what cultures they use to let the labs know what tests to perform. You know, like this little vial goes for diabetes, this little vial is for AIDS," she stated flatly.

Maureen shut her eyes, her mind just floating away on stupid alternative lyrics for 'This Little Piggy', when she felt the nurse pull out the needle and place a piece of cotton and a Band-Aid over the puncture wound.

"The doctor should be in shortly," she said leaving the curtained off area.

She laid her head back, closing her eyes when she heard a familiar voice startle her.

"You sure do know how to make a man's heart beat faster," Bill said gently, moving the curtain away before stepping inside.

"Well, you know me, I like to keep everyone on their toes," she said, attempting to sit up.

"No, lay back. Has the doctor been in to see you?" he asked, pulling up a chair.

"Not yet. They just came in and took some blood."

Bill paused a few moments.

"Maureen, what happened?"

"I don't know. One minute I'm standing on the curb, holding my bag from the Tea Caddy, and the next thing I know I'm going down and staring at the grill of a pickup truck. It all happened so fast, but it was so weird because it was like I was seeing it in slow motion."

Bill nodded. "Okay, I want you to take a deep breath and think. Replay me every moment, scene by scene. It's important I know the facts so I can try and figure out what exactly happened."

"I left the Tea Caddy. I purchased a teacup and saucer and some tea and," she said. "My bag and —"

Bill looked under her bed and reassured her that they were right under her bed.

"I saw your Expedition in the parking lot by the Sherriff's station, and thought about going into say hello, to come in and thank you for," she paused, feeling her face flush with the preceding remark, "tucking me in last night. It was very nice of you, Thank you."

He smiled. "Go on."

"Well, I decided I would stop in to see you, and went to the corner. I was the only one there, and I pressed the crosswalk button. I was watching it flash, kind of staring off into space."

"Okay. How close were you to the curb?" he asked. "Do you remember how you were standing?"

"I was standing there, the bag swinging from my hand, my shoulder bag draped over my shoulder. I was going to make it a point to tell you about the strange vibe I got from this woman at the Tea Caddy. Then —" Maureen suddenly stopped short.

"Maureen?" he asked.

"I maybe I was pushed," she finally managed.

"Why do you think that?" he asked as the curtain opened.

"Hello Miss," the doctor looked at his paperwork before stating "Welsh. I see we had a little accident and now you're experiencing some wrist tenderness?"

Bill moved out of the way.

The doctor was in his late twenties, was wearing hospital scrubs in the same sterile green-grey and typical white lab coat.

He didn't look like he was old enough to be practicing medicine, but Maureen knew doctors were getting younger all the time, or maybe she was just getting older.

"It isn't really in my wrist so much as in my shoulder. It just aches so bad. Like a toothache." she said, wincing as he ceremoniously felt around her shoulder.

He pushed with his fingers, pinched in several places, using his two index fingers to feel around the socket and joint of her shoulder. He moved down her arm, slowly flexing and bending her elbow before he began to examine the lower part of her arm.

"Does this hurt," he would ask occasionally as he came to a new spot.

"My whole arm hurts," she moaned.

"How about this?" he asked, grasping her hand gently and bending it back and forth.

"Not as much as the rest of my arm," she winced as he rotated her arm, his last moment causing Maureen to inhale sharply from the pain.

"Okay, I think I know what the problem is. The good news is that you don't have a fractured wrist or a broken arm. The bad news is that your arm has been dislocated from the socket at the shoulder, and we're going to have put it back."

Maureen didn't like the sound of that.

"I'd like to help if I could," Bill said.

"Thank you. We don't have a lot of nurses on staff right now, budget cuts, and it's imperative that we have someone who can sup-port Miss Welsh's size."

Maureen opened her eyes and looked at the doctor with clouded vision.

"And just what in the hell is wrong with Miss Welsh's size?" she asked tersely.

"Well nothing, but according to the BMI chart, you're few pounds over your ideal body weight. Being overweight can lead to serious health issues," he stated, removing a folded sheet from the cabinet to his right.

"You're right. I feel like slapping a doctor right about now," Maureen frowned, looking down, her curly hair falling forward hiding her face from the embarrassment she felt over Bill having heard the comment.

She watched him fold the sheet lengthwise, over and over and over again until he had a very narrow band in his hands. Then he started to twist it, making the standard white hospital sheet look like a rope.

"Okay Miss Welsh, sit up for me please," he said, slipping the sheet around her middle and moving it up her torso to fit snuggly under her arms.

"This is a pretty weird kind of a sling, Doc," she said looking from the doctor to Bill.

"There are other ways to realign the shoulder and socket, but this is the most commonly used and effective procedure. It's very simple, trust me," he stated, lowering her bed.

Before she could protest or raise a question, he looked at her while readjusting the sheet to fit tightly under her arms, "I need you to lie very still and flat on your back and just relax. The deputy here is going to hold your arm and in just a second, I am going to fix your arm so it's not throbbing anymore."

"I don't know, I think—" but the doctor interrupted her.

"Relax Miss Welsh. Once we get this over with, you'll be good to go. I'll sign your paperwork and you can go home. Now, deputy, I just need you to hold her arm, gently but firmly, by placing," but he noticed that Bill had taken up the standard position. "You've done this before I take it," he looked at Bill.

"Yeah, just once."

The doctor placed Bill's hands where he needed them.

"Okay then, on the count of three. One, two, three."

On three, the doctor, having wrapped the twisted sheet around his hands and forearm for bracing pulled in one direction, while Bill pulled in the opposite direction.

Maureen didn't know what to expect, but she wasn't expecting the sharp burning pain that spiraled through her arm. The pain shot up her arm like fire and centered in her shoulder, where the dull aching throb had intensified into a sharp stabbing that centered on the socket where her arm connected to her shoulder.

She ground her teeth, tears welling in her eyes not caring if she cried out at all. Then a loud pop and blissfully her arm went warm, and the burning hard pressure that had suddenly intensified was gone.

Maureen let her head lob back on the pillow and closed her eyes.

"Miss Welsh, can you hear me?" he asked, pressing the end of the stethoscope to her chest.

"I can hear you fine," she said, her voice was soft and unsteady.

"I'm going to send a nurse in to check your pain level in a few minutes. I'll fit you with a prescription for pain meds, and then we'll go from there."

"I'm fine; I just want to go home. You said that I could go home after this," Maureen opened her eyes, looking at him.

"I also said that it wasn't going to hurt." He offered her a smile and left, closing the curtain behind him.

"Jerk," she muttered, sniffing lightly. She wanted to cry. She really wanted to just sob uncontrollably in the pillow, and blow her nose in the hospital sheet, but she didn't. It took every ounce of her strength not to, but she managed.

"The worst of it's over, Maureen. I think you're going to be fine," Bill said.

"Did you know what was going to happen, when he did that sneaky little trick with the sheet," she turned her head to look at him.

"Yeah I did, but I knew if either one of us said anything, you'd get panicked and freak out, and it makes it that much harder to set. I'm sorry, but I did it for your own good."

She sighed, the tears pooling in her eyes.

"I just want to go home," she managed to squeak out before she started to cry.

"At soon as you're done here, I'll personally give you a ride back to the cabin, and then you can get some rest."

"I don't mean to the cabin, I mean home. Chicago. To my life there. My plants. I want to be able to lock my doors from the tenth floor and not have to wonder if someone is peeking in through the windows. I just want everything to be like it was."

Bill didn't have any words to comfort her this time, so he just sat there silently waiting for her tears to subside.

"Where is your comforting wit now, T.J. Hooker," she sniffed and threw pride to the wind and wiped her nose with the tip of her sheet.

"I have no idea how to take you, Maureen. One minute I want to sit and talk and listen to everything you say, and the next minute, I'm waiting for you to smack me. You're a bundle of contradictions, and sometimes it throws me for a loop," he confessed.

"I get that a lot," she sniffed again as a nurse came in.

"Okay, someone gets to go and get their picture taken." The nurse smiled cheerfully, making the puffiness of her cheeks seem to enlarge even more.

Maureen looked at Bill. "I'm going to have to go with you too, Ma'am."

"I'm sorry. Hospital policy states that only authorized personnel are allowed in the restricted areas of the hospital."

Bill flashed his badge, smiling. "Consider me authorized."

Maureen had to stifle the need to laugh and pretended to smooth out an imaginary crease in her sheet.

"I don't think that's going to be possible, Sherriff. Hospitals have rules for a reason. Litigation and personal lawsuits are what keep insurance costs up. But don't worry; I'll have her back in no time."

"And as I stated, I'll be going with her to make certain her safety isn't put into jeopardy. If it's going to be a problem, go and bring back your supervisor and I'll have a talk with them," his stern words echoing the silent warning to the nurse.

"Fine. But I'm going to have to go and check with my supervisor before I take the patient down for any additional services. I'll be back."

Maureen looked at Bill and smiled gently.

"Ma'am?"

"What?"

"I'm not in any danger, Maureen said. "I probably wasn't paying attention and fell."

"You just told me that you felt pushed." He looked at her. "Now, which is it?"

"What if I'm wrong, Bill? It all happened so fast, I just don't know what actually happened, and my head still hurts."

"Maureen, did anyone talk to you while you were here, I mean, once you left the ambulance?"

"A few people."

Bill looked outside the curtain area and looked around for the nurse.

"Maureen, I'm not going to leave you unattended until I get to the bottom of things."

"Do you always personally watch over every person involved in an accident in your town," she eyed him with some suspicion.

"Stop arguing with me and rest." the doctor walked passed and Bill motioned for him to come over.

"Yes, I was just about to come and see you. How are you feeling," he walked to Maureen, taking her arm and bending it.

"Not too bad, it's still really sore, though," she winced a little.

"It's going to be for about another week or so. We doctors call these kinds of things lucky breaks, meaning that you aren't going to need the standard cast and six to ten weeks of inconvenience of having limited use of your arm. While it's painful, it can be fixed relatively quickly with just some minor inconvenience."

"Gee, lucky me. Maybe I should go and play the lottery as well," she snorted.

"What about the X-rays?" Bill asked.

"Her initial X-rays were a clear indication that her arm was dislocated from its adjoining socket."

"No, I mean the second set of X-rays. The nurse was going to take Maureen for another set of X-rays, and I told her that I have to keep an eye on Maureen because she's a witness to a potential crime. The

193

nurse said she was going to talk to her supervisor to clear me going into any authorized areas, and she never came back."

The doctor looked around, thoroughly confused.

"I never ordered a second set of X-rays," he pointed to her chart and then beckoned another nurse to come over.

Whispering to themselves, the doctor became agitated and finally looked at Bill.

"I'm sorry; there must have been some sort of confusion. I never ordered another set of X-rays."

Bill looked at Maureen, then back at the doctor.

"Look Doc, if she's cleared, I need to be taking her back to the station for an official statement," he urged.

Fifteen minutes later, they were wheeling Maureen through the front entrance of Leewanue County Memorial Hospital and she was still having trouble figuring out what exactly had happened to her.

She felt a wave of depression sinking in around her, surrounding her, suffocating her with the need to render anything hopeful and bright from her life.

Bill signed a release. "I don't want to leave you alone. Think you can walk?"

"I think so." Maureen stood and Bill helped her to his car.

"You've been really quiet since we left the emergency room area. Are you okay? If you aren't, we can go back in and see about getting you looked at again," Bill said.

"No, I'm fine. I mean, I'm as fine as I'm going to be," she said.

"What does that mean?"

"It means I woke up this morning thinking that I was going to do something and find a clue as to what happened to Hannah, and I ended up nearly dying."

"But you didn't die. You're okay, and you're going to be fine. You just need to rest, and you need to take better care of yourself."

Maureen looked out the window of the police cruiser and turned her head in such a way that her long wild curls hid her face from Bill's as silent tears fell.

"I'm sorry about the teacup and saucer. I hope they weren't a gift," he said, desperate to change the subject and get her talking.

"Oh, no I just bought it because," she sniffed, then grabbed his arm frantically, "Bill! The teacup," she shrieked, as Bill tried to make sure that he didn't career off the road.

"I think it's broke Maureen, it didn't sound like it was in one piece when I put the bags in the back."

194

"Can we pull over someplace, someplace secluded?" she asked.

He arched a brow at her.

"I think I have an idea," Maureen said.

Bill nodded, drove another mile to a rest area, then pulled over. It was off the highway and away from the vision of traffic along the state road.

"This is as secluded as we are going to get right now," Bill said, shutting the car off and getting out.

Maureen followed and waited for him to get her bag.

"Bill, remember when I told you I got some sort of weird feeling from that lady at the Tea Caddy? I think maybe that was the reason that I was pushed into traffic."

Grey skies loomed above, and the clouds that moved in looked like snow clouds, their large billowy gray masses holding the icy condensation that would ultimately become snow.

"I'm listening," Bill said.

"Well, she didn't know who I was, and I went in there with the intention to see if she would spill any information about Hannah."

"And she did?" he asked.

"No, it's what she didn't say that got my attention. I told her I was visiting the family cabin. My sister had this wonderful blend of tea, and I had inadvertently drunk the lot of it. Feeling bad, I wanted to replace it. I made the comment that I was also a little jealous of her Victorian Rose tea set that she had and that I absolutely had to have one myself."

"Okay, so you went to buy some tea and this lady gave you a bad vibe about it?" Bill asked.

"Well, she said she had no recollection of who Hannah was, but I could just tell that she remembered. I wasn't getting what I wanted, so I picked up another tea set and feigned that I was torn between the two. That's when I got the hinky feeling."

"Hinky feeling?" he asked. "No never mind, go on," he urged her.

"Well, any good sales lady is going to try and tell me that she remembers my sister, and try and sell me the most expensive set of the two. Especially in a town whose revenue lies heavily on tourism. Yet she didn't try and sell me anything."

"Maybe the sales lady was new," Bill countered.

"No, she wasn't new. When I first got into the store, I made the comment that tea was like wine, and she went into a presentation about the type of tea, how they are harvested and processed. She told me about the Sunday tea parties that they host in the spring and summer."

"Okay, but so far you don't have a whole lot to go on since all you've told me is that she gave you a weird vibe by not selling you an expensive tea set."

"I'm getting to that. I said I really wanted the set just like Hannah's because I wanted to take it back with me to Virginia Beach, and that I was only here for a short visit. She suggested that I call my sister and find out the name of the pattern."

Maureen went on to explain that each of the sets was named and labeled on the bottoms of the cups and saucers as a means to identify each different pattern.

"I told her I didn't want to bother my sister since she has a newborn. Bill, when I dropped the bomb that Hannah had a little baby at home, the color drained from the woman's face."

Bill had his head tilted. "But your sister doesn't have a newborn."

"I know that. Bill, I'm telling you she knew Hannah. She seemed a little upset to find out that Hannah had a small baby at home, but she also seemed to be a little, I don't know if irritated is too strong a word or not, but she did seem agitated that I mentioned Hannah in the present tense."

"Maureen, why would some shop lady want to kill your sister," he challenged, putting up his hand to silence her interruption. "Now, I'm willing to investigate any and all possibilities as to the whereabouts and safety of your sister, but come on. You just can't go out and start accusing random people of murder."

"I didn't accuse her, but what are the odds? Less than fifteen minutes after the weird conversation with the tea lady, I get pushed into traffic? I mean come on, devil's advocate aside, what are the laws of probability that those two events could possibly happen to me on the same day, under the circumstances of my missing sister, and be completely random?"

He was silent for a long time. "Okay, let's entertain your theory. What's the possible motive?"

"Well, I haven't figured that out yet, but it's something, right? I mean, where there's smoke there's fire."

CHAPTER 26

SHAWN WAS WAITING at the dock on the opposite side of the lake, irritated and angry that his only day off that week was being spent do the bidding of someone else. He kept telling himself that it was almost over. As soon as he could wrap up his messy business, he'd be home free.

No more gambling debt and Bill would be gone. Budget cuts would require a reduction in numbers, and though the county would want to keep Bill, Shaun had it on good authority that the mayor would use his pull with county executives to ensure police protection came from the county sheriffs, not the locals.

Bill would be out of a job and sent packing, and Shaun's life would be perfect.

I can't wait for that little prick to leave, Shaun thought bitterly, flicking the butt of his cigarette into the water.

Shaun had his fishing gear with him, just in case anyone asked though in truth he didn't fish. His idea of a recreational sport was seeing how many beers it took to get one of the local waitresses to come home with him.

Shaun was looking forward to starting over and had managed to work out enough leeway with the bank to get a loan to purchase some property. He figured that once Bill got the old heave-ho, he was going to want to sell his place and move to where he could find work, and Shaun would be there in hand to purchase the property.

He'll take what I have to offer to and be at my mercy, Shaun grinned. Feeling cocky, he lit up another cigarette, waiting for his cell phone to ring.

A few moments went by, and he checked his watch.

Shaun heard a car pull up and immediately put out his smoke, and grabbed the pole.

Damn, he thought, *I need to be alone*.

"O'Riley. Where the hell have you been," the angry voice interrupted his silence.

Shaun relaxed a little bit, hearing the familiar gravel like drawl of his contact.

"I thought we agreed that you were going to call me because you said it wasn't safe if we were seen in person?" he asked a little confused and somewhat nervous. He'd left his gun in the car.

"That was the plan, but I was unable to get a hold of you. There's poor service coverage up here. It's one thing that I won't miss when my work here is done."

"Well, I thought of that, so I waited around," he said.

"Shaun, don't patronize me. We both know you aren't bright to think of that on your own. Now then, what have you learned?"

"It's like I told you, the Welsh chic's sister is still missing, and so far Bill hasn't been able to rule out Maureen. At worst, this will take a few months to wait out for the case to get cold. At best, he'll find some evidence to arrest her. I know her lawyer went back to Chicago on business, and poor Miss Welsh had herself an accident this morning."

"Was she killed?" the contact asked hopefully. It would make his work a lot easier if he had one less body to dispose of."

"No, the truck was able to swerve and miss her. She was taken to the hospital, but we have a nurse there who is going to see to it that she has a slight accident."

"What do you mean, accident? I don't want anything that's going to cast suspicion. We need this wrapped up and gift packaged, nice and neat. I don't have to tell you what's riding on this."

"I know what's riding on this," Shaun snapped. "When she fell, she hit her head. Our little friend is going to put a tiny air bubble in the I.V. when she's secluded and one massive coronary later, our witness is silenced. Permanently."

The contact contemplated the information.

Shaun was nervous. The man said little and shared even less in terms of his role in this situation.

Looking like a fatter version of Johnny Cash, the contact stood a mere five foot seven, but his shoulders gave the appearance of a taller man with their depth. Dressed in black on black, he wore a black fedora hat and black sunglasses.

Shaun had tried to remember the man's facial features but was unable to pinpoint any real distinctive marks. The man was a perfect amalgam of every poor soul on the planet. He was average build, average weight, and height.

If push came to shove, it would be near impossible to give a description of the man.

"Fine. I want to know the moment you have her confirmed death. I don't want any more screw-up's Shaun. We have extended you enough credit and leeway in this matter. If anything else happens, I want you to fix it. End of discussion."

Shaun nodded. He didn't have to be a genius to know what would happen if he failed. Shaun knew that Lake Superior was a dark and cold lake, and its bottom was fathomless. It wasn't something that he wanted to experience firsthand.

"I'll be in touch. In the meantime, damage control Shaun. If you want that transfer to the county's offices when this whole thing blows up, I need to know I have a can-do guy who can get it done."

"I'm doing all I can," Shaun muttered through gritted teeth.

"Do better. I have little patience for incompetence and even less for jerk-offs like you. It's a simple task, get it done."

The contact walked off, and Shaun muttered a curse under his breath, taking out his pack of cigarettes and lighting another one.

He watched the shiny black Lincoln navigator pull away, and was half-tempted to follow it.

Reaching for his cell phone, he checked the time. Twelve-fifty. He'd wait until one fifteen before he'd text his contact at the hospital to get an update. Taking a long drag off the cigarette, Shaun got an idea.

Dialing a phone number on his battered cell phone, he waited until the third ring finally solicited a response.

"Dalton."

"Dalton, this is Shaun. How would you and your boys like to earn your weight in beer?" he asked.

Of course, Shaun knew the teen punk at the other end of the line would bite. Too old to be a juvenile, and too young to buy liquor themselves, Shaun had struck gold when he needed some patsies to do his dirty work for him. A couple of cases of beer, and fifty bucks for the teens dope habit, and Shaun had a stooge that would do his bidding.

"Same price as before, but I'll up it another two cases. I need you and your friends to get out their motorbikes for a little trip. I want you to find out what you can about a black Lincoln navigator heading west out of town."

"Sure thing, Shaun. We can do whatever you need us to. When do we exchange the goods, man," Dalton's squeaky yet laid-back voice drooled.

"Later tonight, about eight. I just need to know who these people in the navigator hang out with, where they are staying. License plate numbers too. Got it?"

"Whatever man. Just remember, no lite-beer this time. It gave me and Charlie the shits the last time," and the line went dead.

"Punks," uttered Shaun, closing his phone. Checking the time on his cell phone again, he had another fifteen minutes to wait for what was hopefully good news.

Bill paced back and forth for a few moments, thinking over everything Maureen had told him. He needed a course of action but wasn't sure exactly what to pursue.

In all his years of experience, he hadn't met many old people who turned out to be killers, let alone have them turn out to be female.

There was no motive, no logical explanation for whatever possible reason Maureen's mysterious older woman could have had for possibly killing Hannah. Not to mention that he had trouble believing that an elderly person would be able to subdue a person nearly half her age, and find a way to dispose of the body.

"It's a theory," he said at last. "But it's a long shot at best, and I think that you know it."

"But she's involved."

"She might be, but I don't think she's involved in the manner in which we're thinking. How would a woman in her, what did you say? Sixties? Subdue a woman in her mid-twenties?"

"I know the theory has a snag or two, but I think that there's something there."

"Snags, Maureen? It doesn't have snags; it has holes. It's like Swiss cheese."

She threw up her hands, and just shook her head, wondering else she could possibly say.

"Then how do you explain my accident," she looked at him.

"I can't at the moment, but that doesn't mean that it isn't explainable."

Getting back in the car, they drove in silence until they came to the main road.

"Well, you can't go back to the cabin, Maureen. It isn't safe. We're going to have to put you in a safe house somewhere, somewhere where I can keep an eye on you."

"That isn't necessary. The cabin has deadbolts now, and an alarm system's been installed. I don't need a babysitter. And what for, since there's nothing the matter."

"Maureen, I am not saying that your theory isn't possible, it is just not logical at this point for me to go and question some old lady about you and your crash. I need evidence to link the two together."

"Fine. Just take me home. I'm sick-" but Bill's radio cut her off.

"Base to Downs." It was Edith's loud voice coming over his walkie.

"Go ahead base."

"Sergeant Tucker needs you out at the beach front, near the old boating docks on Arcadia Lane."

"What's the call?"

"They were doing their beach surveillance, putting up the no swimming signs and checking on the closed lifeguard lookouts when they came across some bones."

"I'm on my way."

"Will do. I have that file for you. If you aren't back to the station house before I leave, I'll bring it out to you."

"Copy that."

Bill clicked off his walkie and started to accelerate towards the old boat launches.

"Should I be going with you?" Maureen asked.

"Until I can figure out someplace to put you, yes. Right now, the safest place on this planet is right behind me."

Maureen continued to stare out the window as they drove the rest of the way in silence.

CHAPTER 27

THE BEACHFRONT WAS a ghost town. During the summer, it was nearly impossible to walk down the beach without bumping elbows with someone, yet Bill rarely ever got to the beach during that time of year.

He'd driven the police cruiser onto the beach itself, then told Maureen to wait in the car. He climbed out, taking the keys, then locked the car.

Bill made his way to the careened off area of the beach, and two of the station's deputies, Lieutenant Alan Tucker, and Sergeant Vic Kinsley were already there. Bill also noticed the medical officers van there as well, and he stopped to look at Maureen sitting in the front seat of his car, and held up one finger, trying to convey to her that she shouldn't jump to conclusions.

"What do we have, Tucker?" he asked as he approached.

"Well, we were doing our rounds, same as always, and came across this," he pointed to the two nearly foot long bones and the jawbone.

"Are they human?" he asked.

"I think so. I mean, a lot of the teeth are missing but it's clearly the bottom of a human skull."

"I believe so," Vic stated, running a hand through his scruffy beard.

Bill pause a moment, and asked the question he knew was coming. "Is it the missing girl?"

"Not sure, and to be honest, I doubt it," the medical examiner said, leaning down on her haunches and taking a pen from her jacket pocket, pointing to the jawbone, "This skull has been in the water a long time. Probably too long to be the missing woman you are looking for."

"Are you certain?" asked Bill.

"Yeah. The bone's extremely smooth and worn away."

Bill looked back at Tucker and Kinsley.

Tucker gave Bill a sidelong glance.

"Look, I'd like to end the case as much as you and be able to provide some closer to the family. Because you know if this isn't the missing woman, we have another murder investigation on our hands." Tucker stood, looking at Bill, shrugging then putting his hands on his hips.

Bill sighed, nodding. He waited while the medical examiner processed the remains.

She stood up, signaling for her partner to load up the remains, before turning to Bill.

"At this point, Sherriff, I can't rule out whether this is natural or foul play. There've been a lot of shipwrecks on the Great Lakes. Even boaters nowadays wind up missing. I'll know more once I get the remains back to the lab."

"Are you going to be able to tell anything by the jaw bone?" Tucker asked.

"Possibly. Modern science has enabled to do a lot that we couldn't have done twenty years ago, but to be honest, we may have our work cut out for us."

The petite redhead stood up, nodding to her assistant who secured the remains in the back of the coroners van.

"Can you tell me anything about that skull, something I can go on?" he asked.

"I can tell you that it's too old to be a recent killing, at least from where I stand now."

Bill nodded. "I want a report with anything that you find out." Bill handed her his card. "No one sees the report but me, got it?"

"Loud and clear."

Bill headed back to his SUV, unlocked the car and climbed inside.

He turned to look at Maureen whose hands were gripping her knees.

"Yes or no," she nearly whispered.

"It isn't her, Maureen." He reached out and stroked her hair lightly.

Soft sobs ebbed out, her chest and body slowly shaking inside the comforting warmth of her sweater.

Bill put the car in gear and headed off the beach, the expedition rocking gently as it went over the rough patches of beach.

Once out on the main road, he went in the opposite direction away from Maureen's cabin.

"Where are we going," she finally managed to sniff.

"To my place. I think that you need to relax, and you definitely need a drink."

"Bill," she started.

"Relax, I'm not going there to seduce you. When that happens, you'll know it."

That caught her off guard, and for a moment, she was able to feel a little better about her current situation. When, she thought. Something inside her liked the sound of that.

Bill's cabin was small though tidy, and male.

From the hardwoods, to the solid sturdiness of his wooden rockers and furniture, the cabin held no feminine touches.

Very few knickknacks ordained the cabin, but the ones that did were extremely personal. A single baseball on a tri-stand with a date on it. A few pictures in brassy frames littered a few shelves on the floor to ceiling bookcase that stretched the length of one wall.

A rug, in a thick, woven braid of a rich burgundy color, lay in the center of the floor in the living room. There were a few pillows of a similar color on the couch, which was, in fact a futon. The wooden frame of the couch accented the rest of the rustic wooden feel of the cabin, but there was something more.

The colors were bold, rich, and in textures. The curtains were a thick wine and chocolate brocade, and the splashes of color only brought out the richness of the natural woods furnishings.

The room felt warm and cozy, but there was something else, something that Maureen could sense. Besides giving off the feeling of being homey, the place felt safe. And masculine. Definitely masculine.

Maureen inhaled and was surprised to find the crisp scent of vanilla and something spicy in the air.

"Scented oil warmers," Bill said softly. "Sometimes in the fall and spring, when the rains are bad, the smell of the lake just permeates everything."

"Fish stink," she nodded in agreement. Only people with homes on the water knew about the smell of stinky rotten fish.

"This will calm your nerves," he said, hold out a glass with a small amount of amber liquid inside.

"Thanks," she said softly, reaching out to take the short glass. She sipped the drink, wincing at the liquid fire taste, but swallowed, feeling its warmth spread throughout her.

"I think it smells nice in here," she said. "I mean, I wasn't expecting this."

"What exactly were you expecting?" He smiled at her, taking a sip of coffee.

"I don't know, maybe a bean bag chair, a folding table with chairs around it littered with poker chips, and maybe a pool table."

Bill had to laugh. No matter what happened to her, Maureen's mind was always working, always focusing on something.

"Go on, give me the full picture," he said, trying to lift her spirits.

"Maybe some paper plates for dishes, or they'd be mismatched plastic plates and a beer stein collection for drinking glasses. I was just expecting something a little more, I don't know, Neanderthal."

"Honey, I was born and raised in Michigan. That's north of Neanderthal."

Maureen smiled with sudden realization that she did something with Bill that she never did with Steve. She joked around with him. She was instantly at ease, and she like that.

"You know it's going to be okay, Maureen. No matter what happens, no matter what we find about Hannah, good or bad, you're going to be okay."

She looked into the amber colored liquid floating around her glass, letting it swirl around and around, taking a small sip before she nodded in agreement.

"I'm a horrible person, Bill." She started to sob again.

"No, you aren't," he said, setting his cup of coffee down and sitting next to her on the couch.

She nodded, downing the whiskey in one, quick gulp.

"I am, because if she was found dead, I would be...relieved," she started to sob uncontrollably. "I would...have my life...back and I would...be free of my mother, and Frank...and I would be able to once, not have to worry about looking over my shoulder to see if Hannah is...is able to keep up."

Bill rubbed her back, letting her vent.

"Maureen, it's only natural for you to feel this way. Most caregivers feel like this at one point or another when they're dealing with their charges."

She just hung her head, sobbing into the pillow for a few moments before looking up into his face.

"What about you?" she sniffed, "What's your secret?"

"What secret?"

"You know that I'm a bad sister, what's your secret?"

Bill was quiet for a moment.

"I was a lair, to my mother," he finally said, his voice taking on a softer tone.

Her hazel eyes looked up at him, this time returning the sweet gesture and reaching out to touch his arm.

"My mother had cancer. By the time we found out, there was nothing the doctors could do but make her comfortable. The morphine helped take the edge off the pain, but it didn't give her peace. She begged me," he spoke, picking up his coffee cup and staring into it, "begged me all the time that if the pain got too bad, for me to end it for her. I promised her if it came to it, I would."

"But you couldn't."

"No, I couldn't. No matter how bad it got, how sick and weak she got, I could never bring myself to do anything about it but watch and pray. Even when she was coughing up blood, and her skin grew translucent and paper thin, I couldn't do anything."

"You did enough. You took care of her, you prayed for her. She didn't die alone," Maureen's voice waivered, "and that's more than I can give Hannah at the moment."

"You don't think that Hannah's alive, do you?" Bill asked.

"It's been too long, Bill. She's had no access to any money, at least through her bank accounts, or credit cards, for over three weeks. No phones calls, no letters, no emails. No contact. The only way Hannah wouldn't contact her family is if she were dead."

"You don't know that. There's still hope."

"Is there?"

Bill's phone rang, and he reached onto the large wooden coffee table and picked it up.

"Hello."

A moment later, he mouthed the words Victoria and took out a pen from his pocket.

"Go on. I want to write this down," he said, holding the phone to his with his shoulder.

After a few moments, Bill hung up the phone and looked at Maureen.

"Do you know anything about chemistry?" he asked.

"That's probably the worst pick up line that I've ever heard." She said faintly smiling at his would-be pick-up line.

"No, not that chemistry. But it's nice to know that you're thinking about me in that aspect. No, that was Victoria. She was curious about the webbing that I gave her, so she did some tests on it, and sent it out to a lab. It had traces of a chemical component found in animal saliva."

"So then whatever it was that was in the woods, is an animal," she shuddered.

"Yes, but the saliva has an odd combination of venom, pheromones, and something else that she wasn't able to identify yet."

"What?" Maureen looked up at him.

"A mineral. Iridium. Apparently it isn't a common element found in nature. It does occur sparingly from what she told me, but it's one of the materials that are in the webbing. Too much for it to occur naturally."

"What's that mean, naturally? It if occurs in nature, then it's natural."

"She didn't get into it. She wants me to swing by tomorrow sometime so she can explain it further. Are you up for a trip?"

"Yeah," Maureen stood up. "But I'm tired. I think it's time for me to go home."

"I can't in good conscience let you go back to the cabin. We can't say for certain that someone didn't try and kill you, so until we know for certain, I'm afraid you're under an unofficial house arrest."

"Then why do I need to be here, why can't we go back to my cabin?" she asked, her hands on her hips. Her face was flushed with color, no doubt due to the influence of the liquor.

"Several reasons. One, if you aren't there, they won't know where to look for you. Two, no one knows that you're here. Three, my place has security features put into place that yours don't."

"I have an alarm."

"You have a generic alarm from a general alarm company. My system is a little more advanced than that, and I won't have to worry while sleeping if someone is breaking in."

"Why do you think someone wants to kill me?" she asked, barely able to utter the phrase much less comprehend the reality of it.

"Because as you stated earlier, things just don't happen for a reason. I need to find out what those reasons are, and until I do, you aren't getting out of my sight."

"What do you plan on doing?" she retorted clearly irritated and a little tipsy, "handcuff me to the bedpost."

"Business before pleasure." He said, and took her glass, returning from the small kitchen with a cup of hot coffee.

"I would have preferred more of the whiskey," she snapped, reluctantly taking the mug of coffee.

"I know you would've, which is why I brought you the coffee. Don't start getting into a pattern, Maureen. How do you think your mother started?"

Maureen didn't say anything. She sipped the coffee, and then looked up.

"Where do I sleep?" she asked. "What do I sleep in for that matter?"

He pointed to the master bedroom.

"You can sleep in there. I'm going to take the couch out here. I can get you some sweat pants and a t-shirt until we get over to the cabin tomorrow to get some of your things."

"A button up shirt will do. I get too warm if I wear much else to bed."

"Even in Chicago?" Bill asked surprised.

"Even in Chicago."

Bill motioned for her to follow him to the bedroom, and he reached into the closet and pulled out a long sleeve red wrangler button down shirt.

She took it, smiled and watched as he closed the plantation style shutters and pulled the drapes over them.

"Everything is secure in here. The bathroom is through that door. Fresh towels are under the cabinet in the sink."

"Thanks, but I think I'll wait until tomorrow morning to take a long hot bath. I'm so dead tired all I want to do is go to sleep."

Bill nodded, grabbing his sweat pants and tee shirt from behind the door, pausing to kiss her.

"Get some rest, okay? You've had a long day."

"I feel funny taking your bedroom like this Bill."

"Don't. I insist. Besides, I have some work to do. In the morning, we can head over to see Victoria and check out a friend of mine near Sault Ste. Marie."

"What for?" she asked, stifling a yawn behind her hand.

"Lake Superior has a lot of secrets and it doesn't give up its dead. I want to know more about what else she's hiding," he said, before closing the door.

Maureen changed and crept into bed, smelling the musky male scent of Bill's cologne as it stuck to the sheets. Oddly, Maureen found it comforting. There was just something about being in a troubling situation and having a man around that made a girl think that everything was going to be okay.

Superior Lies

She didn't drift off to sleep right away. For a long time, she laid in bed, thinking about her sister, her mother, and remembered them in her prayers.

Finally rolling over and looking at the clock, she felt the slow tugging of sleep pull at her consciousness and lull into her a deep slumber.

CHAPTER 28

BILL CHANGED IN the small half bathroom that was adjacent to the main room of the cabin. Sitting down, he kept his gun and flashlight on the coffee table and opened a stack of papers trying to shift through them.

He lost interest about twenty minutes into the venture and decided that the paperwork could wait.

Pulling out his laptop from the roll top desk that angled itself in the corner, Bill started to look up as much information as he could find about Iridium. What he had found surprised him and frustrated him.

The data was interesting to know, but it seriously complicated an already complicated case. He'd been hoping for answers, not more questions.

Iridium was a scarcely found mineral, one of the rarest Earth metals known to man. Not found commonly in anything else occurring in the natural world, it is plentiful in only two places: the K-T boundary, and meteors. The K-T boundary was the period between the last surviving years of the dinosaurs to the years where there were no dinosaurs. Many scientists speculated that a six-mile wide asteroid hit the Yucatan Peninsula at Chicxulub and believed to have caused the extension of the large animals.

Bill had the pieces of the puzzle, but they just didn't fit into the picture. The scientific evidence that Victoria had discovered didn't fit into the same frame as Maureen's missing sister, nor did the accidental push off the curb, or the nurse at the hospital who mysteriously disappeared.

Frustrated, tired, and a little irritated, Bill did one final sweep of the rooms, double checking doors and windows before arming the alarm to its fullest degree. He looked at the bedroom door, and opened it silently, checking on Maureen.

Under the deep navy comforter—his navy comforter—Maureen slept. She looked peaceful for once. Always in a state of frantic yet well-organized chaos, this was the quietest and most still, he'd ever seen Maureen.

Closing the door quietly, he went back to the couch and grabbed his gun. Leaning back, putting up his feet, he turned on the television, remote in one hand, revolver in the other.

When he woke up, he had the sense that he wasn't alone and his leg was warm. Unusually warm. He looked around, then down, to see Maureen, wrapped in the comforter off the bed, sitting upright her head resting against his thigh, asleep on the floor.

He watched her, felt the heat from her face against his thigh, and reached out his hand to stroke the loose strands of hair that clung to her sweaty cheek. But, he stopped himself.

He had to admit that it was a nice feeling seeing Maureen, in his button down tee shirt wrapped in his comforter, next to him, sleeping peacefully.

She reminds me of the Scottish women from Rob Roy and Braveheart, wrapped in their man's colored tartan.

That thought brought an instant reaction of his carnal base desires, and Bill was torn between kissing the top of her head versus waking her up.

He never got to make that decision because Maureen lifted her sleepy head, hazel eyes blinking rapidly at him. Her hair was wilder than it was when she was fully awake, with loose curls spiraling everywhere at the same time, but never in the same direction.

"I need coffee, Gomer Pile," she said, getting to her feet and walking to the kitchen.

Bill just watched her, amazed and a little confounded by the woman who only moments before was curled up next to him like a faithful pet.

Opening the cupboards, she turned around and looked at him.

"You don't have any coffee," she turned back around, rechecking the open cupboards.

"No, I don't. I only keep instant around the house and I used the last of it last night. I don't usually drink the stuff. It tends to keep me awake at night, and I find it rather cliché."

"Cliché?"

"Yes."

"Bill," she yawned, "a cop eating a doughnut is cliché. A cop drinking coffee is just a hallmark of good social graces. Besides, how do you possible function in the morning without at least one cup of the stuff?"

"I don't need it. I wake up; go for a run, shower, and head to work."

"Oh God, you aren't one of that 'wake up because Mister Sunshine has given us this beautiful day' people are you? I mean, I really hate people who are just chipper and raring to go in the morning."

"I wouldn't say that I'm that. But I usually wake up before the alarm goes off, and once I open my eyes, I'm wide awake."

"Really? I should try that sometime." Frowning, she tried to smooth her tousled hair.

"I see that sarcasm is part of your natural charm and not caffeine induced."

Rolling her eyes at him, she spotted the bag from her trip to The Tea Caddy and smiled.

"I'm a genius," she said, reaching for the bag.

"It's debatable. Getting the idea to brew tea from tea that you purchased, after spotting the bag out in the open is hardly worth genius status, so let's not start polishing the Pulitzer just yet."

Narrowing her eyes to thin slits to glare at him, she ignored his jabs and went on to make herself the tea, turning the kettle on.

She opened a few cupboards; found the mugs pulled out two. "Do you have a tea ball?"

"A what?"

"A tea ball. You know. The little metal ball you put the tea in so it can steep in the hot water. You got one?"

"Um, no."

"How about a strainer?"

"That I've got. Third drawer next to the oven."

Opened the drawer, she retrieved the strainer. She waited for the water to boil before dropping two generous scoops of loose tea into the kettle.

"So what's our plan for today? What're we doing?" she asked, keeping the comforter around her loosely while she sat at the kitchen table.

"We? We aren't doing anything. I'm going to check on the leads from Victoria, and I put in a call to a friend of mine who works for the University up here. However, you will be happy to know that I agree with you, something is hinky, but I just can't put my finger on it. I'll be right back."

"Where are you going?"

"Just to the bathroom. All right?"

She shook her head and shrugged. "Whatever."

Just as he was finishing his business, Bill heard the smoke detector go off. He ran from the bathroom, gun in hand.

"What the—? He lowered the gun when he saw Maureen standing over the toaster waving her arms, trying frantically to clear the air.

He looked to her, ready to say something when his eyes met hers, sheepish and clearly embarrassed.

"You certainly know how to make a man's life interesting, Maureen."

"Yeah, never a dull moment around me. Wait until you see me when I have the office eggnog in me. Party, party, party."

Smiling, Bill brushed past her, noticing in her haste to get to the burning toaster, she had dropped the comforter and stood in his kitchen wearing only the button down t-shirt.

Bill turned off the house alarm, opening a window to alleviate the smell and accumulation of smoke, then the toaster. He then opened the door and tossed the toaster into the metal trash can. Closing the door and rearming the alarm, Bill turned to look at her.

"You're looking pretty hot right about now."

"Maureen scrambled for the comforter. "Don't kid yourself, she said, pulling the comforter around herself. "I look like a train wreck."

"How about I cook and you just—" he stopped mid-sentence.

Maureen, first smiling as if going to say something to him, stopped and held her breath.

Bill brought his finger to his lips in a silent motion for her to be quiet. He then motioned for her to stay behind him as he slowly moved the two to the window.

They listened.

It was still early, barely past sunrise.

A few birds chirped, but in Michigan in the late fall and winter, the only birds that stayed that far north were blue jays and sparrows.

Bill listened, trying to separate each distinctive sound coming from the outside.

Maureen stood behind him, her breathing shallow and soft, unable to understand what was happening except to know that it wasn't something good.

Bill pressed back against her, butting her up against the wall to shield her as much as possible.

He knew the alarm was on and didn't have to worry about securing his cabin.

Raising his weapon, Bill scanned outside for intruders, a car — something to match with the looming thud he had heard.

But the sound never repeated itself.

The sound changed.

Outside, the soft thud that Bill heard just moments before grew louder.

Thwack.

Thwack. Thwack.

A large shadow passed over the small back porch and clearing that lay adjacent to Bill's cabin and porch.

Behind him, he felt Maureen inhale sharply and afforded himself a quick glance over his shoulder to make sure she was okay, before returning his attention back to the window.

Thwack. Thwack.

The whooshing hollow sound grew closer, then faded, then grew closer again.

If Bill didn't know better, he would have sworn he'd just seen the shadow of an extremely large bird.

CHAPTER 29

HE NEEDED TO be able to see outside, to get a good look at whatever was out there, but he couldn't afford himself the luxury, not while protecting Maureen.

Reaching over, he dropped the blinds on the window and scanned the area.

Thwack.

A loud screech.

"Oh my God, what the hell is that?" Maureen breathed hard against his back.

"I have no idea."

He backed them away from the window, drawing the curtains.

"I need you to think Maureen. I need you to replay each moment, tell me everything and anything."

"I...I was sitting on the couch after I put the bagel in. I was looking at the files on the coffee table. Glancing at them. I heard the smoke detector and ran to the kitchen."

"Okay. That's when I came in and unplugged the toaster. I turned off the alarm and put the toaster outside and came in."

"You set the alarm again," Maureen noted.

"I did. Then what happened."

"I was listening to you, you asked if I wanted you to make breakfast, then you stopped in midsentence."

Bill looked around the small modest kitchen and eyed the two coffee cups.

"When did you make this?" he asked, sipping the mix.

"About ten minutes ago. I put the kettle on when you said you didn't have any coffee."

"This the tea that you bought yesterday afternoon at The Tea Caddy, right?" he asked, picking up the tin.

"Yeah. The woman refilled the tin for me. I told you all that yesterday. Why?"

215

Bill wasn't sure why either, but he was certain that he was holding another piece of the puzzle; he just wasn't sure how it fit into the rest of the picture.

"Bill? Bill?" she prodded.

"I'm thinking. Maureen, yesterday when you were in a tea store, you said that you got a hinky feeling. I need you to tell me exactly what happened, word for word."

Fifteen minutes later, Maureen hadn't only given Bill a play by play of what had occurred the day before, but she had also done what she had in the past with her research in writing an article: she wrote it all down.

"Do you think that lady at the tea shop is involved in Hannah's disappearance?"

"I don't know. There's all these pieces to the puzzle, Maureen. They're all connected, but I don't have a bigger picture to go by to make them all fit. I think it might be worth making a visit to Victoria and my buddy. Until then, I don't want you drinking that tea but I also don't want you to throw it out, either."

"Why?"

"If that tea is laced with something, DMSO or GHP, I want to know."

"You think someone is preying on women and using the tea as a sedative? Like, for human trafficking?" Maureen shook her head. "I don't buy it. That isn't the vibe that I was picking up when I went into the store."

"Maureen, let me handle this, okay? I know you want to find Hannah, find out what happened, but the last thing that I want to do is miss a clue because we have pigeon-holed ourselves into a lead that isn't there."

"Okay, but I want to be with you when you go to these places."

"I don't think that's a good idea, Maureen. You should stay here. I need to know you're safe."

"If I stay here, I'm a sitting duck. The safest place to be right now is right behind you. You said so."

Bill didn't want to say it, but a part of him did feel better if she was within eyesight.

"Fine. Get dressed."

"Can we stop off at the cabin first? I want to pick up a few things, change of clothes, and some toiletries."

Bill didn't think it was a good idea. Whoever was after Maureen might be hidden in the woods at the cabin, or worse, in the cabin itself. He shook his head.

"Bill, I need a change of clothes. I need my deodorant. I need a hairbrush and toothbrush."

He weighed her pleas and started to pace back and forth slowly. It was dangerous, and it was stupid to entertain the idea of going back there.

Heading into the small den, he came back with a large black duffel bag.

"Please tell me you aren't thinking of giving me your ex's left behinds." She almost sounded hurt.

"No. I don't allow women to just shack up with me, and second, why would I keep their old stuff around? That's a girl thing."

"I'm sorry. I didn't mean that. I just...it would be nice to have clean clothes in my size, and a toothbrush of my own."

"No. I don't want you going back to your cabin until I can find out what's going on. You and I both know that nurse at the hospital wasn't a paid member of the staff."

She tilted her head, looking at him.

Obviously, she didn't.

He stood up, and walked over to her, and put his arms around her.

"I didn't mean to tell you like that, I'm sorry. I just assumed you knew. I mean, you seemed like you were thinking the same thing"

"I was just thinking that they were incompetent."

"They might be that, but that nurse had an itch to make something bad happen to you, I know it. That's why I need you where I can protect you."

"Does anyone else know that I'm here?" she asked, staring up at him.

"No, and I plan on keeping it that way. I had your car towed last night into the next town, and it's being stored in a friend's garage. He's a one-man operation, so I don't have to worry about one of his employees seeing the car and reporting it."

Nodding, she sat back down on the couch.

"Relax, Maureen. Worst-case scenario I put you on a plane out of here myself. It won't come to that, though. I have a feeling the reason why someone tried to push you off the curb wasn't just to injure you but to kill you, or at least make you give up the search and leave."

"That doesn't make any sense."

"Did you ever give any thought that maybe Hannah wanted to get you up here? On purpose."

"For what?"

"You said it yourself to me on more than one occasion. You and your sister didn't always get along. What if she had enough of living in your shadow, lured you up here, only to do something bad to you?"

"Hannah would never do something like that," Maureen stared at him.

"How do you know that? People hurt people all the time, for reasons less than this."

"You have no idea how she felt," she snapped.

"Obviously, neither do you," he retorted.

"You're a real jerk, you know that." She stormed off, slamming the bedroom door, only to emerge a few moments later, fully dressed.

"I'd love to know where it is you think you're going," Bill crossed his arms.

"I'm going home. I'm going away from here. Most of all, I'm getting away from you, you pompous self-righteous two faced hypocritical jerk."

Red faced and clearly agitated, her wild auburn curls sprang around her like a modern medusa.

Reaching into her bag, she pulled out three twenty dollar bills and tossed them on the coffee table, briskly walking past him.

"Here's for the hospitality and the maid."

The muscle in his jaw tensed, and he crossed the distance between them in two long strides, blocking her path.

"That isn't what I meant and you know it. Now listen to me, Miss Welsh," he started.

"Oh boy we're back to that," she snipped.

"Shut up. I mentioned it because it's a very real possibility that that might be the case. Whatever the reason, you aren't leaving this cabin or going anywhere without me. Before you respond to me telling you to shut up, I only use the Miss Welsh like you use the colorful euphemisms to describe my line of work."

The corners of her mouth twitched in a vain attempt not to smile at him. It was something that Bill had come to expect in her character, and he found it both irritating and attractive.

Can you imagine living with this walking contradiction the rest of your life? Bill asked himself.

"I know she's your sister. I know that you love her. But we have to look at Hannah as not only a missing person but as a suspect in a bigger picture. I just want you to be prepared should that outcome become known.

She nodded to him, still a little mad, but not fuming as she'd been before.

"I think we'll head over to see Victoria and grab a bite to eat on the way. Then we go see my buddy up at the university."

"What does he do?"

"He's a cryptozoologist."

"English please," smiling gently, tucking a strand of hair behind her ear.

"He studies the creatures of myths and legends when he isn't regularly teaching freshman chemistry. John liked the idea of being the mad scientist when we were kids until he found out it was a lot of work. This way, he can chase the creatures from the comics we loved, and still be a functioning member of the science community."

"It sounds like a made up title."

"It is. But he has access to files that might be helpful, and his intentions are good."

"Is he one of those conspiracy theory people?"

"No, he just never wanted to leave home and had to find a way to support his every growing comic book addiction," Bill said, slinging the black duffle bag over his shoulder before disarming the alarm and opening the door to look around before ushering Maureen out to the Expedition. "The only subject that he didn't ditch class for was science."

"What about you? What subjects did you ditch?" she asked, imagining he was probably going to say something flippant, like 'all of them'.

"None. My mom would have tanned my hide if she caught me cutting class. I held all A's throughout most of school, including college."

"You went to college?" she asked, her voice hinting at the slight tone of disbelief.

"Yes. Bill go to college. Bill done good," he quipped, taking on the deep tone he used to express the inner Neanderthal that Maureen mentioned earlier.

Once inside the SUV, Maureen looked at him.

"The cabin?"

Sighing, and wanting to avoid another argument, he finally relented.

"Fine. But you have to wait in the car until I check the cabin, and we are in and out. No cleaning, no deciding what outfit to wear. Five minutes. Deal?"

"Deal. And thank you."

Bill clutched his chest.

"My heart. It hurts…to breathe," he joked, and she looked at him, clearly not amused.

"Funny, Bill. Very funny."

They spent the short ride from Bill's cabin to Maureen's, in silence.

The clearing of Maureen's cabin looked strange to her without her trusty beat up old Pontiac in the circular dirt drive.

Bill looked around and backed the car up to the front porch as far as it would go.

Reaching into his black duffle bag, he pulled out a pair of thick black binoculars and Maureen just stared at him.

Whether it was his military training, his dedication to his job, or a sincere interest in her, Maureen was grateful that he was both thorough and attentive.

Attention to details meant he cared, at least on some level. It had been a long time since Maureen had truly felt the silent actions of genuine affection.

"Why are you looking at the world through your rose tinted glasses?" Maureen looked over to where he was looking, wondering if he saw anything and if he would bother to tell her about it before reacting.

"These aren't binoculars. They are ultraviolet heat-seeking thermal binoculars. They allow me to see anything that is bigger than a squirrel that might be camouflaged out there in the woods."

"You think someone's in the woods."

"I think it pays to be safe than sorry."

Another ten minutes later, and Bill was satisfied that no immediate danger was lurking in the woods.

Getting out, he kept his hand on the hilt of his gun, prepared to reach for it if needs be.

The door to the cabin was intact, and as far as he could tell, it was safe and secure.

Maureen reached around him to punch in the seven-digit code on the alarm panel, and watched as all exits, windows and doors alike, light up green.

"It's safe."

Bill went in first and pulled his gun, sweeping from side to side.

"Bill, I said we were safe."

"Alarms can be deceiving."

Looking around downstairs, Bill took another ten minutes to sweep the upper level while Maureen waited impatiently on the staircase.

It was almost nine in the morning. They were cutting it close to getting to the maritime museum with their appointment with Victoria, but with any luck, they'd make it.

"Get to it. You have five minutes."

Bill kept his eye on the door as Maureen grabbed her suitcase, and emptied the top drawer of the dresser.

"Ready."

"You only unpacked the first drawer?

"It was all I got around to. I didn't plan to be here this long, remember. I didn't bring a lot of stuff with to begin with."

"Good. Let's get out of here."

Maureen made sure to grab the personal telephone book off the secretary before locking the door. Any mail that came would have to wait as Bill grew inpatient.

Outside, she handed Bill the suitcase, as he opened the back glass hatch to store it.

Something caught Maureen's attention. A subtle wave in her peripheral vision.

She craned her head back, catching sight of something small and white in the top of the tree line.

"Bill, what's that?" she asked, pointing to the white image at the top of the trees.

"I don't know. It might be a plastic bag of some sort. Lots of times people leave behind debris on the beach and it gets blown around in the wind."

"Up that high," she looked. "Do you have a regular pair of binoculars in that little black bag of yours?"

"Maureen," he started, feeling the need to remind her that time was ticking and he didn't want to stay here any longer than necessary, but stopped. Instead, he reached inside the smaller inner pocket and pulled out a pair of binoculars, scanning the tree line where the white object was.

"What is it?"

Bill didn't say anything, instead handed the binoculars to Maureen.

She looked through them, focusing on the small white apparition.

"It looks like a jacket."

"I know."

"It looks like a long sleeved zippered jacket." Her voice betrayed the cool exterior that she was showing.

It looked like Hannah's jacket.

"Come on Maureen. We're leaving. I'll send a crew down there to retrieve the jacket."

"How?"

"We have equipment from the DNR to go up trees to catch poachers."

Thwack.

Maureen didn't get a chance to say anything because overhead, a large squawking roared. The ground around them was momentarily cast in shadow as a predator circled instinctively around them.

Thwack. Thwack.

Bill grabbed Maureen, shoving her in the car.

He jumped in alongside her, locking the doors and starting the car.

"What the hell is that?" Her hands, pressed against the window, craning her neck to catch a better view.

"I don't know, but I'm not sticking around here to find out."

Bill sped out of the dirt driveway, clicking his seatbelt as he drove. As the sped away from the cabin, Maureen started taking a small nip at her fingernails.

"Stop it."

"What." But it wasn't a question.

"You're thinking that the white jacket belongs to Hannah. We've no way of knowing that, and even if it did, we can't be certain that Hannah didn't lose it in the throes of foul play."

"I know."

"So, why are you so quiet?" he asked, veering off onto the main highway heading east.

"Because I don't know what else to do. I spend half my time preparing myself that it's going to be her, and the rest of my time won-dering where else I can look for her."

By the time they arrived at the maritime museum, the sun had passed its early morning stages, rising high in the east making Maureen squint as she climbed out of the Expedition.

The inside of the museum was the same as it had been a few days before, only it smelled different. Warm. Like Cinnamon.

Victoria emerged from the back room, carrying several small holly berry wreaths, and smiled.

"Bill! I thought you military types were the punctual kind," she teased.

"Sorry, it was my fault," Maureen interjected.

"Not at all. I've been busy getting stuff out of storage for the holidays. I wanted to have all of the holiday decorations up before I left for the weekend."

"It smells wonderful in here."

"Thanks. It's the cinnamon sticks in the oil diffuser. A little really goes a long way."

"Victoria, I hate to cut it short, but we have to be somewhere this afternoon."

"I understand. Come on back to the office, and we can go over what I found."

The office was a neat and tidy ten by ten-foot office space that boasted gleaming natural honey oak hardwood floors and plaster textured walls. They were a faded antique white that matched the nautical theme in the rest of the museum.

Victoria pulled out a vial jar that looked like a small test tube, and some papers encased in a manila folder.

"I did analyze some of that stringy moss stuff that you gave me and I came up with some interesting things. First off, I found several components in the makeup of the webbing."

"Like spider webbing?" Maureen asked tensely. She hated spiders.

"Not so much so. However, in a sense, yes. The webbing on one side is tacky and the other isn't. My guess is that it's used for a nest of some sort. I believe the tacky side has two possible purposes that I can derive. One, it acts a way to trap prey for later consumption."

"The other," Bill inquired.

"I believe another possibility is that the tacky side is used to keep whatever is put in the nest, in the nest. It isn't sticky enough to cause serious harm, but for example, if there were eggs in the nest, it would be sticky enough to keep them from rolling out of the nest."

"So you think that whatever made this has nests?"

"It's more than likely. There aren't a lot of animals in the animal kingdom that make their own nests with this type of material."

"Do you know what animal is belongs to?"

"No, sorry Bill, I don't. I don't even know if the animal is native to Michigan or not. You're going to need to talk a zoologist or someone who might be able to narrow your search down more. Remember, these are just educated guesses based on my limited research."

"Is that all?"

"No. I did some tests on it. The residue of the nest has Iridium. There's animal saliva, iridium, and traces of pheromones."

"Pheromones? The chemicals that cause attraction?" Maureen was butting her way into the conversation.

"Not in the traditional sense that you're thinking of, but yes. I can't tell if they're for attracting their mates, or prey, or what. The residue left on the webbing left me only trace amounts to work with, and while I'm no expert at this, I would warrant a guess that it might be some sort of self-defense mechanism that it has. Like snake venom, if you will."

"But it isn't poisonous, though," Bill commented.

"No, not that I can tell, but remember, I had very little to work with. If you had brought me a bigger sample to work with, I might have been able to give you more than what I'm able to now. I have rudimentary equipment and limited resources when it comes to something like this. If you need it for anything official, please by all means, get a second opinion."

"I was more curious than looking for anything official. Besides, this isn't for an investigation, it is for personal use."

"Personal use?" she asked skeptically.

"Bill knows that I like to bird watch, and there are lots of trails around the lake. I just hate spiders and when I saw the webbing —" Maureen shrugged sheepishly, feigning embarrassment, "He knows that I am paranoid about spiders, so he was being a sweetheart and checking it out for me."

"Oh, Bill, that's sweet."

Victoria turned around to grab a book off one of the shelves and Bill gave Maureen a small smile, and she returned it.

"Here," she handed Maureen the book. "This will tell you all about the native birds that you can find on Lake Superior, as well as some of the lesser known creatures of wildlife."

"Thank you." Maureen opened the book, "I'll get it back to you as soon as I'm done."

"Nonsense. Keep it. It was one of several copies that I have here at the office, and it's one less book I'll have to donate or throw away.

This tiny office doesn't afford me much space and I'd rather the books go to a good home than in the trash."

"Have you thought about donating them to a shelter, like for abused women or a group home for seniors? They rarely get donations from the state, and they always can put the materials to good use."

"Thanks, I never thought of that."

"So, back to the webbing. It isn't anything that you haven't seen before then," Bill interjected.

"No, I never said that. Like I said, Bill, I am no expert. You're going to have to talk to a zoologist or another animal expert. I've never seen this type of webbing before in all my life. But again, I don't have much experience in that area of things."

Bill nodded and reached to take over the folder and notes, reading them over.

"So, what is your final word on this, Vic?" Bill asked.

"I'd say you have some sort of predatory waterfowl, or perhaps a new migrating species of spiders. Michigan doesn't get very many breeds of them. In fact, we only have a few, the wolf spider, the black widow, and one other I can never remember the name of."

"The brown recluse," Bill commented.

"But that doesn't mean that another form of species can't take up residence here. We get a lot of shipping in and out the state, and the Soo Locks provide a partial means of transport of exotic goods."

"So this webbing might be from some sort of migratory animal? Do you think that whatever it is that made the webbing, is carnivorous?"

Victoria looked quizzically at Maureen, then at Bill.

"I mean, you said the webbing might have been made to trap prey, so I assumed that whatever made the webbing might be, you know, aggressive," Maureen stammered.

Bill stared at Maureen, and then looked back at the folder.

"Bill, I tell you, she's precious. Here," Victoria pulled a card from the thin middle drawer of her wooden desk and handed Maureen a small business card.

"Tell him Victoria sent you." She smiled lightly.

Maureen looked down and read the card, advertising the name and address of a local hypnotist. Maureen, brow quirked, looked up.

"He's great. He can hypnotize you to get over anything. Smoking, weight loss, phobias," Victoria said making little creepy movements with her fingers as if to simulate spiders legs.

"I'll keep that in mind," she said, tucking the card into her bag.

"I appreciate it Victoria, and I promise that this time I'll call you." He smiled, giving her a warm hug.

Once out in the car, Bill gave a sidelong glance to Maureen, who was thumbing through the glossy mated book of natural wildlife along Michigan's northernmost lake.

"Predators, Maureen. Why didn't you just come right out and ask whether these things ate people for God's sake?" Bill shook his head.

"Excuse me for wanting some answers. Look, there are lots of animals that eat people. You said let's not get caught up in the one theory situation. I just wanted to know if she thought that there might be some reasonable explanation as to what made that webbing."

"Giant spiders?"

"Have you ever seen Stephan King's It? It was a ginormous spider that wanted to suck the face off of half the people in town."

"I actually read the book instead. You should never judge a book by its movie. In the book, it wasn't a giant spider, and it wasn't like the ending of the movie. And as I recall, it only went after the little kids."

"Whatever. It was still a huge spider."

"Well, I think we might end up finding out something more concrete from my buddy at the university."

"All right. It's the reporter in me, always looking for all the angles of a story."

"It's the curiosity in you, and you need to be careful. Look what it did to the cat."

CHAPTER 30

SUPERIOR STATE COLLEGE was a lot like any other college, surrounded by a town full of Coney Islands, cheap burger joints, tons of bars, and coffee houses.

Maureen had never been into the whole college scene even when she'd been in college herself, and she wasn't very impressed with it now.

"So, this friend of yours, what exactly does he do for a living?"

"He's head of the sciences department and we served in the Marines together. He did the four-year stint to pay for college, but we were cool."

"I see. So what're you hoping to get out of him?"

"Scientific answers. I want to know what made that webbing. If I've gone through all this trouble for it to be manmade, it might have cost us valuable time in searching for your sister. If it turns out to be a hoax, I'm going to be royally pissed off."

"I hadn't thought of that," she said, getting out the Expedition.

They had parked in the visitor parking section of the parking lot that was adjacent to a rust colored three-story brick building. Across the parking lot, a small paved road that led to other buildings on campus, and beyond that, a small boat dock, covered in a light layer of snow.

The water of Lake Superior was always a deep rich blue color. Yet now the water looked more gray-blue, with its icy caps slowly cresting over as the waves lapped at the shore. Maureen felt cold even staring at the water and shuddered with remembrance over the infamous one line, she had heard so many times before.

Lake Superior never gives up her dead.

Maureen had never paid much attention to those corny lines that defined the beginnings of urban legends. They were alluring to her at best, a quick thrill from the subtle spookiness that it promised. Like a good tagline for a horror movie, or a teaser paragraph to a mystery novel, it was something that kept Maureen hooked and interested.

227

It was a whole different story when the mystery involved a member of your own family.

When she thought about Hannah, especially lately, she was thinking of her in the past tense.

Maureen had covered a few stories of child abductions, and the parent's desperate need to find their child. In one case, the parents never did. They never had justice, closure, and they were never at peace.

That's all I want, she pleaded silently, peace. *Not for myself, but for Hannah.*

"Maureen." It was Bill's voice.

"Sorry, I didn't hear you."

"I gathered that. What's the matter," he looked at her.

"I was thinking about Hannah again. You know, she spent the majority of her life doing everything under the sun just to get some attention from my mom and Frank. I was thinking," her voice shook a little, "that she's been ignored her whole life, and I didn't want her life, or her death, to be ignored either."

"No one's going to ignore this case or your sister," he planted a comforting hand on her shoulder.

"No, no that isn't what I meant. What I meant was that I just don't want her forgotten about. If we find out, or even suspect that she did die, I want to find her body. I want to know. I want her at peace; I want that same peace for my mom and Frank, too. She spent her whole life living in the shadows, being ignored until it was time to play happy family, and I don't want her disappearance to be forgotten about after a while. She deserves more than that."

Bill nodded, understanding.

"Instead of a reporter, you should have been a nurse."

"Writer."

"What?" he asked, walking along the paved concrete walkway towards a building that read, FACULTY OFFICE AND LABS.

"Writer. I wanted to be a writer."

"Writer, reporter. Isn't that the same thing?" He opened the door, ushering her inside.

"Not exactly. A writer writes whatever they want to, whenever they want to. A reporter has to find the story or write about the story that's given to them. I have to find a way to make it interesting, marketable, and most assuredly, profitable. In many ways, being a reporter is like being in marketing. I'm only as good as my last story."

"I never really thought of it like that. What do you write?" he asked, stopping in front of a wooden door with crazy formulas inscribed all over it. Hanging on the door were two clear plastic holders containing papers and handouts.

"A little of everything. Poetry, lyrics, short stories, novels. How did you know that I wrote, I mean as a hobby?" she asked, blushing slightly that her secret might have been revealed.

"You just told me," he said before knocking.

"Speak friend, and enter," boomed a voice from the other side of the door.

Maureen shot him a half smile and turned the knob, walking into the small office.

Cramped was a vast understatement. Books were stacked neatly on orange crate bookshelves, and wherever else they could fit. Piles of books sat next to the door, under the window, on top of the bookcases, and under the two small chairs that sat opposite the old wooden desk.

Papers lay strewn about the desk, piled in two wire baskets three inches thick.

"Fair lady, what do I owe this dubious pleasure?" The redheaded man said at her, getting up and extending a hand.

"Easy there Paul, she's spoken for."

"Aren't they always? All the good ones are either married or refuse my calls. William Downs, it's been a long time," he stepped out from behind the desk and came over to hug Bill.

The man was thin; Maureen would have guessed that under the tweed sweater and beige corduroy trousers, he was probably a little gangly and scrawny.

"Too long," Bill said, and closed the door behind him.

"So, this is a nice surprise. When I got your call yesterday, I was a little surprised. I mean, you never liked anything to do with science or animals, let alone know anything about them."

"That isn't true. I was always asking you what that animal would taste like, or would it be good with sweet potatoes."

Maureen laughed a little.

"That's mean. You know I'm a vegetarian."

"I know. That's why it's funny."

"I hope you can live with yourself the next time you slice into Bambi's mother."

Maureen could tell that Paul was poking fun, but he was also trying to get his point across. Maureen decided to break into the conversation before an argument occurred.

"Thank you for meeting with us on such short notice; I know you must be incredibly busy this time of year."

"Not at all. It gives me a chance to actually get out of this office for a change. Lately, it seems that the only places that I get to go are class, here, and home. Sometimes I forget that there's a whole other world off of campus."

"Paul's one of those people who liked school so much that they wanted to be lifelong students," Bill nudged her, then pointed to the several degrees on the wall.

"I'm currently working on my second Master's degree."

"Wow," Maureen said, clearly impressed.

"It's nothing, really. I just took my love of animals and harnessed it into a career that I find enjoying. Not many people can say that about themselves," he said, sipping from a mug with Einstein's picture, next to an older woman in a green and white Mumu, and a quote about how everything is relative.

Scientific humor, she noticed.

"So, you said you had some specimens for me to look at?" he asked, appearing hopeful.

"Yeah. We found them on the beach and were wondering what you could tell us about it."

"What were you hoping to find?" Paul reached across the desk, taking the plastic bag from Bill's hand and holding it up to the light.

"I don't know really. Whatever you can, I guess. I mean, knowing what type of animal it was would be helpful. What is the stuff exactly? What it's made of? And how it might be used."

"Well, I can tell you right now it's from a species of waterfowl."

"How can you tell that just by looking at it?"

"Do you see the small green specs on the striations of white webbing? The green specs are a form of algae that's common on the great lakes. It's caused by the fuel from the big tankers that use the locks and the Saint Larry."

"Saint Larry?" Maureen interrupted.

"Saint Lawrence Seaway. Sorry, a little science humor, I can't help it."

"No, not at all. Sorry, I was just curious. Please continue," she said.

"Where was I? Oh yeah, algae. The chemical remains of the fuel that the big tankers use, cause the alga. It seeps into the water and creates a thick greenish alga that floats along the surface of the water. Sometimes it attaches itself to plankton or local foliage in the small causeways, but mostly it sinks to the bottom, where the fish eat it. And what eats the fish?"

"Birds," Bill confirmed.

"Exactly. Did you find it locally?" he asked, reaching behind him for a book.

"Yeah, how did you know?"

"Lucky guess. You only live two towns away. Besides, this alga was a real problem for the Soo locks a few years back, even causing it to shut down some of them."

"I thought it was the mussels that did that?" Maureen asked.

"The mussels did because they were feeding off of the algae. So, this is some salvias webbing that the mothers secrete when they first start making the nest for its young. The white striations are caused by the lactic acid in the lining of the birds' stomachs, and it mixes with the saliva and regurgitated when the birds start spinning the nest."

"They puke it back up?" she asked, a little turned off by the science behind Paul's bird theory.

"Of course. But, this webbing is brittle, and normal webbing should be softer, more flexible. Come on, why don't we take this into my lab and we can do some tests, and hopefully answer your questions."

The lab had the classic the nineteen seventies feel. Black concrete tabletops on wooden legs pushed together in groups of two. Long narrow counters with equipment and containers littered many of the available surfaces.

Once inside, Bill sat on top of a table, and Maureen opted for a chair.

"Did you get a chance to look at those bones that we found, Paul?"

"I did. I have to concur with what your medical examiner said. They're human but too old to be your victim and too short. Those bones belong to a male, a healthy male at that. But I disagree about his time of death, though," he said, setting up a large circular tray and machine.

"Why's that?" Bill asked, putting a hand on Maureen's shoulder.

"Your medical examiner thinks the bones are from a few years back. I think they go back a few decades. There was too much yellowing of the bone for them to have been in the water for a long period of time."

"So you don't think that they just washed up to shore from a boating accident victim or a person overboard?"

"No. Lake Superior is a big, cold lake and temperatures rarely get above sixty-five degrees in summer. Furthermore, Lake Superior is deep. The odds that the bone was somehow on the bottom of the lake somewhere, and just managed to get dislodged and wash up on shore, is slim at best."

"Why?"

"They're too yellow, too oxidized. They've been exposed to the elements for quite a while. In addition, there were no traces of algae infestation or ravages of lake wear. No higher mercury levels, no clinical proof in the drop of bone density. Not to mention, a bone in water that long is probably going to be smooth on the outside, from being soaked in the water for such a long time."

"This bone wasn't?"

"No. This bone was rough on the outside. I'll have to do more tests on it if you want an official statement from me."

"As a matter of fact, I'd like that. So, this webbing," Bill nodded to the microscope.

"I'm getting to it, I'm getting to it. Patience, is a virtue, Bill. One that you never had if memory serves."

"Patience is for people who don't have the ability to step out of line and think for themselves."

"You'll never get anywhere in science without patience," Paul said absently, staring through the lens of the microscope.

After a few moments, Paul looked up.

"It all looks to be normal here. However, that's just the physical. I need to see its chemical composition."

Twenty minutes later, Paul had cut tiny samples and put them into long test tubes, at droppers of various color liquids before placing them in the tube size container in the circular machine.

"What does that do?" Maureen asked.

Bill had wondered how long that was going to take before her curiosity got the better of her.

"It is a chemical spectrograph. It will break down the chemical components of the webbing to allow me to know what it is composed of."

"I see."

As the machine's soft hum filled the room, no one said anything. After a while, Paul looked up.

"It shouldn't take too much longer."

"I appreciate it, Paul. I know that you're busy," Bill said.

"Not as much lately. Budget cuts, so instead of my usual eight classes I'm down to six. But I'm still doing research for a grant, and working on my second masters so I am able to stay busy."

"You need to take time out and go get a drink, maybe somewhere in a social setting," Bill prodded.

Bill liked Paul, but he was worried that he was going to end up alone and bitter, alone with his science manuals and research.

"For your information, I've been seeing the head of the computer science department for the last year."

"Awesome man. Good for you. Is she nice?" Bill wondered aloud.

"Yeah and sweet. She likes to cook and knit. So far, I've gained ten pounds and went up one pants size. It's nice to have someone to go home to, you know."

"Yeah, I know."

"So how is Natalie? Still wild and crazy as ever?"

Bill glanced at Maureen.

"I told you before; I was Natalie's friend, nothing more. She wanted more, wanted to be married to a Marine, and couldn't handle the fact that that wasn't going to happen."

"Man, that's a shame. She was hot," Paul grinned, then cleared his throat as if he forgot that Maureen was in the room.

"Sorry, I didn't mean anything by it. Bill and I go back to the Corp is all, and well, you know how men can be when they get together and start talking about the past. Sometimes we can be pigs."

"I know. Don't worry. No offense taken," Maureen said.

The machine stopped its humming, and the printer spit out a few sheets of paper. Maureen noticed that the first was a graph.

"That's odd."

"What?" Bill asked, impatient for the statistics.

"This says that the main components of the webbing are saliva. In that saliva, there are pheromones, high traces of iridium, which is odd as hell, and triptaphaze."

"English, Paul."

"Sorry. Pheromones are common in some animals. Not just for mating, but they also use it to attract prey. The iridium throws me for a loop, though."

"Why?" Maureen asked.

"Iridium isn't a common element found easily in nature, and when it is, it isn't found in high levels. Usually it's found as a trace element. But there's one place that iridium is abundant, and that's in meteors."

"Is it toxic? I mean, if ingested, can it kill a person?"

"Well iridium metal by itself is mostly nontoxic, due to it be nonreactive, but iridium compounds should be considered highly toxic so I don't recommend eating or drinking them."

"You said something else, the last element," Bill wondered.

233

"Triptaphaze. It's the common problem related to anaphylactic shock. It paralyzes the body, making it veritably immobile, usually for several hours. The interesting thing is that after a while, the triptaphaze is untraceable in the blood."

"Was there blood on the webbing?" Maureen asked, anxiously.

"No, that's the funny part. I shouldn't be able to trace it, but here it is, see for yourself."

Paul handed the papers to Bill, who looked at the graphs and chemical analysis that the computer printed out.

"How's that possible?"

"I'm not sure. You've just handed me a mystery. You know, chemistry isn't my strong suit. Maybe I should call in a colleague of mine."

Bill hesitated a moment, then looked at Maureen. He didn't want her to suffer any more than she already had.

"Yeah, that would be great."

Paul went over to a phone on the desk and made a few calls.

"Vern's available. He's on his way."

A few minutes later, a tall lanky man with sandy blonde hair and smoky blue eyes wandered in. He was tall, but only slightly taller than average. Black jeans and a gray sweatshirt advertising the school's name, he looked like the typical college kid himself, not a member of the faculty.

"Bill, Maureen, this is Vern Chaplin. Vern is the head of the chemistry department and co-chairs the biology department with me."

"Hey, how's it going," he nodded. "So, what's this off the hook formula that you are having trouble with," he leaned over, looking into the microscope then checking over the printouts before looking up to Paul.

"I hate to tell you Paul, but I think that there's a problem with your machine. This isn't right."

"No, there's no problem. I used it this morning, and it was fine."

"Triptaphaze isn't traceable in the blood after a few hours, and there's no blood on the sample here."

"I know."

"Also, there's a high level of iridium. This isn't natural."

"I know."

Watching the two science experts back and forth, Bill had to admire them. They had a way to read numbers and data that Bill envied. Hard sciences were a mark of true intelligence, cut and dry, data and research. Bill was good at intelligence, but his job relied more on human instincts, intuition, and gut reactions to situations.

He knew that he could never be them, and they could never be him, but despite that, neither of them could survive without the other.

"You know, these striations look familiar," Vern said. "I ran a sample similar a few weeks ago from some girl who said she was a reporter."

Bill looked up.

"What do you mean?"

"This girl came to see me, said she had been to a few different places, the library, marina, and couldn't find the answers to what she was looking for. I offered to help."

Maureen looked at Bill, and he knew that she was holding her breath.

"Did she have a name?" Bill asked.

"Yeah but to be honest, I forgot it. I have a lot of students and one meeting with a walk in wasn't memorable."

Maureen turned her head, feeling tears form in her eyes.

Bill removed a picture that he was carrying of Hannah and handed it to Vern.

"Was this the girl?" he asked.

"Yeah, it was. Do you know her?"

CHAPTER 31

"YEAH, I KNOW her." Bill pulled out a badge from his pocket. "I'm Sherriff Downs of Shoshanee County. I'm investigating this woman's disappearance.

"Disappearance? She's missing?" Vern looked shocked.

"When was the last time that you saw this girl?"

"Last time? It was the only time that I saw her, man. She came in here wanted to speak to someone about animals. I helped her the best I could. She said she was a reporter from a local paper, just starting out. Personally, I didn't buy it."

"Why not?" Bill asked.

"Because she was really nervous, and she appeared to not know what she was talking about. No offense, we have a journalism department here on campus and I have enough students who have been in that class to know a reporter."

"Oh?"

"Reporters have an angle usually; they ask a lot of questions, they don't wait to be fed information. She didn't write anything down."

Bill ran a hand through his hair and nodded.

"What else. You mentioned that she was asking questions about animals. What animals?"

"Birds," Vern said. "She said she saw a huge hawk-like bird where she lived, and wanted to know what type of bird it was, and how she could get rid of it."

"A bird?" Bill asked.

"Yeah. She claims she was having these bird issues, and then said a lot of people in town were having the same problems and wanted to know how to help the DNR keep them off of people's property. That is when I knew she wasn't a reporter, probably just someone with a bird infestation. She said the DNR sent her here, which I know is a lie."

"Why?" Bill asked.

236

"Everyone knows that the DNR enforces the protection of the animals in their natural environments. The DNR isn't going to send her here, or any place else for that matter. They'd take care of the problem themselves with live traps and re-release into another similar environment if they deemed it necessary," Vern stated.

"She's a missing person from Lighthouse Bay. We're trying to piece together her whereabouts from the last few weeks. This is her sister, Maureen," Bill nodded towards Maureen.

"Oh. Wow, hey I'm sorry. I didn't think anything was the matter with her when she showed up at my office. Like I said, she was asking about birds and whatnot. I figured she had an infestation of some kind, and wanted some free advice," said Vern. He went over to a chair and turned it around, sitting backward. "Sorry, this is really bizarre. I mean, I'd be glad to help any way I can."

"You didn't think that it was odd she was coming to a college professor for help, instead of a local hardware store, or someplace like Home Depot," Maureen turned to him, looking at directly at him.

"I did, but well, I thought she had a problem with some of the local wildlife. Some of the cranes up near her cabin are on the semi-endangered species list. I thought she was tired of them covering her backyard in crane shit so she wanted to stay off the radar of the DNR"

"How do you know she has a cabin?" Bill asked, putting a hand up to Maureen to keep her quiet.

"She told me. She said she lived in a cabin on the other side of Lighthouse Bay, near Ellington. I know there're cranes over there because our science department does field outreach programs through the DNR there. Hey, you don't think I had something to do with her disappearance do you," Vern looked at Bill, unable to hide the sudden realization that he might have gone from helpful colleague to a prime suspect.

"At this time we're just trying to put together the pieces in an official investigation," Bill said.

"I mean, I only talked to her for a few moments because I had a class at eleven."

"What class?" Bill asked.

"My earth science two class. We're doing midterms that week, and things were crazy. I was here most of the time," Vern looked to Paul for reinforcement.

"He was here; I remember bumping into him a lot in the lounge. I can vouch for him," Paul said.

"But where were you when you weren't on campus," Maureen blurted in.

"I was either at the gym or at home. My wife and mother-in-law can confirm it," Vern said. "My mother in law is going through chemo for breast cancer, so she's staying with us until she's in the clear. I'm sure my gym can tell you when I sign in and out," he reached into his wallet and pulled out a gym card, handing it to Bill. "That's my ID, my club info is on the back. Check them out; I'm there every night from nine to ten doing laps in the pool."

Maureen looked at Vern, and her gut told her that she was telling the truth. She'd reported on enough stories to know that when people volunteer up personal information at the ready, it means that they have nothing to hide.

Usually, she thought.

"We will. You're not a suspect, Vern," Bill said. "We're just try-ing to find out where Hannah Prescott was over the last two weeks. I want to go over the visit, word for word."

As Vern spoke, Bill and Maureen learned that Hannah had shown up early that morning asking around campus, and eventually made her way to the sciences building where she found Vern. She'd been alone, looked a lot like the picture, though Vern had guessed that she looked a little thinner in person.

Maureen took note of what he said, her mind already turning with more questions and ideas. She felt like she was circling the same clues over and over again.

They had another confirmed lead that seemed to dead end. It was frustrating, and all it did was renew Maureen's sense of urgency in the matter.

She knew what it meant if the investigation stayed open too long and what would happen, and she was going to do her damnedest to make sure that it didn't happen to her sister.

It was after midnight by the time Vern made his way to the park-ing lot. He didn't have an assigned space like Paul because he didn't have the tenure yet, so he had to park in visitor parking.

Carrying his leather shoulder bag and an arm full of books, he opened the backseat of his Chevy trailblazer depositing the menagerie of class papers, lesson plans, and books onto the seat.

Getting into the front and locking his door, he pulled out his cell phone and dialed the number he'd committed to memory all those long months before.

He waited until the digital voice prompted to leave a message.

"Yeah, it's me. I sat in on a very interesting meeting this afternoon."

Vern looked around; checking to make the campus parking lot was nearly deserted.

"A police officer was here with some girl, looking for that Prescott woman. I got the impression they think she's run off. Just thought you should know."

He hung up, then went back into his phone's memory and erased the outgoing call. If the phone was ever lost, or God forbid confiscated for any reason, the number he just called would be listed to a phone in his mother-in-law's name. In truth, she knew nothing about the phone. He'd been told to purchase a phone under a family member's name and mail it to a post office box outside of Marquette.

It didn't matter, he reasoned. He was just a middle man. He got paid to pay attention, and tell what he knew if needs be.

Pulling the car out of the parking lot, he headed towards his gym for his nightly routine.

CHAPTER 32

"YOU WANNA TALK about it?" Bill asked once they were safely inside the confines of his SUV. Bill thought Maureen was either going to break down in tears, or start screaming at Vern, or call him a liar.

To her credit, she didn't do either.

And that worried Bill.

"Not really. I mean, what's the point? We only know that at some point in the last two or three weeks that my sister came here to ask questions about birds. Birds that we haven't even seen or even know exist," Maureen looked out the window.

"Not yet, but it is winter up here. Most birds have migrated south. The only birds that stay in Michigan in the winter are the crows and blue jays," Bill said.

"Look, Bill, there's something else I've wanted to tell you, but haven't. I know I should have; I was half hoping you would've uncovered it yourself, but you haven't and well, now seems like a good time to bring it up," Maureen looked at him.

Bill swallowed hard. He didn't like surprises when it came to information about a case. Surprises always meant something bad was coming, like the whereabouts of a body or a confession.

"I'm listening," he said.

"Hannah was married once before, about five years ago. It was annulled after only a couple of weeks."

Bill nodded, and looked at her.

"That it?" he prodded.

"No. There's more. It's about why she got it annulled. The man she was married to was in the military, a Marine. He was really rather nice; I always felt sorry for him being married to Hannah," she said.

"Why?"

"Because he was a sweet boy from Oklahoma who wanted nothing more than a wife and kids to come home to, coach little league — the

240

whole nine yards. But Hannah didn't want that, she only thought she did."

"Go on," he said, taking out his notebook to write down a few things. "This ex have a name?" he asked.

"Well, yeah he does. Wyatt Huxley."

"We'll have to question Mr. Huxley about his whereabouts. I'll have Edith see what she can dig up on him," Bill said.

"That won't be necessary. I know where he is. I mean, where he was."

"Why do I get the feeling that what you're about to tell me is going to make this case a whole lot more complicated than it already is." He shook his head, too tired for games. "Out with it. All of it, Maureen."

"Wyatt was my ex-boyfriend before he and Hannah eloped in Vegas. She took my gown, took my fiancé, and married him. I was out of town on assignment and made it home in time for my birthday to find a message on my machine asking me to wish her congratulations."

Bill blew out a whistle and looked at her. "Please don't take this the wrong way, but with a family like that, why the hell do you bother with her?" he asked in all seriousness.

"She's my sister. I've been doing it for so long that its part of who I am." Maureen knew he was right, but kept on talking. "My parents were thrilled because they thought this Marine could teach Hannah discipline. Give her structure. This is what she needed to straighten up and fly right, as Frank said."

"What about you? Weren't they just a little bit upset and concerned for you that your former fiancé just up and married your sister without a word?"

"They were, yes. But my parents always said I was much too independent and spirited to settle down. I was able to care for myself, and if Hannah and Whyatt were fated—"

He cut her off. "Fated. Please tell me that they didn't take her side in this?" Bill asked. He watched her face. She was so cold in her retelling of it, so numb to the pain that it no doubt caused her that Bill knew she had a hard exterior to crack.

Maureen was the type of women who buried her pain deep, away from others, away from herself. But she wasn't the type of person to let it go either. No, she nurtured it, fed it, learned from it and kept it alive deep inside because it fed her ambition to succeed.

"My mom and Frank knew that with time, I would get over it. They were right in a way," Maureen sighed.

241

"It's not like you had much choice. Why kind of man runs off with his fiancé's sister?'

"What's done is done. It didn't work between them. Hannah left him for someone else, another serviceman I think. The marriage was annulled and he got stationed in Germany for a while," Maureen said.

"Putrid Deb," Bill said.

"What?" asked Maureen?

"Putrid Debs. It's a term that men in the military use to describe the chicks who hook a military man because they're in love with the idea of marrying an officer," Bill said.

"Oh, I didn't know that. I'll have to file that away for future reference. It would make sense, though, with Hannah. I think the only service branch she hasn't dated is the Coast Guard."

"Look, I want to ask you this right out, because I don't like surprises. Was Hannah a drug user of any kind?" Bill asked.

"Not that I know of, but again, it's Hannah, anything's possible," Maureen said, looking out the window.

"I'm sorry," Bill finally said after a few moments of silence.

"For what?

"For the way he treated you. That had to suck."

"It did, believe me. But I learned from it. From then on out, I knew who I could depend on, and trust: myself."

Bill nodded because he didn't know what else to do. For the longest time he wanted Maureen to open up about herself, to give him some clue into Hannah's past, or Maureen's past, but now that she was, it was making him uncomfortable.

Admit it, you want to punch the guy's lights out for hurting Maureen that way.

"Damned right," he said aloud, agreeing with himself.

"Uh-oh, Bill. The first sign of dementia and psychotic behavior is talking to one's self." Maureen smiled.

"No, I was just thinking out loud. Look, what do you say we grab some lunch and then try to put together a time line from Hannah's diary, the phone calls from and to your parents, and her visits around town? It will give us something concrete to work on so we won't feel like we're just circling the wagons."

"Sure, that's fine. I think getting something hot in me would probably do since all I've had for breakfast was coffee," Maureen said.

"Which reminds me." Bill pulled out his phone and dialed.

"Who are you calling?" Maureen asked.

Bill made several calls and after he hung up, Maureen sighed her impatience.

"So, do I get to know who you're on the phone with, or do I get to play twenty questions?" she asked.

"I called around to a few of the other cops I know in various counties around us to see if they had any missing persons."

It didn't take but a moment for Maureen to question why.

"You think it might be a pattern of a killer," she said quietly. Maureen couldn't wrap her brain around the idea that her sister could have fallen victim to a serial killer.

"It's a possibility that I have to look into, Maureen. Not just for your sister, but for others out there who might be in harm's way. Serial killers have patterns and types; they have a specific kind of victim they search for."

Maureen didn't say anything. What was there to say?

"Maureen, we have to check every possible lead. I wouldn't be doing my job if I ignored this lead."

She gave a curt nod, a wispy tangle slipping past her ear and falling towards her face from the sudden movement.

"When will we know?" she asked.

"I'll probably end up hearing back from some of the other counties within the hour."

"And if they have any missing girls who fit Hannah's description?" Maureen asked.

"Not just females, Maureen. Serial killers, though rare, have been known to have both male and female victims."

Ignoring him, she asked again.

"Then we have to coordinate our search efforts with them," Bill stated.

"And if not?"

"Then we keep looking. I gave you my word."

"It's your job," she countered. She traced her finger along the fogged window.

Bill pulled over, steering the SUV off to the shoulder, and turned to look at her.

"I gave you my word because it's who I am," he said. "Yes, it's my job. But I offered my help, and I stand by my word."

Maureen didn't say anything for a long moment. When she turned to look at Bill, she had tears pooling in her eyes.

"I didn't think anything could be worse than Hannah disappear-ing. But," she paused, her voice wavering on the verge of tears, "Thinking about Hannah being the victim of a serial killer is worse."

Maureen started to sob and was lost for words.

He pulled her to him, pressing his lips to the top of her head.

Maureen looked up at him, fresh tears streaming down her cheeks, and that look sparked something inside of Bill.

He leaned down pressing his lips to hers. He breathed in her scent, deepening the kiss. His senses consumed with Maureen, the way her lips tasted, her smell, the feel of her skin.

It'd been a long time since he'd wanted a woman as much as he wanted Maureen Welsh.

He pulled back, staring at her. Her eyes held that mixed look of in-nocence and strength that seemed to deepen the longer he stared at her. "There, now that we got that out of the way, let's get some some-thing to eat."

As Bill pulled the SUV back onto the road, neither of them paid much attention to the dark sedan driving past heading away from Lighthouse Bay.

Chapter 33

THE STATION HOUSE was busy, too busy for Shawn to give a quick look over Bill's desk. The man kept his files under lock and key, and the other officers had fallen in lock step and did the same.

Shawn managed to obtain duplicate keys for all of the desks and filing cabinets but Bill's. He hadn't used the local locksmith; he'd done the work himself.

Bill's attitude for being by the book and accountable only proved to irritate Shawn even more.

They'd gotten into it one day at the office, at the beginning of shift change when Shawn had been twenty minutes late for work.

"If you're early you're on time, if you're on time, you're late, and if you're late, you're unemployable. Remember that the next time you think about wandering into work nearly a half an hour late smelling like you slept on the floor of the Brew Haus."

"What's your problem, man? I was late, no biggie. It's not even tourist season," Shawn balked.

"My problem is that you don't take your job or its responsibilities seriously. We uphold the law, and as such, we owe it to the people who pay our salaries to do the job all the time, not just during tourist season. It's a matter of accountability and integrity, two things which you either have none of or don't know how to use."

Shawn had taken a swing at Bill, but another deputy had stopped it.

It was stupid of Shawn.

He was good forcing his bravado onto local punks and wielding his attitude in a bar fight. But he knew Bill was a Marine, and there was no way Shawn could handle himself and keep his pride.

He went home pending a disciplinary review.

Yet, Bill hadn't fired him. Instead, Bill apologized to Shawn for berating him instead of giving him the tools to become a better officer.

It had only goaded Shawn more.

245

"Smug prick," Shawn muttered.

Edith was busy with the week's payroll and time sheets. Two of the other officers were heading out to court for traffic situations and warrant issues.

Lighthouse Bay didn't see much in the way of crime, but it had its share of locals who refused to pay parking fines, hunters in violation of trespassing, and minor delinquents who used the sidewalk as their own personal freeway.

Most of the locals were friendly. But there were a large number of people, most of them older residents who remembered what the Bay was like before it became a booming tourist town, that didn't like yielding the way for tourists.

Giving up parking spaces for tourists, having to pay to park on the street were constant squabbles that was a part of Shawn's daily grind.

He could time his weekly schedule by the weather and tourist season.

Good weather and tourist season meant citations for drunk and disorderly, missing kids, illegal bonfires on the beach. Winter weather and the off-season brought the regular locals out complaining about the tourists. No matter which way Shawn played his hand, he couldn't win.

What I need to do is get the hell out of this town and move to Vegas.

Shawn had always wanted to move out of the Bay to a town where people could just get lost in the thick of the masses. Anonymity in a sea of people.

Shawn had been thinking about Vegas off and on for the last five years. Since last summer's fight with Bill, the thought of Vegas was near constant.

There was an air of shame that clung to him because of the fight with Bill. No matter how cool and aloof Shawn was, he felt the invisible brand on him just the same.

It was one wrong that Shawn wouldn't be able to cover up or smooth over.

In Vegas, Shawn knew he could start fresh and blend in. He knew the cops out there had to bend the rules a little. The appeal of shows like CSI had only fueled Shawn's desire.

The dry crisp air of the dessert had to beat the smell of stagnant fish that lingered in the Bay every spring.

"Shawn."

Edith was staring at him, a file in her hand.

"What?" he asked casually, pretending to have heard her but choosing to ignore her.

"I said this file is yours. You started it, but never followed up on it," she handed it to him.

Shawn looked it over and flinched. It was his street contact who did the odd vandalism and side jobs for him.

"Yeah, I didn't find any evidence that this kid did any of the allegations that Mrs. Mulder suggested. She probably just scraped the paint of her car in a parking lot or backing out of the garage."

"If you're implying that because she's old she doesn't know how to drive, you can stick it. Mrs. Mulder still has full capacity of her senses, and her car was parallel parked on White Forest. The paint scrapes were on the passenger side door; the side that faces the sidewalk."

Don't start with me, he fumed silently. *I'm not in the mood.*

"Yeah, I'll check into later on," Shawn said, taking the file and tossing it on his desk.

"It's been three months; I think you should check on it as soon as possible. Before she takes it up the commander of the squad."

Edith didn't have to say Bill's name because his title said it all. Whichever way she worded it, she made her point. Do it or someone was tattling to the boss.

Children, Shawn thought.

"And I think you should go back to filing and not tell me how to do my damn job," Shawn snipped.

Edith squared off her shoulders and looked at him.

"I think you best check that attitude of yours because I'll give you the verbal thrashing that your mother never had the sense to. Don't think because you can bully most of the females in this town that you can take that tone with me, Shawn O'Reilly. I'd be able to go back and do my job if you knew how to do yours. Don't even think about apologizing and saving face now, because I wouldn't accept it. But I will allow you the option of not speaking to me the rest of my shift. In the meantime, I'll cool off a little before I mention your attitude to Bill."

Edith walked back to her desk.

Shawn felt the familiar determination to find a way out of the small town. Everyone knew everyone else, and usually, the people in positions of power were there because of whom they knew or whom they were related to.

Shawn didn't like Edith McRainey much, partly because she was the widow of the late Sherriff, and had often voiced her opinion about the ability and quality of work that Shawn would bring to the job as undersheriff. But he also didn't like her because she'd sat on the town council, and public business was a part of her job. Shawn always felt he scrutinized, and he hated it.

I'm a big fish, I need a big pond, he thought.

Shawn grabbed his stack of files and muttered past Edith's desk as he went that he was going to lunch.

CHAPTER 34

MAUREEN'S NERVES FELT frayed. She was overwhelmed. From the situation with her sister, to her mother's fall off the wagon, to Bill's kiss. It was too much.

Normally, her appetite was healthy, but she'd spent the first ten minutes of lunch pushing her food around the plate before Bill finally stilled her hand.

"Maureen," he looked at her.

"Yeah?" she asked, not moving her hand.

"You haven't heard a word I've said, have you?"

"No, not really."

"Well, that's good because I just described in great detail what I'd like to do after I get you alone with a bottle of wine."

He was trying to lighten the mood, trying to take her mind off all the potential horror that might await her at a moment's notice, but it wasn't working too well.

"You're not a wine drinker are you? I don't picture you sitting in some leather armchair with a book and a glass of merlot."

"Oh really," he grinned. "What do you picture me as?"

Maureen thought about it for a moment, then smiled at him.

"I picture you with a beer, maybe a little glass of scotch. Sitting in front of the fireplace, watching the fire."

"Is that an invitation?" he asked lightly, eating the last few spoonfuls of stew.

"What if it was?" Maureen challenged him. "What if I said I want to go back to your place and have the wildest sex imaginable, no strings?"

"Then I'd ask why you're selling yourself short," he said.

"What do you mean selling myself short? In case you didn't know, it's the twenty-first century Cro-Magnon man, and women don't need a knight in shining armor to rescue them anymore."

Bill smiled and pushed his plate aside, and finished his water.

249

"I'm not looking to be anyone's knight in shining anything. Frankly, I'm glad that women of the world are so assertive that they've finally realized that they don't need a man to fix things, especially themselves. But there's a tradeoff to buying into that logic, Maureen. Women who feed into that are giving up on finding themselves someone who completes them, and settling for someone that just meets their needs. It's sad that so many women sell themselves short in the desirability department for the sake of being an independent woman."

The man is smooth, Maureen realized. Half the women in the world would want to tar and feather him, and the other half would be tearing off their clothes and building statues in his honor.

"Maybe. But some of us more level headed girls know from experience that being hopeful in love, usually leads to being hurt."

"If you don't go through the bad ones, how do you appreciate the good ones?"

It was making Maureen nervous, openly discussing relationships between men and women with a man who was blatantly flirting with her, and beyond attractive.

Sure, they had their fun earlier, but she was frustrated and he...well, was being a man. Was he really interested in her that way?

"Let's get back to the point you were trying to make before we traversed to this fun topic," Maureen said.

"I was saying that I'd like to try and find that homeless man I met on the way back from the courthouse. I think I want to ask him some questions about the island. I can't help but feel like we're being pigeonholed into an area of plausibility."

Maureen shrugged and inhaled.

Days had turned into weeks, and in a few days, it would be one month of searching for her sister.

She'd exhausted all of her personal time, her vacation time, and her sick days in Lighthouse Bay searching for her sister.

She'd come up in early November, and it was the middle of December. Maureen couldn't even begin to wrap her brain around go-ing through the holidays without Hannah.

They were no closer to finding Hannah that she'd had been the first day she arrived.

It was growing harder to remember what Hannah looked like, sounded like, without looking at a picture.

"What're you thinking?" Bill asked.

"I was thinking that time is a bitch. It makes us remember the people and moments that are the most horrible, the most wretched. And at the same time, it robs us of the things that we love about them the most."

Bill didn't know what to say because he knew she was right.

"Before we start getting bogged down here, I think we need to look at this from another angle. You're the reporter, you know have the facts, what's your gut telling you to do?"

Maureen thought about it for a moment. "Assuming that I know all the facts, and I've talked to everyone involved, I'd do a landscape of facts, then make my connections to the information I already know. Then I'd start looking where there isn't a connection and see what I could dig up," she said.

"A landscape of facts, you mean like a three-dimensional layout or something?" Bill asked.

Maureen took out a notepad and started making shapes. In the center of the page, she wrote Hannah's name with a box around it. Then she made random circles with the places that Hannah had last been seen at, and the people she'd talked to.

Bill looked at it.

"I think there should be a few more circles on the page."

"What am I missing?"

"To be honest, I don't know. I want to talk to the homeless man if I can still find him. That was a few weeks ago, sometimes vagrants drift on or die. But if we can find him, we can start checking out his story, then possibly the island."

"What island?" Maureen asked, picking up a menu.

"Gull Island. It used to house the old lighthouse, but the Coast Guard moved it in the late fifties because of the increased traffic in the shipping lanes."

"You think Hannah's on the island?"

Maureen hoped he didn't mean buried on the island, but it was a sobering possibility.

"No. No one lives on the island. It's vacant. Some developers wanted to buy it a few years back, but the town council shot them down."

"So what about this homeless man makes you think that there's something that I'm missing?" she asked.

"Nothing. But I believe in signs, Maureen. I was meant to stop that day and grab lunch. I was meant to talk to him. I just don't know what the significance is yet," Bill said.

"So this homeless man's ramblings are a divine sign to the whereabouts of my sister? Come on, Bill, are you spiking your coffee with something because if you are, you should share."

"I'm just thinking out loud," Bill said as Fran appeared at the table.

"In my experience, a man thinking is dangerous," Fran said. "Need a warm up on your coffee?"

"Thanks," Bill said sliding his cup over.

"I need to ask you something, and I need your honesty on this," Maureen looked at him after the waitress left.

Bill nodded but said nothing.

"I'm running out of time. I mean literally, Bill. I've used all my vacation time, my sick time, and my personal time. My editor's a good guy, but he can't keep me on the payroll if I'm not giving him a story. A reporter is only as good as their last story," Maureen sighed, then took a sip of water before continuing.

"I have a couple of weeks left before I'm officially unemployed. I'll have to take a leave of absence. I can pick up freelance work here and there, but it's not going to be as it was. I could start dipping into my 401K, but I don't want to do that. Another option is to ask my parents for money, which —"

"Which you don't want to do," Bill finished for her.

"Exactly. So that leaves me with my only other option."

"Which is?"

"I have to find part time work around here. I'm going to freelance for a while, the benefits of going green, Pure Michigan, the whole she-bang. I'm hoping to sell some of my stories to travel magazines and a few of the local tourist industries here."

"What about family medical leave act?" Bill asked as Fran came over and filled their coffee, then left.

"I'm not sure if I'll qualify. But it just prevents the paper from re-placing me; it doesn't state that it has to pay me for my time off," Maureen said. She held the coffee cup in her hands, absorbing the warmth of the mug, but not drinking.

"I'm sure someone will pick up something. It's coming up on the holiday season. Lots of the small businesses, especially here on Main Street, are always looking to grab some of the easily spent tourist dollars."

"Do you," Maureen hesitates a moment, "do you know of any businesses that might take me up on my services? I mean, I hate like hell to ask you for help, but any leads you might have would be appreciated."

When she looked up at Bill, he was still smiling at her.

"What's so funny?" she asked. Am I blushing?

"Was it really that hard to ask me for a favor?" Bill asked.

"First of all, it wasn't a favor. I don't owe you anything for —"

"Whoa hold on. I never said you owe me anything. I was helping you out because it's the right thing to do."

"Well, don't think that just because of what happened at my cabin that I'm now marked as territory or something," Maureen snapped.

"That's it sugar, make him earn it," Fran teased from across the room.

Maureen's face flushed with embarrassment.

"Thanks, Fran," Bill called back. "She really likes busting my chops."

Maureen kicked him under the table, but Bill kept smiling.

CHAPTER 35

THE BELLS TO the front door of the Tea Caddy chimed a Shawn O'Reilly stepped inside, making Pamela look up from stocking the shelves.

A few customers were browsing, and Pamela played the part of the sweet shop lady.

Only Shawn knew better.

"Why hello, deputy O' Reilly. What can I help you with today?" She smiled with emphasis.

Only those who knew her would've been able to tell that Shawn's unexpected visit had unnerved her.

He, in turn, smiled politely.

"I've been having some trouble sleeping, and I wondered if you'd ever gotten in another shipment of that tea that I bought from you the last time?"

Pamela looked at Shawn, then casually towards the two ladies who were still shopping.

"You know, I'm not sure. It's imported from India — usually too costly for me to get my hands on. And to be honest, we weren't selling enough of it to make the hassle worthwhile. But we have some lovely chamomile and rose hip that I'm sure would better suit your needs," Pamela said. She let her last statement hang there for a moment.

"Really? You don't have any laying around in back somewhere," Shawn pressed.

Shawn could tell Pamela didn't like him discussing the town elder's business so carelessly out in the open.

"Excuse me," one of the women interjected. "Do you have any more tea balls than the ones you have here?" she asked.

Pamela set down the boxes of mint tea she was stocking and went over to the middle-aged woman, steering her in the direction of what she was looking for.

When she turned back around, Shawn was still standing there, waiting patiently.

Shawn knew that she didn't trust him, but he didn't care.

She walked back over to Shawn.

"Would you like to try the orange blossom, deputy? It's very sooth-ing; a mild tea with just a touch of chamomile."

"No thanks," he said. "I was hoping you'd look in the back, see if there's any of the other laying around. I'd sure appreciate it," Shawn said.

Before Pamela could answer, the bell at the counter rang, and she headed to ring up her purchase.

After she started ringing, Shawn breezed past the ladies and waved his hat at Pamela.

"Thanks, Pamela," Shawn said seizing the moment while Pamela was distracted to get what he'd come for. "I'll just grab a box while you're ringing up these ladies."

She could very well cause a scene and come after him, but Shawn knew she'd keep a calm façade in front of customers.

He opened the door to the storeroom and went inside. After a few minutes of searching, he found several boxes of the tea. He picked up a box and headed out.

Pamela said, finished ringing up the sale. "Thank you, ladies. Please come again."

"I've got a call, Pam," Shawn said. "Can I pay you for this later?" He didn't wait for her to respond.

"Of course, deputy. I look forward to seeing you again, soon."

CHAPTER 36

BACK AT BILL'S cabin, Maureen felt the intense attraction, the thrilling pulse of being near someone who was attracted to her, and she to him.

They were too close to each other in the small confines of the cabin, and there was nothing Maureen could do about it.

So, she busied herself sending emails, making phone calls, and trying not to think about Bill.

Or the fact that she wanted him again.

Bill's cabin was definitely too small.

I'm going to jump out of my skin; she thought, craning her neck from side to side. She was starting to fidget, and in a desperate attempt to appear keeping her cool, she would fidget even more.

She tried to focus, making a list of places that Bill had suggested she try. Looking up a few temp agencies, Maureen wondered where she'd be working in the next few weeks, the next month.

"Penny for your thoughts," Bill said, appearing with a mug of hot tea.

Maureen took it, sipping it.

"I don't know how long I'll be here. I can't abandon my life to search for Hannah forever. I mean, at some point..."she trailed off.

"I know. At some point, you have to move on with your life, or else you'll lose yourself in the chaos."

"That's a textbook way to put it. Sounds like maybe you've had a psychology class or two," she sipped at her tea again.

"Several. It's a requirement for a criminology degree."

She nodded, holding the mug for warmth.

"But I've seen this situation before, especially in the Corp. People go missing—it's hard for the family to move on because there's never a sense of closure."

"So, how long do I wait? How long do I give it until I finally leave here, without knowing where Hannah is?"

"That's not for me to decide. That's something you have to figure out on your own."

"What if I never find her? Never find out what happened to her?"

"You might not. As shitty as that seems, sometimes it happens."

Maureen didn't like having her worst suspicions confirmed.

He came over to the couch, sitting next to her.

"Look. I won't pretend to know what you're going through, because I don't. You may leave here never finding Hannah. But grief and death are a part of life. Whatever the outcome of this investigation, I have a feeling you'll be okay."

Maureen lamented on his words, nodding. Reaching out her hand, she traced a finger gently down the side of his face, leaning towards him, her lips skimming his.

His hands reached up, cupping her face tenderly. She broke the kiss, kissing the inside of his wrist before she caught him staring at her.

"Maureen," he said, making her name sound so familiar, his tone casual and welcoming, like he'd been saying it for years. For her, it felt like home.

Seduced by the softness in his voice, she leaned closer, sliding her arms around his neck, pulling him towards her and back against the couch, closing the distance between them.

He took his time, holding her body to his, a contrast between her willowy limbs and his hard muscles. He stopped kissing her, lifting his head to smile down at her, brushing away a loose strand of hair. Her robe in front had come loose, the slit growing deeper as her chest rose. His eyes caught a flash of turquoise, and he ran a calloused finger along the edge of the robe, soliciting a faint moan from her parted lips to peek at what lay underneath.

She arched her back, the cotton robe sliding open just enough for Bill to see the lace at the top of her spaghetti strap nightie. Leaning down, he let his lips and tongue trace where his finger had been, feeling her arch against him as her hands threaded through his hair, pulling at him, silently begging for more.

He peeled her robe off, exposing her bare shoulders, feeling her shudder as the cool wind caressed her skin, her nipples straining against the thin cotton fabric.

She started tugging at his shirt, pulling it free from his jeans, and reaching for his belt before his hand stopped her.

"What," she looked at him, blue eyes tenderly looking at him, reminding him of a lost puppy who just needed to be sheltered and loved.

Love.

That word should have scared the hell out of him.

"Maybe we should slow it down a bit, take things slower than we did last time. I don't want to take advantage of you," he said, his thumb caressing her forehead.

"You aren't taking advantage of anything. I want this. But, if you think the other night was a mistake — "

He could feel her body stiffen, and he kissed her, pressing his lips gently against hers until she relaxed in his arms once again.

"I never said that. I just think we should take it slower this time. I don't want to take advantage of you, under the circumstances. You don't deserve that."

She smiled at him. "What do I deserve, then?"

Bill didn't answer her. He just kissed her again, long, deep, and slow. She pulled at his shirt, sliding it off his shoulders.

His hand caressed her thighs, sliding upwards, teasing and enticing her. She arched against him, pressing her body against his. Head swimming, she wanted him to kiss every part of her, strip her clothes and forget, at least for the moment, the reason they were brought together.

Bill groaned when her hands managed to undo his belt and slide past the waistband of his jeans, fingertips grazing and inching their way lower.

"Bill," she gasped, breaking the magic between them long enough for her to look at him.

He stood, scooping her up and walking towards the bedroom, placing her in the center of the bed. The light from the sun cast the room in amber gold light, creating an immediate softness. Time crawled as he slowly undressed her before shedding his jeans and boxers until he too was finally naked. Kneeling at the foot of the bed, he started planting soft kisses, pressing firmer and lingering longer the further he traveled up her body.

Leaning over her, he watched her face as his fingers stroked her, caressing the slick folds until he slid one, then another finger inside her. Arching against him, she leaned up to kiss her way along his jaw.

Looking up at him, face flushed, she smiled.

She leaned over, grabbing the last condom from the bedside table. Maureen watched his face as her fingers encircled him, sheathing him before she wrapped her legs around him. He leaned up and over her, she savored the way his body felt as he drove into her.

Afterward, Maureen lay with her head in the crook of his chest, his arm wrapped around her shoulder. But she was restless.

"What's wrong?"

"I keep thinking we're missing a piece of the puzzle and its starring straight at us."

"How so?"

"I don't know. I can't put my finger on it. This homeless guy you mentioned. How do we go about finding him?" Maureen asked.

"I figure we can—"

Bill stopped mid-sentence.

He craned his next to hear, but Maureen had already heard it.

Thwack. Thwack. Thwack.

"Oh my God, Bill."

It came out as a whisper. Maureen stopped, sure that her heart beat was echoing off the cabin walls.

Bill leaned over to the bedside table and picked up his gun.

He motioned for her to get behind him. He eased his way towards the front door, checking the alarm.

The panel assured Bill that the system was armed.

Thwack. Thwack.

A whistling rush swept through the open chimney and inside the cabin, filling the cabin with a sooty haze.

Maureen started coughing, covering her mouth with her hand.

Bill ran over, pulling the damper closed, coughing as well.

He grabbed Maureen's hand and pulled her into the bedroom, closing the door behind him.

Maureen yanked the comforter off the bed and jammed it under the space of the door, hoping to keep out some of the hazy smell of the settled fireplace.

"It's trying to draw us outside," Bill said, checking the window.

"What do you mean, it's trying to draw us outside?" Maureen asked.

"Animals have predatory instincts when they hunt. It's like the animals in the wild; they're going to flush out their prey."

Prey.

The sound of the word stopped Maureen cold.

Bill looked out the window and motioned for Maureen.

"Look at this," Bill said, his voice barely above a whisper.

Maureen went over to the window and followed Bill's line of vision to the treetops outside. In the near distance, above the tree line, the darkened shadow of an outstretched wingspan covered the landscape.

For the first time, Maureen and Bill had a glimpse of what was causing the loud thwacking outside.

The backside of the creature was a dark greenish gray, blending easily into the background of the trees that Maureen had to focus so as not to lose sight of it. In the dim light of the setting sun, she thought it was almost an illusion.

A trick of the light, she thought.

The shadow it cast was impressive, almost eight feet. Maureen wasn't sure if she was seeing the creature in its entirety, or if her mind was struggling to rationalize the image into something her brain would recognize.

It didn't have legs, at least not in the sense that most people thought of. They were leg like, but shorter in length. From what Maureen could tell, it looked like the leg had only one section as if ending at the knee.

Its body was covered in the same grayish green coloring as its back and wings, but the underbelly appeared to be lighter in color.

Its head was oval shaped, not quite the roundness of a human's, but not quite the symmetrical oblong of a bird.

Bill listened and leaned in to whisper to Maureen.

"Hear that?" Bill asked. She had to strain to hear him.

"Hear what?" Maureen asked.

"Exactly. No other animals, no birds."

Maureen listened to find his observation correct.

The woods were quiet.

Except for the creature circling the tree line.

Bill went over to the wall panel by the bedroom door and turned off the alarm.

He went over to the window, lowered it, and fired off a warning shot.

The creature screeched, its massive wings fanning the tree line before disappearing.

"We should follow it," Maureen said.

"No. We need to study it first. We don't know where it's going. A good predator would never lead its enemy back to its home. We could be walking into more of those things," Bill said.

"Well, at least we know they aren't nocturnal," Maureen sighed, rubbing her neck as the bottled tension ebbed.

"Not necessarily. It's almost sunset. Bats come out right at dusk. Owls are nocturnal."

"There is no way that thing was an owl, Bill."

"I don't know what it was. Until I do, I'm treating it like I would any evasive threat: with precaution."

Bill removed the bedspread and opened the door, fanning his gun. Most of the haze from the fireplace still hung heavy in the air, but it was breathable.

He opened the windows, airing out the cabin.

Maureen stood in the doorway of the bedroom, looking around.

"What's the matter?" Bill asked.

"I—don't feel very safe here anymore," Maureen confessed. *Do not go all girlie now*, she chided herself.

"Well, you are. The house is secure. I'm here, we're armed. Even if it turns out to be something from a Predator movie, it's still going to be hasta la vista, baby," he smiled turning on the ceiling fan.

"That was from Terminator, not Predator."

"Yeah, but it got you to smile," he said and came back to the bedroom doorway and pulled her into the living room.

"We need to recreate everything that happened, point by point up until just now," Bill stated, handing her a legal pad and a pen.

"Why?" Maureen asked.

"Because something around this cabin was its trigger. I don't think it was hunting game and just came upon the cabin. An animal that size is going to need substantial meat to sustain itself. Deer, bear, a wolf."

"How do you know it's carnivorous?"

"Maureen, there is no way that thing is a herbivore. I'll bet—"

But Bill stopped short.

"You bet what?" Maureen asked.

"Nothing, I'm tired and I'm reaching. It's fiction, science fiction at best."

"Some of the best ideas in modern technology came from science fiction. Cell phones were born out of an idea from Star Trek, so try me," she said, sitting on the couch.

"The bones, the ones discovered on the beach. What if this thing ate someone? Now it has a taste for human flesh, God knows we are easier to hunt than most animals, and it's adapted to its environment."

"Okay, assuming what you think is true, animals in the wild usually only change their eating habits and patterns when something catastrophic happens to their own habitat. It's either adapt or die."

Bill looked at her for a moment, running a hand through his hair.

"I'm going to put on some coffee. I think it's going to be a long night."

Maureen sat on the couch, retracing her movements from the evening, Bill's words echoing in her subconscious.

We are easier to hunt than animals.

CHAPTER 37

DESPITE STAYING UP late cleaning the cabin and making a time-line of events, Bill was up early. Whether it was his military background, or his inability to sleep knowing that something strange lurked outside, Bill was unsure.

By the time Maureen appeared from the bedroom, her auburn hair askew, Bill was on his third cup of coffee. He leaned against the kitchen counter, drinking his coffee amidst the splayed papers he'd help create the night before.

"You are way too organized for this early in the morning," she said, walking towards the coffee pot.

"Sorry, we're out of coffee," Bill said.

Maureen blinked at him, then at the pot, grabbing his cup from the counter.

"No, you're out of coffee. I still have half a cup," she said.

Bill grinned and went to the cupboard, pouring her a full cup and retrieving his own.

"I was only joking," he said, handing her a fresh mug.

"I knew you were joking, I just wanted you to wait on me hand and foot," Maureen said.

She looks good in the morning, Bill thought.

Maureen sat across from him, looking at the timeline they'd made the previous night.

"So, what's the plan for today? More history museums and science professor buddies?"

"No. I've already made some inquiries in some of the state data-bases, and I have a few calls out to some local law enforcement colleagues I know in other counties. I also want to track down that homeless guy today, ask him a few more questions."

263

"What kind of inquiries?" Maureen asked, reaching for a bagel atop the toaster oven.

"Your missing sister can't be the first person in Lighthouse Bay to ever go missing. She can't be the first person to have gone missing under mysterious circumstances. I'm trying to connect the dots, but I feel like I'm spinning my wheels. Half the time I feel like I don't have all the facts, and the other times I feel like the evidence is staring me directly in the face."

"Feeling helpless sucks, doesn't it?" Maureen commented.

"I was thinking this morning—"

"Good. I encourage thinking on a daily basis, Bill." Maureen smiled, taking a bite of her bagel but still listening to Bill.

"I was thinking," he started again, "that there might be a pattern to the disappearances. If we can link your sister's disappearance to any other suspicious disappearances or deaths, we might be able to ascertain a pattern and find your sister."

"Thank you," Maureen said quietly.

"I told you, you don't have to thank me for doing my job. I made a promise, and it's one that I intend to keep," Bill said, sipping his coffee.

"Not that. I mean about not referring to Hannah in the past tense. For assuming that she's still alive."

Bill didn't know what to say, so he didn't say anything. Changing the subject and beating a retreat to safer conversation seemed like the only appropriate course of action.

"I want to find this homeless guy, ask him some questions."

"Do you think that he could be linked to Hannah's disappearance?"

"I don't know. I spent all of about five minutes talking to him so I couldn't really get a sense of whether or not he was telling the truth. But I think he knows something that might be valuable in locating Hannah," Bill said.

"So, when do we leave?" asked Maureen. "Don't even think about leaving me here while you're out playing cops and robbers."

"No, I actually planned on you doing a ride along. Cops have a way of making people nervous just by their mere presence. I figure the reporter in you would be better at making him relax, and find out what we need to know without spooking him."

"Oh," she replied, staring into her coffee. "Well, since you asked nicely, I guess I could free up my schedule."

Maureen went to her bag on the coffee table and retrieved her cell phone.

"I still have no signal," Maureen said. "I mean, I like the remote cabin feel, but I'd be lying if I said I wouldn't feel a little more secure having the means to connect to civilization at the touch of a button."

Bill checked his cell phone.

"Mine too. We are miles from the nearest tower, and most of the places up here have satellite hookup for cable. It usually picks up a signal once we get about a half mile onto the main road heading to town. Besides, I think it did you good not to have to deal with your mother for a night. You needed the rest," he said.

"You're probably right. The last thing I need to be doing is sitting on the phone with her, giving her another update on the same information that I did the day before."

"You need to be able to take a step back and make sure you're getting the bigger picture of things. If you stay too focused on the tiny details of Hannah's disappearance, you may miss something that may be a clue," Bill commented.

"How are you going to get off work today, I mean, I didn't know that Sheriff's got personal time to just go investigate things without keeping the home fires burning," Maureen said checking the contents of her bag.

"That's the beauty of being the Sheriff in charge; delegation is an expected part of my daily job duties, just like investigation. And believe me, Maureen," he said, walking past her to grab her coat and hold it open while she slipped her arms inside, his breath at the back of her neck, "I have no trouble keeping the fire going at home."

Maureen smiled and blushed a little.

Her pulsed quickened slightly like it was skipping along her veins with Bill's blatant innuendo.

The feel of his warm breath on her neck, feeling him close behind her made her involuntarily shiver as she turned and grabbed her bag.

"I just don't want to get burned," she said before heading out the door.

CHAPTER 38

PAMELA WAITED UNTIL the last of the customers left the Tea Caddy and put the closed sign on the door. Locking it, she went to the register, removed the till, and went upstairs to the small attic office. She counted the contents of it, put the excess cash in the safe, made up a fresh till and went back downstairs to the register.

She was gathering the day's sales receipts and holiday inventory list from her suppliers when she heard a faint tapping at the front door.

Gasping in surprise, she dropped the day's totals and leaned over the counter to look at the door.

Sighing briefly, she went to the door and opened it.

"You scared the hell out of me," she said opening the door.

"You said we had problems and I needed to come down and handle it. I'm here to handle it, because I love taking orders from you, Pammie."

She never liked him. Not even when she was having an affair with him. But there was something about his cocky smugness that got under her nerves, made her want to put him in his place.

"Don't call me Pammie. I never like it when we were sleeping together, and I sure as I hell don't like it now."

Pamela locked the door and motioned for him to follow her. Grabbing the pile of loose receipts and the daily totals she took them upstairs to the attic office.

Once behind the large spans of her polished pine antique desk, she felt a little more in control.

"Shawn came to visit me today," she said.

"Well, holy sakes alive, alert the national freakin' guard."

"Shut up, Dwight. He marched into the back room and helped himself to the special reserve blend," Pamela commented.

266

Ten minutes later, after she related the whole story to Mayor Carlisle, he was leaning back in the club chair, holding his chin in his hand.

"I just worry Shawn is becoming careless. He thinks he's getting out by doing this, and erasing his gambling debts. When he discovers it's all a setup, and they were framing him it could come back to bite us," Pamela lamented.

"You were never worried before now," the Mayor replied.

"We never had this many people involved before now. Christ, Dwight. You should have sold the island to that chemical company who wanted to buy it for its research laboratory and been done with it."

"Are you forgetting what lies on that island, Pamela?"

"I know as well as anybody what's on that island. I also checked out that chemical company. It's a fake. Their mother corporation had several federal violations for illegal dumping and wildlife endangerment. They would have destroyed everything on that rock and no one would have been the wiser."

"But the consequences of the biohazards—"he began.

"Would have been small once the feds were tipped off, and after the natural wildlife was depleted and before they could do any serious damage. It would have been nice, neat little package," Pamela threw her pen down.

"We can't worry about that now. I'll have a talk with Shawn. Make him see the light again," the Mayor said as he stood.

"See that you do," Pamela said, standing as well.

"Oh, and see that your little punk grandson stops keying cars. A file came across Shawn's desk; a complaint. If that little punk wants to keep earning his lemonade money he better keep his nose clean."

She'd have to speak to her grandson about keeping out of trouble. He thought he was just an undercover errand boy, paid under the table to do some simple police assistance work since the station was too busy to handle it themselves.

She walked the Mayor downstairs, seeing him out, and relocked the door before heading back upstairs.

The shop was her life. She built it up from the little bakery that had been her mother-in-law's when she married Charlie.

Glancing over at the silver frame, she smiled sadly; reaching out a finger to trace along the dramatic features of Charlie's smiling face.

He'd been gone about six years, but it felt like a lifetime ago.

Things were less complicated when Charlie was alive because he took care of their interest in the business of Gull Island.

Now that burden went to Pamela, and eventually, it'd be left to her son and her grandson.

Some families bequeath wealth and property to future generations. Her's passed on secrets and murder.

Chapter 39

SHAWN GRABBED A burger and ate it in the car, feeling an immense satisfaction in knowing that it rubbed Bill the wrong way. It's the one thing that the rest of the deputies were adamant about, being able to eat in the cars while on duty.

Bill suggested about eating at one of the local restaurants because it not only gave the deputies a chance to mingle with the locals but also made their presence known to the tourists.

In the end, the deputies agreed.

Staring at the file on the seat put a damper on his mood.

Chucky Butler was a good kid to have to do his dirty work, but he was going to have to bite the bullet and apologize to Mrs. Mulder for the damage to her car. If the kid fessed up and came clean, he could close out the report, and then remove it after a few months. No paper trail and everyone involved was happy.

Finishing his burger and tossing the wrapper on the floor he started his car, heading off Main onto Fifth Street before he picked up his collar walkie and radioed to the station that he was going on patrol. He drove towards Piedmont Park, knowing he'd find little Chucky Butler there smoking behind the dumpster with the rest of his degenerate friends.

Its looming shadow grew, circling the cabin. Its senses could smell the faint hints of the lemon and citrus wafting through the air. Even though the tin was well inside the cabin.

Its mouth began to salivate as it senses infused with the scent, engaging the memory of previous kills. Its last prey had satiated the hunger, but it was growing late in the season, and the familiar pangs gnawed around in its belly with a vengeance.

Circling the cabin and swooping lower, it returned the darkened tree lines to lay in wait.

CHAPTER 40

WHEN HER PHONE rang, Maureen looked at the caller ID, instantly regretting it.

Bill knew from her hesitation that it was her mother.

"Hello, mom," Maureen answered, followed by a long pause of silence.

She closed her eyes, her breathing controlled through short inhales.

"No mom, I know. But they're doing all that they can, and I'm —"

More silence before Maureen snapped her phone closed.

"Your mother," Bill commented.

"Like you had to ask, and for the record she plans on writing a stern letter to your supervisor about why you aren't lifting a finger to find her daughter," Maureen said.

"Well, it's not the first time I've had a victim's family get upset with me and threaten to call my superiors, I don't think it's going to be my last. I'll get her number from you and start giving her personal updates myself."

"What are you going to tell her that I haven't already?" she asked.

"Sometimes hearing the news coming from an authority figure makes a person feel like something's getting done. It's my fault anyway for not contacting her on a more regular basis in the first place," Bill said, turning the police cruiser onto West Main.

"Bill, please don't tell her that I'm staying at your cabin it would just really," she paused, "complicate things for you."

"For me? Don't you mean for you?" he asked, pulling into the parking lot for Ida's Café.

"I mean my mother will lynch you herself, accuse you of taking advantage of one daughter while failing to look for her other, she will probably create a huge scene with your boss and one way or another you'll be selling oranges by the freeway off-ramp," she said, looking down. "My mother can be quite embarrassing."

"Most parents are when it comes to the well-being of her children. Don't worry, I'll phone her from the station, and ask Edith to make a courtesy call once and a while; she has a way with people," Bill said.

Maureen made a move to open her door, but he stopped her.

"This is going to be a to-go order. We have a lot of driving to do, and not a whole lot of time to get it done."

Bill closed the door and was walking in front of the car when Maureen rolled the window down.

"Don't you want to know what I want," she shouted from the open window.

"I know what you want, but breakfast before dessert," Bill grinned opening the door to Ida's Café.

Maureen rolled up her window, wondering if Bill making good on his promise was a good thing.

In the car, Bill and Maureen spent the first few minutes eating in silence. She didn't know what to say, afraid that any conversation she started was going to lead to more innuendos.

"So where're we going?" she finally asked between mouthfuls of breakfast sandwich and coffee.

"First, we're heading out of Shoshanee County towards New Winston."

Maureen blinked and put her breakfast sandwich down, staring at Bill.

He caught her look and smiled.

"Relax, we aren't going to the courthouse. Give me some credit, Maureen. Lighthouse Bay is inside Shoshanee County, and New Winston has the gas station that I ran into that homeless guy."

"Do you think he's still around the gas station, after all this time?"

"I hope so. Old transients don't stray too far from their safety zone. I'm guessing either he has a place to come in from the cold, or he frequents a shelter in town. I just want to talk to him. Well, I want you to talk to him. He mentioned he worked on the lighthouse at the Big Island, so maybe you could be all smiling attentive journalist and find out what he knows."

"What are you going as, my assistant?" She asked.

Though Bill wasn't in uniform, it was hard for a man of his physical features not to command respect. Clad in a black turtleneck and blue jeans, down jacket, he still had the look of authority to him.

The man can dress, she thought to herself.

"Well, I like to play things safe, we should be honest. He might recognize you, civilian clothing or not. I'll still be the reporter, but you introduce me to him and we'll use the guise of the restoration of the lighthouse as a means to establish trust."

"Sounds good," he nodded, finishing his apple.

"How sane do you think he is?" Maureen asked, depositing all the trash into the plastic bag.

"He seemed pretty lucid to me when I talked to him. Then again, it was only for a few moments and I wasn't paying close attention. If he was on a bender or on something else, I couldn't tell." He slowed down then turned left toward New Winston.

"Then how are we going to check out if what he tells us the truth or not?" Maureen asked, sipping her coffee.

"Luckily there's a library branch near here, and what we can't find, we can get from Victoria."

Bill pulled into the gas station where he'd seen the homeless man weeks earlier.

They got out, Bill went inside and Maureen looked around, getting a feel for the town. A lot of the towns in northern Michigan were like this. Sparsely populated on the outskirts with their social mecca nestled in town. Most usually consisted of gas stations, a few fast food restaurants, and a couple mega marts with a spattering of mom and pop businesses that had been there long before the mega retailers moved in.

Bill came back out, hands in his coat pocket. It was chilly and windy, but Maureen thought the chilled air felt good.

"He comes here regularly, looking for spare bottles in the trash. The owner inside says she lets him come once a week and break down boxes in exchange for cash and a free meal," Bill said.

"So where does that leave us?" Maureen asked as they headed back to the truck.

"It means we have to find his usual hangouts."

"Did the owner know his name, where he might go?" she asked as they pulled onto the main road.

"His name is Charlie, and hangs out near the Silver Dollar on Maple she said."

Maureen looked around what appeared to be the main thorough-fare, then took her notebook out of her bag and began to write.

"What are you writing?" Bill asked, keeping an eye out for Maple.

"I'm making a list of things to look into," she said, writing.

"Like?" he prodded, making a left onto Maple and searching for the Silver Dollar.

"Just keeping track of the random information as it comes to us. I mean, you never know when some small bit of information is going to become relevant," Maureen stated.

"You're right. I just hope we can locate him. I can't take tomorrow off; court appointments," Bill commented, spotting the Silver Dollar on the right-hand side of the road.

They pulled into the parking lot, and Maureen gave Bill a look of apprehension.

"Please tell me this is a bar, not a strip joint," she demanded.

"I have no idea," Bill said. "You want me to go in and see if Charlie's around, then get him to come out here?"

Maureen thought about it for a moment.

"No. If he's inside, we might have better luck if he was in his own surroundings. Plus, we could always smooth things over by buying him a drink," she said.

"Good thinking, Hutch." Bill smiled, turned off the truck and facing her. "Look, I want you to know, I made some calls today. A couple to the local ranger stations and the DNR offices in the county. Another one to Hank at the Seed and Feed to see if Hannah showed up there. I got in contact with Whyatt Huxley. He's been stationed in Germany for the last eighteen months. Our office verified it with his commander."

Maureen nodded, part of her glad to know that he hadn't been involved in her sister's disappearance, but another part of her upset that another potential lead had run cold.

"If he's not here, we can try —" Bill began, but he didn't have to finish his sentence because the black vinyl door of the Silver Dollar opened, and Charlie staggered out into the cold.

CHAPTER 41

BILL WANDERED OVER to Charlie and nodded.

"Hey Charlie, remember me?" Bill asked, offering his hand.

Charlie looked up from the pavement, his eyes fixating as if to re-member.

"I...think so," he paused. "Yeah, you were the guy with the sand-wich," he nodded. "I remember now."

"Yeah that was me all right. I had so many calls that day after I saw you I didn't end up getting home until about midnight."

Charlie didn't say anything but looked from Bill to Maureen.

"This your wife?" he asked. His hands in his pockets.

"No, she's a friend of mine," Bill said. "Maureen this is Charlie; Charlie, Maureen Welsh. She's writing a book about the lighthouses of Michigan, and she's having trouble locating research and infor-mation on Gull Island. I know you helped the Coast Guard, and I thought—"

"Stay away from that island, missy. Nothing out there is worth put-ting into a book," Charlie commented and started walking away.

"You're right. I was just interested in the lighthouse itself, not the is-land. The book I'm writing is about lighthouses-the different styles and types of lenses they used. It's more like a nautical biography pay-ing tribute to the shores of the Great Lakes."

Charlie didn't say anything, but he did stop.

"Yeah so. What do you want from me?" he asked cautiously.

"When Bill told me you were in charge of the crew who removed the lens from the lighthouse I insisted I had to meet you. Of course, since this book is research for the company I work for, there is a con-sulting fee involved," she said.

"A fee, you say?" he asked. "How much are we talking about for consulting with the likes of me?" he asked, pulling his thin jacket tighter around him.

275

"It's hourly," Maureen said, amazed in her ability to come up with believable lies without missing a beat. "Its industry standard; fifty an hour. I should only need a few hours of your time, maybe over lunch," she said, reaching into her bag and pulling out a business card.

Charlie held the card in his dirty hand, then looked back at Maureen and Bill.

Reel him in Maureen, she urged herself. *You almost got him.*

"It would mean a lot to me. See, this is my first major assignment and if I don't get this one right, I won't be offered anymore," Maureen confessed.

Playing the helpless female worked.

"Well, I'd hate to see a nice, pretty girl like you lose your job. What's a few hours anyway; it's not like I got to get back to my office anytime soon," he said.

Maureen smiled, extending her hand.

"It's a pleasure to meet you. Now, what do you say we go and grab some lunch while you tell me about the lighthouse, preferably some-place where I can grab a beer," Maureen said.

"You paying?" Charlie asked.

"My company is. Lunches are part of my paid expenses," she said.

Charlie wandered over to Bill's truck and climbed in the front seat.

"Guess I'm the designated driver," Bill said while Maureen climbed in back.

They pulled out onto Maple, sitting at the light behind a black Lincoln Navigator.

They picked a small family restaurant for lunch. There wasn't much of a lunch crowd, and being a weekday there wasn't many families inside.

After ordering, Charlie spent ten minutes in the bathroom, finally emerging with clean hands and face, his hair wet and slicked back.

While he was in the bathroom, Bill went to the front and talked to the manager, flashing his badge. He didn't want any trouble for bring-ing Charlie inside. They shook hands and Maureen marveled the way Bill had with people.

When Charlie came back to the table, their orders were waiting. He dug in, eating heartily for a few minutes before flagging down the waitress for a fresh cup of coffee.

"So what do you want to know about the lighthouse, missy?" he asked between mouthfuls of food.

"Well, I know there was a lighthouse on Gull Island up until the late fifties or early sixties. The Coast Guard built the breaker on Lighthouse Bay, moving the lighthouse there. What can you tell me about the lens or the lighthouse in general?" she asked, taking out her notepad and writing.

Bill sat back, eating his meal and watching the conversation enfold between the two. He wanted to stay out the conversation as much as possible, but still paid close enough attention to any details that Charlie could provide.

He had a hunch, and Bill was usually never wrong about his hunches.

"Well now let me think," Charlie said, sipping his coffee. "Well, we moved the lighthouse back in sixty-three or sixty-four. It took us all spring and summer to move the lighthouse and the lens. The water about the island is nothing to be messing with, mind you. There were lots of times I heard about the Coast Guard having to help out stranded boaters who careened onto the island. A couple kids drowned out there the summer after we moved the house and lens."

"That's sad," Maureen commented. "Tell me, was the lighthouse cylindrical, conical, or more like a schoolhouse?" she asked.

"Oh, if I remember the lighthouse where they kept the light was long and narrow," Charlie said.

"So it was cylindrical," Maureen confirmed.

"Yeah. But there was a ramp to the main keeper's quarters, and his home. Made of iron. These huge Y-shaped buttresses that lined the walkway, and the steel handrails that were icy cold, even in the summer."

Maureen wrote, casting a quick glance to Bill.

"Tell me about the lighthouse keeper's quarters," Maureen urged.

"Well, it looked like a little white school house, save for the roof. It was sort of smashed down in front, like a Dutch house," Charlie said, sipping his coffee and he finished his meatloaf.

"Was it a single story? Did it have any unique features to it?" she asked.

"It was a pretty little house out on the island. Naught but a soul to bother you, and the view from the widow's walk beats any of those fancy resorts they got over near Ellington."

Bill smiled to himself, certain that Charlie had for the moment, full capacity of his senses.

"It was two stories and was made of limestone, same as the tower. Had lots of ivy and the like, climbing up one full side of the house. We only had access by boat since it was out about a mile or so offshore, and it was a pain let me tell you. The town was in a pickle, that's for sure," Charlie said, scraping at his now empty plate.

Bill motioned to the waitress and pointed to Charlie's plate. A few moments later, she returned with another order of meatloaf, potatoes, and carrots.

"Eat up while it's hot, Charlie," Maureen said, eating her own meal.

"Well, can't say the last time I've had this much hot food at my disposal, so I think I'll take your advice," he said. "Now, where were we? Oh, yeah. The town was in a bind you see. A couple of years before, they spent a lot of money putting in those new sandy beaches in the state park. Brand new lighthouse and the Bay renamed Lighthouse Bay, but they ran out of money and couldn't afford a new lens. It was cheaper, in the long run, to use what funds they'd allocated towards the purchase of a new lens and retrieve the old one."

"Why was it vacant, Charlie? And when, do you remember?" she asked.

"I don't know why it was vacant; you'd have to ask the Coast Guard that one. It was abandoned sometime after the war, maybe in forty-six or forty-seven. It wasn't even that old to begin with, if memory serves," he said, taking another healthy bite of meatloaf.

Maureen stole a glance at Bill.

"I remember that island like it was yesterday; hard to forget things that leave a man scarred," Charlie said, taking a long sip of his coffee.

As Maureen wrote, Bill looked around. Only a few more people had wandered into the restaurant, and none seemed to pay any attention to Charlie.

"Why, because you weren't used to heavy construction like that?" Maureen asked, trying to find a delicate way to pry into his past.

"No. We lost a few men moving that lens and the lighthouse. Six in fact."

"Oh Charlie, I'm so sorry," Maureen said, putting her pen down to place a hand on his forearm.

The gesture seemed to warm Charlie, whose eyes glistened over for a moment.

"You're not really doing an article on the lighthouse, are you missy?" he asked, his voice dropping to a low sigh.

Maureen hesitated but went with her gut.

"No, I'm not. I am a reporter, though. I'm looking for my sister, who lives along the beach in Ellington. She's missing, and no one knows where she is," Maureen said.

"How long," Charlie managed to ask after a few moments.

"A little over six weeks," Maureen managed.

"It's too late then," Charlie sighed, putting his fork down.

"What do you mean it's too late?" Bill asked and leaned forward.

He caught the nervous, frozen facade that seemed etched on Maureen's face.

"They've done got her, and got her good. You won't find anything; she's gone missy. I'm sorry for it too," Charlie said, stabbing at his meatloaf, but not eating.

"Who has her, Charlie? And how...how do you know it's too late," Maureen finally managed to ask.

"Because those things don't play with their meals, missy. With them its feast or famine, and once they find food, they feed with a nasty ferocity," Charlie uttered.

Maureen dropped her pen, her mouth agape.

"Charlie, we should talk about this somewhere—"Bill started.

"No. I've been carrying it inside me for a lot years now. I think I should tell someone about it, about them out there. That way, you can take up the torch when I'm gone," Charlie said, holding his coffee mug with both hands. "Maybe you can even stop them."

CHAPTER 42

"I'LL STOP THEM, Charlie. You just have to tell me who they are. I need a name, or where they live," Bill said, sitting upright in his chair, taking a much more keen interest in the conversation.

"They live out on the island," Charlie said, taking a small bite of meatloaf and potatoes. Either his appetite had satiated, or he'd lost it among the menagerie of bad recollections of his past.

"Who?" Bill asked, sipping his coffee doing this best to hold back the eager need to find a name, secure a warrant, and find Hannah.

"I don't know what folks call them. One of the men from our crew, John Littlepaw, he called them the baykok."

Maureen wrote and started flipping through the pages of her notebook, making more details.

"What happened?" Bill asked.

Charlie sighed, staring into his coffee.

"I don't know much about Gull Island. I knew there was a lighthouse there. As I said, it wasn't that old. They put in the new house and lens in forty-one or forty-two. In the middle of the war, as a way to protect the Great Lakes from foreign invasion. It was a beauty too. Nice whitewashed stone and concrete. They used the sand right from the beach, and it was a pretty thing to look at because it had that Lake Superior agate in it. Little flashes of red against the white stone. It looked more like a summer cottage than a lighthouse keeper's quarters."

Maureen was still taking notes, and had spread her them into two piles. Bill decided to take over the questioning.

"Did you help build the lighthouse too?" Bill asked.

"Oh no. It was built long before me. Built right on top of the remains of an even older lighthouse. Made some of the men on the crew squeamish, since the last lighthouse was cursed and all," Charlie said, picking at the cherry pie.

"Cursed? Like somebody put a curse on the lighthouse?" Bill asked.

"No. Gull Island is a cursed, wretched place. I know, I spent six years in the merchant marines, stationed near Marquette. Gull Island used to be a traffic route before the Depression. Then the shipping channel was moved eleven miles down the coast past Elgin and the lighthouse that had been there since the mid eighteen hundred's fell into disrepair. The old building wasn't made of concrete like the one that currently rots on the island is," Charlie said.

"What was it made of?" Bill asked, too intrigued to finish his meal.

"Limestone blocks and mortar is my guess. Limestone holds up fine, but the mortar can't hold up against the constant damp and cold of Lake Superior. It's no wonder that by the time the Coast Guard got around to building a new lighthouse on the island during the war that they had to build it from scratch. The elements got hold of the first one and she just crumpled into the lake," he said, taking another bite of pie.

"Of course, we heard that the original cornerstone of the first building was used as the last piece in the new lighthouse, but it's a rumor we heard. We heard lots of things about Gull Island back then," Charlie said, looking around. He leaned closer to Maureen and Bill. "Not like now. No one talks about what happened out there. No one wants to remember."

"Remember what?" Maureen finally asked, lifting her face from her notes.

"That people died out there. Have been dying out there for almost a hundred years, and no one wants to say or do nothing about it," Charlie shook his head in disgust.

Maureen raised an eyebrow, glancing at Bill.

"Why do you think the place is haunted?" Maureen asked.

"Because back in thirty-two, the Gales of November came early, and the banshee of Gitche Gumee came calling hard that winter," Charlie said, draining his coffee cup, and flagging down the waitress who came over and refilled his cup, then left the coffee carafe on the table.

Bill took a deep breath and mulled over what Charlie said. But the more he talked about things on the island, the banshee of the Big Lake, he wasn't sure that Charlie was a credible witness of anything.

"The same Gitche Gumee in the Gordon Lightfoot song? So you think a witch is responsible?" Maureen asked gently.

"No, the Fitz went down, God bless their souls, in a bad storm. The Native Americans have their legends. One of them is of a sea witch who screams her fury to make the gale force winds, and unleashes her

281

anger and makes the waters of the Great Lakes treacherous in winter," Charlie replied, sipping his coffee.

"John Littlepaw talked about them all the time. We were shared an eight by ten bunk space for three years. Said that year, the banshee of the Big Lake came calling."

Back in those days, the lighthouse keepers operated the light by hand, nothing was automated. But the light on Gull Island didn't need manning in the winter since none of the ships traveled the lakes like they do now."

"So, what happened?" Bill asked, pouring himself another cup of coffee.

"The lighthouse keeper, a widower, and his son got trapped in the ice and snow that came early that October. Couldn't get the iron door open to get out. Coast Guard found them the next spring, their bodies just inside the causeway. Windows all broken, and their...remains, were gnawed upon."

"Jesus," Maureen said, taking a long sip of her coffee.

"The old place fell into disrepair, and eventually fell into the lake. Coast Guard built a new lighthouse on the ruins of the old one and set up a light there during the war. But after the war, they used a lighted buoy set out in the lake for channel traffic. I was on the crew that got the order to go out to Gull Island and retrieve the lens," Charlie said.

"What year was this," Maureen managed to ask.

"In the sixties, I don't remember the year. Still had Iris and Jacob, that's my son, Jacob, with me," he said. He grew silent for a moment, pushing his food around with his fork.

"Would Iris or Jacob know the year?" Maureen asked.

"They died, missy," he said, growing quiet. "Car accident."

"I'm so sorry," Maureen said, placing a gentle hand on Charlie's arm. "How long ago?"

"About as long as I've been drinking I suppose," Charlie said, staring into his coffee.

Bill's phone rang, and he looked at the caller ID.

"Excuse me a moment, I have to take this," he said, getting up and walking outside.

Maureen looked at Charlie. For the first time, she tried to gauge his age but wasn't able to make an educated guess. Years of hard living on the street, alcohol, and probably half a dozen other things had shortened his lifespan.

"Don't you worry about me, missy, I've made my peace a long time ago with what happened," he said.

"How do you do that, Charlie?" Maureen asked. "Because I may never find Hannah, and I've always had a sister. How do I go on living my life, day in day out, eating breakfast, watching movies, going on with life when she can't?"

"Because life goes on whether you want it to or not," Charlie said. "After the accident, I didn't want to go on living. I didn't want to wake up in the morning, let alone live another day without them," he said, staring into his coffee.

"But the world keeps turning, and you keep on breathing. The pain is still raw, and it still hurts, but one day you wake up and that pain isn't as sharp as it once was. Then if you're like me, you feel guilty for not being there with them, for being able to save them, and you go looking for solace in the bottom of a bottle."

Maureen sipped her coffee and thought of her mother. She knew her parents loved each other. Her mother's drinking started after her dad died, and hadn't ever really stopped. The only thing that had changed was her mother's social status and the fact that she got drunk at bridge games and ladies society luncheons instead of at bake sales at parent-teacher conferences.

After a few odd moments, Maureen steered herself back into the conversation.

"How many of you were on the crew that removed the light?" she asked.

"Ten of us at first, but when we got to Ellington and saw the small island and the short distance to shore, the crew was cut to eight. Four of us spent three days on the island disassembling the lens and packing it up proper to be shipped back."

"What happened?" Maureen asked. "You mentioned before that only a couple of you made it back on the boat."

"We'd spent three days camped out on the island. It was the end of spring, early summer maybe. It was chilly at night, but not too bad during the day. We camped there for two days."

"Who was on the island with you?" Maureen asked, looking past Charlie out the window at Bill, who was making his way back inside.

"It was me, and John Littlepaw, and two others I don't remember. I used to know their names but, time makes you forget. John was antsy the whole time we were on the island; we all were. Couldn't shake the feeling something wasn't quite right."

"What do you mean?" Maureen asked as Bill sat down again.

"I don't know. We spent a lot of time looking over our shoulder those couple of days. Maybe we were worried about a storm coming in, or the lens breaking. All I know is that we were glad come dawn on the last morning," Charlie said, taking another bite of his pie.

Bill refreshed his coffee and listened, his eyes going from Maureen to Charlie.

"On the third, when the last of the lens was carefully packed in our boat we started heading back. The ride back wasn't long, about a half an hour. But out there, out on the part of the lake, it's quiet. Not a lot boats use that part of the channel anymore, which is why they moved the lighthouse to begin with."

"What type of boat was it?" Bill asked Charlie.

"It was a little trawler, the Emily Anne. It took longer to load the lens than expected, and it was suppertime before we were able to get under way. We thought about spending another night on the island, and head out at first light, but none of us wanted to stay on that island any longer than possible," Charlie said, finishing his last bite of pie.

"Why not?" Bill asked.

"Because there wasn't no sound out there. It's creepy. I remember John saying it was like nature didn't want us out there. There were no birds, no gulls, nothing. Just the water lapping at the shore, and a few miles of stark silence," Charlie said.

Bill looked at Maureen, who was still taking notes.

"We didn't notice much during the day; we were too busy taking apart the lens. But at night, when you expect to hear gulls or owls or something — we had silence. Made us feel isolated all the more."

"Why did it take you three days to remove the lens, Charlie? It's not that big of a light, I've been to the new lighthouse that houses it back in Lighthouse Bay," Bill commented.

Maureen gave him a sharp look, uncertain of what was behind his questions.

"It's not that big of a lens, you're right," Charlie said. "But it took us most of the first day to clean out the bottom two floors of the tower before we could even make our way up to the watch room and lantern room.

"The windows were all smashed out. First, two floors had a ton of dead leaves and things, and tons of netting of some sort. One of the guys thought the cranes were using it as a nesting ground like they did Pelee Island."

"Netting?" Maureen asked. "What did the netting look like?"

"It was sorta yellow looking. Like thin sheer curtains left to rot, all wispy like and frayed. Tons of it. We spent the better part of the first day cleaning it out, then made sure the stairs were intact before we started dismantling the lens."

Bill inhaled, and leaned back in his chair. "Did you see anything else on the island while you were there? Think; it was a long time ago. Could someone else have been on the island with you, and you and the rest of the crew been unaware of it?"

"I don't think so. I mean, no one else lived on the island. The lighthouse was abandoned."

"Is there a forest on the island, or woods of some sort?" Maureen asked.

Charlie thought about it for a moment before speaking.

"I think so. Not a lot of woods from what I remember, but that was a lot of years ago," Charlie said and stifled a yawn.

"Charlie, where are you staying nowadays?" Bill asked.

"I get by. I don't need any handouts or pity," Charlie said, setting his coffee cup down and pushing his plate away.

The waitress came over and started clearing the menagerie of plates, and returned with the check just as Maureen handed her a credit card.

"I'll be right back," the waitress said.

"Charlie, you were a merchant marine. You served your country, you performed an invaluable service. You have benefits coming to you, why not take them and use them to your advantage," Maureen suggested.

Bill opened his mouth to say something, but Maureen cut him off.

"Charlie, there are a lot of veterans who still have a lot to offer, have a lot to give back, but they need help making those first few steps," she said. "Why not let us help you take them, so you can help others."

Charlie looked at her.

"No thanks, missy. I'm not looking for a government handout," Charlie said.

"It's not a government handout. It's using the facilities that you helped create all those years you were in the merchant marines," Maureen pressed.

"I don't—" Charlie started.

"What was Iris like?" Maureen asked, changing tactics.

"Iris? Oh, she was great. She deserved a lot more than ending up like she did," he said with bitterness.

"Did you make her happy?" Maureen asked.

"I...think so. We didn't have much, but she never complained. She laughed a lot. I miss that, her laugh," he said, growing quiet.

"I lost my dad when I was young. It's hard for me to remember even what he looks like without staring at a picture," Maureen said.

"Charlie, if you loved her, and still love her, do this for her, and for your son. Don't let their legacy be just a memory," Bill said.

Charlie sat a moment and nodded.

"I don't know where to begin," he finally muttered.

"Come with us. Maureen and I are heading back to Lighthouse Bay, and I know the guy at the Veteran's Hospital in Ellington. He'll get you squared away," Bill said, extending his hand.

Charlie shook it and stood, excusing himself to the restroom.

"Can I ask who was on the phone?" Maureen asked.

"I checked with the DNR No one at the park in Ellington or in Lighthouse Bay ever heard of your sister," Bill said.

CHAPTER 43

THE RIDE BACK to Lighthouse Bay seemed extraordinarily long to Maureen.

Bill's words still hung in the air, rolling around in her head like marbles.

They never heard of your sister.

Maureen's veins throbbed with anxious worry, running her brain into overdrive.

The muscles in her neck ached with kinetic tension, built up by the possibility of a lead, now gone cold.

How many other leads are going to turn out this way?

If Bill sensed anything about her mood, he didn't let on. The conversation between the three consisted mostly of Bill telling Charlie about the Vets he knew at the center.

As they were nearing Lighthouse Bay, Maureen's nerves received another jolt as her cell phone rang.

"Your mom?" Bill asked.

"No. I don't recognize the number, but it's a Tampa Area Code," she said.

"Let it go to voicemail," he said.

A few minutes later, they pulled into the large parking lot of the Veteran's Hospital.

"I'm going to get Charlie settled in," Bill said to Maureen as they climbed out of the car. "This may take a while," he said.

"It's okay. I'll go to the station house and have one of the deputies give me a ride home," Maureen said.

"I'd rather you didn't," Bill said. "You can either come with us, or you can—"

"Or I can do as a please, Bill. Look, I'm a big girl, it's a small town. The station is less than three blocks away," Maureen reassured him.

"Maybe this wasn't a good idea," Charlie interjected.

287

"No. Let's go, Charlie. Call me when you get to the station house," Bill said to Maureen.

"Roger that, Hooch." She smiled.

"Hooch was the dog," Bill corrected her.

"I know," she said and headed off onto West Main.

"So?" Charlie asked as they walked into the reception area, "how long you two been together?"

Maureen turned onto West Main and was heading towards the station house when she saw the woman from The Tea Caddy slip out of an expensive looking, black SUV.

At first, Maureen didn't think anything of it, but a sharp dressed man got out and went into The Tea Caddy.

The open sign facing the street remained off. Crossing the corner, she went into a tourist shop and purchased one of the overpriced knitted blue berets and a scarf, then went back out onto the street. She pulled out her phone, pretending to be on it to blend in.

Something prickled Maureen's senses that something wasn't right.

Crossing the street, she strolled along; pretending to window shop as she slowly worked her way to the store just before the Tea Caddy. A yarn store, offering a window display of brightly colored yarns, Maureen went in.

Looking at the display on the window, then around the shop, she hoped to find a bathroom or at the very least, an exit that might lead to a back alley, but all she got was a closed door marked for employees only.

Going back to the window display, she found herself idly watching the street.

Out of the corner of her eye, a sales lady started to approach. Grabbing a charcoal black and gray mix mohair blend, and a crochet needle, Maureen made her way to the counter to avoid the sales banter.

Back out on the street, Maureen cast a glance into the Tea Caddy's lace covered windows. The shop appeared empty, though Maureen checked the street only moments before to find the black SUV still parked at the curb.

Something seems off, Maureen thought.

Walking past, she made her way to the station house where Edith greeted her. A couple of unknown deputies who were sitting behind their desks doing paperwork.

"Bill is having a coronary," replied Edith.

Up until that moment, Maureen wasn't sure that Edith knew who she was, but nodded.

"Sorry. It's cold, and I wanted to get a hat and scarf," Maureen said. It was partly true.

"You were in Florence's shop? A great little place for knitters and crochet lovers," Edith said before returning to her paperwork.

Maureen started to dial Bill's cell phone when the station house phone rang.

"Yes Bill, she's here." Edith smiled at Maureen.

My God is the man paranoid, Maureen thought.

"Yes, hold on," Edith said. "He'd like to have a word with you, Ms. Welsh."

"With Bill, it's never one word," Maureen said, walking over and picking up the receiver. "Hello."

"I heard that," Bill said.

"Oh honey, you're so sweet to check up on me like that. What would I ever do without my big strapping man," Maureen spoke, making sure anyone at the station house could hear her sugary-laced sarcasm.

"Stop that, Maureen. I work there, have a heart," Bill said, though if she could see him, she knew he'd be smiling.

"Oh," Maureen purred, "lacy and red. Billy," she said, grinning at the two young deputies who'd long since stopped their paperwork to eavesdrop.

"Maureen, have you heard about paybacks?" he joked. "Anyway, I wanted to let you know it's taking a little longer to get Charlie signed in, so I'd like you to wait there for me, okay?"

"That's fine. Do you know how long you'll be?" she asked.

"Probably another fifteen to twenty minutes. He's having a hard time remembering his social security number, and without it, they can't locate his service record," Bill said.

"Well, what's his last name? I have a friend out of Chicago that can access that type of stuff; I can have her look into it," she said.

Maureen got Charlie's last name and hung up.

"Thanks," Maureen said and took a seat on the bench behind the railed off work area of the inner office.

She spent ten minutes on hold while her friend Delilah found Charlie's social security number. When Delilah asked if there was anything else, she needed, Maureen was struck with a thought.

"Do you still have Ben Dalton's number?" Maureen asked. Ben had been a college friend of theirs who worked in the government sector and could be loyal to his old school friends if persuaded.

"Yeah, but he's married," Delilah joked.

"I don't want to marry him, I just want to talk to him," Maureen said.

Maureen got up to go outside when Edith called after her.

"I got the impression that Bill doesn't want you to leave just yet," she said.

"I'm only stepping outside to make a call. I promise. I won't go anywhere," Maureen gave her the Girl Scouts three-finger salute.

Once outside, she dialed Ben.

"Dalton," a gruff voice said.

"You still smoking two packs a day, Benny Boy?" Maureen teased.

"Maureen, it's been a long time," he laughed. "What do you need?"

"Benny, you always did like things short and sweet. I'm up here in the Upper Peninsula of Michigan, and I need a favor?" she asked, looking around the street. Not much pedestrian traffic, she thought.

"Oh no. I don't do snow, at least not snow measured by the foot. Forget it," he said.

"No, I'd never dream of you leaving your posh downtown view of San Diego. I need to know if there is a way you can track missing persons."

"Anyone in particular, or are you looking for merely statistical data?" he asked.

In the background, she could hear the clicking of computer keys.

"Both. One name of a woman, late twenties. The rest of the information is on any missing persons reported in a hundred miles of my area," she stated.

"Okay, give me a sec," he said. "All right, what's the name?" he asked.

"Hannah Prescott." Maureen waited in silence for the name to resonant its meaning.

"Hannah? Jesus, Maureen I'm sorry." Fingers clicked on keys and sighed.

"Nothing, Maureen. Last known residence was Ellington, Michigan. What happened," he finally managed to ask after Maureen didn't say anything.

"We don't know. She's missing and with Hannah, well, we never know. But apparently, this time, she's run off and who knows where or with whom," she finally managed.

"I got nothing on this end, but I'll keep her file active, see if I get any hits. Now what's the other stuff you're looking for?" he asked.

"I need to know the number of missing persons within a hundred miles of where I am, and their names, next of kin, that type of thing," she said.

"You on the trail of some—" but he stopped short.

"God, I hope not," Maureen said softly.

"Sorry, Maureen. I didn't mean anything by it. You kind of caught me off guard about Hannah is all. Given the nature of what you're looking for, it should take me a day at the most to compile the stuff. You still at the same email address?" Ben asked.

"Yeah. Can you send it in an encrypted file if?" Maureen asked.

"Sure. Password is still the same," Ben said all matter of fact.

"Got it."

"Now where are you so I can start ol' Betsy on the search?" he asked. The fact that Ben referred to his uber fast computer by name was just part of the quirkiness that Maureen found endearing.

"It's Lighthouse—"

"Bay," he finished.

"How did you know?" Maureen asked.

"Our office got a call a few days ago from a sheriff there, asking for similar information. My boss knows him back from his tour in the Marines," Ben confirmed.

"I see," Maureen finally managed. Her temples began a slow throb of angry frustration at Bill's duplicity.

"I'm almost done with the file, so I'll blind copy you on it as well. Sorry about Hannah, keep me posted, though," Ben said.

They exchanged their goodbyes in time to see Bill's SUV around the corner.

Maureen took off walking in the opposite direction.

CHAPTER 44

MAUREEN WALKED A few hundred yards when she heard Bill's breathless shouts calling out after her.

"Maureen!" He finally caught up to her, grabbing her at the elbow.

"When were you going to tell me?" She spun on him, hands on her hips.

"Tell you what?" he asked.

"Please don't play coy with me, Bill. It doesn't suit you. You're obviously intelligent, so feigning innocence is underrated," she fumed.

"Then why don't you use that snotty, upper-class education and explain it to this good old country boy using small words and maybe I'll understand," Bill retorted.

"You're gathering information on other missing person's in the area, aren't you," she demanded.

"It's standard procedure in a missing person's case, Maureen. I told you I'd made some calls so it's not like I kept it a secret, unlike you who kept Hannah's diary from me," he pointed out.

"She's my sister."

"And she's my missing person," he countered.

"What do you care? In a few more months, when all the leads are dead, you'll go back to ticketing speeders and drunken tourists. I'll still be without my sister," she cried.

"Maureen, I don't know if you're aware but I'm breaking all kinds of rules, both personal and professional, with you. Look," he took a deep breath, "we both want the same thing. We just have different methods of getting the information we need to get there."

"You're keeping me out of the loop on purpose. You just want to swoop in like some grand hero and make everything okay. But, you can't make it all okay. You should have told me," she screamed at him on the verge of tears.

"Told you what?" he fired back.

"That she isn't coming back," Maureen answered softly.

Long moments of silence passed between them.

"Look, Maureen, I don't know where Hannah is. I don't know if she's coming back. I don't know that if she does, what that form might be. But I'm in this with you, for the long haul."

He closed the distance between them and put his arms around her.

"Come on, let's go," he said.

"No. I want to go back to the cabin. I want to look around. We're missing something, and I need my sister's laptop."

"Fine, let me get my truck," he said.

"I'm still not following you," Bill said, heading off the main road towards Maureen's cabin.

"I'm not saying that there's really anything to follow, but I got a vibe about the whole scenario. It was hinky," she said.

"See, I don't get that. She's a shop owner in a small town on Lake Superior. He's the mayor of that small town on Lake Superior. It's coincidence," Bill said.

"Then why did she go into the shop, and why did he wait to follow a few moments later. People do that—"she started before Bill cut her off.

"In the movies. Anyone could argue a thousand ways from Sunday why he went into the shop. For one, they both sit on the chamber of commerce. They've been friends for years, and her son married his daughter."

Maureen sat quietly, still in disbelief. Bill's explanation seemed reasonable, but she still didn't buy it.

At the cabin, Bill went in first, checking things out.

The house was just as Maureen had left it.

Bill checked his watch.

"It's two o'clock now. I don't want to spend too long here."

"Bill—" Maureen began.

"No. Someone pushed you off that curb, and they're still out there. Get what you need, and we're leaving. You have thirty minutes," Bill said.

He continued to walk around, while Maureen sorted through the desk again, retrieving her sister's laptop and packing it into her bag.

Upstairs, Maureen looked at the master bedroom. Going through the dresser drawers and nightstand table, she wandered over to the closet again.

After fifteen minutes, she came back downstairs.

"This was on the front porch."

Bill handed her a green receipt from the post office.

"It's addressed to me. Who would send me certified mail up here?" she asked.

"I don't know. But if we hurry, we can make it to the post office and find out."

Maureen looked around and went to the small secretary near the base of the stairs.

"What are you doing?" he asked.

"Leaving a note for Hannah in case—" she started.

"In case what?" Bill asked, walking over.

Maureen was going to write a small note when she noticed indents in the top of the pad. Taking a pencil and gently rubbing over the yellow legal pad, she was able to come up with a partial number.

"What are you doing?" he asked again.

"I was going to leave Hannah a note. You know, in case she comes back." She looked down, biting her lip. "Then I noticed the gouges in notepad and well, here's a partial number."

Bill looked at the paper that held the smudged impression of numbers.

"What do you think it is?" asked Maureen.

"I only have five numbers that are clear. Could be a license plate, could be a phone number. I can try the records at the DMV and get with deputy Haskelll and he can secure a warrant from the phone company," Bill said.

"You don't need a warrant, Bill. I can have Alfie—"

"No. Josh needs to get his feet wet with more complex investigations, and I do things by the book."

She could tell he was serious, so she didn't press him any further.

"I think I'm losing my mind," Maureen said, looking around the living room.

"Why?" Bill asked, looking from window to window with caution.

"I could have sworn that the cabin had a cellar. I was upstairs in the master bedroom closet, and I got a flashback. I was playing hide and seek with another girl," Maureen said.

"With Hannah?" Bill asked.

"No. I think it was a local girl. I remember her sitting on the porch waiting for me some mornings so I could play. I remember hiding in a root cellar, and my mother getting very angry because we knocked over a kerosene lantern, and the smell stunk up the living room," she said.

Walking to the hall closet, she pushed coats aside and looked around.

"How old were you?" he asked.

"I don't know. Maybe five or six. But I remembered it upstairs," she said.

Bill looked around and went to the kitchen door.

"Wait here."

He disappeared outside for a few minutes. Maureen checked the closet, looking for an opening but found none. She pushed the oak paneling near the L-shape stairway, hoping some secret door would pop open but nothing.

Bill came back in a few minutes later, dirty and layered with pine straw.

"What happened?" Maureen asked.

"I was looking around outside. The cabin has a fieldstone foundation, with no windows. But near the back of the kitchen porch, the fieldstone looks like it's been replaced in one spot. Come out and take a look."

Maureen followed.

Bill pointed to a spot on the foundation near where the porch ended.

"See, right here," Bill said as he rubbed his finger along the joint. "See how the cement is flaking here? This was added later than this," he pointed to a different joint. "Something was added or removed after the original foundation was in place."

"The cabin's always looked like this," Maureen countered.

"Didn't you say your parents remodeled?" Bill asked, kneeling.

"Yeah, but that was inside. Nothing on the outside was touched as far as I can recall," she said.

"Something's been changed here. These stones and this concrete don't look like the rest of the foundation," Bill lamented.

"Could it fade from the sun or something?" Maureen asked. "I know the weather up here gets pretty cold."

"I don't think the elements could disfigure in just one spot," Bill said. "Was this always open in the back here?"

"Yeah. My parents used to have these giant white Adirondack chairs that they would sit in, but that's it."

"Look, Maureen. Put your finger here and trace along. See how this mortar is thinner here? They tried to feather it in, to blend it to look like the original, but it's flaked off over the years and you can tell that something is different here," Bill stated.

Maureen traced along joint. Indeed, the concrete felt rough, gritty with a definite edge to it. The concrete felt like it overlapped in parts, which stirred Maureen's curiosity even more.

"Come on, let's get back inside," Bill said, pulling her along.

Once inside, Maureen started to move the rug and push the couch out of the way.

"Still looking for a door?" Bill asked.

"I wasn't imagining it, Bill. I remember very clear that my mother was extremely angry that we had to go in town and spend a few nights while the cabin cleared out. She didn't like touristy motels even back then."

Bill took the hint. She didn't like cheap motels and back in the day before the large commercial chains built, places like Luanne's Hideaway Bungalow's and the Caprice Motor lodge were all the accommodations travelers had.

"Are you sure it wasn't this other girl's house? Do you remember her name, maybe she still lives in the area," he suggested, looking at the floorboards as well.

"No, it was here. I know it was. And I don't remember her name."

"Let's get going. We'll go into town, stop at the post office, and then by the county clerk's office to see if we can find the original plans for the cabin."

"Will the plans show if there was a cellar or basement?" Maureen asked as Bill locked the door behind her.

"If it's on the original plans, it should. But I'm not an architect, so I don't know for certain," he said.

Climbing into his SUV, they headed back towards town, where they stopped off at the post office, then the county clerk's office.

CHAPTER 45

IN THE BACK booth of Ida's Cafe, Bill and Maureen sat across from one another.

"Aren't you even curious as to why your mother sent you a registered letter?" Bill finally asked.

"No. To be honest, it's probably a letter, giving me instructions on what I should be telling you so you can find Hannah. She'll probably go on and threaten a visit, and at the very end, remind me of how much my little sister needs me and it's my family duty. Then there'll be a check. I'd rather open it later when I've built up my defenses."

"Are you going to call her and at least tell her you got it?" Bill asked, sipping his remaining coffee after their meal.

"No, because that means I have to talk to her. You don't get it. These conversations are exhausting and they make me lose focus," she said, staring into her empty cup of tea.

She blinked.

"The tea," Maureen said aloud.

"Do you want me to flag the waitress down for some more?" Bill asked.

"No. I mean the tea is a piece of the puzzle."

"What?" Bill asked.

"I'd been running a lot of errands that day I went into the Tea Caddy. I went to several places, stocking the cabin, groceries, and the usual." She looked at him, waiting for him to make the connection and follow in tow with her line of thinking.

"Maureen, I'll give you a hint: men aren't telepathic, so I don't know what you're thinking. You're going to have to explain a little more."

The familiar banter with which they teased one another provided Maureen with an odd level of comfort.

"At any point during my day out, that person could have pushed me off the curb. Why did they wait until after I walked out of the Tea

Caddy," she stated, waiting for the summation of information to kick in.

"I honestly don't know," Bill said.

"If you were going to push someone off a curb, wouldn't you do it and get it over with?" Maureen asked.

"I generally help little old ladies across the street, not push them into traffic," he said.

"Exactly. I was alone on the sidewalks a lot throughout the day. It wasn't until I left the Tea Caddy and walked to the library that someone came up behind me and pushed me. Why then?"

Bill didn't say anything, just sat pondering Maureen's theory.

"It's a good theory, but we don't have any proof," Bill said.

"Bill, what do you know about the lady who owns the Tea Caddy? Her staff? You said her son is married to the mayor's daughter. What if—"

Bill paid and motioned for Maureen to follow. Once outside, in the open area of the less crowded streets, Bill finally resumed his conversation.

"Maureen, listen to me. I've seen this before. You're becoming desperate and you're starting to grasp at straws."

"No, I'm not. Listen to me. Isn't it possible, no matter how remote that possibility might be, that once I left the Tea Caddy someone started to follow me? Like they were tipped off?" Maureen stood her ground, stopping in mid-stride.

"It might be possible, but it's highly unlikely. She's a pillar of the community and you're missing a little thing called motive," Bill said.

That was the part that Maureen hadn't been able to figure out. There was no plausible reason why anyone in Lighthouse Bay or any of the nearby towns would have a reason to want Maureen dead.

It wasn't adding up, but Maureen was certain that the Tea Caddy was somehow involved.

What if the person who pushed me into traffic had a grudge against Hannah?

"What are you thinking about?" Bill wondered aloud.

"Motives. There's no motive why someone would push me into traffic. I don't know a soul up here. I can chalk it up to a mere accident, except I know I was pushed, and that nurse at the hospital wasn't a nurse."

"I'll agree with you that I don't think it's random. But it doesn't make any sense, Maureen."

"What if the person who pushed me had a grudge against Hannah? Or they mistook me for her?"

Bill thought a moment.

"First off, you two don't look anything alike. I mean no disrespect, but if I put you two in a room full of people I'd never be able to tell the two of you were related. And two, we checked into Hannah's friends. She might have bounced a few checks, and dated a few men, but I wasn't left the impression that Hannah burned a lot of bridges."

She shook her head in frustration.

She knew it, felt like she had a piece of the puzzle, to something of the bigger picture only she couldn't figure out what that was.

"Okay let's retrace my steps from that day. Go over it, bit by bit," Maureen suggested.

"Fine. In the meantime, we need to stop off at a store. I need more coffee."

Back at Bill's cabin, Maureen and Bill had reviewed the notes they'd made earlier while Bill went over a copy of the incident report.

Bill wrote on a dry-erase board, making a timeline.

"Okay, so far as I can tell, by matching your receipts with the average it would take you to walk to your next stop, the only plausible window of time would be before or after you entered the Tea Caddy," Bill said.

His face showed reluctance, but Maureen couldn't tell if it was from being wrong, or because he liked the store's owner.

"I was inside the store between twenty to thirty minutes," Maureen said.

"Did you talk to anyone?" Bill asked.

"One lady in the store. The same one I saw enter the store earlier today with the Mayor in tow. We chatted about teas. I gave you all that information already."

"I know. But I'm trying to find something to make your theory work, and I can't," he said, running a hand through his hair. Out of habit, he checked his watch.

"It's late and I have to work tomorrow. Why don't we call it a night and look at it with fresh eyes tomorrow? We've had a long day," he said, going to the hall closet and pulling out a pillow and blanket.

"What are you doing?"

"I'm taking the couch."

Maureen looked at him puzzled.

"Despite what happened between us, I think I should sleep on the couch."

Maureen didn't know if she should be hurt or touched. Could he really be a gentleman?

"Shut up," she said. "Neither of us is sleeping on the couch." She pulled him into a long, lingering goodnight kiss.

CHAPTER 46

SHAWN LIT ANOTHER cigarette after the bedroom light shut off. From his vantage point up the hill, he could look down on Bill's property and still maintain his cover.

He thought about all of the little things that Bill had managed to do to him to make his tenure as a Shoshanee Sherriff tedious. Before he'd arrived, Shawn had always enjoyed himself as a deputy and felt a certain sense of power in wearing that uniform and driving around.

It helped him intimidate the snotty tourists who came in every season and littered his town, and it didn't hurt with scoring with the women.

Bill's presence and his rules about conduct, his organization and constant speeches about being a presence in the community had drained all the joy from Shawn's job.

"Dumb jarhead," he muttered, taking a long draw off his cigarette.

Bill's insistence for organization had won over the entire office, and many of the prominent locals in town who found Bill's hands on presence to be, as they had mentioned at a city council meeting before giving Bill some award, "a refreshing and welcome change of pace."

Shawn recoiled at the memory, and the physical ill he had to endure to watch the man who took a job that was rightfully his be awarded for his efforts.

"Stupid Podunk townies don't know anything," Shawn cursed, stomping out the cigarette and looking through his binoculars.

The lights in Bill's cabin were still on in some parts, which infuriated Shawn. He planned to wait until the lights were out and then slash Bill's tires.

While Shawn's stunts were juvenile and petty, he did receive a certain amount of satisfaction in disrupting Bill's well-planned and organized day.

The cold and damp had settled in, and the sweater and windbreaker Shawn wore no longer kept out the damp cold. He retraced his steps back to his parked truck on the other side of the hill.

Shawn wasn't afraid of the dark, but he hated the way the whole town seemed to shut down after ten.

Nothing was open, and the local bars were more to suit the needs of tourists and locals.

His thoughts drifted to his future in Vegas, the bright lights, the big city full of opportunity. A fresh start, with thousands of things to do and millions of people, in an urban metropolis that never slept.

Reaching his truck, Shawn noticed another car had parked close to him.

What the hell is going on here, Shawn thought, a tremor of fear shaking him.

Reaching slowly for his gun at his hip, Shawn clicked off the safety and aimed before he heard a familiar voice.

"Careful with that O'Reily, I don't want my damn head blown off because you're spooked."

He recognized the familiar voice and lowered his gun.

"How did you know I was out here?" Shawn asked.

"Old habit of yours. Not hard to pick up. Hell, I bet most of the cigarette butts around here probably contain your DNA you've been up here so much," the older man replied.

"Yeah, well, I like to make sure I stake out my targets well. The Welsh girl's inside. I think they're screwing," Shawn sneered.

"Yes, that's why I'm here."

"Oh," Shawn said, lighting another cigarette.

"Yes, the plans have changed."

Shawn felt the biting sting pierce his chest long before the silencer gave any trace of a sound.

From behind the man's voice, two other men appeared.

"Make sure it's done," the voice commanded.

Wordlessly, the shooter went over, put the end of the silencer to Shawn's forehead and squeezed off another round for good measure.

Shawn's body twitched once, twice, then went limp.

"Put him in his car, and follow us. Stay close, but not too close. I don't know who's on duty tonight and I don't want to have kill anyone else," the man warned.

After a few minutes, Shawn's truck, and the black sedan drove off the secluded mountain road, taking the main road out of Lighthouse Bay.

Superior Lies

Maureen woke a little past three in the morning, climbed out of the bed so as to not disturb Bill and padded into the living room.

She couldn't sleep. The notes they made the night before were pieces of the puzzle, but couldn't make them fit.

She felt an overwhelming sense of panic and had to calm herself. Getting up, she walked barefoot into the kitchen for a glass of water. These attacks had come with familiar regularity lately, and Maureen had to steady her breathing and focus on something soothing to calm herself. Never one for medication and drugs because that would mean admitting she needed help, Maureen tried to help herself.

She stretched and began to get into her yoga poses. For nearly a half an hour, she did the same soothing repetitive motions until she felt centered.

Sitting on the couch, sipping her glass of water, Maureen stared at her bag.

More pieces to a puzzle that I don't know, she thought, struggling to keep the feelings of anxiety from returning.

Pulling out her sister's laptop, she tried to turn it on.

Nothing.

She got up and plugged it in.

Pulling out a copy of the original plans to her family cabin, Maureen felt a little nostalgic, knowing that the cabin had once belonged to her grandfather. She hadn't known him, though she was named after her grandmother.

She flipped though the pages trying to make sense of the boxes and lines, converging to outline the schematics of the house. The original layout didn't look much different than it did now, but Maureen didn't feel confident in her estimation, as she knew nothing of architecture.

She flipped back to the sheet labeled Foundation Plan and stopped

The plan indicted a basement. She managed to translate the slanted writing: excavate to six feet.

Her heart skipped, and she forgot to breathe.

She'd been right, there is a basement.

Was it possible to fill in a basement? She wondered.

Glancing at the door, she wished that Bill was awake. She felt an odd sense of guilt in discovering this and not sharing it with him right away.

Grabbing a sticky note, she made a small note on the page and flipped the drawings back over, deciding to translate all of the slanted writing to see if there was any further indication of where the basement's entrance might be. Halfway through the first page, in the bottom of the right-hand corner was a block of numbers below a county seal.

Maureen grabbed the piece of paper from Hannah's notepad.

All five numbers matched.

Maureen felt light-headed.

Hannah had managed to figure out something about the cabin, about the basement, and managed to get the county's file number for the property's original documents.

Did Hannah already own a copy? She wondered.

Would someone at the county clerk's office recognize her sister? Does that make me a target?

Questions raced through her mind, and Maureen felt an odd sense of comfort knowing that she was on the same path that Hannah discovered.

There was just one more thing to do.

The letter from her mother called to her like whiskey to a drunk.

This is stupid, she chided herself. *Their just words, they can't hurt me.*

Rummaging through her bag, she found and opened it.

It was longer than normal, and contained no check as she had first suspected, but what it did contain was priceless.

Maureen read the letter once, eyes wide.

She wasn't sure what to make of it.

Reading it carefully a second time, the words still dug into Maureen's heart, bringing new panic and fresh tears.

> *Dear Maureen,*
>
> *I hope when you receive this letter, and after you read it, that you will find it in your heart to forgive me. I wasn't always the best mother to you. I don't know what it was like for you, but it couldn't have been easy having a drunk for a mother.*
>
> *You're so independent and strong, Maureen. You get that from your father.*

I miss him; please don't ever think that I don't. Not a day has passed since that I don't wonder how things might have been.

I'm going to give as many names and facts as I can recall, though it's not much. Your father took care of the messy details in those days. I know you; you'll want to check them out to make sure poor old mom isn't on another bender.

Lighthouse Bay is filled with too many sad memories for me, and for a long time, almost my entire lifetime, I've been harboring those secrets. But it's not mine alone, and there are people who'd kill me to keep me silent.

The people of Lighthouse Bay stumbled upon something on a little island where the lighthouse used to be. I think they might have lived on the mainland at some point, but as people began to settle, I believe they moved their location to the island.

I don't know what kind of ungodly creatures they are; I just know what they do.

Your father and I learned what they did when we were in high school. Two classmates, Joanna Davis and William Pearce. Only a few know what truly happened to them, though many in town assumed they'd run off an eloped.

Follow the old mining trails to the cliff face, and dig behind the tree line. There are bones buried there. Human remains. We buried what was left.

Whatever lived on that island, torn Joanna and William to bits. It lives off of humans. I don't know how many there are, or what they are for the matter, but I know they're dangerous.

I fear for your safety and Hannah's. I never liked the idea of her living there fulltime, unprotected and wild.

Life is about choices, and I fear the wrong choices I made are going to cost you and Hannah your lives.

But I had no choice, Maureen. When Dwight and the others confronted us, your father wouldn't back down, and I panicked. You were so little, and I was so naïve at the time I thought things would blow over. They didn't.

Your father knew about how people just went missing from time to time. He learned that the certain families in town had tried, and failed to kill whatever was on the is-

land. But whether it was through science or mercy, they found a way to limit what it hunted.

I remember your father and Dwight arguing. Dwight was convinced that they were acting in the best interest of the town. In those days, if there was a rare species of something, the government would just swoop in and scoop up the land and everyone would be out of their homes, their jobs. Many of the farms have been passed down through several generations.

We were being practical, we thought. At first, your father was okay with it. But I think a few years of playing God with strangers' lives, and the lives of people he knew, played on his conscience and soul. I still say a prayer for your father's soul.

The recession made tourist season difficult. But those things have to feed even if it's a townie. They tried to choose wisely, as if there was an easy to way to choose a sacrifice.

When you were just over a two, you found a length of bone on the beach and I went into hysterics. By that time, your father had had enough and threatened to expose the whole town.

He went to see a friend of his in nearby Beaumont, who worked for the newspaper.

Dwight and the others somehow caught wind and they came knocking at the cabin door while your father was gone.

They gave me a choice: you or your father.

I loved your father, but I loved you too. I didn't know what to do. I panicked. In the end, I made the only choice that I could live with at the time.

I chose my child.

Two days later, your father's car was found off the side of the road. They said he fell asleep at the wheel.

I fear Dwight killed him.

I took you and moved to my aunt's home in Nettles, Florida, where I met Frank while he was studying for law school. Frank was a few years young-er than me, and had money and power, and he adored you, loved me, and I knew deep down, even without telling him what happened; he'd be able to keep us safe.

Superior Lies

I hope you can use this information to find Hannah, and when you do, please leave Lighthouse Bay. It's not safe there.

And Maureen, I pray that you someday find the ability to understand the secrets I've told you, and possibly find it in your heart to forgive me.

I love you, Maureen.

Mom

Maureen felt like throwing up.

Her mother had gone to the trouble of having it legally notarized, though it wasn't Alfie's signature.

There was something in her mother's letter—the carefully detailed wording that made the words reverberate truth.

Bile rose in Maureen's throat and she sprinted to the bathroom, throwing up the contents of her late dinner. After, sitting on the cool porcelain tile, Maureen sobbed into a towel to muffle the noise.

Raw ache overwhelmed her, invaded her bones with a sickening heaviness that felt worse than any flu she'd ever had.

When she emerged from the bathroom, the wall clock read a little before four.

Grabbing her cell phone, she put it on vibrate and set the alarm for an hour before Bill would wake up.

She hated to leave him, but she had to find answers because Hannah's time might be running out.

CHAPTER 47

BILL AWOKE A few minutes before the alarm clock. Years of training had sharpened his internal clock to work with sharp precision.

Switching off the alarm, he wanted to spare Maureen the hassle of waking up before she had to.

He was dressed in his running pants and sweatshirt before he realized Maureen was not in the bed.

He existed the bedroom expecting to find her out in the living room. No dice.

The bathroom door stood open so he checked the alarm panel. Deactivated.

"Damn it," he swore. "How the hell did she figure out the code?"

When I find her, I'm going to handcuff her to the couch, he thought.

Grabbing his cell phone and gun, he looked at the coffee table, and noticed that not only was Maureen missing, so were her things.

Calling the station house, he got Josh, who was pulling midnights in the rotation.

"Josh, I need a trace put on Maureen Welsh. Her credit cards, debit cards, you name it. I want an APB on the make and model of her car, and I want it yesterday."

"On it," the young deputy replied and hung up.

He drove to town, looking around for her car but came up empty-handed.

Nearly twenty minutes had passed when Deputy Haskell called back.

"Talk to me," Bill commanded.

"I put out the APB Nothing so far. Same with her credit cards, but her debit card came up with a hit at the Wal-Mart in Bloomfield."

"That's nearly twenty-five miles away. Call them back, get a me—"

"One step ahead of you. Had them fax me a copy of the receipt. She purchased a shovel, sledgehammer, respirator, and a few other things," Josh reported.

"Copy. Make sure you keep a copy and leave it on my desk," Bill said, steering his car into a U-turn and heading for Maureen's cabin.

"Sure thing. If you need anything else, let me know. I'm going to finish up some paperwork until you, Sid, or Paul gets here."

"Where's Shawn?" Bill asked. He knew that Shawn was covering the morning shift because Bill had made the schedule himself.

"I don't know. Hasn't showed yet, and I figure if he does, he's going to be too hungover and pissed off to be much good. Edith came in, waited until eight o'clock before calling Sid and Paul. One of them will relieve me shortly. Until then, I got paperwork to do."

Bill felt a sense of pride. He'd trained Josh, and the young, green deputy was no longer waiting for instructions on where to go, he was learning to lead.

"Don't think that won't go unnoticed; I appreciate it," Bill said.

"Appreciate what, I'm doing my job. Crime doesn't work nine to five, Bill. Let me know if you need any more help with the Welsh girl, and let me know when you find her so I can call off the APB"

"Will do."

Bill hung up, nearly breaking the speed limits through town as he pushed his Ford Expedition towards Maureen's cabin.

His thoughts jumbled, he needed to focus. He had to find Maureen, and then he'd have to find Shawn. A sickening chill raced through him as he wondered if Shawn was responsible for Maureen's disappearance.

This was the last straw as far as Shawn was concerned. Bill would make a recommendation to have him relieved of duty pending an investigation. The man was unreliable at best and a liability at his worst.

As soon as he turned off Main Street heading out of town, his cell phone rang.

"Downs," he answered.

"Bill, it's Paul, you got a minute," came the high-pitched voice at the other end of the line. He'd recognize Paul's voice anywhere.

"Not at the moment, Paul. Can this wait?" Bill asked,

He was anxious. His temples throbbed, his veins ached with clear certainty that he would find Maureen at her cabin.

"Well, if you're in the middle of something. But it's about that sample that you brought me the other day. I have some information for you, and I have a problem with it," Paul stated.

Paul's words caught Bill's attention.

"I can spare a few minutes," Bill said.

"Good. Listen, are you sure that the sample you gave me was pure? I mean, it wasn't mixed with anything else, and it wasn't tainted in any way?" Paul asked.

"No. I collected it myself; using some of the crime scene bags we have on hand."

"Well, that makes it even stranger. Bill, this webbing is throwing me for a loop. The sample has to be tainted. When you get a chance, I want to come up there and get a sample for myself, so I can rerun the results. Just to make sure."

"Sure of what?" Bill asked.

"The webbing has organic material in it. At least, that's what my results are coming up with."

"So," Bill said.

"Bill, I mean organic as in human. The webbing has about dozen trace elements in it, most of them are common enough not to send up any red flags," Paul said.

"But here you are calling me bright and early," Bill stated.

"Yeah. Most of the elements I found were basic, found in nature. I was expecting this to be the regurgitation of a barn owl, or maybe a hawk. They're fierce predators known for making sturdy nests. But I don't think it's either of those two animals."

"Why?" Bill asked, making a left.

"Because there's something off about the webbing. It had its trace organics in it, leaves, twigs, plankton. Things you'd expect to find in the saliva of an owl or hawk. Basically, any predator that survived off of waterfowl."

"How do you know it eats waterfowl?" Bill asked.

"The presence of plankton in the webbing. But then the chemical results came back and the levels are way off for them to be accurate," Paul stated.

"English, Paul. I wasn't a science major," Bill urged.

"Right, sorry. The webbing sample has a high percentage of pheromones in it. Human pheromones. It also has a high percentage of Iridiumtriclorophate."

"I've never heard of that," Bill said.

"Mining companies are the only ones that do. They don't want people knowing that this is a by-product of their industry, otherwise, the government would come down on them like a ton of bricks."

"But you know," Bill commented. "Why don't you turn them in?"

"Let's just say its best not to make waves, Bill."

"Why not?"

"The university gets a lot of its funding from private donations — mining companies, geological study groups, environmentalists. I don't think they'd take too kindly to have that funding used to out their dirty little secrets."

Bill remained silent in full understanding. Paul made a meager living at a small university in the Upper Peninsula of Michigan. His job and tenure were expendable to a board of trustees.

"Like I said, this stuff is found in mining communities like Copper Harbor, or Houghton — someplace where there's been a lot of mining. It's a residue that lefts behind when the ground has been strip-mined. The dust settles onto the vegetation. Animals on up through the food chain absorb it into their diets, and eventually it's in their system permanently," Paul said.

"Which means?" Bill asked, still unclear of what Paul was trying to tell him.

"It means that whatever regurgitated the webbing is an omnivore. The presence of the plankton and pheromones are proof of that," Paul said. "But there's more. I found traces of Adipocere."

"Adi — what?" Bill asked.

"Adipocere. It's a white, suet like substance that's formed when bacteria, moisture, and heat come in contact with human fat," Paul stated.

Bill was silent for a moment.

"Are you telling me that there's a trace of human fat in that webbing?" Bill asked.

"No. I'm telling you that there are traces of digested human fat in that webbing, Bill. It doesn't make any sense, which is why I want to get another sample and test it for myself, to rule out any margin of error."

Bill digested the information.

"You still there, Bill?" Paul asked.

"Yeah. Look, Paul, was does this mean, laymen's terms."

"I don't know. We should talk. In person, and soon."

Bill understood perfectly. He didn't want to talk about anything else over the phone.

"I'll let you know where and when, Paul, but I've got to go for now."

They said goodbye and hung up moments before Bill turned into the driveway of Maureen's cabin.

Sitting in the driveway was her Pontiac.

Bill called the station and canceled the APB

"Lord, give me strength," he said, getting out of his car.

Maureen was sitting on the couch, going over the blueprints once more before she started her demolition.

She was sure that something was hidden in here, and she had to find it, and soon.

Hannah's life depended on it.

Maureen wasn't having much success in reading the old construction documents, and finally, she got up, heading to the stairs. She began to knock on the walls, listening for a hollow sound.

"Logic would dictate that if we'd had a basement or cellar, the door would be somewhere near the stairs that go up," she said to herself.

"You done playing Bob the Builder?" Bill asked from the doorway.

Maureen screamed and turned around.

Bill had his arms crossed, having closed the front door behind him.

"How...did you know...?" Maureen stuttered.

"I'm a cop, Maureen. The better question would be what the hell are you doing here when I clearly told you not to leave my sight," Bill walked over, grabbing the construction documents.

She reached into her jeans pocket and fished out the letter her mother had sent her.

"Read it," she said quietly, her voice shrinking.

Bill read it, then carefully refolded it and handed it back to her.

"You don't know —"he started.

"I do know. She wasn't drinking; she's sober. Besides, she was right. I did check into a few things. Her two classmates were killed just as she said. Several others, too. A couple of tourists, one merchant marine at a bar in Ellington, and a hunter. Spanning a nine year period or so."

"That doesn't mean anything. Coincidence looks convincing when you're clinging to hope, Maureen. She was probably drunk," Bill said.

"Maybe. But not this time. She didn't tell Frank about how my father died, and why. Frank never understood why she drank so much. Twenty-five years of guilt is a pretty good motive, wouldn't you say," Maureen said, shoving the note back into her pocket.

"It still doesn't explain what you're doing here."

"I want to find out. I know I'm right about there being a cellar here, and if I am, it proves that my mother's letter is right."

"How does that help Hannah?" Bill asked, taking off his jacket.

"I don't know. But if there was a cellar and it's been boarded up and plastered over, there had to be a reason for it. If I can find that reason, maybe I can link it to Hannah and we can find her. Time's running out, Bill, I can feel it. I know the longer a person stays miss-ing the less likely they'll be found."

Bill leaned against the couch, having picked up the dropped docu-ments and turned them around.

"Bill, did you know that if a murder goes unsolved for more than five years, the chances of it ever being solved are not very good?"

"Well, let's see if we can decrease those odds a bit," Bill said and pointed to the wall that the secretary stood against.

Maureen felt tears pooling but blinked them away.

God, he's a good man, she thought.

"See this mark here? This line with the quarter arch? This indicates a door opening, it might be to a cellar, it might be to a small closet," Bill pointed to the blueprints, then the wall.

"I knocked on that wall, and it didn't sound hollow," Maureen stat-ed.

"That only works in the movies, Maureen. Up here, in the winter, if they boarded up the opening, it would have been dry walled and in-sulated to help retain heat in the winter and coolness in the summer. There's a lot of hollow spaces inside a wall," Bill said, rolling up his sleeves and moving the secretary.

"How do you know that?" Maureen asked, moving the Dutch style pine bench and lamp.

"I worked construction in high school before I joined the Marines. Thought I might be a builder or an architect once I got out of the ser-vice," he said.

"What changed?"

"The war. The war changed me. I wanted to do something that made a difference," Bill said and grabbed the sledgehammer.

"What are you doing?" Maureen asked with alarm.

"I have to make a hole to find out if there was a door here. If I hit a pocket of cold air, I know we've found something."

Bill swung, knocking a fist sized hole into her mother's pristine whitewashed walls.

After ten minutes, Bill had made a two foot by two foot opening in the wall. Dust and debris littered the living room, and it wasn't until Maureen saw the thin layer of white dust coating her mother's an-tiques that she worried about how she was going to put the living room back into working order.

"I think I've got something," Bill said.

Maureen stepped closer and ran her hand over the opening. Beneath the layers of dust and dirt, was the smooth solid amber stained wood of a door.

Her heart thumped, missing beats. She felt lightheaded and staggered back to lean against the couch.

"Take it easy, it could be an old closet, Maureen," Bill said. Never the less, he continued for another ten minutes, until the faint clang of metal hitting metal echoed throughout the living room. Bill stopped.

"What?" she asked.

"I hit a doorknob. I'm sure of it."

The removed the rest of the drywall in silence, Maureen focused intently on ripping away the layers of drywall that hid her past.

Stepping back, Maureen got a sudden flashback.

"This is it, I'm sure of it. The whole living room was that color. It changed after my mother remarried," Maureen stated.

She stepped closer, trying the knob.

Locked.

"Let me?" Bill asked.

He stood back and kicked at the rusty metal of the handle that gave way without much resistance.

Maureen took a step closer to open it, but Bill pulled her back.

"Me first," Bill said, drawing his weapon.

Whatever was down here, someone went to great lengths to conceal. Maureen tried not to think about the possibility of someone or something down there; after all, if they were able to get a copy of the blueprints, others could too.

Bill pulled his Maglite from his pocket, flicking it on, his left hand over his right hand, which held the gun.

He jerked open the door, and a rush of cold air hit them. Dust settled, and the wet, muddy smell permeated the room.

As he shined his light around, Maureen saw a simple Michigan cellar with a dirt floor. A single set of stairs — nine total, led to the dirt floor. Dust settled, clinging to the cobwebs that strewn the entryway.

Bill flipped the switch.

Nothing.

Maureen peered over his shoulder, holding a large camping flashlight she'd found and scanned the cellar's contents.

Bill kneeled, testing the stability of the steps.

"I don't think we should use these, they look rotted," he said, holstering his weapon.

"There doesn't appear to be anything down there," Maureen said.

Bill flashed the light around, and looked at her.

"You owe me," he said, and gingerly took the steps descending into the cellar. He flashed the light around and walked the eighteen feet to the back of the wall where the window had once been.

"It's been sealed, you can really tell from inside. There seems to be more work taken to how it looks outside, but in here, they just did a really rough patch job," Bill called.

"Here, take this," Maureen said, holding out her cell phone. "I need photos, as many as you think it will take to document it. It might be important."

As Bill took pictures, Maureen waited by the cellar's opening, kneeling and looking around with the light from his flashlight. Leaning over the stairs to get a better view, Maureen almost lost her grip on the door jam.

"Be careful," Bill warned.

Her flashlight shone directly below the open slats in the stairs.

"Bill, look. There's a crate…under the stairs," she beckoned him over with her light.

Bill saw the wooden crate and used his boot to move it.

"It's empty. Probably left behind by the workers who sealed up the basement. There's an old coke bottle down here too."

Nonetheless, Maureen insisted on him taking pictures of the crate, and she examined it thoroughly before handing it back to Bill. He was climbing up when he noticed a few notches carved into one of the large stones that made up the basements walls.

Shinning his light, Bill felt the stone.

"What is it?" she asked.

"I don't know. This stone looks weird, out of place I think. It's hard to tell in this light, though."

Bill examined the stone, and after a moment noticed that the stone, and the one next to it, moved.

"It moves," he said breathless.

Maureen looked at him, a mixture of hope and excitement drowning out the worry that had been present since the day she wandered into the stationhouse.

He maneuvered the stones, and pulled out a thick plastic bag.

"What is it?" she asked, peering over the top of the steps.

"I don't know. It's a plastic bag. The stones were loose, I moved them around and found it."

Bill climbed the rickety wooden stairs, the weight of his body making each step creak. Closing the basement door, Bill looked at Maureen.

He looked at the package once, then handed it to her.

"Aren't you going to look at this for evidence?" she asked, taking the bag.

"It's not part of my on-going investigation, and I haven't secured a warrant for it."

Bill's matter of fact tone unsettled her a little bit, and the sinking feeling that was in Maureen's stomach this morning was fast returning.

She smiled faintly and looked at him.

"Whatever's in this bag, we'll look at it together. Over some breakfast, my treat since I bailed on you this morning," she said, grabbing her coat.

"I think we should clean up the mess a bit, in case anyone comes by," Bill said.

Nearly an hour later, the mess was cleaned up, and Bill used thumbtacks to hanging a decorative woven throw on the wall to conceal the hole in the drywall. Pushing the secretary back into place, the only way anyone would know was to enter the house and look behind the couch.

"What if someone breaks in and find the hole?" Maureen asked, gathering her bag and the blueprints.

"It all depends on who did the breaking in I guess. Look, I think we have to take a rain check on breakfast for a moment; I have some-thing I have to take care of and I can't do it with you around."

Maureen looked wounded.

"That's fine. I have some calls to make myself, and I have an interview tomorrow," Maureen said, locking the cabin door behind them.

"Oh really, where?" Bill asked, opening the door to her Pontiac.

"The café. Fran wants to generate some press and she said there's a woman's league luncheon that she holds every Tuesday. Some of the other local business owners will be there. Stacy from copy shop, and Pamela from the Tea Caddy," she said. "Word gets around in a small town, and I think they're anxious for a well to do Chicago paper to do a story on them."

"And you're trying to find a way to nose around. I don't want to get any calls about you getting into trouble with Pamela Betts, Murphy Brown. Not that I wouldn't love to slap the cuffs on you a second time," Bill grinned, shutting her door on her before she had a chance to reply.

Once onto the main road, Maureen took Oakwood back to Bill's cabin.

CHAPTER 48

MAUREEN CHECKED HER watch. Fran told her that the business luncheon ended around noon. Maureen wanted to drop into the Tea Caddy and nose around while the owner was out of the building.

She had about twenty minutes to go in ask some questions before going over to the café for her meeting.

"Nancy Drew, eat your heart out," she said at herself in the rearview mirror.

Maureen went into the Tea Caddy and smiled at the woman behind the counter.

Bill pulled up to Shawn's place and sat in his truck. The windows gave a clear view inside the small ranch home.

Shawn's car wasn't in the driveway, but that meant little. His house was only three blocks away from the local bar, and there were a few times he'd gotten calls that Shawn was passed out drunk in the parking lot.

Bill wired the stationhouse and talked to Josh.

"Do me a favor, Josh. Whoever is out on patrol, have them swing by Ray's Roadhouse and see if Shawn's car is in the parking lot; go inside and ask if he was there last night then get back to me."

"Will do, Bill."

Bill got out, looking around the outside.

Beer bottles and cans littered the front porch, and Bill peered inside one of the windows.

Everything looked normal on the inside, but that didn't mean anything.

Bill drew his gun and knocked.

"Shawn?" Bill called. "Shawn, it's Bill. Are you home?"

Silence.

Bill waited, knocked again. Nothing.

He tried the knob. Locked.

The scratchy static came over his walkie and Bill stepped off the porch and into the clearing for better reception.

"Repeat that again?" Bill asked.

"Bill. We have a negative on Shawn's car in the parking lot. Owner told Sid that he hasn't been in a few months. Came in a few weeks ago and paid up his bar tab and left."

Odd, Bill thought. He knew Shawn had reported for work hung over several times in the last few weeks.

Bill pulled out his cell phone and called Mayor Carlisle's office. When the mayor answered, he sounded annoyed.

"Mayor Carlisle? Sherriff Downs. I'd like to have a meeting with you today, if possible."

"I have a lot of work to do, Bill. It's not like I get to ride around all day waiting for some tourist or townie to double park."

Bill shook his head. In the four years Bill had worked as the town's Sherriff, and in the dozen times he butted heads with the Mayor, it never ceased to amaze him how quickly the man resorted to childish tactics.

"Well, just doing what I can to keep the streets of Lighthouse Bay safe. Besides, I think those parking tickets help pay for a few of the improvements around your house."

Bill enjoyed spiking the ball, no matter the occasion.

"What's this about, Bill? I really don't have time today."

"Shawn O'Reilly didn't report to work this morning. It's the third time this month, and several times in the last three months. He's been wrote up twice. You were at the last meeting. Something has to be done," Bill demanded.

A long pause ensued.

"I agree. I'll take care of it."

Bill's brain skidded off track.

Why is this man offering to help you out of a problem he'd been telling you to put up with for the last six months.

"Thanks, but it's something I'm quite capable of taking care of myself. I just need your approval. Faxed to the station house," Bill added.

"It wouldn't be any trouble. Bernadette is doing some filing and faxing. I can have her get a hold of Shawn."

"That's going to be a problem. He's not at any of his usual haunts, and he isn't at home."

"How do you know that?" Mayor Carlisle asked, his voice rising in pitch.

"Because I'm at his home now, and his car is gone. He isn't home. But he isn't in town either; we've looked."

"I see. Fine, I can squeeze you in today, but only for a few minutes."

"Good. Let me know when and I'll head up—"

"No need. I'm heading to the Bay to visit my daughter, I'll phone you when I get a few moments this afternoon."

The line went dead.

Bill kept getting a feeling that he was a part of some colossal joke, that at any moment someone with a camera was going to jump out and yell surprise.

He spent another ten minutes looking around the house, checking in windows and doors for signs of trouble before leaving and heading back to the station.

Maureen recognized the woman behind the counter and her heart sank, it was the Tea Caddy's owner.

"Hello, I'm Maureen Welsh. I'm a reporter for the Chicago Globe. I'm in town visiting family, and my editor loved my photos of the town, and wants me to do a few articles on the local businesses."

She handed over her business card, smiling as the woman looked first at the card, then back to Maureen.

"I'm thinking of a three-part series for travel destinations close to home. You know, a nice three-day weekend jaunt to relax and unwind from the bustle and chaos of the city," Maureen said, pitching her story ideas in hopes of getting the woman to talk to her.

"Sounds fascinating," the elderly woman replied. Maureen couldn't tell if it was sincere of sarcasm, though she extended her hand nonetheless.

"I have some free time now. I have several other business owners whom I'm interviewing for the series, but I have to admit, I can't resist your shop. It's so Victorian, and I'm so disappointed that I've missed your social luncheons."

There, Maureen thought, *a little flattery never hurt.*

"Why thank you. We try to create a nice niche for ourselves. I'm Pamela Betts, I'm the owner."

Maureen extended her hand.

"Nice to meet you."

"Pleasure's mine. Why don't we go down to my office and I can tell you a little bit about the history of the shop. I have some lovely photos you might like to use in your article," she said and gestured for Maureen to follow her.

Maureen did, past rows of glass canisters of tea, porcelain teapots and sets of cups and saucers.

"Getting ready for the holiday season?" Maureen asked casually.

"Oh my, yes. Tourists give us some of our best business during the holiday season. Only the Cherry Festival rivals it," she said.

At the back of the store, they went through a swinging door marked 'employees' and Maureen looked around half expecting to see an office.

"My office is in the basement," Pamela said, opening a door.

"The basement?" Maureen asked. Her gut flipped in a tight somersault.

"Afraid so. We're forced to use the attic for storage for the teas since they can't be exposed to the severe cold or damp. But I don't mind it much," she led the way down the wooden steps.

"It must be hard to work with the lack of light," Maureen said, keeping her hands on her bag.

"Not at all. I have lots of overhead light, and its cooler in the summer time, and no humidity."

She waved her arm, gesturing Maureen to a small wooden oak desk with two standard office chairs.

"Why don't I give you some of our previous publicity photos, and I'll make us a pot of tea," Pamela suggested. "This way, you can sample our merchandise firsthand."

Maureen nodded and watched the woman descend the steps.

She didn't let her breath out until she heard the woman's footsteps fade, the light from the open doorway spilling down the stairs.

Looking half-heartedly at the photos, Maureen started to peer around, casually looking around for a video camera before she started snooping.

There were piles of mail that been opened, and stacks of what looked like invoices.

Two large metal filing cabinets were on the left, with a couple of picture frames of the building in its earlier years.

A pegboard hung behind the desk, a blank calendar with inventory dates inked in.

Maureen stood up, looking around to try to find something that might help her, keeping an ear out for Pamela's return.

Slowly walking around the desk, Maureen gently looked at the mail in the pile, trying to get look for return addresses.

She heard rustling from above and quickly moved to take her seat again.

Maureen was frustrated and tried to calm herself from the irritation. She thought she'd have more time to look, have more time to search for clues and check if this woman's story was truly what it was.

She'd put in the information on background checks, but nothing came back flagged. A recent online search gave Maureen some brief information about Pamela Betts' family and social background, but nothing in the local library's archives that had a red arrow that screamed abnormal.

"I hope you don't mind, I made you our signature house blend," Pamela said, returning to the dungeon office with a small wooden tray and two contemporary teacups in a pink and mocha pattern.

"Not at all," Maureen said, taking hers and sipping it. "It's great." In truth, the tea tasted a little stale and metallic, but insulting the woman's handiwork wouldn't do now.

"Thank you. It took me years to get this blend just right. Everyone tends to think of tea as something in a little bag on a string, but true tea masters would never dream of making teas like that. I went to college, got my horticultural degree, and turned my family's little store into something much more profitable."

"So, this was your family's business before you made it into the Tea Caddy?" Maureen asked, taking out her notebook and taking notes.

"Oh yes, my grandfather's, actually. When he owned the building, it was an apothecary and pharmacy. My father turned it into a general store, but in the late eighties and early nineties, big box stores dazzled people and their paychecks. They wanted to buy a gross of paper towel for three bucks and a dozen bottles of olive oil for twelve dollars."

"So business started to decline?" Maureen asked.

"Somewhat. Then my father's health took a turn for the worse — stroke left him a shell of the person he'd been. He was in hospice, and there were still bills to pay. My mother had passed a few years earlier, so it was up to me to keep the business going."

"I'm sorry. Are you an only child?"

"Yes. My parents had me late in life so I imagine it was a handful to have a toddler in your mid-forties. In any case, when my father took sick, I decided I had to do something, so I completely renovated the place into something I knew could be successful."

"You did this while your father was in hospice? Sounds like you had a lot on your plate," Maureen lamented.

Getting people to open up is a tricky business. Ask them too many questions and you seem intrusive, which creates suspicion and usually clams them up. Ask too few, and it appears you aren't interested, and that usually leaves them annoyed.

"Yes. He was in his final stages. He didn't live to see the Tea Caddy open, but I'd like to think he'd have been proud of me."

Maureen continued to write, sipping away at her tea.

Footsteps echoed on the wooden stairs and an older woman in what Maureen guessed was her mid-fifties came carrying a tray of petit fours and small tea cookies.

"Fresh from Odessa's Bakery two doors down," she said and left.

Maureen eyed the bevy of pastries and couldn't resist the small chocolate petit fours.

"You should interview Odessa if you get the chance. She's a sweet lady. She's been baking in that bakery for the last forty years. Just like her mother, and her mother's mother. They used to sell baked goods and jams at a little roadside stand near the county line when all there was up here were loggers and miners."

Maureen tasted the rich chocolate cake and the luscious caramel mousse inside.

"These are amazing," Maureen said, helping herself to another one.

"So I've heard. I'm allergic to chocolate myself, but if you get the chance, try her carrot cake. It's really quite delicious," Pamela said.

Maureen finished her tea and began to focus on steering the questions towards Hannah.

"I love how the town has seen a resurgence of artisan crafts. When my sister told me about the neat little shops, I wanted to check it out for myself. She sent my mother a basket of artisanal goods that she just raved about. So when I had the chance to come up here for my paper, I took it."

"Who's your sister again, maybe I know her," Pamela said.

"She lives outside of town, on your way to Ellington. She had some difficulties after her pregnancy and she just raved about your tea. I was in here a few weeks back, looking for a tea set like hers."

Maureen had gone fishing, and she had what she wanted.

Pamela's face paled, but she didn't completely lose her composure.

Chapter 49

BILL'S FOUL MOOD did little to help push through his mounds of paperwork. Everyone gave him a wide berth, and the stationhouse was quieter than normal.

Bill pushed aside his current caseload and started making notes.

She's having an effect on you, he thought as he began to map out his information.

Bill still wasn't able to understand the facts in front of him. He had pieces to a puzzle, but he couldn't be certain that he didn't have more than one puzzle to solve.

Picking up the phone, he called the county records office hoping to find a list of people who may have requested copies of the blueprints to Maureen's family property.

The request would take a couple of days.

Bill continued for the next hour, making inquiries on other missing persons, John Littlepaw — the friend of Charlie's who'd help move the lighthouse's lens — and a few other potential leads. He'd even managed to get nail down the kid who'd damaged Mrs. Mulder's car.

One case down, fifteen more to go, he sighed. Bill didn't like loose ends, and a dozen open cases only intensified that drive to get things in order.

Checking his watch, he remembered his previous phone call from Paul.

Grabbing his coat, he muttered to Edith he was going out and asked if she needed anything.

"No thanks, I already asked Santa to bring me a boss with a better attitude."

She smirked keeping her deadpan stoic face, not even bothering to pause from her filing.

Bill shook his head, unable to scold Edith, and unwilling to show she'd gotten a rise out of him.

Superior Lies

Heading in his SUV, he started wondering why all the women in his life had suddenly decided to get on his nerves.

Waves lapped at the small abandoned island in Lighthouse Bay. Gulls screeched overhead, and the clouds rolling in promised gray skies and rain.

The stone rubble of the abandoned lighthouse echoed the faint scratching and clawing of its occupants.

Rusty brown and dark gray plumage rustled about as the creatures large head dipped and bobbed. In its beak, opening and tugging on the fresh kill, pulling away the bloodied meat from the femur bone of a large man.

Savagely tugging, twisting its head and dropping it into the open, beckoning mouths of her two offspring. Their feathers taking on the appearance of down like a newborn chick, their translucent skin starkly reflecting the coal black of their beaks and eyes.

Their bodies were huddled together in the nest of its mother's making—combined bits of twig, leaves, mingling in with the faded hot pink of a scarf, the dusty blue of a jacket, and weathered bones of its cast off meals. Skulls and bones of sheep, chickens, moose, lay amongst the remains of skulls and bones of its given sacrifices—its human victims.

On the side of the nest, tucked in between the faded blue of an old varsity jacket sleeve that read 'Class of '68', was a cross necklace, dirty and slimy, but still glittering in the late afternoon light with the Lord's prayer etched inside.

By the time the soft pelting of the rain had started, most of the remains of the leg bone had been stripped of its flesh and meat, the bone haphazardly discarded as both mother and offspring huddled inside the cozy confines of their makeshift home.

CHAPTER 50

PAUL CHECKED HIS watch, then checked to make sure his office door was locked. He'd felt uneasy since he'd gotten the results back. Gathering the material he'd compiled for Bill, making sure he didn't miss anything. He couldn't shake the uneasy feeling he'd been having all morning, and he thumbed through the material again hoping for a fresh look at the facts.

But the information looked as it had the night before.

His data was off the charts, showing massive irregularities with the samples, though he personally retested each of them twice. Something wasn't adding into the mix, and his frustration at what should have been a simple analysis was trying his patience.

He'd sent his empirical data to a larger research company he used from time to time for bigger research projects and was surprised as he read the fax in front of him.

Their results had concurred with his.

Human pheromones present in the saliva. Large amounts of Iridium-umtriclorophate, along with adipocere.

Whatever it was that Bill found, it was huge.

Not just for the science industry, but on a deeper scale.

As far as Paul was able to establish, the webbing and its sample didn't coincide with any known animal in the natural kingdom.

Pouring himself another cup of tea, Paul opened his filing cabinet and took out the encyclopedia of cryptozoology. He pulled another book off his shelf, this one on Native American legends.

If the samples were accurate, then Paul didn't need to be looking for anything in the known world of animal species, he needed to be looking in the realms of fantasy land.

"It's a start," he muttered to himself. Loathe to admit that he was grasping at straws, Paul couldn't help but feel a little excited about the possibilities that were nestled somewhere in Lighthouse Bay.

Pamela's phone rang, and she held up her hand.

"I'm sorry I have to take this," she said, answering the phone.

"Let me get that invoice and check, can you hold?" she asked, putting the phone on hold.

"I'm sorry this will only take a minute. I've got a vendor in Green Bay who didn't receive his full shipment."

"Not a problem, I'll just go over these old press photos," Maureen said, spreading out the packet of old press releases and pictorials that had been done on the Tea Caddy in the last five to six years.

"Help yourself to more of Odessa's baked goods and tea. I shouldn't be too long," Pamela said.

Quickly opening the filing cabinet, she searched and finally pulled a folder from the filing cabinet, ascending the stairs.

Maureen spread out the photos and looked them over checking to see how much of the Tea Caddy had changed in the last few years. Most of Main Street had stayed the same, but fresh facades had been put on the storefronts, and trendier boutiques had sprouted up in between the older mom and pop businesses were now the main thoroughfare's status quo.

She checked the stairs, listening for Pamela.

Grabbing another couple of baked goods, Maureen ate, drinking the last of her tea before pouring herself a refill.

She picked up a press release and began reading.

When she'd finished the articles, she looked up searching for a clock.

The room felt hot, and when she stood to pour herself another cup of tea, the room swayed.

Panic hit her like a rogue wave. She tried to listen for Pamela, thinking frantically. Putting her phone to silence, she stuffed it into her shirt and struggled to stand.

She made it to the bottom of the stairs, craning her neck to look up at the darkened figures illuminated by the early afternoon sun.

Maureen squinted, willing all her energy to stay on her feet.

Heavy footsteps descended upon her, and a pair of rough hands pulled her back towards her seat.

A throaty, male voice spoke, but not to her.

"Did she have enough?" he asked.

"I believe so. The tea and sweets were both laced to make certain it'd knock her out. I recognized her the moment she walked in the store. She came in a few weeks back nosing around. I told you not to trust Shawn to handle things—"

"Let's not talk about this now. I want to tie up loose ends here, and get her out of here as quickly as possible."

Maureen tried to focus, her vision going blurry and fading the longer she tried to focus.

"What is…going on here…?"Maureen stammered. She leaned across the desk, her head in her hands.

A wave of nausea washed through her and she breathed deeply, tring to calm the rolling in her stomach.

"We're just going to end up taking a little trip, sugar. Don't you worry about a thing," his voice soothed.

"We have to be careful getting her out of here. I don't know who knows she's here, and I know from the gossip around town she's been shacking up with Bill," Pamela said, snatching Maureen's bag and going through it.

"I'm not seeing a cell phone," Pamela said.

"We'll have to pat her down," he said.

"Now Dwight—", she began.

"Dwight…Dwight Carlisle," Maureen slurred, lifting her head.

"What of it?" he asked. His irritation with Maureen was becoming increasingly hostile.

"Dwight, we need to move her soon," Pamela said, listening to the stairs.

"You don't think I know that, Pam? It's almost hibernation time for them. Do you think I want those things leaving a bloody trail after swooping down at the park's Christmastide Festival? Maybe what we need to drum up business is to have one of those creatures snatch some poor tourist's kiddie and take advantage of the national press coverage," he said angrily.

"I know what time of the year it is. I know what has to be done. But you promised that Shawn was going to take care of it, and he didn't. If he'd taken care of the situation in the first place, none of this would be happening," Pamela shouted.

"Keep your voice down, do you want the whole town to hear?"

"Oh please! I had the sense to close the shop after I called you. You think I'd let in customers while I'm drugging some stranger in the basement? God, you can be so dense sometimes."

"Dwight...Carlisle...I know all...about you," Maureen uttered lifting her head off the desk, trying to focus.

"What do you know, girlie?" Dwight asked, spinning Maureen around in her chair.

"I know you were the last one to see Joanna Davis and William Pierce alive."

Pamela gasped, dropping Maureen's coat.

"What of it?" Dwight snarled. "Last I knew, they were going to elope and get the hell out of this pissant town."

"But they didn't," Maureen slurred. "I read the newspaper articles. I did the research. She was tutoring him to keep from failing science. What happened to them, Dwight? What happened to the other missing persons around the Bay? What happened to my sister?" Maureen wanted to scream but couldn't.

"The same thing that's gonna happen to you," he sneered and grabbed her by the arm.

Her hand had curled around the glass paperweight, it took all she had but she managed to lash out, smash him across the face.

"You bitch," he snarled, backhanding her across the face.

She cried out, spinning around and sliding from the chair like a limp rag. Hitting her head on the hard cement floor, Maureen's ear rung with a tenacity before the ensuing blackness consumed her.

CHAPTER 51

PAUL'S OFFICE PHONE rang, pulling him out of his academic trance. Several books lay open, with multi-colored sticky notes in the margins.

"Hello?" Paul answered, still reading over his research.

"Paul, it's Bill. You got time to meet?"

"Yeah. Actually, I think it's better that we meet rather than talk over the phone. I've got some things I want to show you," Paul said.

"I've been on the road for the last twenty minutes; I'll be there in a few."

"Good. While I have you on the phone, can I ask you who else knows about what you found?"

Bill hesitated.

Can I still trust Paul after all these years?

"A few people, why?" Bill finally answered.

"Because I'm getting the feeling that we've only scratched the tip of the iceberg on this one," Paul said.

"Look, I'm pulling into the parking lot now. I'll be up and we can talk then."

"Okay."

The line went dead.

Maureen shifted, and felt a stabbing pain in her temples and a dull ache in her left shoulder. Her body ached, and cold rain gently pelted her face.

Trying to move, she felt her hands tied behind her back. The bonds around her wrists dug into her skin and burned, creating an odd sensation of heated warmth against the bitter cold wind and rain.

It was still light outside, and her head throbbed every time she tried to open her eyes. She didn't know where she was, and attempting to sit up caused her to plunge back into the blackness.

Paul's office looked exactly like it did the last time Bill had been there. Books still piled on every available space, lining shelves, on top of filing cabinets, piled into neat stacks along the floor like baseboards.

Paul looked up at Bill and moved a stack of books off a chair without as much as a 'hello'.

"So, what's so important that we had to meet in person?" Bill asked.

Paul stood up and locked the door, turning on the radio.

Bill arched a brow at him but didn't say anything.

Paul leaned over, speaking in hushed tones that barely allowed Bill to hear him.

"I'm not sure, but I got a feeling about it. The webbing has human pheromones in it. Most animals that make webbing for nests — whether to catch prey or for their offspring, don't contain human pheromones. And not at this level, either."

"What do you mean?" Bill asked.

"Bill, levels this high is usually associated with a trauma or other highly caustic event. Instances that are related to the equivalent of hitting the winning home run, orgasms, winning the lottery — big moments that cause high levels of hormones and adrenaline."

Bill nodded, still uncertain of what Paul was telling him.

"The webbing has several components that lead me to believe that it was animal regurge — "

"Regurge?"

"Regurgitation. But I don't know how the human pheromones got into the mix. That's why I want to take a clean sample myself."

"Your data's probably wrong, Paul."

"It's not wrong, Bill. I checked the samples twice, then sent them out to another lab. The results match," Paul said, grabbing the faxes he was studying earlier.

Bill didn't know how to read scientific charts, but it didn't take a genius to see that the chart on the left matched the one the outside lab did on the right.

"The lab checked its sample twice, too. I need to get another sample, and I need to know where exactly you found this."

Paul pulled out a map of Michigan's upper coastline and gave Bill a pencil.

After fifteen minutes, Paul had a better indication of where he needed to start looking.

"You still aren't giving me much to go on," Bill said.

"Do you remember Mitch Kirk, from the thirty-fifth airborne?"

"I do. Still get the occasional email from him once and awhile."

"Me too. Do you remember when he got injured in that tank explosion?"

Bill was solemn, remembering all too well the tank explosion that nearly cost Mitch his life.

"Do you remember what the medics said, and the doc said about how he survived?" Paul asked.

"That it was his high levels of adrenaline that kept his heart beating. Yeah, I remember."

"When a body is operating in a fight or flight situation like that, it puts out a lot of adrenaline. Adrenaline is laced with pheromones."

"And these other moments, they produce a lot of pheromones as well?"

"Most definitely. Look, Bill, if my data is accurate, and this webbing does carry human pheromones, that means that something out there had to digest it first, get my drift?"

Bill shook his head.

"I think you've been hitting the Dungeons and Dragons game a little too hard, Paul. There is no animal out there that—"

"Before you say 'that can eat a human', I'd like to point out that there are several that can."

"But you said earlier that this webbing had water algae in it."

"Plankton algae, but yeah, so?"

"So? Animals that make web-like nests are usually reserved for arachnoids and avian, right? I don't know any giant spiders or large birds except in Harry Potter and Lord of the Rings."

"Bill, I need you to keep an open mind. There's something else on the chemical analysis that is blowing the sample off the charts, too."

"What?" Bill asked, his patience waning.

"Do you know what isotopes are?"

"Something like protons and neutrons," Bill said.

"A little more complicated. Isotopes are heavier in atomic weight, and there were traces of radioactive isotope number one-ninety-two in the chemical readouts."

"English, Paul."

"Sorry. Certain radioactive isotopes are found in a large number of common elements. But radioactive isotopes, especially isotope number one-ninety-two, are rare."

"How rare?" Bill asked.

"It's found in the mantle and core deep down in the earth. It's more commonly found in meteorites."

"Meteorites. Jesus Paul, please don't tell me I'm looking for freaking extraterrestrials or UFO's because I'm really not in the mood."

"I'm not. However, you are looking for something or someplace that experienced meteor showers, hence the traces of isotope one-ninety-two and iridiumtriclorophate."

"What and where?" Bill asked, sitting back down and looking at the map of Lake Superior.

"Meteor showers happen all the time. In order to give this much trace in a sample, we'd need a significant amount of meteorites to hit. The last massive shower was sometimes after World War Two."

Bill looked at Paul.

"Are you telling me that this webbing might have been around Lighthouse Bay since the late forties, and no one has bothered to notice?" he asked.

"It's possible, but again, I have nothing to compare it to, Bill."

Bill tried to pace in the cramped office and looked at him.

"I think I know where we need to look, but first, I want to make a call. But I can't tell my deputies to start looking for aliens and tribal lore."

"Look," Paul said, grabbing a book and pointing to earmarked pages. "There are several Native American tribes that point out leg-ends of large animals in their folklore."

"Paul, people are missing. I can't go back and tell my deputies that we are looking for mythical creatures and animals of Native American folklore. I need something concrete, and something that will help us."

"Tell me about the missing persons?" Paul asked.

It took Bill nearly thirty minutes to give Paul all the details. When Bill was finished, Paul ran a hand through his hair.

"Look, Bill, I'd like to offer you something more, but I can only offer you what science gives me. We can go out and take another sample if you want," Paul said.

"How long will that take?"

"Depends. If I get a new sample, get it back here and test it, and it matches the results to the first batch I ran, then you have your proof."

"Proof of what?" Bill asked.

"I don't know. But I know that my results aren't wrong, and neither are the labs. The sample has human pheromones in it. It has traces of Iridiumtriclorophate and adipocere. I did the general inquiries into my research. I can't find any other trace of research on the webbing that has all three of those components. I wasn't able to come up with anything. What else can you tell me?"

"You know everything about the case," Bill snapped.

"What about missing animals, unusual inquiries into killed livestock?" Paul asked. "Usually missing animals and slaughtered livestock are indicators of something wrong in a species environment which forces them to go outside of their normal eating patterns."

Bill thought about it.

"I'd have to check with animal control and the livery about the animals, but I'd think if anything was up, I'd have heard about it by now."

"That should be something to look into," Paul said. "Also, I want to comb the beach as well."

"We've done that, and no other evidence was found."

"No, because you weren't looking for it. Bill, I'm a biologist, I know what to look for in terms of animal migration."

"Well, what's your schedule look like—"Bill started before his walkie went off.

"Sherriff Downs."

"Sheriff, this is Josh. I've had the team all over town. No one's seen hide or hair of Shawn. But we did find his pickup truck off of Sumner's Ridge about two hundred yards directly above your cabin. From the looks of things, I think he was watching you for some time."

"You know that for certain?"

Paul had been busy shoving the faxes and data, along with several books into a worn leather satchel.

"Sir, there are at least a few dozen beer cans up here, and probably several cartons of cigarette butts."

"Rope it off and get forensics up there. Put an APB out on Shawn."

"Sir, we also got a call from Fran at the diner. Apparently, Ms. Welsh was due for lunch, in order to do a magazine article and take some photos. She was no show. Fran said she normally wouldn't worry, but after she talked to Edith at lunch—Fran was worried that Maureen wasn't with you and asked me to give you a call to see if she's okay."

"She isn't with me. Send a unit to my place and one to the Prescott residence. I want you personally to go over and talk to Fran and get any details you can on where Maureen could have been headed."

"Already done, Sir. I pulled her credit cards, contacted her attorney Alfred Meyers, and we've got a warrant out for her cell phone records."

"Well done, Josh. I'm heading back there now, keep me posted. Downs out."

Bill looked at Paul, who'd grabbed his coat and keys.

"Where do you think you're going?" Bill asked.

"With you. Look, you said that her family's estate is by water and that the webbing was found on the beach. We should start there."

"We don't have time. Shawn's crazy, but he's not stupid. And now with Maureen missing, I'm walking a very fine line. One missing person is bad enough, but another one and I need some help."

"You need a science guy who knows about animal behavior, and besides, I think there's more to this case than just Maureen and her missing sister. I hate to say this, but that girl has been nothing but a rollercoaster of trouble since you met her," Paul said, locking his office door and scribbling a note on the dry erase board.

"Yeah, good thing for me I like roller coasters." Bill smiled.

Chapter 52

BILL PULLED HIS SUV off to the side of the road, taking a vantage point from behind a line of juniper bushes that provided some privacy between the Greater Lewanee Maritime Museum and the Lewanee Marina.

"What are we doing here?" Paul asked.

"I want to talk to Victoria again, and maybe you two can confer. I have a call that went to voicemail that I need to check."

Bill dialed his voicemail and listened, stiffening in the seat enough for Paul to take notice. After a few moments, he snapped his phone shut.

"Bad news?" Paul asked.

"No. Odd if anything. Did you know that Coast Guard abandoned a small station on Gull's Peak in the early thirties?"

"No, but what of it?"

"It's odd. They up and moved, and the station wasn't just decommissioned, it was on their disavowed list."

The military's disavowed locations lists were for rogue officers and other official personal that turn sides and aided the enemy.

"Buildings don't get placed on disavowed lists, people do. It's probably a clerical error," Paul said.

"That's what I thought, but my source took a deeper look. No, the island was put on the list, but the government retains the rights to the property. Apparently it had a recurring infestation of wolf spiders that they couldn't get rid of, and decided to move the station further up the channel."

Paul took out his map.

"That doesn't seem likely," Paul said. "Arachnoids generally don't like water. Additionally, they don't usually set up house in heavily occupied buildings. Maybe after the station was abandoned. The dates were probably just entered wrong."

336

"No, my source checked. He said that every once in a while, a general inquiry is made through central command, and a Coast Guard cutter goes out to survey the island."

"Again, so?"

Paul told him about Charlie and the lighthouse.

"I don't know, Bill. I don't see how an abandoned lighthouse ties into this missing girl or Maureen."

"I don't exactly know either, but I know it's part of a bigger puzzle. Come on, let's go talk to Victoria."

When Bill and Paul entered the museum, they caught Victoria off guard, pulling out boxes from the attic storage space.

"Bill, what a surprise," she said, giving him a quick hug. "Who's your friend?"

"This is Paul; he's a friend of mine. We were hoping to pick your brain if you have a few minutes," Bill said.

"Actually, I'm due for a meeting soon, and—"

"You have this specimen wrong," Paul interjected, having wandered over towards a curio case display of pelican skeletons put on display.

"I beg your pardon?" Victoria asked, setting the box onto the counter.

"This wing is all wrong. This femur bone is the wrong size for this type of breed," Paul said, looking over the other animals on display.

"Who's your friend again, the museum police?" Victoria asked, not bothering to hide her agitation.

"Lighten up Vic, he's in the field. We wanted to talk to you about Gull Island."

Victoria tilted her head and looked at Bill.

"What's this all about?" she asked, checking her watch.

"We want to know the history of it actually," Bill said, looking around.

"Oh, that's easy," Victoria said. She walked over grabbing a history of the Great Lakes, and handing it to Bill. "There's bound to be something in there on it."

"Vic, I need your help on this," Bill said, looking at the book.

"I told you I don't have time. I have a meeting this afternoon and I can't be late."

"Just a few minutes," Bill pressed.

"You never did know when to take no for an answer, Bill," came a voice from the doorway.

Bill turned around, staring at Mayor Carlisle, his .44 Magnum revolver pointed directly at him.

337

The sun hung low in the autumn sky, the chill increasing as night slowly descended. Maureen's bones ached, the only reassurance that she was still alive.

Above her, she could hear the sounds of scratchy squawking, a mired off-key melody of animalistic caterwauling, and she finally managed to push past the pain enough to open her eyes. Above her, the gray skies of late autumn. Billowy clouds of grayish white hung low in the sky, threatening snow.

She struggled into a sitting position, the bindings around her wrist burning with every minute movement, sawing their way deeper into her skin.

Looking around, she was inside the remains of a bricked, stone building.

A warehouse? A cottage?

Her ears buzzed with an incessant ringing, and her left cheek throbbed. Her lip felt swollen, probably where Mayor Carlisle had backhanded her.

Mayor Carlisle.

It came flooding back to her, her own nightmarish accident playing again in her head in slow motion.

The squawking grew louder, more shrill. Scooting to peer around the crumbled wall of a building, Maureen saw the vast openness of dark blue water.

She listened.

Waves lapped against a shore to her right, and she desperately tried to crane her neck for a better look when out of the corner of her eye, a large shadow loomed overhead.

Maureen kneeled and willed herself to look over the wall. Thirty feet in the distance, its silvery eyes intently focused on the open, hungry mouths of her offspring, was the crouching figure of owlish like bird that she'd seen once before.

In its mouth, hung a bloody piece of meat with a long bone jutting from inside its beak.

She slid back down the wall slowly, willing herself not to throw up, and tried to think of a way not to die.

CHAPTER 53

"SORRY, BILL. I tried to be nice and get you out of here, but you just don't listen," Victoria said, walking from behind the counter and standing near Mayor Carlisle.

Bill looked from her to the Mayor.

She smiled.

"Dwight doesn't like to be kept waiting," she winked and walked over, placing a single kiss on the mayor's cheek.

When the Mayor smiled, his overly white teeth shown through, reminding Bill of why he disliked politicians.

"Where's Maureen?" Bill finally asked.

"What does it matter?" Victoria asked.

"It matters to me. Where's Maureen?" Bill repeated. "For that matter, where's Hannah? Come to think of it, there are a lot of people I'd like to ask old Dwight about," Bill said.

"Don't take another step, Bill," the Mayor warned.

"You're a weasely little bastard, Dwight so I get you part in this. But you Vic? I don't get your part in all this," Bill said.

"Silly Billy, you don't know the half of it. You think Maureen's missing because she was nosing around about her sister?"

Paul looked at the scene, his hand clutching the leather satchel.

"Isn't it?" Bill asked.

Victoria laughed, shaking her head so her hair fanned loosely around her.

"Nope. That's the best part. That's what everyone will think, and they'll never know the real cause, will they, baby?" she asked, smiling at Dwight as she went over to her office and brought out a suitcase and a small duffel bag.

"Shut it, Vicki. The less anyone knows, the better," the Mayor cautioned.

"Don't tell me to shut it; I'm not your damned wife, Dwight. Bill asked me a question, and I'm going to answer him. You see Billy boy, a girl can't make a living as a curator of a museum in a little town."

"So this is about money, then?" Bill asked. "You want a ransom from Hannah's parents for their daughters?"

"No, you moron. It's about earning my part. A few of us had help."

"Help with what?"

"Selecting the ones that would die. When Dwight and I first started our little affair, he got carried away one night after too much cheap wine and spilled the beans. Do you know the things that are out there, Bill? Have you ever seen one?" she asked, going over to the locked cabinet and removing a few pieces.

"I have. Just recently in fact. They're hideous. They eat anything, even rats. Shawn can attest to that," she said and tucked the pieces into the duffle bag.

"What's the skirt talking about," Bill looked at the Mayor.

The Mayor's face appeared to be relieved a little as if he'd been holding in a burden that was making him physically ill.

"We didn't know what was out there, or why the lighthouses could never keep their keepers. My father sunk the town's entire fiscal budget in rebuilding the beaches, trying to create some tourism into this shithole of a town. But we didn't know what was out on the island until we woke it up."

Bill listened, keeping an eye on Paul out of the corner of his eye. There was no time for Bill to draw his weapon, disarm Dwight, and keep Paul out of harm's way.

I'm going to have to play this one out, he thought grimly.

"And I helped.' Victoria said. "It was easy. I helped with misinformation, and as curator, I had a firsthand crack at the town's historical documents."

"Why not just tell the Coast Guard about them?" Bill asked.

"Then those scientists from the government would fly up here, claim imminent domain to study the damned things and the real estate mar-ket plunges. No thanks," the Mayor said, the gun still pointed at Bill.

"So your property value goes down, it's not worth someone's life," Paul said.

"You don't get it. They were here before the town was settled. I heard my granddaddy talk about them to my dad, and then my dad to me. They tried hunting them, but it didn't work. Nothing did. Then we found out by accident what attracted them, and a few of the town's founders decided if they couldn't defeat the beasts, they'd at least be able to pick the victims — keep their own families safe."

"That's barbarous," Bill said. "What gives you people the right to play God?"

"They did what they had to, and I'm doing what I have to."

"How do you choose?" Bill asked, taking a slight step to the left.

"Pamela found out the hard way. She was drying marijuana in her barn along with some of those fancy teas when a few of the things attacked. It took off with a pig, I mean a full-size pig," the Mayor said, his face sweating.

"We thought it had to be something in the barn. Through trial and error, we narrowed it down to the teas. Those fancy teas that she sells are cheap imitations mixed with everyday herbs. The relaxing one she made is made with chamomile and pot for Christ's sake."

"So these things were attracted to the scent of the teas?" Paul asked.

The Mayor snapped his head in his direction, gun along with it.

"Yeah. But only the one, because of the herbs in it. And we'd discovered they had a long hibernation period. We figured if we could select the victims, draw them away from town, and feed them, they'd leave the townspeople alone," the Mayor sighed.

Bill shook his head, his face grim.

"So you selected Hannah Prescott as your next victim," Bill prodded.

"No. The elders get together and we select a victim that way. Usually no more than two or three, and we always try to make sure they're vagrants or tourists; we'd never sacrifice a townie," the Mayor said with an air of pride.

"Gee, how generous of you. I'll be sure to relay that to the victims' families. Hey, you might even get re-elected with that," Bill spat.

"Don't you dare judge me! I did what I had to do, we all did. You think I asked for this life. I inherited this mess from my father, just like he inherited it from his. No one asked for this to happen, we just made the best of it and went on with our lives," the Mayor said. His face had flushed, anger and resentment seeping through his otherwise cavalier exterior.

"So we're going to be the next victims?" Paul asked, leaning against one of the display cases.

"Absolutely. Make sure they're good and fed, and maybe we won't have to have another feeding in the spring," Victoria said.

"Unlikely," Paul commented.

"Yeah, what do you know," Victoria shot. "I've read everything I've could about them from settler's diaries, captain's logs, firsthand accounts. I know them, and I know how they work. We've domesticated them. Face it, some pencil pushing geek like you can't believe that a woman outsmarted you," Victoria smirked.

"Other people know," Bill said.

"Right. Conspiracy theorists have no effect on anything that we are doing," Victoria said, opening drawers and pulling the occasional trinkets and pocketing them into her open duffel bag. "They'll only serve to drive the tourist industry and ghost hunters. Look how many have popped up on Mackinac Island. It's going to spread here as well."

"But those things are still out there," Bill said.

"I know. But the elders control them, Bill. You'd do well to remember that," Victoria sneered.

"Only a fool thinks you can control Mother Nature and her mutations," Paul stated.

"It's worked for us this long. I don't think either of you will stop us," the Mayor said.

"I always knew you were a vain, self-righteous bitch, but I didn't think you had a God complex to boot," Bill said.

"You're just a dumb hick who doesn't know a real woman when he sees one," the Mayor commented.

"When I see one, I'll let you know," Bill smirked, and Victoria marched around the corner and smacked him squarely across the face.

"Victoria, no—"the Mayor shouted.

Bill managed to grab her wrist, snapping before bringing it behind her back, using her body as a shield.

"Let go of me," she shrieked. She struggled against Bill's grasp, flailing her good arm and legs, but it was pointless. Bill easily kept her secured.

"Do you really think you have something to bargain with?" the Mayor asked.

"Put the gun down and kick it over to me, and I'll let her go. You wouldn't want anything to happen to your mistress," Bill breathed, holding her tight.

The Mayor laughed, and it made Bill nervous.

"My mistress. One of many, and if I get bored with them, I have a needy wife at home," the Mayor said, and readjusted his aim on Victoria. "If you ask me, it's one more loose end to tie up. It's been fun, Vicki, but Bill's right; you are a vain, self-centered bitch," he smirked.

Bill ducked, instinctively covering Victoria with his body as the shot rang out, and amidst her screams, Bill could hear Paul shout, "Clear."

Bill's ear rung from being in close quarters with a gunshot.

Bill kept Victoria pressed to the ground, but managed to look up and see Paul standing over the Mayor's body.

A small bloody stain appeared, growing slow and deepening in color. Underneath his portly frame, a brownish red puddle was forming.

The Mayor's lips parted, small gurgling sounds erupting from his opened mouth as his body jerked, convulsing in his death throes.

The thick, metallic smell of blood filled the room, and Bill kneeled, frozen for a moment, staring at the face of one of the last two people who knew where Maureen might be.

CHAPTER 54

POLICE CARS, AN ambulance, and the coroner's van were just inside the tight confines of the roped off area around the museum.

A large gathering of onlookers had formed, and Bill couldn't shake the feeling he was being watched.

Inside in the ambulance, Victoria sat handcuffed with one hand to the gurney, while medics checked her out and taped her wrist.

"Where's Maureen, Victoria? I need to know, and I need to know who else is involved," Bill demanded.

He'd given Victoria her Miranda rights, and she'd remained stoic albeit irritated, refusing to answer any questions no matter how much Bill leaned on her.

"Fine, have it your way. Tell me something, in all of your research into those things, did you ever read anything on women's prisons? You know what they do to petite, assertive little redheads in prison," Bill warned.

It was cliché, but he noticed the sudden stiffness in her posture.

I need to break that pampered reserve.

"There won't be any Chanel suits or time for manicures. No makeup, and no designer bags, Vic," he said, watching her face for signs.

The quick lapse she had earlier vanished, replaced with the same frozen demeanor.

Bill was running out of time. Evidence in a missing person's case grows colder with each passing hour. If police can't find enough leads in the first forty-eight hours, the odds of solving the case cut in half.

Taking another track, Bill called over Deputy Haskell, talking to him briefly before returning his attention back to Victoria.

"So, just a few more questions, Vic. Does Carlos have all his shots?"

"What," Victoria looked at him.

344

"Yes, animal control is going to want to know if he's up to date on his shots. That'll determine on whether or not he'll be euthanized immediately."

"What?" she asked again. This time, that steely iron façade dropped, her face flushing scarlet. "Why would anyone put down Carlos," she demanded.

"It's procedure. This is a crime scene," Bill waved his hand towards the building. "We can't have a cat wandering around our crime scene. We can't lock the poor thing inside the building with no one to take care of him. He went home with you every night, but you're going to jail, at least until you can make bail. That could be days, a few weeks."

Her face drained of color, staring at the building and then back at Bill.

"This way, animal control can put him up for adoption instead of just killing him outright," Bill commented. He watched her face.

Her bottom lip trembled, and she swallowed.

"If I tell you what I know, promise me you'll take Carlos," she said her voice soft with emotion.

"Oh no, I don't have time for animals. I—"

"Do you want to find Maureen, or not. He's a good cat and he's already housebroken, he…" her voice trailed off.

Well, I'll be damned, he thought.

"He what?" Bill asked.

"He doesn't deserve that because I screwed up," she said, her shoulders slumping. She started to cry, and Bill felt the faintest twinge of sympathy for her.

"All right, it's a deal. I'll take the cat. Now, tell me what you know."

"I didn't kill any of them. Dwight did, so did Pamela, the two others they talked to I never met."

"Men, women?" asked Bill.

"Both men. I didn't get names, and I didn't ask. I don't know where they took Maureen, but Dwight did tell someone on the phone that Shawn had been taken care of." She sniffed, as Deputy Haskell brought out the cat inside a cardboard carrier.

"Where's Maureen?" Bill asked.

"I think she's on the island. Dwight called me from his boat, telling me that he had docked and he'd be right over. That's when you walked in. I don't know anything else. Honest, Bill. Can I say…goodbye to him?" She looked at him, pleading.

Bill waved the deputy over, and Victoria called to the cat, telling him to be good, and that she loved him.

345

Paul rejoined Bill as the ambulance took her away.

"Who knew she'd cave over threatening her cat," Paul commented.

"It was a hunch that played off. I've heard of hardened killers crying like babies over the death of their mothers, loss of a dog, birth of their kid. Stranger things have happened," Bill said.

"Where are we heading now?" Paul asked.

"Out there," he pointed, as several uniformed men followed him out of the Marina, where the vast gray-blue water of Lake Superior stretched out before them.

The rocky waters of Lake Superior grew grayer in color, deepening to a coal black casting an ominous haze over the water.

Bill found a GPS unit in the Mayor's boat, and while deputies searched the boat for evidence and clues, Bill and Paul had joined in the search with the Coast Guard for Maureen.

Lake Superior held roughly over a hundred tiny small islands, with about twenty in the immediate area. Ranging from small islands in channels and inlets not more than barren rocks to larger islands overgrown by vegetation.

A Coast Guard helicopter out of Duluth did an aerial search but didn't turn up anything. Bill and Paul were on board a Coast Guard Cutter 47-970, known affectionately to her crew as Little Hawk, as it headed out of the Lighthouse Bay.

The GPS coordinates ended ten miles due west once out of the bay. But there were six islands in that vicinity and they had maybe an hour to ninety minutes of daylight left.

Temperatures dropped, and the chill seeped into Bills bones.

If Maureen was alive and out here, the odds were stacked against her. Hypothermia, the elements, and....

...them.

Those giant creatures that he knew little about, let alone how to fend them off, were out there.

And they were hungry.

"Tell me again what they're looking for," Paul said, stepping out onto the observation deck of the cutter.

"We've got the last known GPS coordinates from Carlisle's boat. I'm hoping that wherever he went, will be where he's keeping Maureen," Bill said.

He pulled his jacket further around him.

"Assuming he had Maureen," Paul said, handing Bill a cup of coffee.

Bill took it, sipping it.

"It's the best lead I have. Deputies went over to Pamela's house and shop and found Maureen's coat and bag in the dumpster. If she's out here, she won't last long in the elements."

"And if she's not?" Paul asked.

Bill didn't want to think about it. About the possibility that Maureen would end up like Hannah.

God, I can't imagine Maureen becoming another victim.

"Sherriff Downs," his walkie crackled.

Bill went inside and answered.

"Downs here."

"We pinged her cell phone and got a hit." It was Deputy Walker.

"Go ahead, Sid."

"Deputy Hopson went through the Ms. Welsh's cabin and Magnus picked up her scent, but it stops in the driveway. We've combed the beach but found nothing. Deputy Fielder has Pamela Betts in custody. She's lawyered up, and her son and Mayor Carlisle's daughter are with her."

"What about the cell phone trace, Sid? Any luck?"

"I've sent the coordinates to your phone now. It's on, but it goes straight to voicemail."

"Good. Keep me informed. Downs out."

"Is it good news?" Paul asked.

"We got a ping on Maureen's cell phone. It's on, but it's going straight to voicemail. I'm hoping we can triangulate her whereabouts from the coordinates in Carlisle's GPS and her phone."

Bill and Paul headed to the command deck, giving the new coordinates to the Coxswain, who steered the boat to an oblong island off of Prestwick Pointe.

Twenty minutes later, Coast Guard had dropped anchor, and a small rescue boat had roared towards shore.

The sun was setting, the wind had picked up, and Bill couldn't shake the sinking feeling in his gut that he was too late.

CHAPTER 55

MAUREEN'S LIMBS ACHED. Her teeth were chattering, and she was bone cold. Even the ropes around her wrists and ankles that lacerated her skin as she struggled to free herself from her bonds, no longer burned as they cut fresh marks into her skin.

She'd dozed in and out of consciousness, and from the looks of the setting sun, Maureen guessed she'd had about a half an hour daylight left.

The thought of being in total darkness scared her. The overwhelming sense of isolation had shaken her early on, and it hadn't left. Fear crept through her in unsuspecting waves, making her shiver.

She tried to do like they do in the movies in bring her tied hands under her and over her feet from behind, but it was easier said than done. After two failed attempts, Maureen had spent nearly twenty minutes searching the ground for a sharp rock, a piece of glass, anything that might allow her to cut through her bonds.

Pushing herself into a sitting position, she'd scooted quietly along the wall at the far end of the stone remains, nestled amongst the dried overgrowth and fallen debris. It helped to block some of the wind and gave her a better vantage point of her surroundings.

She knew she was on an island, but which one? Lake Superior was a big lake.

Slate blue water, marked by icy caps of white, stretched around her on all sides.

Even if I do manage to get free and swim off the island, which direction was land?

The thought of dying on the island, torn apart by the huge owl-like creatures wasn't any more appealing than drowning or hypothermia in the chilly waters of Lake Superior.

Maureen wanted to cry and then cursed herself for doing the clichéd girlish response she'd seen in countless horror movies.

The sun was sinking low in the sky, its coppery light turning the afternoon sky shades of soft pink and purple.

It'd be beautiful save for the whole death and dying part.

She hadn't been paying attention to closely, but something in her subconscious clicked, and she stopped to listen.

Her breathing stilled, and she heard the gentle rustling of the thing in its nest.

Maureen didn't know what to call it.

She crouched down, trying to wiggle as best she could into the thicket of brush and rubble for safety. Through the cracks in her line of vision, Maureen saw it again.

The large head was covered in rusty brown and gray plumage, the shortness of the feathers made it look more reptilian than avian. Yellow eyes with wide pupils stared out at her, and Maureen closed her eyes to avoid making eye contact.

Her heart thudded in her chest as it tilted its head back, but it didn't cry out.

Instead, it lifted its oblong head into the air and deeply inhaled, loudly sniffing and snorting at the air, craning feathered neck at the faint scent that wafted through the air.

Opening its mouth, Maureen saw a thick line of drool ooze from its beak.

A deep gurgling inhale, wet and heavy, with a light hissing like a teakettle only deeper in tone—the sound of it made Maureen's blood curdled.

She jerked in response, and its large oblong head craned instantly at the sudden noise.

It stood up, and Maureen guessed that it was probably eight feet tall or better. Its body was long and lean, the feathers matching the same pattern as the feathers on its head, and it heaved its form over the fallen rock wall and started making its way towards her.

Maureen pressed herself against the fallen rock wall, her hands tied as she desperately tried to take cover.

It hissed, and the noise made Maureen's blood turn cold.

She lay on her side, her face pressed against the dirt and watched as its claw-like feet, slightly webbed, stomped towards her.

Bill and Paul offloaded onto the island aiding the Coast Guard crew with their search.

Paul had briefed them as much as possible on what things were on the island, and Bill provided a description of Maureen.

Daylight waning, the wind had whipped around the island with renewed fierceness.

"We can't stay here long, Sherriff. We'll do a thorough search, but the water's dangerous at night."

"She's here, we have confirmation of her cell phone," Bill said.

"With all due respect, we know her cell phone is here. Hawkins, Graham, you flank that path and walkie back with any signs of the women. Hoyt, go with him and keep your gun drawn. The people who dumped the women may still be here."

"Aye aye, sir."

They split up; leaving Bill, Paul and Commander Wilson veered to the right and resumed their search. Ten minutes later, the tall pines gave way to a clearing, where the shadowy remains of the fallen stone lighthouse stood against the pastel sky.

Commander Wilson walkied the others, instructing them to maintain radio silence and proceed with extreme precaution.

Bill was armed with his Glock, Commander Wilson with his Beretta, and Paul was armed with the Coast Guard's Orlean flare gun, with spare flares shoved into his pockets.

Bill started to take point before Commander Wilson stopped him. "Sorry Sherriff, this search is under Coast Guard authority, so I have point. You," he said to Paul, "take my right and hang back. Bill, you bring up the lead."

They moved in, making their way with stealth like precision towards the ruins.

Wind blocked out any sounds, and Bill resisted the urge to call out to Maureen.

Twenty feet from the remains, they took cover behind some wild raspberry bushes to assess the situation when all three stopped cold.

Nestled inside a large nest roughly four feet in diameter, were two brownish red creatures. Their chest cavities rose and fell, sleeping soundlessly.

Paul was the first to break the silence.

"My God, it looks like a pterosaur," he whispered.

"A what?" Commander Wilson asked.

"A pterosaur. An early version of a pteranodon," Paul said, risking his safety for a few brief pictures on his camera phone.

They moved towards the remains of the fallen lighthouse, getting closer to the nest. The rest of the boat crew joined them as their path merged on the other side of the ruins. Mouths open at the sight of the sleeping, feathered creatures nestled not more than twenty feet away, they looked to their commander to lead.

The warrant officer pulled his gun, and Paul held up his flare gun. The other two men were armed with only pepper spray.

They didn't see what made the noise, they felt it.

A large boom resonated over the ground, shaking the men were they stood.

Then another.

Bill inhaled slowly, his heart thudding in his chest. The sun was setting giving the team another fifteen minutes of daylight if they were lucky. If they were caught out here in the pitch black, it would be a hell of a run back to the safety of the anchored boats.

A sinking feeling settled in the bottom of Bill's stomach. He didn't like being out here on a rescue amongst a team of lightly armed officers who weren't expecting this.

Diminishing light, unfamiliar surroundings, and lack of firepower against something that he didn't quite believe, pushed his nerves to the breaking point.

He hadn't heard or seen Maureen, but this was his best shot.

You might lose her, a little voice inside his head warned him.

The men took cover, and Commander Wilson advanced, turning back to Bill. He held up his first two fingers, pointed at the wall and then back as his own eyes.

He'd made a visual on Maureen, and Bill gave a thumbs up, relaying the same signal to the rest of the crew.

The creature stood on its hind legs, dominating its eight-foot tall presence as it stalked towards her, grunting and sniffing.

Bill couldn't tell if it had picked up Maureen's scent or the scent of the rescue team.

Paul moved towards Bill, whispering in his ear.

"Mayor said it was attracted to the scent of those teas. If they fed them to Maureen or laced her person with them —"

Paul didn't get to finish his sentence as the rustling in the nest grew louder, following by a wet squawking hiss.

In an instance, the creature turned its head at the noise of its offspring and caught sight of the rescue team.

It turned, outstretching wings and hissing loudly at them, and everyone received a bone-chilling full frontal glimpse into the vestige of its macabre physique.

Its wings, a coal black covered in small feathers. Its torso was lean, its physique slim and taut, showing no signs of gender specification. The arms were short, maybe one-third of the length of its legs, and its webbed claws looked opaque in dusky twilight.

"It looks like it's covered in steel," one of the boat crew said, taking a few steps back.

"That's a big goddamned moth," the warrant officer cursed.

"It's Quixilcoebus...or the Birdman...it's...breathtaking," Paul stammered.

"It's toast," Bill said, as he flanked around Commander Wilson.

It hissed at the crew but made no motion to follow Bill. Its large, lidless eyes were almond shaped, spanning around the contours of its face.

"It's torn between us and protecting its young. Carlisle said that feeding season was almost over; that they're going to hibernate soon. It needs Maureen to sustain them through the winter," Bill said, trying to make a visual on Maureen.

He spotted her, crouched under the fallen debris and underbrush.

"Maureen, can you make it to me," Bill shouted, his gun pointed at the creature.

"I can't," she called. "My hands are tied behind me, so are my feet. Get out of here! That thing's going to kill you."

"Not without you," Bill shouted. He turned to Commander Wilson.

"If you can get to Maureen, untie her feet, we can make for the boat and I'll provide cover."

Commander Wilson spoke to warrant officer Hoyt.

"Give me cover, and keep it coming. If I go down, get them back to the boat and radio for air support. Do not, I repeat, do not attempt to rescue me."

"Aye, sir."

Commander Wilson hunched to the ground, gun drawn as he cautiously made his way to Maureen. She could see his figure getting closer, and held her breath as the sun started to sink into the west.

CHAPTER 56

DARKNESS DIDN'T ENVELOP them all at once, it settled upon them like fog, slowly blanketing them in shadow.

Maureen sat up, half waiting for her rescue, half-waiting to die.

She watched, every second stretching on before her like an eternity before a uniformed man made it to her and kneeled, watching the creature from the corner of his eye as he turned his attention to the rope binding Maureen's feet.

"Who are you?" Maureen asked.

Taking out his pocket knife, the man said, "Commander Wilson, US Coast Guard. " He sawed at the rope.

Maureen was desperate and whimpered in pent up anticipation and fear as she saw the creature turn its head toward them, drool covered its face and chest.

"Over here," Paul shouted and waved his hands at the creature.

It snapped its head back, raising on its sturdy haunches and sniffing at the air again.

"Oh God, get me loose," Maureen breathed.

He freed her feet and hands.

"Stay behind me," the Commander ordered.

Maureen crouched down, following his footsteps as Commander Wilson, keeping a watchful eye on the creature, made his way back to the crew.

Halfway between her hiding spot and the rescue team, it whipped its head back in Maureen's direction and started that same rapid sniffing.

It stood up on its frame, its wings shaking as it uttered another high-pitched hiss that shattered the night.

"They drugged me," Maureen said. "It wants me."

Boom.

It took one-step towards Maureen.

Commander Wilson fired off a warning shot.

353

The fledglings in the nest started to hiss and spit, reminding Maureen of the sounds that a newborn kitten makes.

It turned back to the cries of its offspring and Commander Wilson and Maureen started to close the gap.

Boom.

Another step towards Maureen.

"Oh God," she breathed and kept making her way step by step towards the rescue team. She could see Bill, and Paul yet their presence gave her no comfort.

Even if she made it to the boat with them, it could fly.

The thought of being swooped up out of the boat like a fish by a hawk made Maureen's knees buckle.

"Stay alert," Commander Wilson beckoned.

Images of its oblong head and rows of razor teeth flashed in her mind.

I'd never be able to fight it off, she thought.

What if I do make it to the boat, and we get back to land, will it always be able to find me?

The fledglings screeched and hissed, and the mother creature flapped her large wings, creating a whirlwind of dust as she started to take flight.

"Shoot it," Bill said.

Warrant officer Hoyt fired off two rounds.

It was midair, and circled around the lighthouse, her nest of offspring, and the rescue team that separated her from her meal.

Flying upwards, turning, and swooping down, Maureen screamed as it made a beeline for her.

Even in the near darkness, Maureen could sense the charge in the air.

Evil carries a different scent.

The thing hissed at her and circled around them. Officer Hoyt and Bill fired at it, one shot hitting its wing in the shoulder joint as it desperately tried to stay a flight, spiraling the thirty feet to the ground with a loud thud.

Silence.

The fledglings grew silent.

Maureen and the Commander made it safely to the rescue team, climbing down the hill as quickly as the dark would allow them.

Then around them the hissing erupted again, a bitter venomous to it as the creature leapt over the wall remains and charged them.

"Shoot it," Bill yelled.

Bill pushed Maureen to the ground as he, Wilson, and Hoyt fired off rounds into the near pitch-blackness at the towering monster.

A loud whooshing went past Maureen as the night sky suddenly lit up hitting its intended target with a pelting thwack that followed by a scent of burned animal flesh.

She turned to look over her shoulder to see Paul, reloading a flare gun.

The flare had lodged itself in the middle of one of its wings, and it shook itself back and forth trying to free the burning flare from its singed flesh.

Bright red light lit up the terrain of the lighthouse and its remains, allowing the rescue team clear sight of the path back to the boat.

The unarmed officers grabbed Maureen, who was followed by Bill and officer Hoyt.

Commander Wilson brought up the rear with Paul, who had his flare gun aimed onto the creature with the rest of the men.

It struggled, but kept advancing, the hissing and sputtering of its offspring growing louder, like thunderous ovation from a mutant audience of bystanders.

Craning its neck, sniffing the air wildly, the crew was able to disappear into the safety of trees and into the boat before it roared up through the tree line.

Even wounded, it still managed flight.

Paul shot off another flare, illuminating their target.

Maureen screamed, and the men opened fire.

The boat's engine roared to life as Commander Wilson climbed in, ordering them into their life jackets and to hang on.

Barely fifteen feet from shore, the creature swooped down again.

Hoyt shouted he had to reload as Bill and Wilson gave a volley of bullets. It was Paul's last flare that managed to sink into the creature's neck.

Its baleful, high-pitched hissing turned to a sonorous gurgling as the creature stopped mid-flight and flew into the blackened waters of Lake Superior.

Even in the water, the flare continued to burn, its haunting and surreal image disappearing into the fathomless murky depths.

Jennifer Gifford

A long day, followed by an even longer night of boat rides, emergency room visits, statements and depositions, and many questions.

By the time Maureen was done, her voice was hoarse; she had downed nearly an entire pot of coffee although the caffeine did little to stave off the imminent exhaustion that clung to her bones.

State police had cairned off the island.

None of the fledglings were found, the nest abandoned and empty by the time police had found it.

But they did find an abundance of skeletal remains, many which were rumored to be human.

Desperate for a hot shower, a hot meal, and sleep, Maureen was released shortly after dawn the following morning.

Bill left the wrap up of the investigation to Sid and the others, stating that he and Maureen were going back to his place, and he was taking the next two days off.

CHAPTER 57

SHE SETTLED FOR a hot shower and two cheeseburgers from Burger King.

They wordlessly climbed into bed that night.

Though tired, sleep eluded her.

"Bill?" she asked, staring up into the dark.

"Yeah," he said.

"Is Paul going to come out of this okay?" she asked.

Paul's deposition had been the hardest since it was he who had killed Mayor Carlisle.

"Yeah. It's going to be a case of self-defense."

"That's it? A simple case of self-defense?"

"Well, not simple. The mayor's daughter is married to a wealthy attorney, who happens to be Pamela Betts's own son. But I don't think Paul has to worry what with the kidnapping and attempted murder charges she's facing."

After a brief pause, she had finally amassed the nerve to ask Bill.

"Did you find Hannah?"

"No. I'm sorry."

Bill didn't say anything else, and he didn't have to. Maureen was certain that her sister was probably among the bones on the island.

Bill fell asleep to the soft sounds of Maureen crying.

In the morning, Bill was up before Maureen and was on his third cup when she wandered out into the living room.

Never one to like sharing his space, he had to admit to himself that the sight of her walking into the living room, wearing one of his plaid buttons down shirts and a pair of socks appealed to him.

"Morning," he said, offering her a cup of coffee.

357

"Feels like afternoon," she said.

Neither knew what to say.

"Sid called this morning. You're no longer a suspect in the case, and are free to leave town."

Nodding, she sat cross-legged on the sofa.

"Is Hannah's case still open?" Maureen asked.

"As a formality, until we get a positive ID on the remains at the island. We have two so far."

"Who," she looked at him.

"A missing woman from New Winston, and Shawn."

"Oh God, Bill I'm so sorry," she said.

"Don't be. He had a part in this, I'm certain. It's what probably got him killed and dumped there."

"How many do you are there?" she asked, referring to the victims.

"Last count for missing persons was thirty-three, with a couple more pending. Not all of them might pan out, but I'm willing to bet that at least a dozen are going to match up to people we have in the database."

"At least it will bring their family some closure," she said.

"Closure comes from being able to finally let go because your heart's ready to move on," he said, sipping his coffee.

She smiled faintly at him, sipping her coffee.

"Edith called as well. Seems several council members want me to step up and take Dwight's place until they can hold an election in January."

"You thinking about it?" she asked.

"No. I've no interest in politics."

"I can't see you in a suit and tie, sitting behind a desk. You need to be out there, hands on."

"I prefer it that way. What about you?" he asked.

"I phoned my editor. I'm going to be doing a four-part segment on the dead and missing. Whether they like it or not, Lighthouse Bay is going to become famous for all the wrong reasons," she said.

"So you're staying then, at least for a little while." He said.

"Yeah, at least the next few months. I'm going to try and identify all the victims, and I was thinking about holding a bagged tea light vigil on the beach in remembrance of the missing."

"Not the island?" he asked.

She shook her head.

"No, I have no desire to set foot on Gull Island ever again."

"I don't blame you. You know you're welcome to stay here as long as you like," he said, coming to sit next to her.

"I'd like that."

Slipping an arm around her, he turned on the TV.

Epilogue

MAUREEN FINISHED TYPING, hitting save and closing her laptop.

This had been the hardest article she'd written since Hannah's disappearance, and she rubbed her temples desperate to relieve the throbbing pressure that had settled there.

The first article had been purely background, on the people and the history of Lighthouse Bay, ending it with the allure that small towns sometimes hold big secrets.

In the second one, she'd outlined the many missing persons, weaving in the town's conspiracy and finally introducing the creature that had yet to be physically seen by any member of the scientific community or even the DNR

That one article, which ran in the Chicago papers, local papers, and had brought every Bigfoot hunter, alien conspiracy theorist, and crypto-zoologist to Lighthouse Bay in search of the thing that was being reported as being partly responsible for the deaths so many people.

A good number of the people in town had turned a cold shoulder to Maureen, but that didn't bother her. They may not have liked her reporting, but they didn't complain about the tourism it drummed up in the offseason.

The third article proved the most difficult for Maureen because it began the ordeal of her missing sister all over again.

Her mother had a nervous breakdown, but she'd finally stopped drinking. In the midst of the investigation, she'd found out that Frank wasn't who he appeared to be.

Frank was Dwight Carlisle's half-brother and knew full well what lived on Gull Rock. He knew what hunted the people of Lighthouse Bay.

Frank had gone off to college when Maureen's father was murdered, and her mother had left town with her young child.

He'd been giving the task of finding them and making sure they didn't talk about the secrets of Michigan's Upper Peninsula. However, no one had intended for Frank to fall in love with her.

At first, he'd been steadfast in his protection of his new family and refusal to help his father or the town council do anything. The years went on and her mother's drinking got worse, and his perceptive business deals went south. Frank had been desperate.

The plan had been for Maureen to go up and settle the cabin for her sister, who'd agreed to go into treatment for a multitude of afflictions.

Maureen was the actual intended victim, as Frank couldn't bear the thought of sacrificing his wife and own child. It hadn't been a great loss to him if his stepdaughter had died.

In the wake of Maureen's death, the property would have reverted to Frank and her mother. Frank had medical conservatorship over his wife, and could, therefore, sell the property — prime real estate along Michigan's picturesque coast, for a pretty penny and rid himself of the thorn in his side in one fell swoop.

The one thing he hadn't intended to happen did and the blow had been crushing to Frank. When the authorities had uncovered his part in the plot, Frank had crumbled under the pressure and told the police everything.

Her mother began divorce proceedings and the rest was soon going to be history once a judge stamped his decree ending their marriage. Frank was going to prison for a long time.

Bill hadn't been able to determine if Hannah had been a victim of the town's fear of the creature, or if she'd been mistaken for Maureen.

No one had been able to identify the people in the dark sedan, although Bill believed it was the same people who pushed Maureen into traffic. Bill figured that they realized they'd gotten the wrong individual and tried to correct things.

Maureen organized a tea light vigil at the beach, creating a single row of lit tea lights nestled into a mound of sand inside brown lunch bags up the coastline.

Several larger bags were lit to honor the memory of those whose remains were identified.

It surprised Maureen that Edith had made a bag for Shawn.

"I don't like to speak ill of the dead," Edith had said to her, "but just because Shawn was a jerk, doesn't mean he shouldn't be remembered."

Maureen liked her, despite her gruff exterior.

The only thing that had been missing from the tea light ceremony was a bag in Hannah's honor.

None of the remains had matched DNA taken from Hannah's hairbrush.

To this day, the case remains open.

Bill came into the living room, where Maureen sat at the kitchen table. She'd been at his cabin for the last year, leaving her post at the paper opting instead for freelance work.

Maureen didn't know the status of their relationship, but she knew she loved him. Whether or not he felt the same, she couldn't tell, but he did let her buy scented candles for his cabin.

It was a start.

"Penny for your thoughts," he said, freshly showered in his jogging pants and sweatshirt.

"I was just thinking," she said.

"Good. I encourage it daily." He smiled, passing her a mug of coffee.

"You're funny," she teased, but his one sentence had eased a great amount of the tension that had found its way back into her neck muscles. "No, I was just thinking about Hannah."

"I know."

"It's going to be winter soon...almost a full year without Hannah. This holiday," she said, shaking her head. "I was in town yesterday, and I saw a brightly colored knit sweater in the window of Knit Knacks, and I had to stop myself from going in because it still hasn't sunk in that she isn't here this Christmas."

"I'm sorry," he said, coming around the table and hugging her to him.

"It's okay. I should be used to it by now. I mean, we may never know. I've gotten good at coping with the anxiety, the pain, and loss. Holidays are still hard. Birthdays, too. I just wanted some peace for Hannah, some justice."

"You know I'm going to do everything I can to investigate the case, and find Hannah, one way or another," Bill said.

"I know. But all those people missing, some of them identified. Some might never be. I guess I just wanted all this mess to have a happy ending."

"Not all endings are happy ones, Maureen. Sometimes life is about separating and coming together, then breaking apart to become whole again. Don't let Hannah be their sacrifice, because she's been victim enough. As long as you hold onto one piece of her and continue to tell Hannah's story, she's never truly gone."

Maureen smiled.

www.ingramcontent.com/pod-product-compliance
Lightning Source LLC
Chambersburg PA
CBHW060156260626
47160CB00001B/289